"I THINK YOU PERFORMED A GREAT SERVICE TO YOUR COUNTRY, MR. PARTINGTON."

Sweet Claire. Always his champion. He wondered if anybody had ever bothered to champion Claire. . . .

It surprised him when he heard himself say, "I think I need to kiss you for that, Miss Montague."

Her eyes opened wide. "You do?"

"I do."

He settled one hand lightly on her shoulder and another on her soft cheek, guiding her head toward his. His lips barely skimmed hers. She didn't know a thing about kissing, but kept her lips shut tight. She was scared; Tom could tell. He whispered gently, "Open your mouth a little, Claire."

She did. When his lips touched hers again, he found them soft and meltingly sweet under his. . . .

Nothing could have prepared him for his reaction to having Claire Montague in his arms. Her tentative response ignited him, and he discovered himself wanting to teach her the art of love, to coax her secret passion into fire. . . . He wanted to make her burn for him as he burned for her. . . .

Dell Books by Alice Duncan

WILD DREAM

SECRET HEARTS

SECRET HEARTS

Alice Duncan

A DELL BOOK

Published by
Dell Publishing
a division of
Bantam Doubleday Dell Publishing Group, Inc.
1540 Broadway
New York, New York 10036

ISBN: 0-440-22364-4

Printed in the United States of America

Published simultaneously in Canada

February 1998

10 9 8 7 6 5 4 3 2 1

WCD

This book is dedicated to
romance writers and readers everywhere.

Like Claire, we often find our
reading choices disparaged.
I figure that's only because the disparagers
don't know what they're missing.

1

*B*ullets whined through the still morning air, striking with alarming accuracy the boulder behind which Tuscaloosa Tom Pardee hunkered. War whoops and vicious curses rent the air. The woman cowering next to Tom wept piteously.

"We know you're there, Tuscaloosa Tom!" a whiskey-voiced malefactor exclaimed.

"Ah, but goodness and right are on my side," Tom declared stoutly. "You, villains, are the devil's spawn!" He punctuated his declaration with a volley from his trusty firearm.

"Oh, Tom!" the woman sobbed.

"Fear nothing," the heroic man assured her. "I will rescue you!"

"I know you cannot fail me," Miss Abigail Faithgood choked out, flinching at each new auditory assault upon her senses. Oh, my, she was frightened! Yet she knew—she knew—Tom would not fail her. He had never failed in his life.

Suddenly, with a bloodcurdling howl, an Indian brave

leaped from the boulder above them to confront Tom, the feathers in his headdress bristling, his war paint vivid in the noonday sun. Miss Abigail Faithgood screamed.

Without flinching, Tom . . .

"Tom what?" Chewing on the end of her pen and patting at the hair coiled over her left ear, Claire Montague stared at the paper on her desk. "Botheration. And how can it be a clear morning if it's noon?"

"Miss Montague?"

Claire jerked in alarm, and the pen dropped from her fingers to clatter on the blotter. She hadn't heard the door open. Well, why should she? She herself had oiled those hinges faithfully every single Monday of her life for ten years now.

"Good heavens, Scruggs, you frightened me to death."

The butler's lugubrious expression lengthened. "I beg your pardon, Miss Montague. But he's here." Scruggs sounded as though he were reporting the arrival of doom. "His carriage just drew up outside."

Claire's hand flew to her throat. She didn't need to ask who *he* was. Her palpitating heart thundered so violently that for a second she feared she would lose consciousness. She pulled herself together. This reaction was absurd; she knew it.

"Thank you, Scruggs. I shall descend immediately."

"Very good, ma'am. Mrs. Philpott is preparing refreshments." Scruggs's face, which Claire often thought more nearly resembled that of a morose moose than anything else, disappeared.

Mrs. Philpott was the cook, and Claire suspected she was at this moment weeping into her teakettle. With a big sigh she rose from her desk, slipped her work in progress into its special drawer, and locked it away with the key she kept on a chain around her neck.

Composing herself with some effort—after all, it wasn't every day one met the man of one's dreams, the man who haunted one's every daylight hour and filled one's nights with alluring fantasies—Claire stood up straight and tall, entirely too tall, in fact. For at least the thousandth time she regretted her unladylike inches. Oh, well, there was nothing she could do about them. Patting her severe hairstyle once more to make sure no unruly strands poked out, she adopted her best housekeeperish expression.

Then, gulping an enormous breath for courage, she walked out of her room and prepared to greet the new master of Partington Place.

Tom Partington wished it weren't so blasted dark. He'd love to get a glimpse of his new home. But it had been twilight when his rented coach barreled him through Marysville. The night was black as pitch now and raining fit to kill as well. A couple of his many old wounds had begun to ache earlier and now throbbed in earnest. Tom was used to pain, though. Besides, nothing could subdue the excitement bubbling within him tonight.

Oh, he knew life was what one made of it. And he certainly didn't expect to be handed anything else on a silver platter anytime soon. Once was plenty, more than life generally offered a fellow, in Tom's experience.

Excitement gripped him, though. There was something about this place that made one dare to dream, an atmosphere of unrefined excitement. Confidence bubbled in the air. This land wasn't so much raw as it was untamed. The clinging vine of civilization had yet to choke the life out of California, and the climate fairly vibrated with energy.

Tom felt a liveliness here, had felt it as soon as his ship docked in San Francisco. The atmosphere wasn't like that of the cities back home: stifled, stuffy, lifeless. There was something in the wind here that felt like a promise, if not of hope fulfilled, then at least of hope eagerly pursued. It was a promise that assured him that if he couldn't achieve his dream, he could damned well chase it for all he was worth. Tom had never felt so optimistic in his life.

Staring into the impenetrable night, he couldn't keep the smile from his face. It had been there ever since he'd learned the terms of his uncle Gordon's will. Tom still couldn't believe the old buzzard had left his entire fortune to him.

When the carriage slowed, he couldn't even wait for the horses to come to a full stop before he pushed the door open and jumped out. His bad leg gave a tremendous throb when he landed on the graveled walkway, but Tom didn't care. He took the steps to the grand double doors of his new house—house, hell! It was a damned mansion!—two at a time and yanked the bell-pull with an exuberance he hadn't felt in years.

Several minutes had passed, and Tom was on the verge of tugging on the pull again, when the door creaked open. A man who looked as though he'd walked straight out of an Edgar Allan Poe story peered at him. Tom figured him for the butler.

Silence reigned for several seconds before Tom broke it with a broad smile and said, "Hello, there. I'm Tom Partington."

The ghoulish man took a step backward and pulled the door open. "Please come inside, sir."

So Tom did. In spite of the butler's gloomy demeanor, Tom's sunny mood prevailed. "Thanks. It's cold as the dickens out there."

Claire stopped at the top of the wide staircase, the voice at the front door having momentarily stunned her. It couldn't have been better if she'd selected it herself. Deep and resonant, a rich, pure Alabama drawl, it touched Claire in places she'd never dared hope would be touched.

She devoutly prayed the face, frame, and character that went with the voice would not disappoint. After all, she'd often been told photographs did not tell the entire story. Claire had invariably laughed and said she provided her own stories, but tonight was different. She wanted former Brevet General Thomas Gordon Partington to live up to her expectations more than she'd ever wanted anything in her life, barring a genteel background and great literary talent. She already knew those two commodities had been denied her.

Drawing in one more deep breath and exhaling it slowly, Claire put her hand on the polished banister and began her descent.

"Miss Montague will be with you in a moment, General Partington," the butler said drearily. "She will see you to your room."

"*Mr.* Partington will do quite well," Tom said, trying to keep the acid out of his voice. He looked around the foyer of his new home and nearly laughed out loud when he saw the fancy Oriental carpet and all the polished wood and marble. Great God, this was fantastic! He'd scraped and slaved and saved for fifteen years now, hoping he'd one day be able to afford even a small place to call his own, and now, with a few magnanimous strokes of his late uncle's pen, he'd been handed all this.

"Very good, sir."

Tom thought the fellow sounded as though he were agreeing to commit murder. "And what is your name, my good man?"

"Scruggs, sir."

Just Scruggs? Oh, well, who was Tom to argue? Anyway, it didn't matter. "Just Scruggs" was *his* butler now. His very own butler. Ha!

"Right, Scruggs. Well, will you please take my coat and hat somewhere? They're dripping onto the carpet." And what a carpet it was! Tom knew absolutely nothing about carpets, but he'd seldom stood on anything this thick. And it was *his!* With difficulty he checked an exultant laugh.

"Very good, sir."

Shaking his head, Tom watched as Scruggs bore his coat and hat away as though each item weighed a thousand pounds. Good grief, what kind of people had Uncle Gordon employed here anyway?

On the other hand, what the hell did he care? After all, he was rich as Croesus now, thanks to Uncle Gordo. As Tom had been dirt poor all his life in spite of the Fine Old Family Name, the change delighted him. Not even that death's-head butler could blight his happiness.

He heard the stairway creak. Looking up quickly, he discerned a tall, elegant, albeit severe-looking, female making her way down the staircase.

Aha, the housekeeper. Tom had heard about her. According to the letters Uncle Gordon had written to Tom's mother, people in the town of Pyrite Springs had at first been quite scandalized about the relationship between old Uncle Gordo and his housekeeper, Miss Montague. They'd soon gotten over it.

Peering at the woman descending the staircase toward

him, Tom had a hard time crediting the rumors. Unless his uncle's taste had improved since Gordo had fallen in love with Tom's mother, this woman seemed entirely too majestic a female to have been the focus of salacious gossip linking the two of them. Maybe the citizens of Pyrite Springs possessed lively imaginations.

This creature certainly did not appear to be the stuff of romantic tales. Granted, her features were fine, her nose was small and straight, and her mouth quite prettily shaped. Still, she appeared quellingly rigid. Spectacles glittered across her face in the lamplight, and she wore her hair in a dreadful style, braided and coiled into two tight little knots above her ears. Her hair reminded Tom of a pair of rattlesnakes about to strike, although that thought was undoubtedly the product of too many years on the frontier.

Nevertheless, he had been reared to be polite to ladies, no matter how regal their manners and no matter how far his life had divided him from his gracious youth. He walked to the foot of the stairs and smiled.

"Miss Montague?"

"Yes," Claire breathed. "I am she."

Good heavens, the man was perfection. His limp, though barely perceptible, hinted of gallant deeds and suffering. His blond hair was just a bit too long for fashion but perfect for *him*, and it glimmered like gold in the candlelight. That famous mustache of his outlined lips too beautiful for words although God and the whole country knew Claire had used enough of them in her many feeble attempts to do them justice. His eyes were blue as cornflowers. In this dim light she could barely perceive their color, but their size, depth, and luminosity were spectacular. And his smile. Claire swallowed. His smile could melt a heart of ice.

Southern gentleman, fearless soldier, brave frontiers-man. Brevet General Thomas G. Partington was the living personification of Tuscaloosa Tom Pardee. Claire very nearly fainted. Taking several careful, deep breaths, she spared herself the indignity of tumbling down the staircase and landing insensate at his feet, but she managed to negotiate the few last steps with a modicum of dignity.

Her hand shook when she extended it to accept his, and he helped her into the foyer. Good heavens.

Dianthe, she thought suddenly . . . a little sadly. *I must introduce him to Dianthe. They were made for each other.*

"You are Claire Montague? My uncle's housekeeper?"

"Yes. Yes, I am the housekeeper," Claire replied breathlessly.

"Good. I'm very pleased to meet you. Mr.—er—Scruggs told me you'd show me around my new home."

Claire told herself sternly to get a grip on her senses. At the moment they were fluttering in her middle like deranged butterflies. This would never do.

She tried on a smile and decided it fitted. "I should be happy to do so, sir. It's such a chilly, rainy night, though, perhaps you would like to take tea in the parlor first. I believe Mrs. Philpott, the cook, is already preparing refreshments. I'll be happy to tell you about your new home over a cup of tea before we attempt a grand tour."

If she didn't faint and drown in her own teacup. For a woman with such a dull exterior, Claire often thought the fates had teased her most unkindly when they'd given her these exalted sensibilities. She maintained her smile, though, and tried her best to appear unruffled. In truth she'd never been so ruffled.

"Thank you. I would like a chance to dry out and have a nip of . . . something."

"Yes, well, please follow me, Mr.—General—oh, dear."

Well, so much for aplomb. Claire could feel heat rise to stain her cheeks.

" 'Mr.' will do nicely, thank you, Miss Montague." Tom paused. "It is *Miss* Montague?"

Flustered, surprised he'd even bothered to ask, Claire murmured, "Yes. Yes, it is." Then, impulsively, she added, "You see, Mr. Partington, your uncle spoke so glowingly of you that we denizens of Partington Place have become quite used to thinking of you as the Young General."

"My uncle was, I'm afraid, much given to exaggeration, Miss Montague."

Surprised by his tone of voice, which sounded exceedingly dry, Claire decided she'd best not respond lest she say something inappropriate. Opening the door to the parlor, she stepped aside and allowed her new employer to enter before her. She hoped he'd like the way she'd kept the house up. Even though her obligations to her publisher and her readers took a good deal of her time, Claire had always put her responsibilities as housekeeper at Partington Place above all else and hoped desperately to keep her job. Partington Place was her home. She was also proud of her skill at housekeeping because it was one at which she excelled, in spite of her tawdry origins.

Tom looked around the room with apparent interest. Claire trusted he would not object to the dried flower arrangement she'd set on the side table. The late Mr. Partington had enjoyed her attempts at flower arranging, but she had no idea what other men might appreciate. The only men she'd ever known in her life until Mr.

Partington employed her were her father and her brother, neither one of whom counted.

Claire was so nervous it was an effort to keep her hands demurely clasped in front of her. They wanted to wring one another in agitation.

"This room is quite charming, Miss Montague," Tom said, making Claire's knees go weak with relief. "I expect your influence has held sway in Partington Place? I can't imagine Uncle Gordon having this much taste."

Surprised, Claire blinked several times before she managed to say, "Oh, no, General—I mean, Mr.—Partington, the late Mr. Partington had exquisite taste. He was a man of the most refined sensibilities."

"Really?" Tom leveled a perfectly gorgeous smile at her, and Claire's hands tightened around each other.

Swallowing, she said, "Yes, indeed. He was a most worthy gentleman."

A knock sounded at the door, and Claire blessed the interruption as she dashed to open it. Sure enough, it was Mrs. Philpott. Claire noticed the poor old cook's swollen, red-rimmed eyelids and gave her a commiserating smile as she took the tea tray.

Claire had already promised the cook she wouldn't introduce the new master until the following day when, Mrs. Philpott assured Claire, she would certainly have stopped weeping. Claire hoped so, although she didn't dare be too optimistic. Mrs. Philpott went through life as though pursued by her own personal storm cloud. No matter what the circumstances, Mrs. Philpott could find *something* to worry about.

"Here's your tea, Mr. Partington. Do you care for cream and sugar?" Pleased that her voice sounded steady, Claire dared smile at the devastatingly handsome man staring at the portrait of his uncle hanging over the fireplace.

He turned and smiled back, making Claire catch her breath and turn her attention to the tea things.

"Thank you, Miss Montague. I do take cream and sugar. One lump, please. I can understand why my uncle spoke so highly of you. You're a veritable paragon of housekeeperish virtues."

Claire's "thank you" sounded squeaky to her ears. She picked up Tom's teacup and prayed her hand wouldn't shake.

He murmured another polite "thank you," took the cup, and Claire was pleased to note she hadn't spilled a drop.

"Tell me, Miss Montague," he said after a sip of tea, "do you have any idea why my uncle left me this place?"

Startled, Claire said, "Why, no, sir. I just assumed it was because you were his only nephew."

"Hmm. No, he has others."

"I'm afraid I wasn't in the late Mr. Partington's confidence when it came to his personal financial matters."

With a grin Tom said, "No? Well, perhaps it doesn't matter."

"I do know that he held you in the greatest esteem, though." Claire was shy about telling him that but felt compelled to do so.

"Did he now?"

"Yes, indeed. Why, he read me every one of the newspaper accounts of your career." Claire stopped speaking suddenly, as though unsure she should have divulged so much.

"Ah, yes, the reporters," Tom said dryly. "Many's the times I was forced to save some citified newspaperman from his own folly." He took another gulp of tea. "Tell me, Miss Montague, I know the estate grounds are extensive. I'm interested in pursuing certain, oh, business matters and wondered if you knew the exact acreage."

Tom put his teacup down on an end table, reached into his coat, and, with a smooth, elegant gesture, withdrew a slim cigar. Claire watched, eyes widening. That was it!

Without flinching, Tom reached inside his fringed buckskin garment and withdrew a slender dagger. With one swift, graceful lunge, he dispatched the ferocious brave. Miss Abigail Faithgood screamed.

"Miss Montague?"

With a start Claire realized Tom had just spoken to her. "Oh! I'm so sorry, sir. My mind wandered momentarily." Good heavens, the man would think she was demented if she kept this up. Frantically Claire fought for composure.

Tom watched Claire's mental struggles wage themselves on her expressive face and revised his initial impression of her. Miss Claire Montague might be a sobersides, and she might favor a dreary hairstyle and boring garb, but she certainly was not dull. In fact, Tom had seldom seen such an animated countenance. She seemed charming, and not nearly as stuffy as his first impression had led him to believe. He gestured her into a chair and sat himself down on the sofa, trying not to sprawl.

"Do you have any idea what the full acreage encompassed by Partington Place is, Miss Montague?" he asked again gently.

"No. No, I'm afraid I don't. But I'm sure Mr. Silver, the late Mr. Partington's man of business, will be happy to go over all that with you. He has agreed to visit you tomorrow morning if it suits you."

"That will be wonderful. Thank you."

In some agitation Claire took a sip of tea, and Tom wondered what on earth the matter was. All at once it hit him why she must be so nervous. Of course. What a fool he was. But hell, he wasn't used to dealing with servants.

"Miss Montague, I would like to reassure you that I don't plan to make any staff changes immediately, if at all. My uncle got along quite well with you, Scruggs, the cook, and the rest of the employees here at the Place, and I'm sure I shall do the same."

She looked relieved, and Tom was pleased.

"Thank you, Mr. Partington. I fear Mrs. Philpott was worried about losing her situation. In truth, while she is a good, plain cook, she does rather lack experience in more extensive presentations."

"More extensive presentations?" What the hell did that mean?

"Well, if you were to invite your friends in for a gala ball or a theatrical evening or some other affair of that nature, you see, she's worried that she won't be able to cope. I tried to assure her that any family chef accustomed to cooking for a single gentleman would need help under those circumstances and to remind her that the late Mr. Partington used to hire people from the village for parties. Mrs. Philpott, however, seems determined to believe that you would expect her to be able to create elaborate pastries and ice sculptures on an everyday basis."

"Good God."

"I mean, I'm sure a gentleman such as you must be used to entertaining on a grand scale, but I believe Mrs.

Philpott can handle your day-to-day requirements if they aren't terribly elaborate. And even parties, with help."

"What on earth makes you think I'm used to giving big parties, Miss Montague?" Tom asked, genuinely curious. "I've been living on the frontier for fifteen years."

"Oh."

She was obviously startled by his brusque question, and Tom wished he'd phrased it more delicately. That was what came of living in the rough, he reckoned, and vowed to try to conduct himself more appropriately, as befitted his new station in life.

"I beg your pardon, Miss Montague. I didn't mean to sound so blunt. But I can assure both you and Mrs. Philpott that I am not in the habit of entertaining—on any scale at all. Nor do I have a bevy of friends who will expect it of me."

Good Lord on high, the buffalo hunters, half-breed scouts, and mule skinners he'd been associating with for the past several years would probably faint dead away if they even set foot in this mansion. And after taking a good whiff of them, Miss Claire Montague would undoubtedly join them. Tom suppressed his chuckle at the image his thought evoked.

"I see. Well, then that's fine." Claire looked at him over her teacup, a puzzled expression on her face. Her spectacles gave her a grave, studious look, strangely appealing to Tom. He had an urge to tease her out of it.

"You seem surprised, Miss Montague."

"I suppose I am, actually." Her studious expression intensified. "I mean—well, your uncle used to love relating tales of your derring-do, Mr. Partington, but he also indicated you were used to fairly lavish entertainments when you got back to civilization from the wild frontier."

Tom shook his head in disgust. He couldn't help it. "As I said, Miss Montague, my uncle was given to exaggeration."

"Was he really?"

She looked at him, big-eyed beneath those lenses of hers, as though he'd just denied the existence of God, and Tom was momentarily taken aback. Curious, he asked, "Just what did my uncle say about me?"

Peering at him earnestly, Claire said, "Mr. Partington, your uncle was so proud of you. He followed your career with great interest. He cut out every newspaper article and magazine reference he could find and read letters from your—oh, dear."

"From my mother?" Tom gave her an understanding smile. "It's all right, Miss Montague. Uncle Gordon's undying love was probably my mother's greatest pleasure in life. I'm aware that they corresponded regularly."

He could tell she was relieved when a big sigh gusted from her, making her seem much less austere than before.

"I'm so glad. I didn't want to—to make any indiscreet references." Obviously embarrassed, Claire took another sip of tea.

With a little chuckle he said, "And if he read you her letters, I'm not surprised you believed me to be a hero."

Claire opened and shut her mouth twice, then took another sip of tea. "At any rate, Mr. Partington, your uncle used to delight in telling me tales about you. He thought the world of you."

"I'm not sure I liked his way of showing it," Tom muttered sourly. Then he recalled that he was now sitting in the parlor of this very lavish estate—his estate—only because of Uncle Gordo's generosity or, more probably, guilt, and he sighed. "I beg your pardon. I didn't mean to sound churlish. I gather you and my uncle were, ah, great friends."

"Yes, indeed, Mr. Partington. The late Mr. Partington was very kind to me. He took me on—that is to say, he hired me—ten years ago, knowing I hadn't a particle of housekeeping experience. We became more in the nature of father and daughter, I suppose, than employer and employee." She heaved a tiny sigh. "He was a kind man, and I miss him very much. He used to delight in sharing your adventures with me."

She looked at him shyly, and Tom felt a twitch of tenderness in his heart.

"I would carry the tales of your exciting adventures to the kitchen and regale Mrs. Philpott and Scruggs with them. They were every bit as fascinated by them as I was."

Oh, Lord. This was worse than Tom thought. On the other hand, he decided, taking another look around, he guessed he could stand it. He settled for a short "I see" and decided to drop the subject.

They drank tea in silence for a few more minutes. Tom said, "Are you, Scruggs, and Mrs. Philpott the only . . . employees on the estate, Miss Montague?" Unused to having dependents, Tom wasn't entirely certain what to call them.

"Good heavens, no, Mr. Partington. Why, there are two housemaids, Sally and Dolores—we call her Dolly—a chief gardener, Mr. Hodges, his two helpers, Carlos and Rodrigo, and a host of people who work on the farm. Mr. Silver can explain the workings of the farm to you, I suppose. I'm afraid my expertise is limited to the house itself." Peering demurely into her teacup, she added somewhat bashfully, "And the garden."

"I see. Well, Miss Montague, if you're through with

your tea, perhaps you wouldn't mind taking me on a tour of my new home."

Claire put her cup and saucer down with a clank and popped up from her chair. "Certainly, Mr. Partington. Nothing would give me greater pleasure."

Good grief. If that were true, she must lead an extraordinarily dull life. But no. It was probably an empty social cliché and not to be taken seriously. Thinking he really should have studied civilization for a few more days before he tried living in it, Tom followed Claire Montague out of Uncle Gordon's parlor.

No. *His* parlor. Tom sighed with satisfaction.

Claire escaped from Tom Partington's company as soon as she could. Not that she didn't find him utterly fascinating; he was all too fascinating for her peace of mind, in fact. It was just that being in the company of the real Tuscaloosa Tom Pardee inspired her to greater heights of literary fancy than she ever could have imagined even two or three hours earlier.

With a feeling bordering on ecstasy, she sat at her desk and unlocked her special drawer. After pulling out the manuscript of her latest dime novel, she bent industriously to her task, writing far into the night. Even when she finally forced herself to climb into her bed and pull the quilt up to her chin, she stared at her ceiling, too excited to sleep.

He had come at last. And he was everything Claire had hoped he would be. More. Polite, handsome, cultured, elegant: He was perfect.

Tom pulled out every drawer and opened every cupboard in the library and then in the pantry before he found a bottle containing distilled spirits. He took it into the library with him and, after staring at the label in bemusement for several seconds, poured himself a stiff one.

Lifting his glass, he saluted his uncle's portrait. "To you, Uncle Gordo, damn your eyes." After a big swallow and a shudder, he added, "Good God. Why on earth did you ever start drinking cognac?"

His tour of his new home had been unremarkable except that Tom felt like pinching himself every now and then to make sure he was awake and this wasn't a dream spawned by years of backbreaking work and desperate wishes.

He'd also found himself enjoying the company of Miss Claire Montague. Oh, it's true she was starchy, reserved, and majestic. Still, she seemed remarkably efficient, and she hadn't appeared to be offended by his occasional gaffes. Like when he'd called his "boudoir" the dressing room. Or when he'd asked, upon being shown the wine cellar, if his uncle hadn't kept any regular booze around the place.

He guessed he had a lot about gracious living to get used to. He'd manage, though. Sighing deeply, he sank into an armchair, still gazing at his uncle's portrait. His contented expression gave way to a frown after another sip of the fine aged cognac.

Tom knew the old story, about how Gordon Partington had wooed the beautiful belle Melinda Grace Hartwell and how, on the eve of their engagement party, Gordon's dashing older brother, Grant, had swept Melinda off her feet.

Tom often thought marrying his father wasn't the brightest thing his mother had ever done. Of course marrying his mother wasn't the brightest thing his father had ever done either. But then, Tom was a practical person, unlike either of his parents. God alone knew how he'd managed to end up that way; he must have been a throwback to an earlier generation.

Barring his love for Tom's mother, Uncle Gordon had been practical too, and he'd done really well for himself. Tom's gaze swept the room yet again. The furnishings of this room alone were worth more than his parents' entire household in Alabama; Tom would bet anything on it if he were a betting man. Being the practical person he was, however, Tom didn't gamble.

It was practicality that had seen him into the army even though he knew the Confederacy was doomed. He'd had to get away from home, and the army was the only way he could see to do it without breaking his parents' hearts. They, being the fanciful, addlepated fools they were, had thought he was being noble.

Tom rested his head on the back of the chair and stared moodily at the ceiling. Noble! Lord. Well, he guessed his old uncle Gordo had thought he was noble too. Why else would he have left him this magnificent estate?

Now Tom would have to figure out how to help his parents without giving them money outright. If he simply handed them cash, they'd fritter it away, sure as anything. With a heavy sigh he decided he'd tackle that problem later. Right now he planned to wallow in fine cognac and newly acquired riches.

And horses. Tom grinned as he contemplated Jedediah Silver's visit on the morrow. Silver would be able to tell him if his dream was doomed or if Tom could at last indulge his fondest wish.

Good old Uncle Gordo. Even if he had made Tom's life miserable in some respects, the old fellow had certainly done him a good turn by leaving him his estate and his fortune. Perhaps unrequited love, the very thought of which stirred Tom's pragmatic soul to wry amusement, wasn't such an idiotic waste after all. It had benefited Tom Partington, for a pure fact.

Tom pulled out another slim cheroot, sipped his cognac, and wrinkled his nose. The wretched stuff had probably cost a damned fortune. With a grin he decided he could get used to it.

2

At Tom's request Claire took breakfast with him at eight o'clock the following morning. She was in the dining room, in fact, when Tom pushed the door open. Claire looked up eagerly—and dropped her fork.

"You shaved off your mustache!"

Tom stopped dead in the doorway and, obviously startled, blinked at her. Claire was too shocked to be appalled by her shrill bellow.

How could he have done such a dastardly thing? Why, Tuscaloosa Tom Pardee's mustache was dashing. It was gorgeous! It was what distinguished Tuscaloosa Tom from a thousand other, inferior frontier scouts. How in the name of heaven could he have shaved it off?

"I beg your pardon?"

Tom's puzzled voice gradually penetrated Claire's rage and astonishment, and she realized she'd just shrieked at her employer. Immediately she felt her cheeks get hot, and she knew she'd turned beet red. Good heavens, what on earth was she thinking of? She sucked in a deep breath.

With the cheerless knowledge that her breeding had again blindsided her, Claire tore her gaze away from her employer's naked face and bowed her head. "I'm so sorry, Mr. Partington. I don't know what possessed me to shout at you like that. Please forgive me."

Humiliation still burned her cheeks. Claire wouldn't have been surprised if he'd fired her on the spot. She was therefore doubly amazed when she heard his throaty chuckle. Although she feared what she might see, she dared lift her head a fraction and looked at him.

He'd recovered from his shock at her indignation and was grinning broadly as he headed to the sideboard and began heaping his plate with food. "Sorry to startle you, Miss Montague. Didn't know anyone would miss it."

Didn't know anyone would miss it? Good heavens, Claire loved that mustache. She'd written about it endlessly. Depending on the circumstances her hero faced, that dashing mustache of his bristled or drooped or lifted or dripped or sparkled with ice crystals in winter. Claire swallowed hard. "I beg your pardon, Mr. Partington. How foolish you must think me!" She tried to laugh, but a laugh wouldn't come.

As breakfast progressed, Claire kept shooting surreptitious peeks at Tom's face. In truth, his mouth, which was a work of art in itself, actually looked quite good without the frame of its famous mustache. Claire discovered herself staring in a most unbecoming manner at his lips. She frowned and tore her gaze away. Her low breeding was again exhibiting itself.

Claire told herself to stop being foolish and concentrate on efficiency. Efficiency was what Mr. Partington expected of her, and efficiency she would give him.

"Mr. Silver will be arriving at ten, Mr. Partington." She took a bite of ham, although she really was too nervous to eat. Merely being in the same room with this man, this ideal of her heart, made her stomach flutter.

His spectacular blue eyes sparkled at her from across the table. His mustache, Claire thought with a pang, would have drooped just enough to give him the air of an antebellum southern gentleman getting ready to ride to hounds. Somewhat grudgingly she decided he carried the air off rather well even without the mustache. Also, his broad shoulders filled the master's chair much more fully than his uncle's had. Claire decided maybe she didn't miss his mustache too much after all. She tried not to stare.

The breakfast room was much more intimate a chamber than the dining room. It had the capacity to seat only twelve people easily. This morning, with her senses completely overwrought, Claire would have felt more comfortable with twenty feet of mahogany between herself and her new employer, especially since she'd already managed to make a complete fool of herself before the day had barely begun.

"I'm looking forward to meeting him, Miss Montague. I have all sorts of questions to ask."

"I'm sure you will find him very forthcoming, Mr. Partington. The late Mr. Partington said he'd found a treasure in Jedediah Silver."

"I'm certain he said the same of his housekeeper," Tom said gallantly, making her blush like a schoolgirl.

She sputtered something incomprehensible and felt like an idiot. What a noble soul he was, to say such a thing after her behavior only minutes earlier!

He continued. "After breakfast, perhaps you'd do me the kindness of showing me the estate grounds. I know you don't have much to do with the farm, but you mentioned gardens. I've always wanted a garden."

Tom took a sip of coffee. Gordon Partington had imported his coffee from Jamaica, and it was generally considered excellent. Tom seemed to like it, for which Claire was glad.

It surprised her to detect the note of unalloyed excitement in her new employer's demeanor. She'd have expected such a well-traveled, heroic man of the world to be used to grand estates and elegant appointments.

Nevertheless, she met his smile with one of her own that she hoped didn't declare too openly the adoration she felt for him. "I'd be happy to, Mr. Partington. Your uncle allowed me quite a free hand in the gardens. I hope you will approve."

In truth, about the only skill Claire prided herself on besides housekeeping was horticulture. The gardens at Partington Place were famous in the small town of Pyrite Springs. Even people from as far away as Sacramento sometimes visited the grounds during Partington Place's Spring Open House or on the Fourth of July, when Gordon had hosted an annual party for the public. Claire wasn't sure she dared hope Tom would continue some of the traditions she'd come to cherish at Partington Place.

They walked outside as soon as they'd finished breakfast, Tom graciously allowing Claire to lead the way through the solarium, across the marbled terrace, down the stairs, and into the small rose garden. Her heart was thundering like cannon fire by this time. She prayed he'd like what she'd done here.

The small rose garden led, by way of a cunning rose arbor, to more extensive gardens. Claire had overseen that various beds were stocked year-round with annuals and perennials so that the grounds seldom looked completely bare. Now, in the chill of autumn, the roses no longer bloomed, and there were no gay blossoms or sweet fragrances to caress the senses. The wisteria trellis seemed blank and cold to her, and she frowned at it critically. Even without the roses and wisteria blooming, however, green abounded, and one could appreciate the beauty of the grounds.

At least Claire could. She hoped to heaven Mr. Tom Partington would be able to share her enthusiasm. Peering at him from the corner of her eye, she thought she detected an expression of approval, and she contained her sigh of relief with difficulty.

She led him under the rose arbor's arches, bare now except for canes that would in April and May come alive with cascades of sweet-smelling blossoms, and into the flower beds. She wished it were April and the daphne were in bloom so he could smell the precisely pruned hedge lining the flower beds. It wasn't April, though, and she held her breath and clamped her hands together in front of her.

"The gardeners have already planted ranunculus and anemone bulbs, and the tulips, hyacinths, and daffodils come up year after year. In early spring they'll begin to bloom, and it will be quite colorful out here, and very fragrant."

As he looked around, Tom's eyes sparkled with pleasure. "This is wonderful, Miss Montague. I'll bet the place is spectacular when everything's blooming."

"Indeed, it is, Mr. Partington," Claire said in a rush. "Why, I—I believe the gardens of Partington Place are truly inspirational. At least, I have done my very best to make them so." Embarrassed at having said something so clearly bespeaking conceit in her own accomplishments, she ducked her head.

Tom didn't seem to mind. His expression held respect, even deference, when he turned to look at her. "You are truly a woman of many talents, Miss Montague. My uncle was very, very fortunate to have found you."

"Thank you, Mr. Partington," Claire whispered past the lump in her throat.

All at once the solarium door opened, and boots clicked on the marble. Claire viewed Jedediah Silver with pleasure. A young man, Jedediah was inclined to be overly serious. Yet he possessed a sense of fun that surfaced every now and then. Claire had a feeling the young accountant had raised himself up by dint of his own hard work from meager beginnings. He never spoke of it, and she had never asked. She herself came from a background she would prefer to forget, and she respected Mr. Silver's reticence.

Grateful for the accountant's interruption, Claire hurried toward him with her hands outstretched. "Mr. Silver! It's so nice to see you again. You haven't visited Partington Place for much too long."

His smile for Claire was very warm. "Miss Montague, it's a pleasure to see you again too." He looked up, smiled at Tom, and held out a hand. "I see Miss Montague has been giving you the grand tour, General Partington."

"I prefer 'Mr.' Partington," Tom said gently. "And you, I assume, are Mr. Silver."

Later that same day Claire was yawning over the household account books in the tidy office she'd made for herself in a small back parlor in Partington Place when

Dianthe St. Sauvre came to call. Hearing the soft click of the door leading out to the yard being opened, Claire looked up and smiled when she beheld her friend.

"Good afternoon, Dianthe."

Dianthe didn't so much walk as waft toward Claire. As she sank into a chair, her flowing skirts settled around her like a soft cloud, and Claire sighed. She was past envying Dianthe, she guessed, but it did seem somehow unfair that such beauty as Dianthe possessed couldn't have been shared more equitably among God's creatures instead of being bestowed exclusively upon this one exquisite woman.

What used to depress Claire even more than her abundant beauty was that Dianthe enjoyed genuine artistic genius. Unlike Claire herself, who wrote hack dime novels for so sordid a commodity as money, Dianthe created magnificent romantic verses, which she then interpreted in dance. Naturally she was poor as a church mouse, as befitted a True Artist.

Without returning Claire's greeting, Dianthe lifted her head and breathed, "Did he arrive?"

Even her voice was beautiful, Claire thought resignedly. There wasn't a man alive who wouldn't be stirred to gallant deeds by Dianthe's voice.

"He came last night." Claire sat forward on her chair and leaned over the desk. "And, oh, Dianthe, he's everything I expected him to be."

Dianthe's eyes grew round. She tossed her blond curls and whispered, "Oh, Claire, truly? He's truly the hero of—you know."

The very few of Claire's friends who knew her dark secret were extremely kind to her. None of them ever mentioned Tuscaloosa Tom Pardee to her face; they honored her friendship too much.

"Yes. He's simply wonderful. You must meet him, Dianthe. You and he would be—well, you'd be perfect together. I just know it."

Dianthe blushed becomingly, as she did everything. Claire couldn't suppress a wistful sigh. If only she'd been given a fraction of Dianthe's glorious femininity. Ah, well. As her father had told her more than once, each person was given gifts suitable to his or her abilities. It was probably the only sensible thing her father had ever said, in fact, but that was another matter entirely. Claire guessed it was her lot in life to be practical. She wished she'd been given a practical soul to go along with her practical looks.

"Do you really think so, Claire?"

"I truly do, Dianthe. He's every bit as handsome and noble as the newspaper and magazine accounts depict him as being. Why, he even tried to disparage his achievements when Mr. Silver came to call this morning." She decided not to mention his mustache.

Dianthe pressed a hand to her bosom, a feature as gloriously lush as the rest of her. "He's modest as well as heroic? Oh, Claire!"

"Indeed he is. Why, he insists upon being called merely Mr. Partington, as if his achievements in the war meant nothing at all to him. Also, he claims to know nothing about business or farming or running an estate and has very humbly begged Mr. Silver's guidance in those matters."

"Truly? My goodness."

Dianthe rose from her chair, and Claire discovered she hadn't entirely overcome her deplorable tendency to envy her beautiful friend. Graceful as a sylph, Dianthe circuited the room, fingering objects delicately, her lovely face thoughtful.

"He even offered Mr. Silver a generous bonus if he'd spend a few weeks here and teach him everything there is to know about the farm and grounds. Apparently he has an idea about breeding horses but doesn't want to embark on such an enterprise unless the estate is well able to support it." Claire approved such a pragmatic attitude.

"Horses," Dianthe breathed, endowing the word with all the mythic properties of Pegasus. Claire wished she could make her voice do that.

"Indeed. He seems to be interested in a particular breed. I believe it's called Appaloosas. At least I think that was the name."

Dianthe stopped wafting. "Appaloosas?" Her flawless forehead wrinkled when she spoke, as though she did not find the word aesthetically pleasing.

"Yes. The breed was evidently developed somewhere in the Northwest. I understand they're spotted."

"Spotted?" Dianthe's brows dipped over her crystal blue eyes.

Sensing her friend's disapproval, Claire hastened to say, "I asked about them this morning, Dianthe, and they're not nearly as awful as they sound."

Still frowning, Dianthe resumed her chair in front of Claire's desk. "No?"

"No, indeed. Why, in fact, I understand they possess a princely temperament, and their spots are primarily confined to their rear quarters. Although," she added conscientiously, "I don't really know much about them. I'm hoping Mr. Partington will permit me to learn along with him, so that I may be of some help to him in his new enterprise."

She tried to keep her galloping heart from giving her words any special emphasis. She knew her new employer could never find it in himself to view her as anything other than an employee, but if he would allow it, perhaps she could make herself *useful*. Long ago Claire had given up hope for anything more out of life.

"You're interested in *horses?*" Dianthe sounded faintly appalled.

Quelling a spurt of indignation, Claire said rather tartly, "Horses are noble beasts, Dianthe. Frankly, I'm surprised at your attitude."

Waving a delicate hand in the air, Dianthe said, "Of course, Claire. But horses with *spots?*" She shook her head, endowing the gesture with an elegance it probably did not deserve.

As it often did while Claire was writing, inspiration struck her now. She carefully schooled her expression to betray only indifference. "I believe the first persons to develop Appaloosas as a separate breed were Indians, Dianthe."

It did not surprise Claire that Dianthe's expression of distaste was immediately transformed into one of rapt interest, even awe.

"*Indians?*" Again she made this word sound mysterious, glorious, magical.

"I believe so." Claire smiled, pleased that she'd crossed that hurdle so easily.

"Oh, my." Dianthe sank back in her chair, adopting a pose Claire had seen captured on canvas by great artists. Her own little sigh was unintentional.

She was surprised into an unladylike start when a brisk rap came at the door. Dianthe of course expressed her alarm in a much more elegant manner, merely lifting an eyebrow and sitting slightly forward. When the door opened to reveal Mr. Partington, her lips parted and her eyes grew round.

Claire was not astonished when Tom glanced at Dianthe, looked away, swiveled his head back as if it had been wound by a spring, and stared, going somewhat bug-eyed.

She said calmly, "Mr. Partington, may I introduce you to my very good friend Dianthe St. Sauvre. Miss St. Sauvre is a poet whose works are soon to be heralded worldwide." She gave Dianthe a smile that Dianthe returned warmly.

Having risen from her chair as Venus might have risen from the sea, Dianthe glided toward Claire's dumbfounded employer, her hand held out. Claire's heart contracted when she saw the man of her dreams swallow, draw himself up straight, and give Dianthe a smile Claire would have died for had it been directed at her.

She'd been right. They were perfect together.

"Mr. Partington, it's such a pleasure to meet you."

"The pleasure is all mine, Miss St. Sauvre," Tom said feelingly. "Believe me." He drew her limp hand to his lips, and Claire experienced a pang of regret. There wasn't a gentleman alive who would kiss *her* hand that way, and she knew it.

"Claire has been telling me about your interest in horses, Mr. Partington."

"Has she now?"

Tom's smile for Claire was brief and friendly, not at all akin to the one he'd bestowed upon Dianthe.

"Indeed, it sounds like a fascinating venture," Claire said, aware even as she spoke that she'd lost his attention to Dianthe again.

"So you're a poet, Miss St. Sauvre?"

"Yes. I do my poor best." Dianthe lowered her lashes in a becoming manner.

"She's not a mere poet, Mr. Partington," Claire said

hurriedly. "Dianthe writes brilliant odes to nature and then creates evocative dances to go with them."

Tom said, "Really," in a lost-sounding voice.

"Oh, yes." Claire drew in a deep breath. This seemed as good a time as any to beg the new master of Partington Place's indulgence, possibly better than most. Might as well hit him with it while he was under Dianthe's spell.

"In fact, the late Mr. Partington used to support the arts in several extremely practical ways."

"Did he now?"

Claire watched Tom watch Dianthe as she floated to her chair and drifted into graceful repose once more.

"Yes, indeed. He was a great supporter of the Pyrite Arms."

"Beg pardon?" Tom's gaze, which had been stuck like glue on Dianthe, lifted. He looked quizzically at Claire.

"The Pyrite Arms. Several fine, fine artists live there. It is a hotel endowed by the late Mr. Partington specifically to give talented individuals a home. They are provided room and board at a modest cost and are given the freedom to devote their energies to art without the mundane world stifling their creative sensibilities."

Claire and Dianthe shared a smile. Dianthe whispered, "Mr. Partington was truly an enlightened benefactor."

Blinking, Tom murmured, "Was he now?"

Warming to her subject, Claire said, "Oh, yes, sir. Why, Dianthe is only one of five truly gifted artists who live and—and create at the Pyrite Arms."

Tom cleared his throat. "A truly noble enterprise, ladies."

Dianthe breathed, "Truly noble."

"Yes," Claire continued. "And your uncle used to enjoy hosting Artistic Evenings for residents of the Pyrite Arms too, Mr. Partington."

Claire looked down at her blotter, worried lest her passion for the Pyrite Arms enterprise give away her fervent interest. Yet if she could enlist the support of Mr. Partington to his uncle's pet project, she would be so happy. Somehow it seemed to Claire that when she helped the artists at the Pyrite Arms, she was making up in some way for Tuscaloosa Tom Pardee. Using her paltry skills in making so much money in so crass a manner embarrassed her. She tried at every opportunity to enlist support for the Pyrite Arms. Besides, keeping the Pyrite Arms project alive would keep Gordon's memory alive as well. Claire sometimes felt the Pyrite Arms would be her absolution.

Good Lord. Tom had never seen a woman as lovely as the creature draped in the chair across from his housekeeper. The contrast between the two ladies was almost painful to observe, and Tom felt a tug of sympathy for Claire. She was a good woman and was quite taking in her own subtle way.

It seemed a shame, however, that she should have become friends with the ethereal Dianthe St. Sauvre, who must eclipse her in any setting. Yet they obviously shared a strong friendship. That puzzled him in more ways than one, as Claire seemed infinitely brighter than her more beautiful friend. Dianthe reminded him in all too many ways of his own lovely but empty-headed mother. He wondered what the two women found to chat about.

"Well, perhaps you will do us the honor of visiting again, Miss St. Sauvre."

A glance at Claire assured him he'd said exactly the right thing, and he was irrationally pleased with himself. Although Tom had never had much truck with poetry, preferring the bawdy verses warbled in the countless seedy saloons he'd frequented in his impoverished days, he found himself saying, "I'll speak with Miss Montague about one of your—your evening art things."

"Artistic Evenings," Dianthe murmured. She gave Tom another dazzling smile.

"That would be so wonderful of you, Mr. Partington." Even though Claire knew Dianthe's beauty, not her own eloquence, had nudged her employer into making the offer, she was very grateful. After he had witnessed for himself the wonderful work the denizens of the Pyrite Arms created, he would surely be swayed to further generosity.

Dianthe left shortly after Tom's arrival. It seemed to take Tom a few minutes to recover. Claire thought dryly that he looked as though he'd been punched. With an internal sigh she guessed he had been. They discussed the business of the estate for a half hour or so before he took himself off for another chat with Mr. Silver.

As for Claire, her accounts settled, her work done, she went up to her room, fetched her work in progress, toted it downstairs to her office, and immersed herself in the further thrilling adventures of Tuscaloosa Tom Pardee. She knew it was shameful to take such delight in the unedifying pastime but guessed it was only to be expected, considering her origins.

Tom couldn't remember another time in his life when he'd eaten dinner alone. Or in such luxury. Sitting at the head of his magnificent dining table—capable of seating thirty with room to spare—he stared at a vast, empty expanse of polished mahogany that seemed to go on forever.

His uncle hadn't had the place piped for gas, and the

glistening wood faded away into the shadows. An arrangement of dried flowers banked by two candles leaped into view about the middle of the table and saved it from looking utterly desolate, but even that one clump of flowers seemed a mile away. The room was gloomy, lit only by candles set far apart. Tom felt ridiculously alone.

Hell, he'd been around people his entire life. Scads of people. Hordes of people. Even when he'd been scouting for the railroad in the vast emptiness of the American frontier, there had been people around. In fact, the fellows in the railroad camps had been like a big, rambunctious family to him. He'd never been alone like this.

Occasionally Scruggs would bring in another dish or refill his wineglass—God, what he wouldn't give for a mug of beer—but the butler didn't speak to him. Rather, he slumped around the room like a condemned man. Tom still hadn't decided whether Scruggs's attitude was fostered of animosity toward Tom or if he was merely a naturally morose man. He guessed Claire would be able to tell him. He also couldn't figure out how Scruggs could find his way around in the dark.

At least the silly cook had stopped crying. Claire had introduced him to Mrs. Philpott that morning, and it had taken Tom a good forty-five minutes to convince the woman he wasn't going to cast her off like an old shoe.

As he gazed moodily at all the gleaming wood stretched out in front of him, he was struck by the happy thought that Dianthe St. Sauvre would add a stunning note to his elegant dining room. He lifted his glass in a silent salute. He'd never seen anything like her in his life. She was the most dazzling female he'd ever encountered. Maybe he could invite her to dine with him some-time. Then he frowned.

If she came to dine here, he'd have to talk to her. Tom wasn't at all sure what to say to a poetess. Besides, there were societal strictures against single gentlemen inviting single ladies for dinner, weren't there? He couldn't recall if his mama had ever spoken to him on the subject. If she had, it was so long ago the rules had slipped his mind.

Claire would know. He'd ask her. Claire was such a comfortable woman, and she seemed to know all about stuff like that.

Finally Tom couldn't stand the silence. Wondering if he was breaking a cardinal rule of Partington Place, he asked the butler, "Did my uncle always take his meals alone, Scruggs?"

It seemed to take forever for his question to register and for Scruggs to put the dish of potatoes he'd been holding on the sideboard and turn around. Tom was on the verge of asking again, more loudly in case the butler suffered from deafness when Scruggs answered.

"No, sir."

"Did he have friends in often?"

"No, sir."

Frowning, Tom asked, "Well, who'd he eat with then?"

"Miss Montague always took her meals with your un-cle, Mr. Partington." He sounded absolutely hopeless.

Tom digested Scruggs's information. "Well, why isn't she taking her meal with me?"

"I couldn't say, sir."

"Did she eat alone tonight?"

Tom felt a little miffed at the thought. He wondered if Claire was so heartbroken by the death of his uncle that she couldn't stand to see Tom taking his place. She hadn't seemed heartbroken, but what the hell did he know about women *or* heartbreak?

"No, sir."

Tom looked at Scruggs expectantly, but the butler didn't seem inclined to volunteer information on this subject or any other. With an itch of irritation, he asked, "Well, where'd she eat then?"

"In her office, sir."

Poor Claire. Tom wished he'd had the presence of mind to ask her to eat with him. Not for the first time he cursed the circumstances of his life. They'd brought him honor and unwanted fame, but the nuances of polite behavior seemed determined to elude him.

But wait a minute. Scruggs had said she hadn't dined alone.

"Did you and Mrs. Philpott eat with her?"

"No, sir."

Rolling his eyes, Tom barked, "Well, who the hell did she eat with then?"

Scruggs's face seemed to lengthen with Tom's show of incivility, and Tom was annoyed with himself. "She dined with Mr. Addison-Addison, sir."

"Who?"

"Mr. Addison-Addison, sir. I believe," Scruggs added, for the first time answering an unasked question, "that the gentleman is an author."

Tom took a gulp of wine. Damned stuff tasted like vinegar. So much for Claire's missing her uncle. "One of her artists, is he?"

"I believe so, sir."

Scruggs stood by the sideboard, staring at Tom in resignation, as though he expected the inquisition to continue. Tom felt guilty for having snapped at the fellow. He just wasn't used to having a butler, was all.

He said, "Thank you, Scruggs," and was relieved when the man shuffled off.

Well, hell. So now what was he supposed to do? Tom looked around glumly. He wasn't in the habit of amusing himself. He was used to having friends around to talk to, drink with, play cards with, go carousing with. This being rich wasn't all it was cracked up to be. He wished he'd asked Silver to dinner.

After pushing himself away from the table, Tom moped on his way to the parlor, poured himself some of the port Scruggs had thoughtfully left for him there, and took a slug. It tasted like fermented prune juice, and he shuddered.

Finding nothing of interest with which to occupy himself in the parlor, he took his port and paid a visit to the library. There were books aplenty, many of which Tom had not read, but he didn't feel like reading tonight. He wanted to talk to somebody. Hell, this was the evening of his first full day in his new home, enjoying his new wealth, and he felt as though the world had died and left him orphaned.

He threw back the last of his port, grimaced, and wondered if he'd ever get used to the trappings of a gentleman. Tomorrow he was going to lay in a supply of booze, whether it was considered refined or not. He couldn't stand this cognac and port nonsense another day.

He wished Claire were here. She was delightful to talk to.

After circuiting the library twice, staring out the window at the black night for ten minutes, sitting at his desk, and thrumming his fingers on the blotter for what seemed like an eternity, he gave up solitude and headed for Claire's office. He hoped his presence wouldn't be unwelcome.

Claire felt a defeated sense of resignation as she sat on the sofa in her parlor-office and mended a torn pillow slip. It wasn't that the mending hadn't been piling up shamefully. Actually mending was the one job she'd neglected during her tenure as housekeeper at Partington Place.

No. The reason she felt unsettled this evening was that she longed to be sitting here alone in her office, as she had been all afternoon, writing. Writing trash. Heaving a sigh, Claire decided she was truly an unworthy plebeian. After meeting Tom Partington, though, she had an almost ungovernable urge to write about him. She couldn't seem to help herself.

Still, the chapter Sylvester Addison-Addison had come over to read was quite . . . thrilling. In its own way. She glanced up from setting a stitch to observe Sylvester poised as though balancing on the deck of a ship in high water, holding his manuscript to the oil lamp, a fervent expression on his handsome face. Light from the fireplace licked him artistically and highlighted the moodiness of his features.

Claire smiled. Not only was Sylvester a true author, but he—like Dianthe—possessed the looks of an artist as well. And the sensibilities. Why, even in the late autumn Sylvester had managed to find lilies. He'd brought her some this very evening, and they now graced a vase on the table next to her. They'd probably cost him a fortune, she thought, eyeing the flowers with a pang, but a true artist measured cost in terms other than vulgar coin.

Besides, it wasn't his money anyway, or not much of it at any rate. Sylvester did have to work part-time at the local mercantile—unlike Dianthe, who received a modest competence from a dead relative—but he reaped much more from the endowment of the Pyrite Arms than from his employment. Not that Claire grudged him a penny, for Sylvester's genius deserved everything Gordon had had to give.

She sighed again and guessed she possessed the sensibilities of a hack dime novelist. Frowning, she resumed sewing and tried to concentrate on Sylvester's stirring prose.

His glorious voice gave life to his words, but Claire still couldn't help wishing those words were describing something possessing more natural animation than Grecian ruins. With a twinge of regret for her wretched lack of artistic vision, she bent to her stitching.

The knock on her door came as Sylvester had just launched into a detailed description of the marble scrollwork on the tomb of his tragic hero's equally tragic father. He looked up, tossing his tousled locks impatiently.

"Who in God's name is that?"

Claire put her mending down. "I'll go see, Sylvester." Her heart hoped she knew who it was; her practical nature told her not to be silly.

This time her heart won.

3

"**M**r. Partington!"

Tom felt very ill at ease. He'd brought the port decanter with him, thinking to offer Claire and her guest a glass of wine, but now he wasn't sure how his gesture would be received. Claire's exclamation of surprise didn't make him feel any more comfortable. She stood in the doorway as though shocked, and Tom felt like an interloper. He had to remind himself that he was master in this house.

Suddenly leaping backward, Claire yanked the door open. "Oh, my goodness, Mr. Partington! I'm so sorry. Do, please, come in."

With a glance at the young man glowering at him from the fireplace, Tom murmured, "If I'm not intruding."

Another, sharper look revealed the fellow was holding a sheaf of papers in one hand and a wilted flower in the other, pressed to his chest. Must be some sort of new fad, Tom supposed. He'd been out of society for a long time and had a lot to catch up on. But wilted flowers? He shook his head.

"Heavens, no! How could you possibly be intruding? It's a pleasure to see you this evening." Claire took another step back, almost stumbling over a magazine basket in her haste.

"I brought some port, if you'd like a glass."

"Thank you. How kind." Claire stared at him for a minute, marveling again at how perfect he was.

Then she recalled there was another gentleman in the room. "Mr. Partington, please allow me to introduce you to Mr. Sylvester Addison-Addison. Mr. Addison-Addison was just reading me the latest chapter in his epic historical novel *The Solitary Journey of a Grecian Soul.*"

Claire's epic novelist was definitely not happy about having been interrupted. Sylvester slammed his manuscript onto a table, threw his wilted lily on top of it, and thrust a lock of hair back from his white brow. Nodding curtly, he mumbled, "Partington."

All at once Tom felt a familiar tickle in his chest. It had been years since he'd had to deal with surly boys, but he used to get a kick out of it in the army. Setting the port decanter down on a side table, Tom pasted a big smile on his face and walked toward Sylvester Addison-Addison with his hand outstretched.

"Good evening, Mr. Addison-Addison. A writer, are you?"

"I am an author, yes." Sylvester had been practicing his superior sneer, Tom thought. He shook Tom's hand but obviously wasn't pleased to have to do so.

"Mind if I sit down and join you for a while?"

Tom smiled at Claire, who swallowed nervously. He was sorry to see that, apparently a little worried about her author's manners, she'd taken to wringing her hands. Tom could hardly blame her.

"Of course not, Mr. Partington. Why, it would be a privilege to have you sit with us."

Tom sat docilely. "Mr. Silver will be joining us for a few weeks, Miss Montague. I trust that won't inconvenience you?"

"Certainly not, Mr. Partington."

Claire gave him a smile that made her seem younger and prettier than she had until now. A dimple played at the corner of her mouth, and Tom approved.

"I'll have Sally fix up the blue room upstairs tomorrow morning. Do you know how long he plans to visit?"

"At least until Christmas. He's going to show me the ropes around the estate." He wished she'd do her hair another way. Those two braided knots definitely did not flatter her. Tom, admittedly not an authority when it came to females, thought she'd do well to pile her hair on top of her head. If she were worried about maintaining a housekeeperish appearance, that would do it, and much less severely.

Picking up her mending with a shaking hand, Claire said, "I'll let Mrs. Philpott know to expect an extra diner then."

"Speaking of that, I understand you used to take your meals with my uncle, Miss Montague."

She peeked at him over her pillow slip. "Why, yes, I did, Mr. Partington. The late Mr. Partington, well, he—he was very kind to me and treated me more as a member of his family than as an employee."

"I think that's a fine idea myself. I'd be delighted if you'd join me for meals. I must admit to having been sadly lonely at dinner tonight."

Tom heard the angry rustle of manuscript pages at his

back. Apparently the Author was getting peeved at being left out of the conversation. He cast a negligent peek over his shoulder and took note of Addison-Addison's stormy expression. Ignoring him, Tom poured Claire a glass of port and handed it to her.

"Thank you, Mr. Partington." She dropped her pillow slip and lunged for the port. "And I should enjoy joining you for meals."

Tom was surprised to see a hint of pink stain Claire's cheeks, as though she were embarrassed.

The papers rattled again, more loudly, and Tom swiveled to look at Sylvester. "Want a glass of port, Addison?"

"It's Addison-Addison, Mr. Partington. There's a hyphen in the middle."

Nodding wisely, Tom murmured, "Parents came from the same family, did they? Works sometimes I understand, as long as they don't breed idiots." He ignored Sylvester's offended snort and poured a glass of port. "Here you go."

"Thank you." Sylvester's voice was as stiff as his posture when he took the proffered glass.

Claire took a quick gulp of wine, choking slightly. "Mr. Addison-Addison was just reading from his latest work, Mr. Partington. Would you care to listen for a while?" Glancing at the ruffled artist standing next to the fireplace, she added in a conciliatory voice, "I believe he's almost at the end of the chapter."

"Perhaps we should continue another time, Claire," Sylvester said heavily. "I can't imagine Mr. Partington having much interest in great historical literary works."

With a sweet smile Tom said, "I haven't read many, to tell you the truth."

Sylvester muttered, "What a surprise!"

Immediately Claire spoke up, trying to cover the moment. "You know, the historical novel is a fine art form, Mr. Partington, and Mr. Addison-Addison does it very well. You of all people should enjoy such novels since your own career is the stuff of legends."

"What?" The exclamation slipped out before Tom could stop it.

"It's inspired a series of dime novels at any rate." Sylvester's sneer faded into a sullen frown when Claire shot him a look.

"Ah, yes, the dime novels." Tom took a swig of port. He frowned too.

"It's hardly surprising that Mr. Partington should have inspired such literary works, Mr. Addison-Addison. After all, his career is renowned the world over."

"Literary works!" Sylvester downed his port too, then grimaced, as though he hadn't expected it to taste so bad.

A little put out, Claire said, "They may be mere popular fiction, but they are not entirely without merit, I believe. But your career truly has been thrilling, Mr. Partington. Brevet general at only twenty-two. My goodness." She gave him another shy smile.

Tom had encountered that expression of hero worship before. He'd never much liked it, although he found it almost tolerable in Claire Montague. "Everybody else was dead, Miss Montague, or I'd never have been so honored. Believe me."

He felt a little bit as though he'd kicked a kitten when Claire's eyes opened wide, and she uttered a breathy, unhappy "oh!"

"I'm going home," Sylvester announced suddenly. Tapping his manuscript into a tidy pile, he bowed to Claire and then to Tom, although he evidently resented the necessity of the latter. "I shall return at a more convenient time."

"Don't go on my account." Tom grinned in a friendly manner as he took another sip of port.

"Oh, dear. Well, if you feel you must. Do come back tomorrow, Sylvester. Perhaps late morning before luncheon would be a good time." Claire offered him a nervous smile.

Swiping a dark curl from his brow, Sylvester murmured, "If I have risen by then. I feel the muse upon me this evening. Perhaps I shan't sleep."

Tom rolled his eyes.

Claire said, "Of course. Well, do come again when you can. I really can't wait to hear the rest of your chapter."

Another sharp bow, and Sylvester was off into the night, his lily dangling from a white hand, his papers fluttering. Claire watched him stride away and wished she'd handled things better. Sylvester was such a sensitive soul. Turning around, she smiled tentatively at Tom.

"He'll carry off his world-weary suffering a little better when he's got a few more years under his belt," he said with a wink and a smile.

Momentarily stunned by his candor, Claire was too startled to react. When she did, it was with a giggle that took her by surprise. "He was quite silly, wasn't he? And so rude to you. I'm awfully sorry, Mr. Partington. Artists are such sensitive people, you know."

"It's not your place to apologize for a sulky child, Miss Montague. Please sit down. I'm sorry to have intruded. I hope he wasn't in the midst of a particularly moving passage."

With a sigh Claire resumed her chair and her mending. "Actually, Mr. Addison-Addison seems to dwell upon architectural description to the exclusion of almost everything else. I can't even recall the name of his hero."

"Sounds pretty dull to me."

Claire's spectacles glittered, giving her the look of an immensely serious owl. Tom was charmed.

"I very much regret to say I find much of his work rather boring, Mr. Partington." She sounded sad.

"Why do you regret saying that? Sounds like a sensible reaction to me."

"I fear it is only one symptom of an underlying weakness in my character."

"Come now, Miss Montague, I can't imagine you possessing a weak character," Tom said bracingly. "Why, you seem a fine, honorable, sensible young woman to me."

"Thank you, Mr. Partington." Claire gave him a melancholy little smile. "What I expect you mean is that I am such a poor drab thing you'd expect me to enjoy dull passages describing Greek architecture. Well, I wish I did. Unfortunately my taste in literature is not as—as refined as I wish it was."

Since he wasn't sure what to say, Tom only murmured, "I see."

"Now, mind you, I'm not saying Mr. Addison-Addison isn't a brilliant writer. Indeed he's one of the most prolific authors in the Pyrite Arms, and his prose is—is—well, his prose is truly edifying."

Tom managed another "I see."

"I fear my mind is not of such an elevated nature that I can listen to very much of it without yawning."

Since she appeared genuinely grieved about what seemed to him a logical reaction to the pompous young Addison-Addison's mind-numbing drivel, Tom tried not to crack a smile. He opted for a mild "no?"

She shook her head. "No. I much prefer Dianthe's interpretive verses. Or even—or even dime novels."

Her last confession was rendered in such a dismal tone Tom had to take a quick gulp of port to keep from laughing out loud. The resultant choking fit effected a change in the topic of conversation.

After Claire finished patting him on the back and his eyes quit watering, he said, "Thank you, Miss Montague."

"Of course, Mr. Partington." She was flushed when she sat down again.

"Er, anyway, what I came in here for—or, not the only reason, of course, but—" Oh, Lord. Tom hated having to be polite. He wasn't used to it. Funny. For the first several years of his life his mama had drilled him on gentlemanly behavior until he'd behaved like a little gentleman with every waking breath. His manners sure hadn't improved in the past fifteen or twenty years.

"Yes?" Claire asked helpfully, blinking at him from behind her lenses.

"Er, well, I wondered about what you said this afternoon."

She cocked her head, giving her the look of a curious barn owl.

"I mean"—Tom struggled on—"about asking people to dinner."

"Oh." Claire's head turned, and she seemed to be observing her stitching very carefully. "You mean, you would like to invite Dianthe St. Sauvre to dine with you?"

"Well, actually, didn't you mention arty evenings or something like that?" Tom downed the last of his port and poured another glass.

"Oh!" Claire brightened immediately, her eyes going

round and reminding Tom of big brown marbles. "I had no idea you'd really be interested in continuing the tradition of Artistic Evenings, Mr. Partington. I'm thrilled to hear you say so. Absolutely thrilled!"

Tom felt like a fraud—not for the first time—but was glad anyway since he'd made Claire's downcast countenance lift. "Yes, I do think that would be a good plan, Miss Montague. I don't know anybody in this area, and I suppose it would be a nice way to meet people."

Actually he wasn't sure how many artists of Sylvester Addison-Addison's stamp he could stomach in one evening, but he expected the ravishing Dianthe St. Sauvre's face and Claire Montague's conversation would keep him from smashing the insolent puppy's pretty nose flat.

"I'm sure of it too, Mr. Partington. And through them you'll meet many like-minded people in Pyrite Springs. And even Sacramento. Why, we often have visitors from as far away as San Francisco."

"We do?"

Claire blushed rosily, giving her a youthful appearance Tom was astonished to see. Why, she looked quite attractive when she blushed, quite attractive indeed. He simply had to get her to do something about her hair.

"I mean—I mean the people at the Pyrite Arms do, you see. I guess I've taken to thinking of myself as one of them." She let her head droop and was obviously embarrassed. "Of course that's silly of me, as I have absolutely no turn for the artistic."

Out of the blue Tom murmured, "You possess the soul of an artist, Miss Montague." He didn't know what had come over him to make him say such a stupid thing, but there it was.

She looked at him as though he'd just bestowed sainthood upon her. *"Thank* you, Mr. Partington."

It was Tom's turn to blink. "Well, you're welcome, Miss Montague."

Claire seemed much happier now. "That was a perfectly lovely thing to say. And I do believe you're right. Even though I'm not able to express myself in words of an edifying, exalted nature, my soul is stirred by the works of great artists."

"Is it?"

"Oh, yes. Yes, indeed."

Although he thought she seemed a little fanatical on the subject, Tom said, "There. You see? It shows. Your soul's stirrings, and all." He felt like an idiot.

She said, "Thank you," in as fervent a voice as he'd ever heard, and he guessed he'd said the right thing. He felt oddly as though he'd passed some sort of test.

"Er, so when do you suppose we could have one of these evening things, Miss Montague?" A troubling thought hit him. "Is this the sort of thing Mrs. Philpott was afraid of?" Lord, he didn't want the cook to start bawling again.

"No, indeed. Mrs. Philpott was used to the late Mr. Partington's Artistic Evenings, Mr. Partington. Why, if we invite the entire population of the Pyrite Arms, that would only be five extra people. She wouldn't mind that. It was a *big* gathering she was worried about."

"I see." Tom was glad to have that puzzle cleared up. He wondered what constituted a big gathering if five extra people were nothing at all.

"And if you wanted to invite some of the other citizens of Pyrite Springs, which the late Mr. Partington often did, then we could hire a couple of the girls in town to help."

"That sounds like a good idea," said Tom, who guessed it was.

"When would you like to have the first evening, Mr. Partington? I'm sure all the denizens of the Pyrite Arms are dying to meet you."

He grinned. "Especially after Addison-Addison tells 'em all what a Philistine I am."

"I'm sure he wouldn't say such a thing."

Claire looked horrified, and Tom wondered if a sense of humor lurked somewhere beneath her starchy exterior. He thought he'd seen glimpses of one from time to time but wasn't sure. "I was only joking, Miss Montague."

"Oh. Of course." She smiled uncertainly.

"Well, let's see. Silver's coming tomorrow. I don't suppose that would matter. He's undoubtedly met some of your artist friends before."

"Yes, indeed. I'm sure he'd be very happy to join us. He's often expressed an interest in the Arms."

"Has he now? Well, then, how about in two or three weeks? Would that be enough time to fix things up?"

"Oh, Mr. Partington, that would be simply lovely! I'll run over to the Pyrite Arms tomorrow and tell them all we have a special treat coming."

"All right. Sounds fine with me. Er, where do you hold these little shindigs anyway? I mean, did Uncle Gordo—Gordon—have a little theater tucked away somewhere in this pile that I haven't found yet?"

"No, I'm afraid not, although we had discussed building one. The entertainments are generally held in the small ballroom."

"I see." Tom cast about, trying to locate the small ballroom in the warren of rooms cluttering the map in his brain. He thought he'd succeeded, but wasn't altogether sure. This house was so damned big. And it was his. A thrill of satisfaction made him sigh deeply and smile.

Suddenly Claire put a hand on his arm. "Mr. Partington, I can't begin to express to you the honor you'll be showing the fine young artists at the Pyrite Arms. I was afraid the patronage would end with your uncle's death. Although I know it's not an object with you, I must tell you how very happy you've made me."

To Tom's utter horror, he saw tears sparkle in Claire's eyes. Fortunately for him, Claire was too proper to shed them. Blinking furiously, she returned to her nearly forgotten pillow slip. "I'm sure you must think me quite demented, Mr. Partington."

"No, no, not at all, Miss Montague. I'm happy to do it."

"Thank you." She gave him such a glowing look that Tom couldn't stand it. Searching blindly for something to say, he blurted out, "So you like dime novels, do you?"

Claire looked up from her mending stunned. Dime novels? Good heavens. Her heart began beating against her rib cage like a military drum.

"I, uh, well, yes, I do enjoy reading a good potboiler every now and then." Her laugh, she realized with distaste, sounded like that of a fatuous adolescent. She cleared her throat. "Do you care for them?" Then she held her breath. If he admitted to relishing having been made a hero through her books, how would she acknowledge her authorship without fainting?

Sipping his port, Tom cocked a brow. "Well, now, Miss Montague, I'm not entirely sure."

"No?" Claire dared a smile. How she wanted him to know it was she who'd written those books! It was she who'd made him the idol of America.

"I have to admit to being somewhat . . . embarrassed by the *Tom Pardee* novels."

Claire's hammering heart did a crazy swoop, and her mouth went dry. She dropped her pillow slip like a hot rock, grabbed for her port, and took an enormous gulp. *Embarrassed?* Oh, no. "I—I'm sure they were meant as—well, as praise for your brave deeds, Mr. Partington," she said when she could.

"Hmm. Maybe."

Oh, dear. He looked very much as though he were brooding, and Claire, who had never encountered a broody gentleman, wasn't sure what to say. She decided upon: "But well, you must admit your career has more than lent itself to—to acclaim, sir."

"Do you think that's what those books are, Miss Montague?"

"I'm absolutely sure of it, Mr. Partington," she declared, because she was.

"Hmm."

"Certainly they are. I mean"—Claire rushed on, worried about so many hmms—"just think about your heroic action at Gettysburg, sir."

"I'd rather not."

"But you were so noble, so gallant. Leading that charge, saving General Lee's life was—was magnificent. Simply magnificent."

Tom peered at her over the rim of his glass. "I don't suppose you'd believe me if I told you it was a mistake? That I was really trying to get the men to retreat and that the air was so full of smoke I steered my horse in the wrong direction?"

Claire gave a tinny laugh. "Of course not, sir."

Returning his moody stare to his port, Tom muttered, "No, I didn't think so. Nobody else did either."

"And you can't tell me that stealing into enemy territory to rescue Colonel Fosdick was a mistake, sir."

"No, I meant to do that all right. That bast—er, the colonel owed me too much money to let the damned Yankees kill him."

Claire looked at him hard but didn't detect a hint of teasing in his expression. He appeared in fact annoyed. Nevertheless, she forged on. "And then, after the war, when you became a scout for the railroad, why, your accomplishments were legendary."

"My accomplishments, Miss Montague, were minimal. It was the circumstances that were extraordinary."

"I don't believe that for a minute, sir."

With a frown Tom said, "Well, I wish people *would* believe me. It would make my life much less difficult."

"Difficult?"

"Yes. Those books. They've made my life hell."

Good heavens. This was a new slant on her novels, one she'd never considered. "I—I don't know what you mean, sir. How have they made your life difficult?"

"I suppose if the author hadn't written that note in the first book telling the world that Pardee was modeled after me, nobody would have made the connection. But do you have any idea what it's like to be among a group of men, all trying to do the same job, and have one of them break out a *Tuscaloosa Tom Pardee* novel and read it around the campfire at night? There were nights I wanted to crawl away and hide."

"You mean, they mocked you?"

"I guess it wasn't me so much as the exalted prose. Luckily we all got along well. It was just being singled out that made it embarrassing. I pretended to laugh it off, but it was pretty awful."

"But your friends must have known that your exceptional behavior would foster praise, Mr. Partington. Surely they didn't object to the novels on that ground."

"That's just it, Miss Montague. My behavior wasn't exceptional. We were all just trying to do a job for which we got paid a moderate amount of money. I didn't do anything anybody else wouldn't have done—didn't do, if it comes to that."

"Not even when you conquered that Indian village single-handedly, Mr. Partington?" Claire thought she had him with that one. He'd have to confess to having done a heroic deed this time.

"That village consisted of twelve people. Three women and nine children. I didn't conquer anything."

"Oh." Claire digested this daunting piece of information. "That's not the way the event was reported in the press," she said in a small voice.

"Of course it wasn't." He sounded disgusted.

"And the lady you rescued?" Her voice seemed to be getting smaller as the conversation continued.

"That was no lady. That was a wh—a woman of—of easy virtue who'd managed to get drunk and fall off her horse. They're always following the railroad. I just picked her up and poured her back into her tent."

"Oh." Claire stared, unseeing, at her pillow slip for a moment. "But what about the war party? The one you diverted from attacking the railroad by clever stratagems?"

With a big sigh Tom said, "My only clever stratagem was to let the poor souls know where they could find food, Miss Montague. The railroad workers had taken to killing the buffalo for sport. The Indians needed them for food. I'd found a small herd of buffalo and showed 'em where it was. That doesn't sound terribly clever to me, but perhaps Clarence McTeague thought otherwise."

The way he spoke her pen name made Claire's heart take a nosedive.

"I'm sure Mr. McTeague meant no harm," she said tentatively.

Tom threw his head back so that it rested against the antimacassar on the chair. He stretched his legs out in front of him and crossed them negligently at the ankles. His shirt was unbuttoned at the throat, exposing a tantalizing hint of curly golden chest hair. His pose was at once casual and elegant. He was the most magnificent male Claire had ever seen in her life, and her poor tattered heart throbbed in response.

"He may not have meant any harm, but he made me a damned laughingstock." He looked at Claire ruefully. "Sorry, Miss Montague. I'm used to rough company. I didn't mean to offend you with my profane language."

"No," said Claire, struggling to keep from bursting into tears. "No. You didn't offend me."

His smile just about did her in. "I'm glad. You're a very comfortable woman, Miss Montague. I'm afraid you're so easy to be with that I allowed myself to say more than I should have. I hope I haven't shattered too many illusions."

Comfortable. She was comfortable. Well, Claire guessed being comfortable was better than nothing. She tried to smile. "Thank you, Mr. Partington. No, you didn't shatter my illusions. I already knew you were a modest man."

His little snort didn't surprise her.

"I don't know how modest I am, but I'll tell you this, although you might think it shocking. If my uncle Gordon wasn't already dead, I might just be tempted to put a bullet in his brain for writing those blasted *Tusca-loosa Tom Pardee* books. They've made my life a living hell for five years."

Now *that* surprised her.

4

laire's brain raced. As if determined to keep up with it, her feet sped her toward the Pyrite Arms until she was nearly running down the road.

Tom Partington hated her books. Not only did he hate them, but they had made his life miserable. What was even worse than that was he thought his uncle had written them and despised him for it!

Good heavens. She'd been so upset after their conversation, she'd barely slept a wink all night long, worrying about how she'd ever be able to confess that it was she, not his uncle Gordon, who had created Tuscaloosa Tom Pardee. Yet she didn't feel it right that Tom should continue blaming his innocent uncle for them.

She wished she could apologize to Gordon Partington. It was all her fault that his nephew had not esteemed him as he surely would have done had not *she,* in her innocence, created a monster. But she hadn't meant Tuscaloosa Tom as a monster; rather, her novels had been meant as praise for her hero.

If she confessed her authorship, Tom would undoubtedly hate her. Claire didn't think she could stand it if he were to dislike her. She loved him, for heaven's sake. The whole situation didn't bear thinking of.

So why could she think of nothing else?

Not only that, but her latest creation, *Tuscaloosa Tom and the River of Raging Death,* was scheduled for release in January. Mr. Oliphant, her publisher's representative, would be arriving any day now with her advance copies and to finalize arrangements for the one book remaining to be written under her current contract.

If Claire had not learned early in life to disguise her emotions, she might have burst into tears. As it was, she jumped a foot when she rounded the hedge separating the grounds of the Pyrite Arms from the prying eyes of the rest of the community and almost collided with Sergei Ivanov.

Sergei, a portrait artist and resident of the Arms, had been occupied in glaring at an empty canvas. When Claire uttered a stifled shriek and skidded to a stop, a hand pressed to her hammering heart, Sergei's glare transferred to her, and he lifted his paintbrush in a sinister manner.

Claire stared at him, her thoughts instantly congealing into a scene of riveting intensity.

As the ferocious brave fell dead at his feet, Tom swirled around to behold yet another peril. A villain stood over Miss Abigail Faithgood, his dagger poised threateningly.

"Stop, fiend!" Tom demanded.

"Never!" the miscreant retorted. "Not until the wench agrees to give up her foul sheep!" He grabbed Miss Faithgood by her flowing tresses, eliciting another scream from her ruby lips.

"Claire? Miss Montague?"

Her attention thus jerked back to the here and now, Claire realized Sergei's attitude had changed from one of belligerence to one of concern. Pressing her forehead, momentarily disconcerted, she said, "I'm so sorry, Sergei. I got lost in a fog there for a minute."

Turning to resume glowering at his canvas, Sergei muttered, "Fog is to be chosen over a tarnished soul."

Since Claire didn't know how to respond to that cryptic utterance, she chose to say instead, "I see you're beginning work on another project, Sergei. Who will be honored by your artistry this time?" She gave him as sunny a smile as she could manufacture.

With a gloomy sigh the artist said, "Mrs. Humphry Albright."

"Mrs. Albright?" Triumph replaced despair in Claire's breast. "Why, Mrs. Albright is one of Pyrite Springs's leading citizens, Sergei. What a wonderful achievement for you!"

Scowling at his canvas, Sergei said darkly, "A tarnished soul will out, Miss Montague."

Her sense of triumph diminishing rapidly, Claire said uncertainly, "Do you mean you believe Mrs. Albright to be the possessor of a tarnished soul?"

His look rubbed the rest of the shine off Claire's moment.

"Oh, dear, Sergei. Are you absolutely certain? I'm sure she's a very nice lady. I can't believe her soul can be so *very* tarnished."

Another darkling glance from her friend assured Claire that while she might not believe such a thing, Sergei certainly did.

"Sergei, you must remember that there are many people who prefer to keep their soul's imperfections to themselves. Are you sure you must paint them?"

Sergei scowled at her as if she'd just suggested he sell his firstborn. "I paint what I see, Miss Montague. I will not prostitute my art for fools."

With a sigh Claire said, "No, I suppose you won't. Well, just don't be surprised if Mrs. Albright objects. You remember the ruckus Mr. Gilbert kicked up."

Throwing his head back, Sergei barked out, "Ha! Barbarians!"

Claire decided to leave Sergei to his gloomy reflections. Shaking her head, she made her way up the gravel path to the front door of the Pyrite Arms. With a brisk tug at the bellpull, she pushed the door open and called out, "Mrs. Elliott, it's just Claire. Is Dianthe in?"

A harassed-looking woman scuttled through a door on the other side of the hallway and smiled at Claire. Waving in the appropriate direction, she said, "She's in the parlor, Miss Claire. Creating a dance to go along with that dreadful picture Mr. Sergei painted last month."

"Thank you, Mrs. Elliott."

"Think nothing of it, dearie. Why anybody would want to dance around in front of that thing is beyond me. Worse than wild Indians these artists are." Mrs. Elliott hurried off.

Another hearty sigh saw Claire into the parlor. She stopped, mesmerized, at the scene that greeted her eyes. There, on an easel in front of the fireplace, in a place of honor, resided Sergei Ivanov's portrait of Alphonse Gilbert, mayor of Pyrite Springs and proprietor of the Pyrite Springs Mercantile and Furniture Emporium.

Although she admired Sergei as an artist of rare ability, Claire couldn't help wincing as she gazed at the countenance on that canvas. Sergei, who claimed to paint the souls of his subjects, had evidently discerned sins in the jovial Mr. Gilbert's soul that Claire couldn't even imagine.

Before the portrait, prostrate amid a buttery froth of chiffon, lay Dianthe St. Sauvre. When the door clicked shut, Dianthe's head lifted, and Claire found herself being scrutinized by two glorious blue eyes in a beautiful face set into a head topped with tumbling blond curls.

"Hello, Claire. What brings you here?"

All at once Claire wondered why Miss Abigail Faithgood's tresses should be flowing if she was hiding out behind a rock in the wilderness. Such a circumstance didn't seem right somehow, but she decided to put her mind to the matter later.

Dianthe rose from the floor and fluttered onto the sofa. Claire couldn't contain a tiny, virtually nonexistent stab of envy.

"I spoke with Mr. Partington last evening, Dianthe, and he told me he is definitely interested in continuing the tradition of Artistic Evenings."

"How wonderful!"

Claire sat in a wing chair, trying very hard to keep her gaze from straying to the ghastly painting by the fireplace. She couldn't stop herself from saying, "I can't imagine why Sergei always seems to see one's soul as black. Do you understand it, Dianthe?"

"He's a Russian, Claire."

"Do you think that accounts for it?"

"Of course. You know how somber and dank the Russian spirit is."

"I hadn't actually thought about it, to tell you the truth."

"Oh, yes, my dear. Positively *centuries* of oppression lurk behind Sergei's wounds."

"His wounds!" Claire sat up, distressed that one of her artists could have been hurt without her having been told about it.

"His spiritual wounds, Claire, darling," Dianthe murmured, sinking back against a pile of pillows on the sofa.

"Oh. Of course." Claire shot another nervous glance at Mr. Gilbert's portrait. "What a terrible shame!"

"Mr. Gilbert thought so too."

"I know. Has he had second thoughts about pressing charges? Perhaps I should speak with him again."

"Well, since Sergei gave him back his money, he isn't *as* angry, but I'm afraid he's threatening legal action should Sergei ever show the portrait. At least he didn't smash it, as he wanted to do."

Claire made herself look at the picture. "Maybe smashing it isn't such a bad idea." She giggled.

Dianthe giggled too. "Perhaps not. But wait until I finish my dance, if you please."

"I wouldn't dream of smashing it, really. But I do hope it won't sit in the parlor forever. It's so *very* . . . tortured. I think I'd prefer to have a series of Mrs. Gaylord's marigolds. Marigolds are at least cheerful."

Glorietta Gaylord, another Pyrite Arms artist, painted marigolds to the exclusion of all else. And if there was anything Claire needed at the moment, it was cheer. She gave another heartfelt sigh.

"Is something the matter, Claire?"

Glancing at Dianthe, Claire detected concern in her vivid blue eyes and was touched. While she honored all the artists Gordon's funds supported here at the Pyrite Arms, she had yet to discover among them much compassion for their fellow sufferers. Except for Dianthe, whose beauty went through and through and who genuinely valued Claire's friendship.

As though the agitation of the last several hours had waited until Dianthe's worry pushed it over the edge, tears trickled from Claire's eyes, and she pulled her handkerchief from her pocket. "Oh, Dianthe, he *hates* them!" Hastily she wiped at her leaky eyes and blew her nose, utterly humiliated by her childish display.

Dianthe, however, was suitably horrified by Claire's news. Nor did she need an explanation of what might have been considered a conversational non sequitur. Pressing one hand to her bosom and putting the other on Claire's knee, she leaned forward and whispered, "Disaster!"

Claire could do no more than nod unhappily as she tried to get her emotions under control.

After her concise summation of Claire's problem, Dianthe sat back against her cushions and tapped her lovely chin with an equally lovely finger. "But not, I think, an impossible one."

Sniffing in a manner she knew Dianthe would never do, Claire said, "N-no?"

Dianthe leveled her magnificent gaze upon her, and Claire took heart. If there was anybody who possessed the secret to a man's sensibilities, it was Dianthe. Why, she had men dropping at her feet all the time. They practically littered the drive. Dianthe would know how to tame Tom Partington's savage beast if anybody would.

"Not at all, my dear. Let me put my mind to it. I'm sure I'll think of some way to reconcile him with your novels." Dianthe's exquisite nose wrinkled a bit as she spoke the word "novel," but Claire felt a swell of gratitude.

"Thank you, Dianthe. You can't know how much I appreciate this. I know you'd much rather be working on your expressive dance. Although," she added with another peek at the painting, "I can't imagine what you're managing to dance about in Mr. Gilbert's face as painted by Sergei."

Dianthe rose to her feet and swirled to the painting where she draped a long, flowing sleeve over a corner and made Mr. Gilbert appear to be leering horribly at Claire from behind a yellow gauze curtain. "I'm creating an 'Ode to a Tortured Soul,' using Mr. Gilbert as my inspiration." She smiled, and the contrast between her heavenly features and the grotesque painting struck Claire as almost alarming.

"Oh. Well, do you suppose your dance will be ready to be performed a couple of Saturdays from now at Partington Place? That's when Mr. Partington wants to hold the first of *his* Artistic Evenings."

Sighing, Dianthe sank to her knees in front of the portrait and stared up at it lovingly. "No, I don't believe so. Besides, Freddy is working on a musical accompaniment, and I'm sure it won't be ready by then."

"No, I don't suppose so," Claire said thoughtfully. "Perhaps if he were to learn to read music, his compositions would flow more smoothly."

Dianthe looked at her reproachfully. "You know Freddy doesn't believe in adhering to traditional musical forms, Claire. He's afraid that learning to read music conventionally will stifle his creativity."

"Yes, I do know that, Dianthe, but I can't help wondering sometimes whether there aren't *reasons* for such conventions as standardized musical notes and so forth. I think of them sort of as musical—well—letters, as it were, used to form words, which then can be used to create literature. If you see what I mean." Unsure how her revolutionary ideas would be received, she peered doubtfully at Dianthe.

Dianthe, however, did not seem inclined to disparage them. Instead she sighed, plumped down onto the sofa again in a much less graceful manner than she had before, and said, "You're probably right, Claire. But you'll never convince Freddy. The way he does it is so slow!"

"Well, he *is* talented," Claire said in mitigation of their musical friend's odd compositional style. "Do you have another work prepared that you can perform, Dianthe? I'm sure Mr. Partington is particularly interested in your work."

"I think I shall do 'In Praise of the Spotted Horse.'" Dianthe smiled at Claire in a conspiratorial manner. "I took what you said about his spotted horses to heart, my dear, and have written what I believe is rather a wonderful poem. My dance in accompaniment is quite lively as well."

Secretly relieved when Dianthe admitted her "Tortured Soul" would not be ready for presentation, Claire was lost in admiration when told about her "Spotted Horse" work. "That will be wonderful, Dianthe. Mr. Partington will be thrilled. I'm sure of it."

"It was nothing, really," Dianthe said, flicking a purple paint fleck fallen from Mr. Gilbert's nose from her yellow chiffon. "And, Claire, I shall give every attention to your problem. No challenge is insurmountable when looked upon creatively."

"I suppose you're right, Dianthe. Will you tell Freddy about the Artistic Evening? And Sylvester, of course, and Glorietta. I'll tell Sergei on my way out." Giving a thought to the morose Russian's tormented sensibilities, she added, "Although it wouldn't hurt to mention it to him again at supper tonight. You know how he is."

"I shall be happy to, Claire. Thank you so much for dropping by."

Dianthe led Claire to the door. Claire followed in Dianthe's drifting yellow wake, feeling very ordinary in her plain brown calico gown.

Her eyes opened wide when she passed Sergei, lost now in the throes of creativity. She saw slashes of red cutting across his formerly pristine canvas. They reminded Claire of knife slits, and she stopped dead, mesmerized.

With a sudden downward slash, the evil man cut through a handful of Miss Abigail Faithgood's beautiful blond curls. She screamed.

Tuscaloosa Tom cried, "Villain!"

That was good, if she could figure out how Miss Faithgood's hair had come to be unbound in the first place. The paltry creature seemed to be screaming a lot too. Perhaps Claire should work on that. Ah, well, one thing at a time.

"Sergei."

The artist, concentrating intently on his canvas, did not respond. Claire tried again, a little louder. "Sergei!"

He heard her that time and turned with a blood-curdling yell. Claire leaped back, startled.

"My goodness, I beg your pardon."

Wild-eyed for only a few seconds, Sergei calmed when he beheld Claire. "I beg your pardon, Miss Montague. I was lost in thought."

Peering at the red-smeared canvas, Claire decided not to ask what his thoughts had been. "The young Mr. Partington is hosting an Artistic Evening, Sergei. He would be honored if you would attend."

Drawing himself up straight and striking a noble pose, Sergei declared, "I shall paint him, Claire. I shall paint his soul's deepest stirrings."

Claire patted his arm. "Perhaps you'd better wait until you're through with Mrs. Albright, Sergei."

Frowning, Sergei considered for a moment before allowing, "Perhaps."

Claire left the Pyrite Arms in a much sunnier mood than when she had arrived. Just knowing Dianthe was working on her problem made her feel better.

A visit to the lending library, also heavily supported by an endowment from Gordon Partington, provided Claire with a book about horses. She looked in the table of contents for a chapter on Appaloosas, but since the book was an old edition, she was unsuccessful in finding information about them. When she asked Mr. Johnson, the city librarian, she was informed that he'd never heard of the breed but that the book in her hand would give her lots of information on horse ranching.

"You may check it out for as long as you need it, Miss Montague, although most patrons are allowed to keep our books for only two weeks. *You* of course needn't worry about that."

Mr. Johnson smiled at her warmly, and Claire felt a pang of regret that she couldn't feel more than tepid friendship for him. He obviously admired her. It was just her fate, she decided, to be attracted to a man who could only see her in the light of a competent housekeeper rather than to this kind, albeit somewhat stuffy, librarian.

Still, being Tom Partington's housekeeper was not a task to be sneered at. Perhaps one day Mr. Partington would consider her his friend, and that was a good deal better than nothing.

Besides, it was an absolutely spectacular day, and Claire decided it would be foolish to spend it moping. November clouds galloped across a sapphire blue sky like white horses. Mountains, green, brown, and magnificent, a miracle of nature, rose majestically in the distance.

She strode toward home feeling quite happy. Inhaling a lungful of crisp Sierra air, she viewed Partington Place with real pleasure. It was a lovely house, set in parklike grounds. Spread out behind it was the farm, acres upon acres of fields, fallow now in the clutches of fall, but bearing rich crops in season. Soon, perhaps, beautiful spotted horses would grace at least one of those fields. Claire hoped Mr. Partington could achieve his dream here.

Partington Place was the grandest house in Pyrite Springs, and it had been built with gold Gordon Partington had mined out of the rich California lodes. Claire frowned, wondering if the pursuit of wealth was as much of a sin as the artists at the Pyrite Arms wanted her to believe. Certainly Gordon had never caviled about how he'd made his fortune.

"Gold has its place in the world, Claire, as much as art does," he told her. "It's one of the most useful commodities a person can have, and it can do a world of good if used judiciously."

He was right. Why, if Claire had not made lots of money with her books, she'd never be able to support her garden or the arts as she did now. A sudden pang made her remember how much she had loved Gordon Partington. They had shared so many viewpoints, so many ideas and aspirations. *Gordon* had liked her books. He'd even told her they had literary merit when she'd seen them only as a means to an end.

Happy memories of Gordon accompanied Claire down the lane. One recollection led to another and another and eventually to her work in progress. The first thing she had to do was solve the problem of Miss Abigail Faithgood's unbound hair. She could tackle her inclination to shriek at the least provocation later.

"Perhaps she lost her pins while riding on the back of Tom's horse," she mused aloud.

"Who was riding on Tom's horse?"

The deep voice startled her, and Claire whirled around to behold her hero, in the flesh, astride a big black horse. She wondered if she would ever become inured to his masculine beauty and had a sinking feeling the answer was no. There wasn't a single thing about him that didn't proclaim his maleness, even without his mustache. A frontiersman through and through, he put in the shade Jedediah Silver, a handsome man in his own right, who was riding next to him.

"Mr. Partington." She felt her face heat up and knew she was blushing.

He dismounted and led his horse, with which Claire was familiar, up to her. She patted the horse's nose in order to do something with hands that felt suddenly clumsy. "Good morning, Ebony." The horse snorted.

"How are you this morning, Miss Montague?" Tom asked pleasantly. "I missed you at breakfast."

Claire looked at him quickly. "Oh, I'm sorry. I ate early and then went to town for a while."

"There's no need to apologize. I'm sure you have many duties. Please feel free to dine with me, though. I'd enjoy your company."

"You would? I mean, thank you, I will be happy to take breakfast with you in the morning. Most mornings."

Looking around with a smile, Tom said, "This is really a beautiful place. If I'd known how pretty California was, I might have visited Uncle Gordon once or twice. As it is, especially in light of his remarkable generosity to me, I regret that I didn't."

"He would have enjoyed your visits," Claire said softly. She smiled at Jedediah, who had joined them. Tom was, she noted, taller than Jedediah. His limp gave him an aura of intrigue sadly lacking in the kindhearted accountant. Jedediah Silver, while an admirable person, was not a man to stir one's passions. At least he left Claire's passions unstirred.

"Yes. Well, my life didn't allow much time for visiting, I'm afraid."

"No. I'm sure that was the case."

"Mr. Silver and I were discussing how much my uncle Gordon valued your services, Miss Montague."

"You were? How very kind!" Claire felt ridiculously pleased.

"Indeed, the late Mr. Partington held you in the greatest esteem, Miss Montague," Jedediah said. He smiled at her too, and Claire decided the day wasn't half as bleak as it had been earlier, even without the glorious weather.

"We were going out to the barn, Miss Montague. Would you like to join us? Mr. Silver thinks my ambition to breed Appaloosas might be on its way to being realized."

"That's wonderful, Mr. Partington. I went to the library and found this book about horse ranching. I'm afraid there isn't anything in it about Appaloosas." She felt silly talking about horses, although in truth she knew quite a bit about them because she'd had to research horses in order to add veracity to her novels.

"Why, for heaven's sake!" Tom exclaimed. "Thank you very much. May I take a look at that book, Miss Montague?"

"Certainly. It deals primarily with equine ranching and mentions only a couple of breeds in depth."

He gave her such a warm look Claire could not maintain his scrutiny but felt compelled to drop her gaze.

"I feel honored that you would go to the bother, Miss Montague."

"It was nothing, really," she said in a stifled voice. He was *such* a gentleman! Why, he just took her breath away.

He walked beside her all the way to the barn, which perched atop a grassy slope. It was used at present to house the Partington cattle, two Morgan horses Gordon had kept for riding, two mules used for plowing, and a big rawboned farm horse.

With a sweeping gesture Jedediah said, "You see, these fields are generally planted with alfalfa, but that's not a crop Gordon found particularly profitable. You could build stables here and a couple of corrals over there. I think it would work quite nicely as a horse ranch, Mr. Partington."

"My, yes," Claire added, getting into the spirit of Tom's new venture, "and if you needed to grow fodder for the horses, why, the old beet field could be converted. I don't believe Gordon cared much for beets."

Tom chuckled, sending a warm feeling sliding around Claire's middle. She looked at him and found him smiling at her.

"You truly are a paragon, Miss Montague."

"Nonsense!"

"Well, Claire has a sensible idea there anyway." His attention diverted, Jedediah stopped speaking suddenly.

Squinting toward the house, he murmured, "I say, isn't that somebody drawing into the drive?"

They all turned to look down the hill, where sure enough, a carriage had just been driven down the circular driveway. It stopped in front of the door, and a gentleman emerged. He appeared to be carrying a large package under his arm.

"Oh, good Lord, I believe it's Mr. Oliphant." Horrified, Claire turned to face Tom and Jedediah. "If you two gentlemen will please pardon me, I'd better see what he wants."

Without giving them time to answer, she hurried down the hill.

"Who's Mr. Oliphant?" Puzzled by Claire's abrupt departure and her even more abrupt descent into nervousness, Tom stared after her. She'd seemed really excited about the horses. When she relaxed like that, she was an extraordinarily appealing woman. Not a beauty perhaps but attractive in her own way. She'd actually seemed to be interested in horse ranching. He breathed deeply of the fresh morning air and decided there was more to like about California than the weather.

"I've met him here before, but I don't know much about him," Jedediah added with a grin. "He mentioned publishing once. Maybe he has something to do with those books you hate so much."

"Oh, no! You don't mean to tell me Uncle Gordon wrote one that's going to come out now, even after he's dead?"

"Well, as to that, I couldn't tell you."

"You're his man of affairs. Don't you know about his books?"

Shaking his head, Jedediah muttered, "I don't know a

blessed thing about any books. If he wrote them, he sure kept it a secret from me."

Tom looked at him puzzled. "I don't understand. I wonder if he kept separate ledgers and accounts for his writing enterprise. He must have made a fortune with those damned books."

"I expect so. They're everywhere."

"I know."

Jedediah laughed. "Aw, don't sound so gloomy about 'em! You're famous now because of those books."

"Maybe. But I didn't want to be famous. All I wanted was to do my job and someday raise horses."

"Well, it looks as though you're getting your wish in spite of the books."

Tom smiled, his moment of irritation lifting. "You're right. And I guess I shouldn't be too hard on Uncle Gordon. He did all right by me. And he brightened my mother's life a lot. There's something about knowing you're making a man miserable that seems to make women happy."

Tom's words provoked another hearty laugh from Jedediah. "I'm afraid I don't know much about that. I don't know much about women, in fact."

"You're not alone there," Tom said with a sigh. "Miss Montague's about the only good woman I've talked to for five years or more. I'm afraid the frontier attracts a certain type of man, and a certain type of female generally follows."

Jedediah went so far as to blush, a fact Tom considered astonishing until he remembered that this part of California had been more or less civilized for a number of years now. He muttered, "Didn't mean to shock you, Mr. Silver."

"No, no, of course not."

Now he was embarrassed. Tom could tell. He turned back to a view of his pastures to be and said somewhat cynically, "But there are several genuine ladies around here. I have to watch myself."

Jedediah cleared his throat. "I see. Well, yes, I can understand how it must be."

Chuckling, Tom asked, "Can you?"

Blushing even more hotly, Jedediah said fervently, "No. Actually I can't. I'd give anything to have had your experiences, Mr. Partington. My life has been so—so—so damnably dull!"

Tom could tell it took a lot for Jedediah to utter his mild blasphemy, and he felt like sighing. "You've read those lousy books, haven't you?"

"I must admit that I have."

"And you believed them."

Looking terribly embarrassed, Jedediah mumbled, "Well, I suppose I did. To a degree."

"Hmm."

"You have to admit your life has been more fascinating than that of an accountant, Mr. Partington."

"I'd love to have had the opportunity to be an accountant, Mr. Silver."

"I don't believe it for a minute."

This time Tom did sigh. "It's the truth, though. But let's talk about something else for a while, shall we? Tell me, Mr. Silver, do you know many of the residents of the Pyrite Arms? Miss Montague seems to set quite a store by the artists who live there."

Taking his cue with good grace, Jedediah said, "Yes. The residents of the Pyrite Arms are all well known in Pyrite Springs. Miss St. Sauvre, well . . ." Jedediah's words trickled out. Tom got the impression he didn't quite have the proper ones with which to describe the angelic Miss St. Sauvre.

"Yes, indeed. I understand Miss Montague is going to be setting up one of her evening art things, and Miss St. Sauvre will attend. With the rest of them, of course. You are cordially invited too."

Jedediah brightened, embarrassment forgotten in a flash. "That would be splendid, Mr. Partington. I'll enjoy that."

All at once Tom decided there was one custom prevailing in civilization that annoyed him. "Do you suppose I could convince you to call me Tom, Mr. Silver? I'm not used to being called Mr. anything."

"Of course. If you will reciprocate and call me Jedediah."

Jedediah looked pleased, and Tom congratulated himself on having performed a civil social function without blundering. He actually rubbed his hands together.

"Good. Well, then, Jedediah, let's talk horses."

5

Claire's heart was battering her ribs like an artillery barrage and her lungs were fairly bursting by the time she reached the house. Corsets, she decided, were not designed to assist ladies in the act of running.

She couldn't stop, though. Panic propelled her. When she'd seen Mr. Oliphant with those books under his arm, sheer terror had seized her, and she'd felt compelled to reach him, thrust him into the house, and hide him somewhere—anywhere—before Tom Partington could discover her black secret.

Mr. Oliphant apparently heard her dashing down the drive toward him because he whirled around, his round, usually benign face registering alarm. When he saw Claire, he smiled, and his plump cheeks turned rosy.

"Miss Montague! What a delight to see you, my dear."

Gasping for air, Claire managed to wheeze, "Mr. Oliphant!" Then she grasped the pillar supporting the porch awning, pressed a hand to her heaving bosom, and hoped she wouldn't faint and disgrace herself.

Scruggs opened the door and blinked at her. Then he blinked at Mr. Oliphant. Claire couldn't speak yet but managed to wave her hand in a gesture entreating Mr. Oliphant to enter the house. She wanted him off the porch this instant in case Tom should happen to decide to investigate the visitor.

"Are you all right, Miss Montague?"

Mr. Oliphant's polite question bespoke only honest concern for her health, but Claire wasn't in a mood to be impressed that a publisher's representative had exhibited a spurt of human kindness. She actually stamped her foot and whispered raggedly, "Get into the house!" Then, using her last ounce of energy, she shoved him. Mr. Oliphant stumbled into the cool tiled entryway of Partington Place, bumping into Scruggs, who danced backward under the blow.

When both men stopped staggering, they gaped at her. As Claire caught her breath, she realized they'd been staring at her in silence for at least two or three seconds. She smiled, hoping the expression didn't look as sickly as it felt.

"I'm so sorry, Mr. Oliphant. Scruggs, please forgive me."

Palm flattened against his solar plexus, which is where poor Mr. Oliphant's well-padded shoulder had connected, Scruggs uttered blightingly, "I'm sure I shall survive, ma'am."

Mr. Oliphant's cheeks had deepened in hue from rose to burgundy. "Are you quite all right, Miss Montague?"

"Yes. No. Yes." Striving for a calm that seemed to elude her every grasp, Claire finally announced, "Mr.

Oliphant, you are the only person in the world who can save me!"

Mr. Oliphant's eyes, which were so dark a color that they resembled ripe olives to Claire's inventive mind, widened until the pupils were surrounded by a halo of white. "Good heavens, my dear Miss Montague, whatever can the matter be?"

Feeling more foolish than she could remember feeling in a good many years, Claire grabbed Mr. Oliphant's arm and dragged him down the hall toward her office, leaving Scruggs behind, his moose's face longer than ever. She wasn't sure how she was going to do it, but she knew she must enlist Mr. Oliphant's support. Mr. Oliphant was unfortunately another of her admirers. She generally regretted the fact, but today she experienced a thrust of gratitude for his unrequited affection.

"Please come into my office, Mr. Oliphant."

He did as she requested and probably would have done so even if she'd not had a firm grip on his coat sleeve and yanked him inside. He fell rather than sat in the chair at which she launched him. The books he'd brought her were still clutched to his chest, and Claire snatched them now and thrust them behind a chair cushion. Fortunately there were only three of them, and they were small.

Then Claire stood before him, wringing her hands and wondering how to explain her bizarre behavior. Looking almost frightened, he stared up at her. Claire didn't blame him.

"My goodness, Miss Montague! Are you ill?"

Immediately Claire perceived she would have to honor Mr. Oliphant with some version of the truth. She didn't want to.

"No. No, Mr. Oliphant, I am not ill. I—I—I—" She

swallowed hard and pressed a hand to her cheek, unable to think of a single thing to say. How could she ask this man to lie for her?

All at once Mr. Oliphant sat up. His look of terror vanished in a trice and was replaced by an expression of almost unctuous concern. Heaving his bulk out of the chair, he snatched her free hand in both of his. Claire looked at his chubby fists in surprise. His palms were sweaty, and she had the unladylike impulse to snatch her hand back and wipe it on her skirt. She refrained, because she'd treated him so oddly already.

"Is it the books, Miss Montague?" Mr. Oliphant's voice vibrated with solicitude. "Do you fear your employer may object to the books?"

Vastly relieved, scarcely able to believe her luck, Claire said, "Oh, yes, Mr. Oliphant! However could you know?"

He patted her hand and nodded wisely. Claire tried to draw her hand from his again, but he held firm. Since his palm was soft and still rather moist, she wished he'd not do that. Nevertheless, he seemed on the verge of handing her an excuse when her own usually fertile brain had failed her, so she didn't tug.

"Ah, Miss Montague, I'm not surprised to hear it. Of course, being the dear innocent creature you are, you can't possibly understand a gentleman's sentiments at a time like this."

"I can't?"

He patted her hand again, and this time Claire almost succumbed to her urge. She didn't and felt proud of herself.

"Of course not. You're too sweet. Too pure."

Mr. Oliphant was somewhat shorter than Claire and shaped like an eggplant. Claire peered down into his round little face and was unhappy to see adoration shining there. Good grief. Why couldn't a man she admired adore her? Why must it always be the Mr. Oliphants and Mr. Johnsons of the world who cherished her?

"What does my being pure have to do with anything, Mr. Oliphant?" She was beginning to feel a little miffy and knew the emotion to be irrational. After all, she'd wanted a good excuse for her peculiar behavior. Besides, she didn't dare annoy Mr. Oliphant, who held great power over her if only he knew it.

"Miss Montague, you've been sheltered for entirely too long. I fear the late Mr. Partington might have given you a false impression of men."

It was Claire's considered opinion that the late Mr. Partington had saved her from the hideous misapprehension that all men were beasts. She did not say so to Mr. Oliphant, but her peevishness increased. Nor did she speak for fear she might utter an indelicacy.

"Not all men, my dear young lady, would be so complacent as the late Mr. Partington at having a young woman in their employ who was in the habit of penning popular fiction."

Claire's mouth dropped open.

"You see, my dear, writing novels, especially novels in the genre that you as Clarence McTeague produce, is considered by many to be rather indelicate."

"Indelicate?"

"Improper."

"*Improper?*"

At last Mr. Oliphant released Claire's hand so he could stick his finger in his ear and wriggle it. Claire knew he had done so to dislodge her shriek, but she didn't care. Her temper soared like a lark ascending.

"What on earth are you talking about, Mr. Oliphant?

Clarence McTeague's novels are most assuredly *not* improper. Nor are they indelicate!"

"My dear Miss Montague—"

"No! I can't believe you said such a thing, Mr. Oliphant. Why, you represent the publisher who has been producing Clarence McTeague's novels for five years now. It's a fine time to be telling me you think they're indelicate!"

Furious, Claire whirled around and stormed to the door. Then, recalling that Tom Partington lay beyond the door—somewhere—she whirled around and stomped the other way.

"Please, my dear Miss Montague," Mr. Oliphant said, obviously ruffled by Claire's discomposure, "I didn't mean to disparage your work per se. Why, I know I speak for most of the publishing world when I tell you that Clarence McTeague's books are probably the finest in the genre."

"You do?" Slightly mollified, Claire stopped stomping. She yanked her spectacles from her face and wiped them on her handkerchief, something she did when agitated. She didn't entirely trust Mr. Oliphant's seeming change of heart and glared at him. "Why did you say they were improper then?"

"What I meant to say, my dear, although I'm afraid I fumbled terribly—I'm not after all a writer, you know, and haven't your gift for words, and I trust you won't take what I have to say amiss because I mean it only for the good—"

"Will you please just get on with it?" Claire could have bitten her tongue when an expression of grave hurt entered Mr. Oliphant's beady eyes. She'd forgotten what an old windbag he was. She muttered, "I beg your pardon. My nerves are a bit unsettled today."

"Certainly, my dear."

He sniffed and still looked hurt. Claire wanted to scream when he didn't continue speaking immediately but turned to pace back and forth in front of the fireplace several times. Governing with difficulty her urge to shake an explanation out of him, she said through gritted teeth, "Pray continue, Mr. Oliphant."

"Yes. Well, my dear, what I meant to say is that I believe there may be—in spite of the excellent arguments propounded by various females who support suffrage and equal rights for ladies—valid reasons to account for the disparities one encounters between the sexes. Ladies, as you well know, possess exalted sensibilities, unlike us mere men, who are slaves to our intellects. Ladies' powers of reason are invariably influenced by their extreme emotions."

To the best of Claire's observations, about the only thing enslaving men was their cursed stupidity. Vanity and lust perhaps. Her lips tightly compressed, she could barely squeeze out an "oh?" Her own extreme emotions were telling her to pick up the fireplace poker and batter Mr. Oliphant with it, and she wondered cynically if he'd forgive her for succumbing to the urge and chalk it up to her exalted sensibilities. She suspected he wouldn't.

His benevolent smile made her want to scratch out his beady black olive eyes.

"You of course are a paragon among females, Miss Montague. You have somehow overcome your natural feebleness of nature and have produced some of the finest literature of this or any other age."

Claire, exasperated, glared at him. "They're dime novels, Mr. Oliphant. Mind you, they're good dime novels, but I don't believe they qualify as elevated literary fiction."

"Exactly, my dear." He beamed at her as if she'd just made his point for him. Again Claire experienced the urge to shake him. Fortunately he continued his belabored explanation before she could do so.

"You see, a normal female would not find the wherewithal to create a hero like Tuscaloosa Tom Pardee. Females do not generally possess the strength of character required to understand the nobility of Tom's temperament, nor would they be able to overcome their natural timidity of nature to write about the violence inherent in Tom's exploits."

"You mean most ladies would faint when confronted with peril, Mr. Oliphant?"

"Exactly!" he exclaimed again, obviously pleased that Claire understood him so well.

Claire had to take several deep, sustaining breaths. She spared a thought to the idols of her youth, Clara Barton and Florence Nightingale, two ladies who had not merely faced the violence of men but dared to mop up after it and endeavored to heal the wounds such violence had inflicted. Then, still not trusting herself to speak without screaming, she forced herself to smile at her publisher's representative. "You mean to say that young Mr. Partington would be shocked to learn his housekeeper writes dime novels because such an occupation directly challenges the role nature intended for a female?" No honey was sweeter than Claire's voice.

"With your usual astuteness, Miss Montague, you have captured the essence of the matter in a nutshell."

Claire nodded, wishing Mr. Oliphant were always this succinct. He again made a lunge for her hands, which she avoided by a quick maneuver to her right. Tucking her hands demurely under her apron, she cast her gaze down and tried to look sweet and ladylike. "That's it all right, Mr. Oliphant. You have discerned the situation exactly. I couldn't have said it better myself."

She politely refrained from pointing out that she had said it herself, having finally plowed through Mr. Oliphant's mountain of words to find the kernel of meaning underneath. Not that she didn't appreciate him for it, as she'd been too panicked to think of a suitable lie by herself.

Thwarted in his desire to hold Claire's hand, Mr. Oliphant had to satisfy himself by looking compassionate. "So that's the problem, is it, Miss Montague? You fear Mr. Partington will experience disgust for you if he discovers you to be a writer of popular fiction? That he may censure you if he ever finds you to be, in your literary guise, Clarence McTeague?"

Taking a deep breath and a chance, Claire tried to sound pitiful. "It's even worse than that, I fear."

Mr. Oliphant's remarkable eyes blinked rapidly several times. "What can be worse than that, my dear?"

Claire wished she could see without her spectacles. She was sure she would present a more affecting picture if her long lashes were not obscured by her lenses. None of her heroines ever wore spectacles, and for good reason. Nevertheless, she did her best. Schooling her voice to a mournful whisper, she said "He—he hates the books, Mr. Oliphant!"

Mr. Oliphant actually staggered backward, a circumstance for which Claire could only be grateful, as it put him farther away from her. It also gave her a brilliant idea.

With lightning speed, Tom thrust his booted foot outward and upward, catching the villain in the chest. He staggered back against the boulder. A quick lunge, and

Tom was upon him. They grappled furiously for the deadly weapon yet clutched in the outlaw's fist. Miss Abigail Faithgood screamed.

Bringing her mind back to her present difficulties, Claire nodded and sniffled sadly. Since she was too angry to summon tears, even false ones, she turned, grasped a curtain, and pretended to gaze soulfully out the window. "It's the truth. I—I daren't tell him it is I who have written the books he claims have made his life miserable, Mr. Oliphant."

"Good God. I had no idea."

Claire heard the genuine horror in Mr. Oliphant's tone and sneaked a peek at him over her shoulder. He looked utterly dumbfounded as she turned and gazed at him pleadingly. "So, you see, Mr. Oliphant, while the late Mr. Partington always enjoyed your visits a good deal, I fear it may be necessary to prevaricate slightly with the young Mr. Partington. I don't believe it would be wise to introduce you as Clarence McTeague's publisher's representative."

"Good God, no. If he knew who I was, he'd probably kick me out of his house and never invite me back again."

"Exactly." Claire hastily turned toward the window again to hide her grin of triumph.

"Does this mean you wish me to stay at a hotel, my dear?"

Mr. Oliphant did not try to hide his disappointment. Claire didn't much blame him. The accommodations to be found in Pyrite Springs, while adequate in their way, were nowhere near as elegant as those achieved at Partington Place. Thinking quickly, she said, "I don't believe that will be necessary, Mr. Oliphant."

"What about the servants, Miss Montague?" He sounded very glum. Claire almost forgave him his loquacity and affection for her. She knew how much he liked Mrs. Philpott's chocolate soufflé.

"Neither Scruggs nor Mrs. Philpott is in my confidence, Mr. Oliphant. The only person at Partington Place who knew the true identity of Clarence McTeague was the late Mr. Partington."

Brightening, he said, "Is that so?"

She moved away from the window, her brain now awhirl with plots and schemes. "Yes." Turning suddenly, she asked, "Do you suppose you could be one of the late Mr. Partington's friends from New York, Mr. Oliphant, instead of one of my acquaintances?"

His mouth opened and shut several times, giving him the appearance of large fish gasping for breath. Claire tried not to dwell on the similarity for fear she'd laugh.

At last he said with remarkable humility, considering Mr. Oliphant was not normally humble, "I'd prefer to be a suitor for your hand, Miss Montague."

The very thought made Claire shudder inwardly. However, since she did not wish to alienate him, she said, "I believe that would be unwise. Not if you wish to spend your visit to Pyrite Springs at Partington Place." She smiled, letting not a drop of spite mar the expression. "I am after all only the housekeeper. It would be odd if a suitor to my hand were to be invited to stay here overnight."

"Oh." Mr. Oliphant frowned. "I take your point. Perhaps you're right, my dear. I shall become the late Mr. Partington's friend from New York."

"You can still be a publisher's representative, Mr. Oliphant," Claire offered magnanimously. "The young Mr. Partington needn't know the whole truth." Even as she spoke the words, a stab of guilt smote her. She shook it off, telling herself she really did plan to confess everything. Someday. When she knew Tom Partington better.

For the first time in her adult life she wondered if a taint ran through her family. She'd tried so hard, since she'd escaped, to live a good life. Yet now, the first time her honor was tested, she'd taken refuge in falsehood and deceit. Savagely she thrust the thought aside, vowing to atone somehow.

A knock came on her office door, startling Claire into a small shriek of alarm. Frantically she looked at Mr. Oliphant and whispered, "Will you do it?"

He nodded and opened his mouth to confirm his decision at length. Claire didn't wait but darted to the door and flung it open. She'd armed herself with a welcoming smile and was glad of it when she perceived Tom Partington and Jedediah Silver outside her door, smiling back at her.

Tom spoke first. "Jedediah and I have come up with some plans, Miss Montague, and Jed suggested I discuss them with you."

"You've got more common sense than a dozen men, Miss Montague," Jedediah said. "I told Tom you'd be happy to give us some advice."

Casting a superior glance at Mr. Oliphant, Claire opened the door wider and allowed graciously, "I'm sure Mr. Silver is wrong about that, Mr. Partington, but I should be pleased to hear your plans. Please come in and meet the late Mr. Partington's friend Mr. Oliphant. Mr. Oliphant," she said deliberately, "represents a publishing company in New York. His firm publishes inspirational literature."

Oliphant gaped at Claire for a second or two until she gave him a quick scowl. Then, with a jerk, he smiled and stammered, "Oh! Oh, yes. Why, indeed, I was terribly sorry to hear about the late Mr. Partington's demise."

All at once Claire remembered the books she'd hidden behind the chair cushion. It looked as if Jedediah were aiming for that particular chair. She bolted for it, almost running him down, and sat down in a fluff of petticoats. Jedediah looked surprised, but Claire only smiled winningly up at him. Far better he think her rude, even insane, than the author of those wretched books.

"So you knew my uncle Gordon, did you, Mr. Oliphant?" Tom sat on the sofa. "You and Jed and Miss Montague will have to tell me all about him since I didn't know him very well."

Jedediah sat at the other end of the sofa. "He was quite an excellent fellow, Tom."

"Indeed he was."

Mr. Oliphant looked around the room, obviously searching for a place to sit. The only chair left was the one at Claire's desk. She stood at once.

"Please take this chair, Mr. Oliphant, and I shall go get refreshments for you gentlemen."

With a meaningful look for Oliphant, she made her escape. Because she felt guilty, she took quite a while preparing an especially fine assortment of tea cakes, coffee, and tea. She wanted to impress Tom Partington.

When she returned to her office, Dianthe St. Sauvre had joined the gentlemen. Oliphant had given up his seat for her and now stared at her, his expression reminding Claire even more of a gaffed trout than it had before. Jedediah Silver too gazed at Dianthe, captivated by her beauty. Tom was smiling at her. None of that surprised Claire, who expected men to swoon over Dianthe.

What surprised—or, rather, terrified—her was that Dianthe held in one graceful hand a slender volume bearing a portrait of Tuscaloosa Tom Pardee at his most valiant. The title *Tuscaloosa Tom and the River of Raging Death* was emblazoned above the portrait on the front cover. Claire almost dropped the tea tray.

"My God!" she whispered.

Her gaze swept the room, eventually colliding with that of Tom Partington. He smiled at her, and her frantic brain immediately tried to decide if it was an ironic smile, a bitter one, or a friendly one. Unfortunately, discriminating between a virtual stranger's various smiles was a task beyond her brain's capacity at the moment.

"I do believe you were trying to keep something from me, Miss Montague."

Claire's panicked gaze shot from him to Dianthe, who looked apologetic and gave a little self-deprecatory shrug. It didn't help.

Claire said, "I'm so sorry."

Chuckling, Tom rose from the sofa and took the tea tray from Claire's trembling hands. "Here, Miss Montague. You don't really want to drop all that fine-looking food on your office carpet, do you?"

She shook her head, unable to speak. She watched Tom place the tray on her desk and felt the craven urge to bolt. She might even have done so had her feet not suddenly turned to lead and her knees to water. When Tom straightened and turned to look at her, she couldn't make herself move but stood stock-still and prayed for deliverance.

When he walked back to her and placed a warm hand on her shoulder, she could only repeat, miserably, "I'm so sorry."

He looked concerned. "Please, Miss Montague,

you're taking this entirely too much to heart. It's not your fault another one of these books is coming out."

Claire felt her world seem to tilt. "It—it's not?"

"Of course not." Tom began to steer her toward her desk chair. "My goodness, you're shaking like a leaf. One would think you were responsible for those *Tuscaloosa Tom* books. You mustn't take this so seriously."

Since Claire *was* responsible for the *Tuscaloosa Tom* books, she found it difficult to formulate a suitable response. Dianthe fluttered up from the armchair and floated to Claire's side. Claire saw Tom smile at Dianthe, a smile as big and warm as the day, and her misery was complete.

"Let me pour you some tea, Claire, dear. I was just telling Mr. Partington that you were undoubtedly trying to spare his feelings when you hid those horrid books behind the chair cushions."

"You did?" Since she knew Dianthe to be somewhat less than quick-witted, Claire gaped at her. Then she frowned as her rattled brain assimilated the word Dianthe had used to describe her books.

"She did indeed, Miss Montague," Mr. Oliphant said quickly. Claire decided to take umbrage later, looked at him, and found him winking at her as if he had a tic.

"You didn't have to spare my feelings, Miss Montague. I'm sure I'm used to those books by this time. Even if I can't like them, I certainly don't expect you to hide them from me. Besides, I'll warrant Uncle Gordon has made a tidy sum from them, and I'm benefiting now."

Claire gazed up at Tom in astonishment. For the second time that day she felt as if she'd been tossed a life raft as she was about to go under for the third time. She grabbed at it for all she was worth and could only bless fortune and good friends.

"I—I didn't want to upset you during your first days in your new home, Mr. Partington. You seemed so pleased with how things were going for you. I didn't want to spoil your good mood."

"Thank you, Miss Montague. That was very thoughtful of you, but you know there's no way I could have avoided finding out about this latest book indefinitely."

Tom took one of the offending volumes from Dianthe's hand and looked at it. At least he didn't glare; he seemed merely exasperated and slightly bemused. Claire shot Dianthe a desperate glance. Dianthe smiled sweetly.

"How did these arrive, Miss Montague? They seem to be in advance of the publication date, which is January of next year. That's two months away."

Claire looked frantically at Mr. Oliphant, whose gaze seemed to have stuck fast to Dianthe. No help there. Striving to adhere as much to the truth as possible, she stammered, "Mr.—Mr. Oliphant brought them, Mr. Partington. He—his publisher is the same one, you see, and he knew how much the late Mr. Partington loved those books." She added almost defiantly, "As do many of us, who don't consider them horrid in the least. Didn't you, Mr. Oliphant?"

Hearing his name, Oliphant jerked out of his Dianthe-induced stupor. "What? Oh! Why, yes. I brought them for the late Mr. Partington. My publisher is the same one indeed."

With a soft chuckle Tom said, "I guess the author gets early copies. Not exactly in the inspirational line, though, are they?"

Feeling slightly stronger, Claire sat up straight and patted her hair, a nervous gesture that was entirely unwarranted as no stray wisps ever escaped those repressive coils. "Actually, Mr. Partington, I believe many people might find inspiration in the strong character and noble nature of Tuscaloosa Tom."

"She's right there, Tom," Jedediah said with a grin. "This Clarence McTeague fellow has created a real hero in those books."

"Surely not 'created,' Mr. Silver," Claire said, still feeling a need to justify her hymns of praise to Tom. "Tuscaloosa Tom is modeled after the career of our own Mr. Partington."

Tom shook his head. "Nonsense. McTeague's created a monster, if you ask me."

"Surely not a *monster*, Mr. Partington."

That Dianthe's soft exclamation lacked conviction irritated Claire. She said, bridling, "No, he certainly did not create a monster. Why, those books were intended as an homage to a gallant soldier and an honorable gentleman. Any lad who attempts to emulate Tuscaloosa Tom Pardee can only improve himself by following a splendid example. If—if the books embarrass you, Mr. Partington, I'm sure Mr. McTeague would be perfectly wretched to learn it."

Tom laughed again. "Yes, I already know you were fond of my uncle and are a hot defender of the novels, Miss Montague. You're such a sensible woman in all other respects I can only believe you've perceived something in these books that has eluded me."

"Perhaps you're just too close to the subject matter," Claire muttered, feeling terribly defensive, not to mention at a tremendous disadvantage.

"I'm sure that's it, Miss Montague." He patted her hand in a brotherly fashion. "Are you feeling better now?"

Claire decided it was past time she pulled herself together and began to perform the duties for which she was paid. Standing and clearing her throat, she declared, "Yes, thank you. I'm sorry for being so silly, Mr. Partington. Please allow me to pour tea."

"Thank you. That would be wonderful."

Dianthe wafted back to deposit herself in the armchair, and the three gentlemen settled themselves like sardines on the small sofa, the plump Mr. Oliphant in the middle. Claire handed out tea and cakes, then sat behind her desk, wondering how long she could keep up this dastardly deception and how, now that she'd begun to lie about it, she would ever be able to confess.

6

Tom found it ironic that Claire Montague, while not as lovely as her friend, was the one who possessed the truly lyrical soul. Claire spoke only to add something meaningful to the conversation. Moreover, her tidbits were insightful, elegantly rendered, and made him laugh. He'd always appreciated people who could make him laugh.

The beautiful Dianthe, on the other hand, while splendid to look at, prattled a mind-numbing stream of drivel, and most of her stories seemed to revolve around herself. Moreover, when she undertook to tell one of them, she seemed to find it necessary to start from creation itself. By the time she got to the point, Tom invariably found himself yawning, if not itching to throttle the ultimate point out of her.

Sipping his tea and glancing at his fellows, he discovered they did not suffer from his ennui. Undoubtedly they were more accustomed to the type of idle social chitchat he'd missed out on during his active life.

He did notice Claire drumming her fingers on her

desk once or twice. Both times he caught her eye, and she looked guilty until he winked and grinned. Then she smiled, and a little dimple peeked from beside her mouth. That silly dimple delighted him. He was finding more and more to admire about Claire Montague with each passing hour.

He guessed the thing that attracted him the most was her practical nature. It didn't hurt, either, that she seemed to be taking an active interest in his enterprises. He'd always hoped to find somebody with whom to share his enthusiasm.

But she didn't have to be such a dowd. It looked to him as if she deliberately tried to make herself appear dull. During another of Dianthe's boring stories he studied Claire's face. It was the hair, he decided, that did the most damage, and he began to plot ways in which to get her to try a more flattering hairstyle. She'd be quite charming if she loosened up a bit.

Overall, he was pleased with how things seemed to be working out here at Partington Place. There was plenty of room for him to build stables and fence pastureland, and he could still keep a profitable farming operation going. Now all he had to do was make arrangements to get the horses delivered.

He jerked to attention when he realized everybody was looking at him expectantly.

"Don't you think so, Mr. Partington?" Claire asked, her expression serious.

He scanned their faces for clues to the question he was supposed to be answering. They didn't tell him much. Except for Claire, their eyes seemed almost glazed. From that he deduced it had been Dianthe who'd last held the floor.

He decided there was no hope for it but to tell the

truth. "I beg your pardon, ladies and gentlemen. I'm afraid my mind wandered off the subject for a moment."

Claire's expression of incredulity surprised him. He guessed she wasn't used to anybody masculine not paying attention to Dianthe.

"I merely asked if it would be appropriate for me to dance my new work, 'In Praise of the Spotted Horse,' at the Artistic Evening, Mr. Partington," Dianthe purred. She fluttered her lashes and smiled.

" 'In Praise of the Spotted Horse'?"

"Yes. I created the poem to honor your horses and would of course recite it as I dance."

"Oh." Tom didn't know what to say. After a moment's pause he told her so. She smiled as if he'd just handed her a compliment.

"Dianthe is such a talented poet, Mr. Partington. Anybody would be flattered to be the subject of one of her verses."

Wondering if Claire was being deliberately ironic, he mumbled, "I'm sure the horses will be delighted, Miss Montague." Encountering her blank stare, he guessed he couldn't count satire as one of Claire's manifold virtues. He admired the affection she seemed to have for a friend whose beauty put hers in the shade, but he wondered if Dianthe didn't occasionally take advantage of her. "In Praise of the Spotted Horse"? Good God.

Since everybody was still staring at him as if he held the answer to all the world's questions, he said, "Er, that sounds like a great idea, Miss St. Sauvre."

Dianthe's smile never wavered. Claire's, on the other hand, burst upon her countenance like the sun after a storm, and Tom realized she'd been worried for her friend. He gave her an encouraging grin, wondering if she cared about all her friends so much. He could appreciate loyalty more than men who'd never seen duty in a war or had to depend on their fellows on the frontier as he had. But he did appreciate it. A lot. He gave Claire Montague another point for her loyalty to Dianthe.

Claire wasn't entirely sure how she managed to get through the rest of the evening, but she couldn't remember a time when she'd been so happy to retreat to her room.

Dinner had seemed endless. The late Mr. Partington's great dining table was not suited to intimate dinner parties, but Scruggs had rebelled at serving the meal in the breakfast room.

"The Young General deserves all the respect we can give him, Miss Montague," Scruggs said stolidly. "He has guests this evening and will wish to have them entertained with the deference due his stature."

"But, Scruggs, truly, he tends to discount his own valorous reputation, and he doesn't seem to appreciate all this formality. He's even told me so."

Scruggs looked down his long nose at Claire. "It is an honor to be in the employ of the Young General, Miss Montague, and until given specific instructions to the contrary, I shall continue to serve him with the esteem due his station."

She, Oliphant, Silver, and Tom therefore shared the gleaming mahogany table in the dining room. Candles did their best to illuminate the room, but it was a battle destined for failure. As the autumn's night was deep and heavy curtains had been drawn across the windows, obscuring any hint of moonglow and starshine, the lighting was poor at best.

More than once Claire saw Tom lean close to his plate and squint to determine exactly what it was he was going to be putting into his mouth. A candle flickered at each place, but so much table separated the diners that to Claire's fertile brain, it looked as if they all were seated at points of an invisible cross.

Candles in the wall sconces each lit approximately a foot square of wall. The light never made it to the floor. Even Claire wondered how Scruggs managed to serve the meal without tripping. She guessed he'd had so much practice he could negotiate the room blindfolded.

She wasn't surprised when Tom, obviously vexed, asked at one point, "God bless it, can't we get more light in here?"

"Yes, indeed," Claire had responded promptly. "I attempted to get Scruggs to bring in several lanterns, but he deemed them unfit for a formal dinner party."

"But this isn't a formal dinner party. It's a few friends dining together."

"I agree, Mr. Partington," Claire said with a sigh. "But Scruggs is Scruggs, you know."

"Good grief."

"Actually, if you wouldn't feel it beneath your dignity, you could even entertain small parties such as this one in the breakfast room. It's a delightful room and can be made to look quite elegant."

Tom goggled at her, and she knew she'd phrased her suggestion improperly. "Beneath my dignity? What are you talking about, Miss Montague?"

She felt herself flush. "I beg your pardon, Mr. Partington. I didn't mean it that way. It's just that Scruggs thought it would have been insulting if he had taken it upon himself to serve your guests in the breakfast room without a direct command from you."

Tom put a hand to his head as if Claire's news had stunned him. Claire felt her eyes open wide.

Wresting the knife from his adversary's hand, Tom plunged it into the villain's chest. Distraught at the violence so rudely displayed before Miss Abigail Faithgood, he put a hand to his noble brow. Miss Abigail Faithgood screamed, and a soft prayer that the delicate maiden would be spared further brutality left his lips.

On the other hand, Claire thought sardonically, perhaps poor old Tom merely had a headache from Miss Abigail's constant screeching. She really *had* to do something about that.

Returning to the problem at hand, she said, "Perhaps if you were to speak to him, he would understand your desires in the matter."

Tom looked troubled. "But, Miss Montague, I really have no experience in dealing with servants and honestly don't want to learn. I believed you to be the one who would take care of these little matters."

Her heart plummeted, and he apparently discerned her distress. He hurried to add, "Not that I don't think you've done a magnificent job here. You certainly have. I've seldom seen such a well-run household."

"Hear, hear," said Jedediah, raising his wineglass to her in salute. At least Claire was sure it was a wineglass. Since the object he lifted went beyond the range of his feeble candle, she wasn't sure. For all she knew, it was his fork.

"Thank you," she said in a tiny voice.

"But I don't know the first thing about giving instructions to butlers."

"Maybe you should simply tell Scruggs that you expect him to take his orders from Miss Montague from now on, Tom," Jedediah suggested.

"Why, that's brilliant, Mr. Silver!" Claire beamed at

Jedediah. "If Mr. Partington follows your advice, it could save me hundreds of hours."

"Good grief, is Scruggs that bad?"

Now Claire felt guilty. "He's not bad, Mr. Partington. He's merely—merely—" "Obstreperous" was the word that popped into her head, but it seemed too harsh. She said instead, "Set in his ways."

"Do you think something as simple as my telling him to take orders from you would solve the problem?"

"Absolutely. You see, Scruggs is used to looking upon you as something of an ideal of perfection, as indeed we all are, and he believes your gallantry and heroism deserve only the finest. Scruggs is, I am afraid, inclined to consider any relaxation in the rules of the conventional protocol he learned in his youth as a rank indignity."

"Good lord."

Since the topic of their discussion entered the room at that moment, conversation stopped.

Scruggs looked particularly ghoulish as, backlit by candle glow from the pantry, he came through the door. He bore a tray of Mrs. Philpott's floating island desserts and stood in the doorway for a moment, probably to get his bearings before attempting to serve them.

The dinner seemed interminable, and Claire excused herself as soon as politely possible from after-dinner tea and brandy in the parlor. Her head aching, she sank onto the chair in front of her vanity table and propped her chin in her cupped hands.

"What have I done?" she asked her reflection, which did not offer an opinion on the matter. Nor did it give her any hints on how to undo the tangle of lies in which she'd enmeshed herself. Feeling like a fly caught in a spider's web, she crawled into her bed and prayed for guidance.

* * *

Tom felt wonderful when he awoke the morning after what might be considered his first real, albeit small, dinner party in his new home. In spite of the terrible lighting, he believed they all had enjoyed themselves. And after Claire had left them in the parlor and he'd broken out some of Uncle Gordo's Havana cigars and French brandy, the conversation had become very mellow indeed.

At first it had centered on his plans for Partington Place and his ambition to establish an Appaloosa horse-breeding ranch. Naturally, other topics arose. Even more naturally, since there were only the three men present, Miss Dianthe St. Sauvre's name was mentioned.

As he sat back in his chair and listened to Oliphant and Jedediah, it became clear to him that these two gentlemen had yet to see past the ethereally lovely Dianthe's exterior to discover the equally ethereal intellect inside. Shaking his head, Tom had listened to them extolling her virtues in language that would have done his nemesis, Clarence McTeague, proud.

Well, a dim-witted, decorative female might do for either one of these gentlemen, but Tom Partington required a good deal more than beauty in a lady. Or anybody else, for that matter. Especially if that body were to become a partner of his.

Claire Montague, now, there was a lady of an entirely different stamp. She seemed equally at home with the insipid Dianthe as with the razor-sharp Jedediah Silver. Why, she was up to anything and anybody, and Tom appreciated that quality in an ally. Even if she did like those damned silly books.

He was chuckling as he made his way into the breakfast room, where he discovered Claire and Scruggs in an animated discussion. At least it was animated on Claire's part; Scruggs was stiff as a cold marble statue. The door didn't so much as swish, its hinges were so well oiled, so neither of them realized he had joined them.

"I shall go into Pyrite Springs today, Scruggs, and purchase lanterns more fitting to the dining room's elegance. You simply can't expect diners to eat in the dark. It's stupid and really not fair. Why, the gentlemen couldn't even find their plates last night." Claire's voice was sharp. Tom got the impression she'd lost her temper some time ago, and he grinned. He enjoyed seeing her proper demeanor ruffled occasionally.

"The late Mr. Partington did not care for lanterns, Miss Montague, believing they conveyed an inelegant atmosphere and one not conducive to artistic conversation. Besides," he added as if to put the cap on the conversation, "lamps smoke."

"That's ridiculous, and you know it, Scruggs. Why, I've seen perfectly beautiful lamps, and if you use the right oil and open them properly, they won't smoke. I believe I've even seen lantern holders crafted from scrolled metal that are positively works of art."

Scruggs looked as rebellious as a cold marble moose could look until he spotted Tom. Then he snapped to attention like a precisely disciplined soldier. Strolling away from his vantage point at the door, Tom smiled at both parties.

"I think Miss Montague's right, Scruggs," he said casually, and watched Scruggs's mouth tighten. "We need more light in that room if we're going to eat in there very often. Lanterns sound like the right idea to me until I can get the place piped for gas."

"How wonderful, Mr. Partington! Do you really plan to install gas?"

Claire looked ecstatic, and that pleased Tom. "Indeed I do. I'm all for the modern conveniences."

Something that sounded like a groan emanated from Scruggs, drawing Tom's attention to his gloomy butler. The poor man already looked as if he'd sustained a punishing emotional blow, but Tom, never one to shrink from necessity, decided he'd better land the knockout punch right now. Maybe the butler would recover by dinnertime tonight.

"Since I've got lots of other things to see to, Scruggs, I want you to take your instruction from Miss Montague. You can consider her my voice in the running of the household from now on." With one of his most companionable smiles he cocked his head to one side and asked, "That all right with you, Scruggs? It'll save me a lot of time and bother."

Scruggs had to clear his throat before he could answer, in a suspiciously hoarse voice, "Yes, sir."

Then he tottered out of the room like a broken man, leaving Claire to gaze after him anxiously.

Her concern over the butler's wounded sensibilities touched Tom. "Will he be all right, Miss Montague? I hope I didn't shatter the poor fellow's feelings."

She left off wringing her hands, for which Tom was grateful. "I believe he'll be better soon, Mr. Partington." She gave a huge sigh. "He was actually used to taking his instruction from me, you see, but your . . . approach to things is at great variance with what he's used to, and I believe he's worried that he will give offense if he departs from the traditions of Partington Place."

"I see," said Tom, who didn't. He'd always figured servants merrily went about doing what the boss wanted and didn't worry about traditions. Showed how much he knew about servants.

He rubbed his hands together happily. "At least I'm glad you got him to serve breakfast in the breakfast room. This is much cozier." Waving his hand toward a chair, he said, "Have a seat, Miss Montague. Let's have breakfast together and plan our day."

She looked pleased, and that pleased Tom. He liked her better when she smiled. She'd seemed so troubled yesterday afternoon and evening, he'd become worried about her.

Mr. Oliphant entered the room, along with Jedediah Silver. The breakfast dishes had been set out on the sideboard, so they served themselves.

"Did I hear you say you were going into Pyrite Springs today, Miss Montague?" Tom asked after swallowing a mouthful of eggs prepared with a delicious creamy cheese sauce. He was very happy that Mrs. Philpott, while obviously high-strung and prone to tears, could at least cook up a storm.

"Yes, indeed, Mr. Partington. My friend Mr. Addison-Addison works at the Pyrite Springs Mercantile and Furniture Emporium. I'm sure he'll know just where to find lamps for the dining room that won't offend poor Scruggs's feelings."

She giggled, and Tom paused with his fork halfway to his mouth. She could be utterly enchanting, this dowdy housekeeper of his, and he wondered if he could somehow persuade her to stop hiding her light under a bushel and bring it forth so that the world could appreciate it.

"Great idea, Miss Montague. It'll be nice to be able to see what we're eating on the Artistic Evening, when there are lots of people here. Of course," Jedediah added dreamily, "it will also be pleasant to be able to see each other."

Tom and Claire exchanged a glance, and Tom knew they both knew Jedediah was thinking about Dianthe. He grinned and winked at her, taking her by surprise. He saw her eyes go round before she tucked her head down and tackled her breakfast.

Ah, well, she'd get used to him. Tom finished his bite of eggs. "Would you mind company on your trip to town, Miss Montague? I'd like to see my new home, and I'd appreciate having a guide along on my first visit."

Was it his imagination, or did the color in her cheeks deepen? Tom couldn't be sure.

"I'd be happy to show you the town, Mr. Partington. I have a few duties to attend to first, and then I shall put myself at your disposal."

"No need for that. I'll just tag along. Maybe I can make myself useful by carrying things for you."

"Thank you," Claire said, her voice stifled.

"I'm afraid I won't be able to stay for your Artistic Evening, Mr. Partington." Mr. Oliphant's voice conveyed real sorrow. "I must leave today."

"I'm sorry to hear that, Mr. Oliphant. I was hoping to learn more about the publishing business."

Before Oliphant could utilize the breath he was drawing for speech, Claire broke in. "I'm sure Mr. Oliphant has hundreds of clients to visit, Mr. Partington."

Puzzled, Tom looked at her. "I'm sure you're right, Miss Montague."

Now he *knew* she was blushing. Her cheeks flamed a bright pink. He shook his head and wondered why she seemed so fidgety. She hadn't seemed this nervous the first time they met, and he wouldn't have blamed her for being nervous then. By this time she must know he wasn't *that* exacting an employer.

They set out for Pyrite Springs shortly after the morning meal ended. The late-November morning air was crisp and clean and tickled Tom's nostrils pleasantly. A slate blue sky hung above them, cloudless and cold. When he looked to his right and left from his front porch, Tom could see nothing but his own land, and his spirit rejoiced.

He'd been scraping and saving for years so he could buy a piece of land somewhere. Not for Tom the feckless, reckless, insecure life of his parents, hanging on by their fingernails to the necessities of life, flinging opportunities away like so much chaff because they didn't fulfill their exacting notions of what "proper" folks did.

All that their worthless pride had ever gotten them was poverty, as far as Tom could tell. He knew they despaired of him and believed he'd forsaken his gallant old southern roots for wages earned at the demeaning profession of scouting for the railroad, but Tom couldn't make himself care.

Not for a minute. His entire adult life had been spent in making something of himself so that he could make something *for* himself. He'd have been happy with a little dirt farm in the Arizona Territory with room for a horse or two. Never in his wildest imagination had he envisioned this.

Thank God for Uncle Gordo. And thank God for those silly books too if they'd played any part in landing him this magnificent estate.

Lighthearted, feeling better than he expected he had any right to feel, he crooked his elbow and smiled at

Claire. He thought it was charming when she blushed and took his arm.

Mr. Oliphant walked with them, since he had arrangements to make in town. Tom wasn't sorry when they parted ways at the telegraph office; he wanted Claire to himself for a while.

"So, please tell me more about these Artistic Evenings, Miss Montague. Are they formal affairs?"

"I don't believe you would call them extremely formal, no."

"I'm relieved to hear it," he said sincerely.

Her spontaneous giggle enlivened an already pleasant morning. Tom smiled at her.

She smiled back, her dimple flashing. "Apparently you don't enjoy the pomp your uncle used to favor."

"I'm not fond of pomp, no."

"Well, here in Pyrite Springs I suppose even our most elegant soirees would fade when compared with the elaborate entertainments one finds on the East Coast."

"I wouldn't know," Tom murmured. He hoped she wouldn't start harping on his supposed sophistication again. He thought they'd already covered that topic thoroughly. Maybe he should invite some of his old scouting buddies for a visit. One gander at them would drive any remaining misconceptions about his refinement out of these people's minds.

"The ladies of course will wear formal gowns, but nothing elaborate." Claire continued, warming to her subject. She apparently set a good deal of store by her artistic friends.

"Black ties for the gentlemen?"

"Yes."

Tom guessed he could stand it. Besides, it would be interesting to see how Claire took to formal attire. He'd be willing to bet she'd polish up just fine. Glancing down, he noticed that her rattlesnakes seemed to be supporting her sunbonnet this morning. He wondered if she'd change her hairstyle for formal occasions and, feeling intrepid, decided to ask.

"I've been out of civilized society for a long time, Miss Montague, and I'm not up-to-date on current modes. I notice you favor a hairstyle my aunt Minnie in Alabama used to wear. I'm surprised hairstyles haven't changed all that much in twenty years."

When Claire didn't answer, he peered down again to find her looking mortified. Immediately he regretted his bold comment.

"I beg your pardon, Miss Montague. I didn't intend to embarrass you. It was rude of me to speak so personally." With a rueful grin he added, "I guess you'll believe me now when I say I'm not used to polite company."

"Please don't apologize, Mr. Partington. I, ahem, don't suppose my hairstyle is particularly flattering, but I believe it suits my position. A housekeeper isn't generally expected to be a fashion plate."

Was it his imagination, or was there a hint of a snap to Claire's answer? If there was, he was delighted. About all she needed to be perfect was a little fire. Risking her further wrath, he said, "I suppose that's true, but I don't think it would hurt your reputation any if you were to adopt a little color every now and then. Or even a new hairstyle."

He felt her hand stiffen on his arm. "I had no idea you objected to my appearance, Mr. Partington."

Her voice was as crisp as the weather. Taking yet another chance, he patted her hand and was encouraged when she didn't immediately draw it away and slap his face with it. "I don't object to a single thing about you, Miss Montague. I just think it wouldn't hurt to loosen up a little every now and then, is all."

"Yes. I'm well aware that you do not approve of formality."

Even her spectacles seemed angry as they reflected the sun's rays. Grinning, Tom decided if she stiffened up any more, she'd snap in two. "And you don't approve of me apologizing either, but I'm going to do it again anyway. I really didn't mean to rile you, Miss Montague. You're a paragon among housekeepers, and you can do your hair any old way you want, even twisted up like snakes. And if you want to wear drab brown gowns, it's perfectly all right with me."

"Thank you" fell like sleet from Claire's lips.

"I'm afraid you're really mad at me now, and I'd like to make it up to you."

"I'm sure there's nothing for which you need to make up, Mr. Partington."

Tom knew better. He'd seen her blush before, but he'd never seen those two red flags of anger displayed on her cheeks until this minute. Hell, he really had to practice his manners. All he'd meant to do was get her to fix her hair another way. What he'd evidently succeeded in doing was humiliating her. Civilization wasn't all it was cracked up to be, he guessed. None of the women he used to know were this touchy.

"We've come to the Mercantile and Furniture Emporium, Mr. Partington. I believe we can find suitable lamps for your dining room here."

Tom saw the striped pole of a barber's shop next to the mercantile and decided if he couldn't do anything about Claire's abysmally coiffed hair, he could at least take care of his own. "Would you mind if I left you to choose the lamps, Miss Montague? I see a barbershop there and have been meaning to get a haircut for a month or more."

"Certainly," she said frostily, snatching her hand from his arm.

Tom impulsively reached for her hand and held it in both of his. He had a feeling she wished she could yank it back again but didn't want to appear foolish. "Please forgive me, Miss Montague. I'd like to make up for my boorishness by taking you to luncheon after our shopping expedition is over. There must be a place to dine here in town."

"That's completely unnecessary, Mr. Partington."

"I insist, Miss Montague. Besides, I'm the boss, remember." He left her with a roguish smile. He'd known that smile to reduce women to quivering jelly. He wasn't sure what effect it would have on Claire, who seemed to have more backbone than most of the females he'd met in his precarious career.

Claire watched until the door of the barbershop shut behind Tom Partington's finely tailored rear end, then whirled around and stalked into the Mercantile. Sylvester Addison-Addison stood behind the counter, moodily rolling two spools of thread back and forth on the polished surface and ignoring Mrs. Jellicoe, trying to catch his attention by waving from the fabric aisle.

Claire ignored her too. Marching up to the counter and slamming her reticule on top of the black spool, she barked, "Sylvester, tell me the truth. Am I dull?"

7

*S*he swirled away again just as quickly, her reticule sweeping the spool off the counter and sending it bouncing across the floor. She eyed it malevolently as it rolled in front of her and gave it a savage kick.

"Here, Claire! Stop kicking the merchandise. You know that old Philistine Gilbert will have a fit if I lose his thread."

Moving faster than Claire had ever seen him move, Sylvester hurtled over the counter and dashed after his thread. Claire watched him, scowling, as he rooted under the notions shelf for the spool.

"Oh, bother the thread, Sylvester. I'll pay for the stupid spool. What I need to know is if I present a dull appearance."

Of course she presented a dull appearance, Claire thought murderously. She'd spent the past ten years of her life attempting to appear dull. Anybody would have, given her reasons.

So why did it make her so furious to have her boring

exterior pointed out by Tom Partington? Why did it hurt so much?

She wished Sylvester would unearth the stupid thread so she could kick it again.

Ultimately he did, but he held it in his fist so her desire was thwarted. Naturally. When had Claire Montague ever entertained a desire that *hadn't* been thwarted? She opened her reticule, grabbed her handkerchief, and blew her nose.

Slapping at his trousers to remove the dust, Sylvester frowned at her. If Claire wasn't so upset, she might have been amused by his slightly disheveled appearance since he'd picked up quite a bit of lint as he'd groveled after the thread. She was upset, however, and didn't so much as smile at his smudged nose and chin.

"Now what are you ranting on about, Claire?" Sylvester asked, annoyed.

"I am not ranting! And do take care of your customers, Sylvester," Claire advised sharply, gesturing at poor Mrs. Jellicoe, whose arms had apparently tired. She drooped disconsolately onto a stool next to a bolt of striped seersucker. "What do you think you get paid for?"

She watched with satisfaction as his dark eyebrows arched in shock. Without another word, he strode to Mrs. Jellicoe. Claire couldn't recall the last time she'd spoken unkindly to one of her friends, but at the moment it felt good to rid herself of some bile. She got very, very tired of being proper all the time.

Besides, as much as she honored his literary talents, Sylvester was a miserable failure as a mercantile clerk. He not only refused to pay attention to customers but treated them like dirt under his artistic feet when forced to do his duty.

While Mrs. Jellicoe attempted to deal with the surly Sylvester, Claire reviewed her conversation with Tom. He hadn't meant to be cruel, she decided, even though his words still stung. Why they should sting she couldn't say. After all, she'd obviously succeeded in transforming herself from the alluring shill her father had used in his medicine shows to the prim, intellectual housekeeper Claire Montague. She should be glad, not glum.

She *was* glum, however. This was the first time she'd had occasion to rue her spectacularly successful self-re-creation. Claire remembered her early years with an internal shudder. They seemed so far removed from her life today that recalling them was akin to viewing a bad melodrama through a stereopticon. She'd been so unhappy as a child and as a girl. And so embarrassed. She'd never been as comfortable an actress as she was a housekeeper and author.

Of course, if the purpose of her father's shows hadn't been to cheat unsuspecting innocents out of their hard-earned money, this might not have been the case. Claire had never taken to her father's credo, Caveat emptor. Nor had she appreciated his favorite quote from Tennyson: "Ah, why/Should life all labor be?" She often wondered if she'd inherited her appreciation of security and her basically honorable nature from the mother she'd never known.

Not to mention the fact that her father had never allowed her to wear her spectacles when she worked and she'd been operating blind half the time. It had been frightening to deal with all those men and not be able to see them clearly. She'd been indecorously pawed many times by men whose intentions she might have anticipated had she been able to see them.

Men!

Until she met Gordon Partington, Claire had not held a very high opinion of men. He was the first real gentleman she had ever met, and looking back, she was surprised he'd taken her under his kindly wing. She'd been so frightened when she'd tiptoed up to his enormous double doors and knocked that long-ago day. Then, when the morose, imperious Scruggs had opened the door, she'd very nearly fled without even stating her business: that she was responding to Mr. Partington's advertisement for a housekeeper in the *Pyrite Springs Weekly Gazette.*

Ten years could be a long time, Claire guessed. Ten years ago she'd been fleeing her past and doing everything she could think of to make up for it. Right now she wondered if she might have overdone it a trifle.

Eyeing Miss Thelma's Frocks and Bonnets, a small shop directly across the road from the Pyrite Springs Mercantile and Furniture Emporium, Claire wondered if it was necessary that she continue to strive so hard for respectability. If the opinions of her acquaintances were anything by which to judge, she'd apparently already achieved it. Perhaps if she were to don the occasional ribbon or frill, she wouldn't be sent tumbling back into the behavior of her scandalous past.

Miss Thelma was a skilled hairdresser as well. Even Mrs. Philpott had her hair cut at Miss Thelma's. The startling idea that she might wear her hair in a less severe style without sacrificing her carefully created image crossed Claire's mind.

Her anger returned, thundering into her heart like a rampaging bull. "He's surprised hairstyles haven't changed in twenty years, indeed!"

"I beg your pardon?"

Claire had been so involved in her thoughts that Sylvester's interruption made her jump.

"Oh, nothing, Sylvester."

Sylvester appeared to be out of sorts, but that didn't surprise Claire. He always hated it when he was commanded to perform the function for which he was paid his wages. The only time Sylvester was truly happy was when he was writing or reading his own words. Well, she guessed he also enjoyed being supercilious to his friends.

Right now, however, he was dreadfully peeved. "What were you prating on about earlier, about being dull? Has that barbarian you work for been stuffing your head full of nonsense?"

"He's not a barbarian! How dare you speak of Mr. Partington in that demeaning manner?" Claire conveniently forgot she had herself only moments before harbored violent thoughts about her employer. "For heaven's sake, his fortune may help keep you alive in the future, and I suggest you not forget that. Anyway, I doubt you'd recognize a barbarian if you saw one. You never get out of the clouds long enough even to look at us lesser mortals."

"Don't tell me you've begun to believe the drivel you write about that ridiculous man, Claire."

His imprudent reference to her work, here, in the public forum of the Mercantile and Furniture Emporium, made Claire gasp for a split second before her anger bubbled over. Stabbing Sylvester in the chest with her gloved forefinger, Claire hissed, "Don't you *dare* disparage my work, Sylvester Addison-Addison! And don't you dare speak of it in public either. If you ever make such a mistake again, you'll not merely be seeking employment elsewhere, you'll be seeking another place to live! Don't forget whom the late Mr. Partington left in charge of the Pyrite Arms."

Sylvester's mouth dropped open. Claire glowered at him for a moment or two before sniffing haughtily and stalking out the door. She was angry enough to spit tacks, and Sylvester had deserved every blistering word. She hoped he'd choke on them! She headed directly to Miss Thelma's Frocks and Bonnets.

An hour later, flushed and surprisingly pleased with herself, she stepped out of Miss Thelma's and made her way back across the street. When she opened the door to the Mercantile the first thing she saw was a red-faced, furious Sylvester Addison-Addison. The second thing she saw was the object of his fury, Tom Partington.

"Well, take heart, Addison," Tom was saying in that nonchalant way he had, "maybe someday you'll sell a book, and then you won't have to wait on people anymore."

After sputtering helplessly a time or two, Sylvester burst out, "My prose is art, Mr. Partington! It exists on a higher plane than that which the world now knows. Only a hackneyed, insensitive boor would write for money."

Tom shook his head, as if in sympathy. "Too bad. Means you'll have to work as a clerk for the rest of your life."

Claire decided it was only ethical to interrupt before Sylvester worked himself up so far that he fainted. It had been known to happen when he began breathing in that rapid, heated manner. As far as she was concerned, he deserved to collapse.

Of course Tom wasn't exactly in her favor at the moment either. It might serve them both right if Sylvester were to faint dead away at Tom's feet.

She cleared her throat and strode toward the counter. "Good morning, Mr. Partington. I see *you* had *your* hair cut, at any rate."

She didn't appreciate the way he eyed her coiled braids and lifted her chin to show him so. She'd show him even more on the Saturday after next, when she had an appointment to have her hair styled in the afternoon—right before she dressed for the new Mr. Partington's first-ever Artistic Evening. Her new gown was to be delivered tomorrow afternoon. She smiled inside. She didn't feel like giving either of those irritating males the benefit of a pleasant expression.

"Good morning again, Miss Montague. Yes, I got myself a haircut. None too soon. Addison here and I were just discussing literature. He plans on having his talents abused for the rest of his life."

Sylvester uttered an agitated sound that might have been a stifled roar of outrage. Claire was sure she heard his teeth gnashing. She didn't care. Nor did she care to contribute to this particular conversation. She stared at her employer stonily.

He smiled back and asked, "Did you find some suitable lamps?"

Claire decided it was unfair of God to have given Tom Partington such a glorious smile. He was the masculine equivalent of Dianthe St. Sauvre, and Claire resented it. So as not to succumb to the effects of his smile, she turned away abruptly and said, "No."

She didn't see him blink in astonishment, but she could guess at his reaction by the silence that greeted her answer. She spared him a response. "No, I concluded you should be the one to decide upon the furnishings for your house, Mr. Partington. After all, this will be your first purchase for your new home, and I thought you should have the final say. Sylvester can show us some suitable lanterns," she added, with a pointed look at her friend.

"Oh. All right then. Sure. Show us some lamps, Addison."

"My *name* is Addison-Addison."

Claire finally condescended to offer Tom a tight smile. He took her arm, and they followed Sylvester to the lamps. Claire couldn't recall another time that Sylvester had walked in so stiff a manner. His usual pose of world-weary languor had vanished entirely.

Tom supposed he really shouldn't have baited Sylvester Addison-Addison the way he had. It was hard to resist, though, because the man was such a nonsensical specimen of humankind. He wondered what the novelist would do if he ever had to face real peril. Undoubtedly he'd scream. Or faint. Still, Tom knew Claire set quite a store by these boring artists of hers, and he'd already riled her once today. Her pinched lips and stern demeanor nudged him to try to jolly her out of her bad mood.

"I think those lanterns we chose will be really pretty in the dining room, Miss Montague," he ventured to say with one of his patented smiles.

She'd been maintaining her air of rigid dignity ever since she broke up what might have become an all-out brawl in the Mercantile. Not even the ever-so-proper Claire Montague could withstand the Partington charm, though, Tom was pleased to discover.

He could tell she was trying not to smile when she said, "I believe you're right, Mr. Partington."

"If you're not still mad at me, would you mind showing me the rest of the town?"

Claire responded to his roguish expression with a blush. Her brown eyes opened wide beneath her spectacles, her thick lashes fluttered, and her dark brows rose. The sun struck her rattlesnakes, and they shot burnished sparks into the late-morning sky. Insecurity showed clearly on her face, and Tom's heart quivered unexpectedly. He'd been mean to her and was sorry for it.

"Please forgive me, Miss Montague. I truly didn't intend to embarrass you."

Her dimple gave him hope—for what he wasn't sure. "Well, all right then." She slanted him a rather roguish look of her own. "Although I'm sure I'm being far too easy on you."

"I'm sure you are." And he was too.

Nevertheless Claire condescended to give him a tour of Pyrite Springs. She pointed out the cobbler's shop, the butcher's, the post office, the bank, the local attorney's office, the farrier (to whom Claire introduced him), the bakery, the florist, the jewelry store, the livery, the Pyrite Springs Hotel, the courthouse, the tobacconist's (complete with a ferociously painted wooden Indian), and even, from across the street and with a moue of distaste, the Fool's Gold Saloon.

They had their lunch at Sam Wong's Gem of the Orient because Tom said he'd never eaten Chinese food before. The Chinese cook who'd worked for the railroad had prepared American fare.

"I hope you'll like it," Claire said, nervously inspecting the menu. "I'm quite fond of Chinese cuisine myself."

Tom thought it was sweet that she cared whether or not he'd like his lunch. "Even if I don't take a shine to it, Miss Montague, I will have had a new experience, and that's the important thing."

"What a marvelous attitude, Mr. Partington!" Claire exclaimed. She looked startled for a moment, as if her thoughts had suddenly been diverted on to some other course entirely. Then she gave a little shake and beamed at him. "Yes, indeed. I think that's the attitude we all need."

A little puzzled, Tom thanked her. She needn't have worried. He enjoyed his lunch.

Dianthe dined with them that evening, and Claire was pleased to find the new lamps did their job well. Even though Scruggs had again seated them in the formal dining room, they could at least see one another and their food.

It had not taken her employer any time at all to restore himself in her good graces, and she worried about that. Was she so easily swayed because of some intrinsic flaw in her character? It seemed to her that if she possessed true grit, she should have stayed annoyed for a little longer anyway.

For some years she hadn't had occasion to think about her life before Partington Place. Recently, however, her doubtful upbringing had been fretting her a good deal. She'd believed she'd left her father's haphazard morals behind her; she'd forsaken them and him ten years before.

Yet in the past few days not only had she found herself being coddled out of perfectly reasonable bad moods by nothing more than a smile, but she'd also told more falsehoods than she could remember having uttered in ages. She'd lied and lied and even drawn her friends into her lies. She was, moreover, attempting to mislead her employer, to "put one over on him," in her father's vulgar vernacular.

What was even worse was that Claire knew Tom believed Gordon Partington to have been the author of the books he hated so, and she had done nothing to disabuse him of the notion. She was deliberately allowing him to think poorly of his wonderful uncle, and her conscience ached in consequence.

Eyeing Dianthe askance, Claire knew her perfidy went even deeper. She had succumbed to petty jealousy. Oh, she'd long since stopped wishing for Dianthe's graceful beauty. But with the advent of Tom Partington, Claire found herself actually longing for him to look beneath Dianthe's glorious exterior and discover the poet underneath to be insipid. Claire knew Dianthe was brilliant, and she suspected her own shortcomings led her to find Dianthe's work inane. She knew it was base of her to want Tom to find them silly too. She did, though.

At least Tom's comment about his Chinese luncheon had given her a good idea about what to do with the forever shrieking Miss Abigail Faithgood.

Rising from the rocky floor of the cliff where she'd fallen, Miss Abigail Faithgood clapped a hand over her mouth. She would not scream again, no matter what horrors manifested themselves before her. Watching the noble Tuscaloosa Tom, she vowed to be worthy of his regard.

"Are you all right, Miss Faithgood?" the chivalrous Tom inquired. He thrust the bloody knife away from him, aghast at the violent acts he'd been called upon to perform this day.

Squaring her shoulders, Miss Abigail Faithgood lifted her chin and averred nobly, "I shall be, Mr. Pardee. Lead on. I shall not waver."

There. That should do it. If only her own problems were so easily solved.

"Is everything all right, Miss Montague? Are you feeling well?"

Claire hadn't realized how heavily she'd sighed until the kindhearted Jedediah Silver asked about her health. Good heavens, she simply must get a grip upon her nerves.

"I'm fine, thank you, Mr. Silver. I was . . . just admiring the new lighting."

"Yes, it's a pleasure to be able to see the food on one's plate, isn't it?"

She shared a gentle laugh with Jedediah and glanced at Tom under her lashes. He looked amused and was staring straight at her, a circumstance that made her pay attention to her crab soufflé.

"I think Claire and Mr. Addison-Addison must have had a tiff today," Dianthe murmured in a voice as delicate as swansdown.

Claire looked up from her crab, guilt stabbing her like a knife. She *had* been mean to Sylvester, and it was all because she'd allowed herself to fall back into the evil ways she'd struggled so hard to overcome. What a wicked web she'd begun to weave.

"Actually I'm afraid it was I who ruffled old Addison's feathers this morning, Miss St. Sauvre."

Claire's gaze swung to Tom, and she stared at him in astonishment.

"I'm afraid I can't resist teasing him because he takes himself so seriously. He reminds me of some of the young boys I used to serve with in the army."

"Really? How fascinating."

Dianthe batted her eyelashes at Tom, and Claire resisted the urge to throw a dinner roll at her. "He can be difficult," Claire muttered, trying to keep her tone sweet.

"He's an insufferable bore, is what he is," said Tom, not mincing words.

"Certainly not insufferable, Mr. Partington," Dianthe suggested gently.

"Well, maybe only a bore," Tom said with a grin.

"Which certainly can't be said for our present company." Jedediah's expression spoke of worship. It was of course directed at Dianthe, who blushed becomingly.

"Of course not," Tom mumbled right before he took a bite of his soufflé.

Claire's wineglass hit the table with a snap. "All the residents of the Pyrite Arms are admirable artists," she said when her dinner companions turned to look at her. Her smile felt brittle; she hoped it didn't show.

"I'm sure that's true, Miss Montague. Maybe I just don't have a proper appreciation for the arts."

Claire felt her eyes narrow and opened them up again. Just because she felt guilty and touchy was no reason to be ill humored. She couldn't recall the last time she'd had such a time governing her temper. "Don't you care for any type of literature, Mr. Partington? There must be some writer somewhere who has managed to capture your fancy."

"Yes. I like to read. I'm fond of Mark Twain and Dickens. And I like Ouida's novels too sometimes."

"You mean to say you prefer Ouida to McTeague?" Claire's voice had risen, and she made an effort to control her passion. But honestly! This was a man who claimed he hated Clarence McTeague's works, yet he liked Ouida? Outrageous! Clarence McTeague was ten times the writer Ouida was. Or, Claire meant, *she* was ten times the writer Ouida was.

Tom shrugged.

"Really, Mr. Partington, I fail to see why you should not respond to Clarence McTeague's works if you enjoy Ouida. At least McTeague's works aren't totally fantastic." She took a vicious bite of her crab.

"No?"

"Certainly not. Why on earth do you prefer Ouida over McTeague?"

"Well, for one thing, Ouida hasn't made my life miserable."

"Oh." Her anger dissolved, and Claire studied her plate. Suddenly the scrumptious meal Mrs. Philpott had prepared took on the flavor of ashes.

"But that's not the only reason."

"No?" She braced herself.

"McTeague writes about places I know. Ouida writes about exotic places. Lush South Sea islands and far-off Arabian deserts. The French Foreign Legion and adventure."

"McTeague's books contain some pretty exciting adventures if you ask me," said Jedediah.

Claire felt illogically gratified by his words. She said, "Thank you, Mr. Silver."

"You're more than welcome."

Jedediah looked surprised, and Claire realized she'd almost made a monumental blunder. "I—I mean, I don't like to think I'm the only one who likes a rousing dime novel set in the Americas every now and then." She hoped the new lighting wasn't so bright that her burning cheeks would show and give her away. "After all," she added with what she thought was admirable logic, "the American frontier is exotic to most of us."

"Hmm, you might be right there," said Tom judiciously, drawing attention away from her. "I can't say that I object to McTeague's writing. In fact, I think he had quite a way with words. It's just that he chose me to idealize, and it was embarrassing. I guess if I wasn't the brunt of those ridiculous books, I might even like them. He was better than Buntline anyway."

"Buntline is a hack," Claire declared flatly.

Tom laughed. "Now, Miss Montague, I know you were very fond of my uncle, but you needn't belittle Ned Buntline for Uncle Gordon's sake. They were both pretty good."

Claire sat up straighter. She had very firm opinions on some issues, and Ned Buntline was one of them. "I believe that if you were to judge Buntline and McTeague solely on the merits of their literary talent, you would find McTeague's work offers infinitely more real value for your dime."

With a sigh Tom said, "Well, I guess it doesn't matter anymore. Poor old Uncle Gordon's gone to his reward." He lifted his wineglass. "How about a toast to him? He must have been a fine man to have earned your approbation, Miss Montague."

His smile could melt a heart of ice. If Claire hadn't already fallen in love with him years before, when Gordon had begun reading to her about his thrilling exploits and noble deeds, his smile alone might have sent her over the edge.

"He was a fine man," Jedediah said. He lifted his glass too.

Claire and Dianthe followed suit.

"He was a saint," Dianthe whispered.

Claire saw tears sparkle on Dianthe's lashes and felt a twist of uncharacteristic disbelief. She told herself to stop it. Dianthe was a good friend and possessed a sympathetic heart. She couldn't help it if she was perfect in every respect and wept at all the appropriate moments.

"He took me under his wing and treated me as a daughter," Claire said softly. "I loved him very much."

"No man could ask for a finer tribute."

Claire looked at Tom quickly to see if he was joking and was astonished to discover he wasn't.

They drank to the late Gordon Partington.

"At least I won't have to endure any more of those books of his. I expect this *Tuscaloosa Tom and the River of Raging Death* will be the last."

Claire, who knew very well it wouldn't be the last because she had the one more book to write in order to fulfill her contract, choked on her wine.

"I'm not so sure about that."

Unable to speak, holding a napkin to her lips to prevent her from coughing, her eyes watering, Claire gaped at Jedediah. Could salvation come from that quarter?

"Why not?" Tom demanded. "Uncle Gordon's dead, for heaven's sake. He couldn't write any more of those books if he wanted to."

With a shrug Jedediah said, "Well, you know, Tom, publishers will often hire other writers to carry on a series if the original writer becomes unavailable for some reason. If the books are doing well—and I expect they are—then you might have to face more of them."

"Oh, Lord." Tom propped his elbows on the table and ran his fingers through his hair. "Please tell me you're joking."

"I wish I could."

Claire finally managed to catch her breath. Watching Tom's genuine despair, she felt a terrible mixture of unhappiness and exhilaration. She'd never expected to get a reprieve such as the one Jedediah had just handed her.

On the other hand, she was mortified to have caused Tom such misery. She knew herself to be beyond redemption when she thought with a thrill that maybe she'd *never* have to confess!

She caught Dianthe's eye and almost forgave her friend for being perfect when Dianthe winked at her.

"I believe Mr. Silver is correct, Mr. Partington," Dianthe said in her angel's voice. "I understand that to be a common practice among successful publishers."

"Why, it may be that even Mr. Buntline's output is augmented by hired writers. I understand he does drink to excess." Claire was appalled when her venomous words sailed into the air. Good grief, she truly must be evil! Not only was she grasping at excuses to continue her deception, but she had now taken to maligning her competition.

"Oh, Lord," Tom moaned again.

"Cheer up," advised Jedediah with a laugh. "All the money from those books must be ending up in Gordon's estate somewhere, and that only benefits you and your plans for the horse ranch. We'll figure out the bookkeeping one of these days. If all else fails, I can always write to the publisher."

Claire stared at him, wondering how in the space of seconds her savior could have turned traitor.

8

Tom had never been attracted to proper females. He was at a loss therefore to understand why Claire Montague appealed to him so much. Maybe it was because he sensed something hidden in her, something that, if he could tap it, would make her blossom. Even though she'd never given him so much as a hint, he had a feeling she wasn't as prim as she wanted the world to believe.

She'd sure gotten mad at him yesterday. And she'd been really peeved when he'd told her he liked Ouida's novels too. He grinned as he looked out over the meadow now being fenced for horse pastures. Shoot, any woman with a temper and a taste for those idiotic dime novels must harbor passion in her soul somewhere.

Hearing footsteps, Tom turned to discover Jedediah Silver loping up the grassy slope toward him. He lifted his hand in salute. "Morning, Jed."

"Good morning, Tom. These plans for the paddocks and barns were just delivered from the carpenter's shop." He waved a roll of papers in Tom's face.

"Great. Let's look 'em over."

"Do you want to discuss these with Miss Montague? She'll probably have some useful ideas on the size and placement of the feed storage areas, accesses, and so forth."

"Good idea, Jed. I'd like to keep her informed of my plans anyway and let her know when the work will begin. Maybe she'll even agree to help me word a letter to the breeder. She seems to be so sensible about things. And she's apparently quite fond of the written word."

Jedediah gave Tom an approving grin. "I'm glad you think so. Your uncle thought the world of her, and it's been my experience that while she is only a woman, her advice is invariably well considered and helpful."

"I've noticed that too."

Which completely contradicted everything Tom knew about women. His own mother had been even less useful than his father. He expected Dianthe St. Sauvre, to whom Jedediah seemed to have taken quite a shine, was cut of the same cloth as his mother. Most of the females he'd known in his life were like that, in fact, except a couple of the scarlet women who'd followed the railroad, and he didn't think they counted.

In his experience, respectable women were decorative and totally useless on a practical level—well, unless you married one of them. Even then they were good for only one thing that Tom could think of, and marriage carried burdens he didn't care to contemplate at the moment. Those burdens more than outweighed the brief pleasures the marriage bed assured a man. Actually, from what he'd heard from his married cronies, those pleasures weren't even assured by marriage.

No, until he'd met Claire Montague, respectable women had held no allure at all. He supposed most proper females' relative helplessness had more to do with the world's expectations of them than from anything nature had intended, but it didn't make much difference. The result was the same.

As he scuffed along beside Jedediah, eyeing his new kingdom with satisfaction, Tom decided it was undoubtedly his odd approach to life that made him appreciate useful people so much. Anybody who wasn't proficient in Tom's line of work didn't stay alive very long. If the elements didn't get you, the Indians or outlaws would. Male or female, old or young, if you weren't alert and capable, you were coyote fodder in short order.

But Claire Montague—well, Claire was another matter entirely. She was alert, capable, and cute as a button when she wasn't watching herself. It was fun catching her off guard.

"What's so funny, Tom?"

Tom hadn't realized he was grinning. "Oh, nothing, Jed, nothing at all."

His heart swelling with admiration, Tuscaloosa Tom declared, "Then come with me, Miss Faithgood. I shall lead you to safety."

Actually, Claire reflected sourly, his heart had probably swelled with relief when she didn't seem to be opening up to shriek again.

Admonishing herself not to allow circumstances to make her bitter, Claire continued.

Miss Abigail Faithgood took the hand Tom held out. A thrill shot through her at his touch. She swore she would be strong. These villains would not wrest her ranch away from her and make her give up her sheep. She owed it to her beloved father's sainted memory [here Claire allowed herself a brief snort] *not to waver in pursuit of her goal. With Tom Pardee on her side, how could she fail?*

The canyon echoed with hoofbeats as Miss Abigail Faithgood and the gallant Tuscaloosa Tom Pardee rode away from the scene of their ambush. Tom's golden hair shimmered in the sunlight. His posture was straight, his eye keen, and his . . .

Patting one of her braids in thought, Claire chewed the end of her pen and scowled at the page. She'd been scowling, in fact, since she'd arisen this morning.

Somehow or other, she had to ensure that Jedediah Silver didn't write to her publisher. But how?

She commanded herself to stop thinking about that awful problem and to concentrate on one disaster at a time. Right now she had to wrench the idiot Abigail's sheep ranch back from the evil men who were trying to snatch it away from her.

. . . his very bearing proclaiming him a hero.

Claire paused to consider if one's bearing could do such a thing. Had Tom Partington's bearing proclaimed him a hero when she'd seen him standing at the foot of the stairs on the night of his arrival?

Yes. She remembered it well. In fact, she remembered everything about that fateful night. She stared dreamily out the window at her winter-bare garden, recalling the momentous occasion of Tom's arrival into her life. He'd certainly lived up to her expectations.

Heavy footsteps in the hallway outside her office jerked her to attention. In a flurry she stuffed her manuscript into her desk drawer and slammed it shut. She leaped to her feet, patting her coils madly, as the door swung open after a short tap.

The sight of Claire Montague nervously whacking at her rattlesnakes made a warm, slushy emotion puddle up in Tom's innards. He certainly couldn't have told anybody, least of all himself, why that should be. He'd always thought he favored shorter, more voluptuous, more overtly feminine females—Dianthe St. Sauvre, for example.

But Dianthe made him yawn. Even the thought of her in his bed didn't do much more than faintly titillate. But Claire—well, he sensed depths to Claire that he'd like to tap. In fact, if he had to choose between Claire and Dianthe, there would be no contest. He'd snap Claire up in an instant.

Fortunately for him, there was no reason to make such a choice. He couldn't think of any reason Claire shouldn't wish to stay on indefinitely as his housekeeper. That would keep her close at hand without entangling him in any kind of commitment.

Dianthe he could admire from a distance. As long as she didn't open her mouth, she was quite lovely. And he was sure to find a willing widow or a scarlet lady to take care of his more earthy needs once he knew his way around Pyrite Springs. That should keep him from fretting about Claire's untapped depths.

Life, in short, was grand. It was even grander after he and Jedediah had consulted with Claire about his paddocks, stables, barns, and pastures. With every contact, his admiration for Claire grew.

"Miss Montague, I can't tell you how glad I am that you finally decided to come in and let me have at this hair of yours."

Claire wasn't sure she appreciated Miss Thelma's choice of phrasing, happy as she was to have brought pleasure into her life. She deemed a small smile the most appropriate answer under the circumstances since the scissors Miss Thelma wielded were perilously close to her ear.

"You have beautiful hair, Miss Montague. Simply beautiful. Why, Mrs. Humphry Albright would kill for hair like yours."

As she gazed into the looking glass in front of her, Claire saw her own eyes open wide even though she'd had to remove her spectacles. Mrs. Humphry Albright? Good heavens. Mrs. Humphry Albright was one of Pyrite Springs's leading citizens.

She allowed herself a brief "Really?"

"My, yes. I always have to supplement Mrs. Albright's hair with false pieces, you know. You didn't really think all that hair was hers, did you?"

Miss Thelma giggled, causing Claire to catch her breath in trepidation. Apparently the hairdresser knew what she was doing, however, because Miss Thelma's hand never trembled and Claire's skin remained unbroken.

"I had no idea."

"Oh, my goodness, yes. But you! Why, I'll be able to do a Roman knot with this magnificent chestnut mane of yours with no trouble at all, and we'll have plenty left over for curls in front."

"I don't wish to appear frivolous now." Claire cautioned Miss Thelma for about the fifteenth time since she'd set foot in the hairstylist/modiste establishment at one o'clock that afternoon.

"My dear Miss Montague, I don't believe you could look frivolous if you tried."

"No," Claire said after a moment, not altogether happily. "I suppose you're right."

"But you'll look perfectly charming, my dear. Just you wait."

Repressing her impulse to ask what Miss Thelma expected her to do besides wait, Claire again produced a smile.

"How does the gown look, dear? Were the alterations done to your satisfaction?"

Claire's nervousness about having her hair cut for the first time in ten years was supplanted by her nervousness about appearing in her new evening gown at Tom Partington's Artistic Evening. It was the first gown of its nature Claire had put on her body since she'd deserted her father's medicine show, and it frightened her.

There was nothing intrinsically shocking about the dress; it was quite tasteful. But it was so different from what she usually wore. A deep golden yellow that went splendidly with Claire's complexion and hair color, the gown had short puffed sleeves embellished with russet velvet ribbons. The bodice sported a triangular insert of the same russet velvet, and the skirt's ruffled flounces were drawn back and tied with more of the ribbon and adorned with silk roses.

"I love the gown," Claire said truthfully. "But it's— it's so different from the kinds of things I usually wear."

"It certainly is."

Claire was almost certain Miss Thelma would love to enlarge upon the theme but was too discreet to do so.

"I think it looks quite good, considering I'm rather tall and—and—"

"You're regally slim, dear," Miss Thelma said tactfully.

"Er, yes. And I'm sure it will look even better now

that my hair will be done in a more—more appropriate style. To the gown, I mean."

"Of course, dearie."

Claire had tried her new dress on every evening since it was delivered. She'd stared at her reflection in the mirror and imagined herself on Tom Partington's arm, greeting guests to their very first Artistic Evening together. Invariably too she'd lectured herself on the stupidity of spinning daydreams, but she couldn't seem to stop herself.

Tom Partington really was the man of her dreams. And to discover that his nature was every bit as sensible as her own had been frosting on the cake, as it were. There didn't seem to be a purposeless bone in the man's body, and Claire approved. She'd had her fill of worthless charmers long since.

"You know, Miss Montague, Mrs. Pringle tried on that same gown earlier in the week."

"She did?" Priscilla Pringle, a wealthy widow, was as close to an object of gossip as Pyrite Springs boasted. A supporter of the arts, she was frivolous and charming and flirted outrageously with all the men in town. She would also be coming to Partington Place this evening.

A ghastly thought struck Claire. "She didn't buy one like it, did she?" That's all she needed, was to have the merry widow show up at the Artistic Evening in the identical gown Claire wore. Mrs. Pringle, with her dashing red hair and coy manner, would make Claire look ridiculous if they both wore the same ensemble.

"Good heavens, no. It washed her out completely. Made her look like a sack of onions."

"Onions?"

"Oh, you know. All sallow and pasty. No, that gown

needed you, Miss Montague. And I'm so happy you found each other."

Miss Thelma giggled again at her wit. Claire gave her a smile. Then, taking her courage in both hands, she blurted out, "Perhaps you can help me augment my wardrobe further, Miss Grimsby. I've decided to—to add a little color to my life." Exactly as Tom Partington told her she should do. She wondered if she was being a perfect fool.

No, nobody in this world was perfect. Except Dianthe St. Sauvre.

"Oh, Miss Montague! I'm so happy to hear you say that. Why, I used to watch you walk past my shop several times a week and just *long* to get my hands on you."

Miss Thelma's words did not make Claire's heart sing. She did manage to murmur another "Really."

"Oh, yes! We can fix you right up. We have a lovely selection of demure gowns, skirts, and shirtwaists. Any of them would be suitable to your profession without being dowdy. Why, Mrs. Humphry Albright and I were discussing you just the other day, and we agreed that all you need is a little fixing up to be *very* attractive. You'll see."

Even without her spectacles, Claire could see Miss Thelma beaming at her and returned her smile because she knew Miss Thelma's heart was in the right place, even if her foot seemed to be lodged rather securely in her mouth. She asked tightly, "You were discussing me with Mrs. Albright?"

"In nothing but the highest terms, I assure you, Miss Montague. Mrs. Albright agreed with me too. We both think you'll be one of the elegant ones."

"One of the elegant ones," Claire repeated faintly.

"Mercy, yes. You see, we think there are five types of

females. Of course there are the vulgar ones, and we shouldn't even speak of them."

"Of course not."

"Then there are the fairy princesses, like your friend Miss Dianthe St. Sauvre."

"Do you do Dianthe's hair?" Claire had never even wondered before.

"Yes, indeed. Then there are the flighty ones, like Mrs. Pringle."

"I see."

"But you and Mrs. Albright are elegant. Or will be when you fix yourself up."

Claire didn't appreciate all this talk about "fixing herself up," as though there were something wrong with her that needed improvement. Nor was she altogether sure she liked being lumped together with the stout, stately Mrs. Albright. She did, however, mutter a grudging thank-you.

"You're perfectly welcome, my dear."

Miss Thelma clipped and snipped in silence for a minute or two. At last Claire asked, "What's the fifth one?"

"Beg pardon, dearie?"

"What's the fifth type of female you and Mrs. Albright classified?"

"Oh." Claire saw a faint tint stain the cheeks of the amorphous blob that was Miss Thelma's reflection in the looking glass. "Well, we, ah—we—oh, dear, I don't seem to remember right now."

"Yes, you do."

"I do?" Miss Thelma's twitter seemed forced.

"The fifth type was unfashionable, wasn't it, Miss Grimsby? Or, perhaps, dreary. And I suppose I fit nicely into that category, don't I?"

"Well—"

"That's all right, Miss Grimsby. I'm not angry." Not very angry anyway. Claire supposed Miss Thelma's assessment was no more than she deserved for having striven so hard to conceal her venal roots. Perhaps she needn't have tried so hard.

This evening should tell the story. This evening she would see once and for all if her new persona, carefully crafted over the past ten years, could withstand a little gilding without shattering completely.

Claire could scarcely recall a time in her life when she'd been so anxious.

9

The stain on Claire's cheeks owed nothing to the
rouge pot. Her blush attached itself to her all on
its own as soon as she entered the parlor before
dinner and Tom, seeing her, dropped his cheroot onto
the Persian carpet. Jedediah Silver stared too.

"My God."

The duet of awed masculine voices checked Claire at
the door. Clutching the doorknob in a death grip, she
looked anxiously from man to man, trying to read the
significance of their expressions.

Actually she didn't much care what Jedediah's expression signified.

Tom's mouth shut with a clack, and he swept his cigar
off the floor before the rug could catch fire. Thrusting
the cheroot into an ashtray, he almost tripped over the
velvet ottoman in his haste to reach Claire's side. He
snatched her hand away from the doorknob and said
breathlessly, "Miss Montague, you look wonderful this
evening. You look—you look elegant. Grand. Superb."

Cheeks afire, Claire murmured, "Thank you, Mr.

Partington." Silently she gave Miss Thelma her due. Miss Thelma had said Claire was one of the elegant ones; Claire guessed she was right. Thank God.

After a moment, during which he looked as though he'd been turned to stone, Jedediah rushed up to her too. He grabbed her other hand and pressed it. "Miss Montague, I don't believe I've ever seen you in formal attire before. You're stunning this evening. Absolutely stunning."

Elegant. Superb. Stunning. Claire guessed she could stand such descriptions. When Jedediah released her hand, she forced herself not to scramble for the over-stuffed armchair and cover herself with the Chinese cushion resting there, but to walk in an august manner to the chair and sit gracefully. Of course it helped that Tom held her elbow the whole way. She was glad she'd remembered to air out her long gloves; they'd smelled dreadfully of camphor when she'd unpacked them earlier in the week.

Tom sounded hoarse when he croaked, "Your hair, Miss Montague. I believe you've had your hair done in a different style."

Peeking up at him, Claire thought he looked dazzled. "Do you recognize it as one your aunt Minnie used to favor, Mr. Partington?"

He shook his head and didn't smile. "Aunt Minnie never looked like this. Not once."

Recalling her days with her knavish father, Claire smiled coyly. "And is that a good thing?"

This time Tom nodded. "Yes. Yes, indeed, Miss Montague. It's a very good thing."

It was Jedediah's turn to shake his head. "You look perfectly ravishing, Miss Montague."

Ravishing. Ravishing was good. Claire liked ravishing

too. Resuscitating all the tips her father had taught her in a childhood she'd done her best to forget, Claire smiled first at Tom and then at Jedediah. "My goodness, gentlemen, I can't recall ever having received so many lovely compliments."

Tom poured her a glass of sherry, and she took it, feeling a heady combination of happiness and worry. She wasn't worried about the success of the evening. Mrs. Philpott had prepared a delightful dinner for the three of them, and a variety of refreshments for the guests who would be arriving shortly after dinner. The artists coming from the Pyrite Arms were primed and ready; she'd visited the Arms this very morning to be sure. She also knew herself to be an obsessively organized hostess. All was set for the evening's entertainment.

No, she was worried about herself. She hadn't tried to be anything but a stuffy housekeeper for years; she wasn't sure she could turn the housekeeper Claire into an attractive young woman without shattering her or sending her slipping headlong into perdition. Achieving balance was certainly proving to be a nerve-racking proposition.

"Well, you're quite magnificent this evening, Miss Montague. The perfect hostess. You do Partington Place—you do me—proud."

"Thank you very much, Mr. Partington."

"You certainly do, Miss Claire. Why, I don't recall you ever looking so lovely for one of these things."

Daring a mischievous grin, Claire murmured, "Mr. Partington suggested I add some color to my life, and I took him at his word."

Peeking at Tom, she found him staring at her as if enraptured, and she glanced away again quickly. The look on his face frightened her; it reminded her of the looks on those men cheated by her father—when they'd gotten close enough for her to see. She pushed her spectacles up on her nose; they hadn't slipped, but they were familiar and gave her a feeling of security. They also provided a barrier—admittedly transparent—between herself and the world.

"I never expected you to take my words so much to heart, Miss Montague. But I'm very glad you did."

At least he didn't sound like those other men. His voice was perfectly respectful, not at all coarse or suggestive. She murmured, "Thank you," again.

"I had Scruggs raid the wine cellar. He said Uncle Gordon was especially fond of this sherry, so I hope it passes muster." Tom lifted his glass. "To the admirable Miss Montague, without whom neither Uncle Gordon nor I could manage."

"To Miss Montague," Jedediah repeated.

Claire felt her cheeks burn hotter.

Tom's sherry almost got stuck in his throat. He hadn't been so taken aback since he'd heard about his uncle's legacy. Claire took his breath away. Jedediah had been right: She was stunning, even with those spectacles perched on her nose. They didn't detract from the overall impression of attractiveness Claire exuded this evening; rather they added a unique finish to a perfect picture.

Tom didn't understand it, nor could he have explained it. All he knew was that Claire Montague appeared this evening to be the personification of everything he'd worked so hard to attain in his life. She was the embodiment of all that he'd ever struggled, fought, and toiled for, the diametrical opposite, in fact, of his frivolous, unpromising roots.

He wanted to throw his head back and laugh and then

throw his arms around Claire and kiss her. This was it; he'd attained perfection, and it was Partington Place and Claire Montague.

The door opened, and he had to leave off staring at his housekeeper.

"Dinner is served," Scruggs announced as though he were proclaiming the end of the world.

"Thank you, Scruggs."

With an imprudent leap up from his chair, which jarred his scarred leg, Tom managed to offer Claire his arm a scant second before Jedediah could perform the same service. "Miss Montague," he said through gritted teeth.

He was almost grateful for his foolishness when she clutched his arm with both hands and cried in alarm, "Good heavens, Mr. Partington, are you all right?"

Her gown was not low-cut, but when she held her arms just so, Tom could detect a delicious hint of cleavage. He gave her a reassuring smile. "Fine, fine, Miss Montague. My leg acts up when the weather's cold or wet."

"Goodness, and it looks as if it's going to start snowing any day now. I'm so sorry, Mr. Partington. Is this from the wound you sustained at Gettysburg?"

Tom decided having Claire's bosom pressed against his arm was almost worth his having aggravated one of his old injuries. "Actually that one's in the left leg and doesn't bother me too much. This one's from the arrow I took in '74 up in Wyoming."

"My goodness, Mr. Partington, what an incredibly adventurous life you've lived."

For the first time Tom forgot to be sorry that his uncle used to romanticize his life to Claire. It felt pretty good to be idolized by her this evening.

"It's had its moments," he said, patting her hand. He wanted to pat further but knew she'd object. "I appreciate your concern, Miss Montague."

She blinked at him, her chocolate brown eyes wide and beautiful beneath her sparkling lenses. "Anything I can do to make your life more comfortable is my prime concern, Mr. Partington."

As her proximity and sweet cosseting had begun to awaken exceedingly improper urges in Tom, he declined to suggest the most appealing way in which she might consummate her prime concern. Instead he saw her to her chair as a gentleman should and seated himself at the head of the table.

They dined on escalloped oysters, roast beef, and, at Claire's suggestion, Yorkshire pudding made the way Mrs. Philpott's mother used to make it back home in England. Also at Claire's suggestion, champagne was served in honor of Tom's first Artistic Evening in his new manor. Scruggs poured the bubbling wine as though he were doling out poison.

Sipping his champagne, Tom looked from his new friend, Jedediah Silver, to his new housekeeper, Claire Montague, and wondered how she'd take to fulfilling another role in his life.

Tom breathed a sigh of relief when the handsome, albeit grumpy-looking, Sylvester Addison-Addison passed under the archway and into the small ballroom and Priscilla Pringle spotted him. She dropped Tom's coat sleeve, to which she'd been clinging, and darted away to greet Sylvester.

Tom brushed the wrinkle out of his sleeve and cocked a brow at Claire. "Good Lord, I didn't think I'd ever be happy to see that surly puppy."

Her giggle warmed Tom's heart. "It's merely that Mrs. Pringle admires you, Mr. Partington."

"She seemed bent on tormenting me."

"Nonsense! She finds you handsome and fascinating. Indeed who can blame her? You look very elegant this evening, which only adds intrigue to your magnificent reputation."

"You can't get out of it that easily, Miss Montague. The woman was plaguing me, and I expect you to take better care of me than that for the rest of the evening."

The flush in Claire's cheeks deepened, and Tom felt a mad impulse to sweep her into his arms and make off with her, and to hell with these silly artists. Of course he did no such thing.

This whole scenario seemed right to him, though: he and Claire, greeting visitors to his home, playing host and hostess to what passed for high society in Pyrite Springs. Even the flirty Mrs. Pringle had added an amusing interlude. He could imagine if he and Claire were, say, a married couple, they'd laugh about Mrs. Pringle's antics over breakfast on the morrow.

What was he thinking of? Good Lord. They'd laugh about it over breakfast tomorrow anyway. They didn't have to commit anything as foolish as marriage in order to do that. Thank God.

People were pouring into the room by this time. The small ballroom was small only when compared with the large ballroom on the floor beneath. It was actually a very big room, with a bank of floor-to-ceiling windows leading out onto a pretty balcony where folks could stroll in warm weather. The curtains were drawn over the windows tonight, and Tom didn't expect the balcony would see much use. Except, maybe, by him when the crush of people got to him and he had to flee. The chilly weather didn't daunt him; he'd lived through blizzards on the prairie countless times.

"Oh, there's Dianthe!" Claire rushed over to her friend and clasped her hands. Dianthe seemed equally pleased to see Claire. Her smile would have made Michelangelo's heart palpitate and his palms itch to paint her.

Watching both ladies critically, Tom decided that while it was true Dianthe was the more classically beautiful of the two, Claire possessed more natural animation. Probably because she possessed a bigger soul. And a bigger brain.

Tom sensed undercurrents to Claire, undercurrents he'd like to explore one of these days, by hand. The only thing he'd sensed thus far in Dianthe was physical beauty, which he granted she possessed in abundance. He guessed she'd never had to strive for much of anything, however, and the blandness of her life expressed itself in her personality. He was looking forward to her poetic rendition this evening as an opportunity either to confirm his opinion or to berate himself as being far too critical.

Good old Jed didn't seem to care about Dianthe's relative lack of intellect, Tom noticed with a grin. He was already hovering over her like a good angel. Well, that was fine with Tom. Jed could have her. After the struggles he'd been through, the thought of being saddled with a mere ornament made Tom's teeth clench and his flesh crawl. His mother had been an ornament, and Tom recalled with a shudder how much use she'd been to anybody. Of course his father hadn't been much more than ornamental either.

Maybe that was what he should do for his parents, he thought suddenly, bring them here. The notion held little appeal, but at least if they were in his house, he could keep an eye on them and make sure they didn't get into trouble. Of course, if he invited them, they probably wouldn't come. It would take an act of God to pry them away from Tuscaloosa, where they lived amid the fallen grandeur of a lost civilization, trading on the family name for the necessities of life.

"God, what a pair," Tom muttered, scowling into the milling throng filling up his ballroom but seeing his parents in his mind's eye.

"Is anything the matter, Mr. Partington?"

Startled, Tom turned to behold a nervously fidgeting Claire. She looked worried, and Tom's heart was stirred by her concern.

"I beg your pardon, Miss Montague, I didn't mean to appear disobliging. I was thinking about Alabama."

"Oh." Claire was obviously perplexed.

"I'm afraid I don't harbor too many fond memories of my childhood home," Tom said by way of explanation.

"You don't?"

"I don't."

A crease appeared between her eyes, and she said seriously, "I don't either, Mr. Partington, but I've always envied people who have pleasant memories of their childhoods. Such memories sound almost golden to me."

This time it was Tom who was perplexed. Before he could question her, she took his arm. "But do come along with me, Mr. Partington. Why, I do believe everybody to whom I sent an invitation is here this evening. Let me introduce you to the mayor, Mr. Gilbert. Mr. Gilbert is a supporter of the Pyrite Arms. At least," she amended darkly, "he was."

"Did something happen to make him lose interest?" Tom asked curiously as he allowed Claire to lead him across the floor.

"Not exactly. In fact, his interest is probably keener than ever. Unfortunately." She muttered, "It was Sergei, you see."

"Sergei?"

"I'll explain later, Mr. Partington." They had apparently reached their destination because Claire tapped a portly gentleman on the shoulder. He turned around, revealing an apple-cheeked countenance framed by gray-flecked muttonchops and a similarly embellished mustache.

"Mr. Partington, please allow me to introduce you to one of Pyrite Springs's leading citizens, Alphonse Gilbert. Mr. Gilbert is our esteemed mayor."

"How-do, young man. I was right pleased to hear you'd be taking over the running of the Place here. Your uncle made a great contribution to our community, and I expect you'll continue his good work." Mr. Gilbert smiled broadly and gave Tom's hand an almost too-hearty shake.

Reflecting that politicians were the same the world over, Tom returned the mayor's smile. "Thank you, sir. I've appreciated what I've seen so far of your fair city."

"Silver tells me you're going to breed horses. I think that's a fine ambition, sir, a fine ambition. I expect a horse ranch will bring a lot of trade to the neighborhood."

"Thank you," murmured Tom.

Mr. Gilbert turned to Claire. "And just look at the changes you've inspired already. Why, I declare, I've never seen our Miss Montague look so splendid. I expect we owe this transformation to your influence, Mr. Partington."

Alphonse Gilbert possessed a politician's voice, booming and genial, and Tom supposed there was really no good reason for him to want to punch him in the nose. Nevertheless, when he saw the mortified look on Claire's face, it was all he could do to keep from grabbing Gilbert by his bow tie and slapping him down like a bad poker hand.

Since he was in the very civilized environs of his own small ballroom, he had to content himself with blowing a cloud of cigar smoke in the mayor's face and saying tightly, "Miss Montague always looks charming, Mr. Gilbert. My uncle could not have managed without her, and neither can I."

Gilbert managed to choke out, "Quite, quite. I'm sure that's true."

Tom didn't wait to chat further with the oafish mayor. He clamped a hand on Claire's elbow and steered her toward Sylvester Addison-Addison. "Don't mind him, Miss Montague. The man's a blockhead."

Claire still seemed somewhat embarrassed. She murmured, "Maybe Sergei was right after all."

Tom looked at her inquiringly, and she shook her head. "I'll have to explain later, Mr. Partington. Here, please let me introduce you to Mrs. Gaylord."

On the way, they passed Sylvester, who turned to glower at them. Mrs. Pringle clung to his arm like a leech, and Tom hoped to God she'd keep her predatory eyes turned in that direction. Tom, who had been contemplating finding an obliging widow not more than a day or two earlier, wanted nothing to do with the pretty, fluttery, widowed Mrs. Pringle.

Sylvester sneered, "I see you've been led to visit that tedious harpy Thelma Grimsby, Claire."

Before Tom could snatch his arm away from Claire and deal with Sylvester Addison-Addison as he deserved to be dealt with, Claire said pleasantly, "Glorietta, do turn around and meet the young Mr. Partington."

She ignored Sylvester, who frowned harder, and Tom decided perhaps Claire's method of handling the sulky twit was superior to his. Old Sylvester seemed quite peeved about being ignored.

"Oh!" came a high-pitched squeal from a clump of people milling around Sylvester.

Then, in front of Tom's very eyes, an enormous orange marshmallow emerged from the jumble. Forgetting all about Sylvester Addison-Addison, he peered more closely and discovered the creature to be in reality a person of the female sex, but amazingly fleshy and draped in a brilliant orange fabric. It might have been silk, and it hung from beneath the woman's several chins, washing over her plump flesh like orange ocean waves and sluicing to the floor, where it puddled at what he assumed were her feet.

"Mrs. Glorietta Gaylord, may I present Mr. Tom Partington. Mr. Partington, as you may have assumed from this wonderful gathering, plans to continue his uncle's good works at the Pyrite Arms." Claire beamed at Tom, admiration shining from behind her lenses.

Tom managed to shut his mouth, which had fallen open at the bursting forth of Mrs. Gaylord. He felt his eyes go round again when, from the voluminous folds of orange, a chubby hand emerged. He took it, and his eyes traveled up the amazing garment to discover a face wreathed in a smile. The hair surrounding the face was nearly as orange as the garment, and dyed orange feathers had been stabbed into its upswept curls. He mumbled, "How do you do, Mrs. Gaylord?" and felt quite proud of himself.

"I'm very well, thank you, Mr. Partington," she said cheerfully. "And please don't be shy about revealing your astonishment at my colorful appearance. At the moment my entire life is an homage to the marigold. I honor the magnificent marigold in dress as in art. In fact, I have brought you one of my renderings this evening as a welcoming gift."

"How nice of you, Glorietta!"

Claire clapped her hands together and looked so pleased Tom found himself murmuring, "Er, yes. Thank you very much." All that vibrant orange was making him feel a trifle bilious. He hoped they wouldn't have to chat long with the ebullient Mrs. Gaylord or his oysters might rebel.

"I gave it to Scruggs on my way in, dear," Mrs. Gaylord said to Claire.

"I'm sure he's put it somewhere safe."

"Maybe we'd better go check, Miss Montague," Tom suggested, grabbing her arm and yanking her away. "Nice to meet you," he called over his shoulder.

Claire's soft laugh made him look down at her. "Are you laughing at me?"

"I am sorry, Mr. Partington. Perhaps I should have warned you."

"Maybe so."

"She's really a lovely woman. But she claims she wants to perfect the marigold before she moves on to other flowers. I'll actually be glad when she gets to roses, because they come in more colors. Perhaps anemones would give her even broader scope."

"I don't think her scope needs to be any broader," Tom muttered.

Claire laughed and smacked his arm gently in reproof. "But she truly is a fine artist. I'll be curious to see the painting she brought you."

"Will it be orange?"

"I expect so. Orange and perhaps yellow."

"I see. I suppose we can hang it in the downstairs washroom."

"Oh, there's Sergei," Claire said suddenly, pulling him along behind her.

"The one you don't blame?"

She shot him a teasing look. "Exactly."

"Is there anything I need to know about this one before we're introduced?"

"Just don't get him started talking about souls."

Souls. Tom looked at Claire's gleaming hair bouncing along before him and mumbled, "I wouldn't dream of it."

After Claire's introduction Sergei ignored Tom's outthrust hand, clicked his heels, and bowed from the waist, his arms held rigidly at his sides.

"Sergei," Claire whispered to Tom by way of explanation, "is Russian."

"I see," said Tom, who wasn't sure he did.

With a sweeping look at Tom that encompassed his person from the top of his head to the tips of his evening shoes, Sergei declared, "I shall paint your soul."

"You shall?" After Claire's brief warning about Sergei and souls, Tom was surprised to have the subject thrust at him so abruptly. He wondered how one went about painting somebody's soul. Were souls as easy to get at as, say, barn doors? "Er, how do you paint somebody's soul, Mr. Ivanov?"

Sergei slapped his chest. "It is in here."

Tom looked at the hand spread over Sergei's evening jacket. "It is?"

"*Da*. I look into the eyes and see the soul. I put the soul on canvas."

"Perhaps you'd better wait until you know Mr. Partington a little better before you attempt to do his portrait, Sergei. Remember what happened with Mr. Gilbert."

"Bah!" Sergei cried with evident contempt. "I paint the truth, and he cannot bear it!"

Claire patted his shoulder sympathetically. "At least I understand he's dropped charges."

Sergei muttered another "Bah!" and turned to stare morosely into the fireplace.

"Oh, dear," Claire whispered into Tom's ear. "I think he's going to brood now. You know these Russians."

Tom grinned at her. He liked having her lips so close to his ear. "Well, no, Miss Montague. Actually I don't."

"Oh, look!" cried Claire.

This time she reached for Tom's hand. He wasn't sure if she knew she'd done something so intimate, but he wasn't about to point it out to her.

Chuckling, he asked, "And just what's in store for me this time? Another mad Russian?"

"Certainly not. It's Freddy. And he's brought his flute. That must mean he's managed to compose an accompaniment to Dianthe's poem."

"Really." Tom guessed he was pleased, although he couldn't imagine what kind of music would go with a poem called "In Praise of the Spotted Horse." Particularly on a flute. He could understand a drum, maybe.

"Freddy!" Claire called.

When a tall, angular redheaded man turned around to smile at Claire, an action that lifted his drooping mustache considerably, Tom decided it was foolish of him to be surprised. All her artist friends were odd to varying degrees; he guessed Freddy March might just as well look like a hunting hound in a plaid coat as an orange marshmallow. Still, it was rather disconcerting to be looking at a fellow who might have passed as a younger version of Tom's father riding to hounds. He summoned up a smile and shook Freddy's hand politely.

"Oh, Freddy, I'm so eager to hear what you've composed for Dianthe's poem."

"I hope you'll be pleased, Claire. It took me forever."

As soon as the first word left Freddy's mouth, all resemblance to his father fled from Tom's mind. Whereas Tom's father spoke in a silky southern purr, Freddy March twanged. Tom wondered that he hadn't chosen to play the banjo.

He didn't have time to ponder the vagaries of human nature, however, because Mrs. Gaylord, who had been elected by some process beyond Tom's ken as the mistress of ceremonies, whistled from the staging area erected in the front of the ballroom. He clapped his hands over his ears and noticed others doing the same. Shoot, he hadn't heard a whistle like that since he was a boy. He was impressed.

After her whistle had silenced the room, Mrs. Gaylord spoke. "Friends, as you know, we are gathered here today at the invitation of Mr. Thomas Partington, new owner of Partington Place."

Cheers and applause burst forth. Surprised, Tom waved and smiled and hoped he wasn't expected to perform.

After the clapping died down, Mrs. Gaylord continued. "We five artists at the Pyrite Arms have long been in debt to the late Mr. Gordon Partington. Even though sweet Gordon has endowed the Arms in perpetuity through a magnanimous gift in his will, I was perfectly thrilled when Miss Montague told me the young Mr. Partington would be continuing his uncle's patronage of the Arms."

More cheers. More smiles. Another wave. He'd had no idea being rich could be such a pain. When he looked at Claire, however, and found her positively glowing at him, he decided acting the gent for this pack of fools was a small price to pay.

"Since Sergei and I alone among the residents of the Arms are not performance artists, I wanted to take this opportunity to present Mr. Partington with a gift." Mrs. Gaylord turned—a process that sent Tom back into his boyhood when he and his cousin George used to inspect pumpkins before carving autumnal jack-o'-lanterns—and called, "All right, Scruggs. You can bring it in now."

It took all of Tom's control to keep from shouting with laughter when Scruggs, looking as miserable as a man had any right to look, slumped out onto the stage, bearing an enormous painting.

"Good Lord, it *is* orange."

"Marigolds are orange, Mr. Partington, when they aren't yellow," Claire murmured apologetically.

"I suppose. Well, the downstairs washroom's too small, I reckon." He peeked at her and grinned. "I'll let you find a suitable place for the thing."

With a distinct twinkle she whispered, "There's always the bare spot over the dining room fireplace."

"Please," Tom said with a shudder, "consider our digestion, Miss Montague."

"Very well."

She giggled again, and Tom's heart went all mushy. Damn, he liked Claire Montague.

10

Halfway through Dianthe St. Sauvre's rendition of "In Praise of the Spotted Horse," complete with flute accompaniment by Freddy March, Tom still liked Claire Montague. He had, however, begun to harbor serious doubts about her sanity.

He couldn't figure out what any reasonable person could find entrancing about the lovely Dianthe doing her dainty best to make horse-clomping motions onstage while reciting banal rhymes.

"The spotted horse exalted/ On the plains where Indians roamed/ His majesty undaunted/ Under ebon skies star-domed," Dianthe recited, her whispery voice almost drowned out by the flute's piping. Then she whinnied, and Tom had to slam the figurative lid on his sense of humor or burst out laughing. His eyes teared up with the effort.

Yet every time he glanced at Claire, he found her bright-eyed and gazing with rapt attention at the stage. A peek at his guests revealed that they seemed to be enjoying themselves too. Deciding to ignore the rest of the audience, he concentrated on Claire.

He didn't understand it. While he had to keep from sticking his fingers in his ears to blot out the tuneless tattoo of flute notes battering his eardrums, Claire seemed enthralled. Eventually he found himself more enchanted by Claire's reaction to her friend's poetry than by the performance itself.

Appreciation of loyalty was one of the few absolutes in Tom's life. Truth, justice, peace, security, wealth—he'd lived without those commodities countless times, but without the loyalty of his fellows, in battle or on the frontier, he'd have been dead a long time ago. He'd been loyal to his comrades too, no matter what he thought of them as individuals, and he honored the attribute when he saw it. In this case, given the idiocy of Dianthe's poetry, he awarded Claire extra points for her allegiance.

The lights in the ballroom had been dimmed by judicious snuffing out of selected candles in the wall sconces. The faint light flickered against Claire's lenses as she leaned forward so she wouldn't miss a single word of her friend's rendering. As Tom examined Claire's features critically, he decided their overall effect was intriguing rather than beautiful. He recalled his first glimpse of her and wondered how he could have thought her dull. First impressions often led one astray.

He'd never have guessed, for example, that in the brief time he'd known Claire, he'd have started to have fantasies about her. But he had. He was having one right this minute, in fact.

She must have sensed his scrutiny because after one of Dianthe's more ridiculous verses, she turned her head, smiled at him, and whispered, "Are you enjoying your first Artistic Evening, Mr. Partington?"

"Er, yes. Yes indeed."

"Dianthe's poem is stirring, isn't it?"

"It certainly is."

It almost, in fact, stirred him to sleep when he decided he'd better pay attention to the stage for a while. A burst of clapping jolted him out of the first stages of slumber. He hoped he hadn't been so gauche as to snore.

Next to perform was Sylvester Addison-Addison, who not only held a lily but also took great pains to inform his audience that he considered it beneath him. At least that was the impression he left with Tom, who shook his head in wonder. Sylvester read several phenomenally boring pages from his opus, and this time Tom actually did fall asleep.

Claire wondered if she would ever get used to the sight of Tom Partington. She hoped so because if she had to endure these incredible pangs every time she looked at him, she wasn't sure how long she could last. Alert, he was magnificent. In repose, he was perfect.

He hadn't seemed to find Dianthe's ode banal but had watched her performance with evident pleasure. With a sigh Claire told herself she'd expected as much. Indeed she was glad her spiteful wish hadn't been fulfilled.

She wasn't surprised he'd fallen asleep during Sylvester's chapter. Sylvester's prose, while uplifting, was geared to an audience that hadn't led the exciting life Tom Partington had lived. Sylvester also had a mean streak, and Claire wondered why she'd never noticed it before. She was frowning when he finally stopped droning on about those wretched Greek ruins of his. The applause was polite rather than enthusiastic.

At the first clap she turned to Tom, who jolted awake

in an instant. She wanted to put her hand on his arm to calm him but knew it wasn't her place to do such a thing. Instead she smiled.

Blinking, he murmured, "Did he finally shut up?"

She couldn't help chuckling. "Indeed he did, Mr. Partington."

"Thank God."

The audience had begun to rise, and Tom and Claire did likewise. Scruggs, Mrs. Philpott, and a boy from the village had begun spreading refreshments on a long table against the wall. Tom offered his arm to Claire and led her over to the champagne.

He handed her a glass and lifted his own. "To you, Miss Montague."

"Heavens, no, Mr. Partington. The toast must be to you. After all, if it weren't for you, this evening's entertainment could never have taken place."

With a crooked grin that nearly made Claire's knees buckle, Tom said, "Oh, no, you don't. You're not going to pin this one on me."

"You mean you didn't enjoy it?"

"Don't look so scandalized, Miss Montague. I told you I wasn't used to polite company. You enjoyed it, and that's what matters. Drink up. Anything that gives you pleasure is a pleasure to me."

"Those are very pretty words, Mr. Partington, but I was so hoping you would take an interest. . . . Oh, Mr. Partington, did you *hate* it?" Claire felt a foolish urge to cry.

His expression was sweet when he said, "Of course I didn't hate it, Miss Montague. I enjoyed the evening very much. In fact, I'm still enjoying it. Now drink your champagne, my dear."

"Thank you."

Still feeling shaky, Claire sipped her wine. She wanted to question Tom further, to determine if he was merely humoring her or if he truly cared about the arts. She thought she'd die if she discovered he had agreed to this entertainment for no better reason than to amuse his housekeeper.

As the idea that he might have done such a thing for her began to settle in her heart, however, she almost choked on her champagne. Good heavens, could it be true?

All at once Claire realized how foolish she was being. Of course he hadn't put on the Artistic Evening for her. He'd done it for Dianthe. Beautiful Dianthe. Brilliant Dianthe. Ethereal, lovely Dianthe. Of course. Silly Claire.

There was no time to repine, however, because the refreshment table had been discovered and seemed to draw Tom's guests like a magnet. Or like maggots, her father might have said.

She frowned, wishing she could stop remembering her crafty father's crude sayings. She wished she could stop thinking about her father. She'd had no reason to think about him until she'd begun to lie to Tom Partington. Maybe her unhappy suspicion that bad blood ran in the family was true.

Tangled web, sang in Claire's brain to the ugly tune Freddy had played on his flute, and she felt unhappy for a moment. A voice intruded into her despair.

"I'm sorry about what I said, Claire."

She turned to discover Sylvester Addison-Addison at her elbow. Priscilla Pringle's talons were firmly attached to his arm, and his lily had begun to droop.

Since she wasn't sure she should believe what her ears had just heard, she stammered, "I—I beg your pardon?"

"About your hair. I didn't mean to sound churlish. It actually looks very nice. I like the curls in front and the twist in back. It's quite elegant."

If Claire hadn't been so stunned by Sylvester's apology—the first she'd ever heard him utter—she might have taken note of the word "elegant." It had been used to describe her quite often recently. As it was, she mentally filed it away and planned to take it out to examine more closely later. Right now she allowed her mouth to drop open in astonishment.

"Thank you so much, Sylvester. How nice of you. I don't believe you've ever begged pardon of anyone for being churlish before. I feel honored."

Sylvester's face crumpled into petulance at once. "Well, by God, I—ow!"

Startled by his cry of pain, Claire opened her eyes wide when she saw Mrs. Pringle's fingers loosen on his coat sleeve. Her nails were long, and they must have pinched terribly.

"I mean," said Sylvester after dragging in a deep breath, "I do like your new hairstyle, Claire. It suits you admirably."

To spare him further pain, Claire said simply, "Thank you, Sylvester. Your reading tonight was . . . flawless." She expected that might be true.

"Wasn't he wonderful?" Mrs. Pringle asked. She fluttered her lashes at Sylvester, who gave her a smile that made Claire's eyes open wide again.

"Yes. Yes, he was wonderful," she murmured.

"And he's quite right, you know, Claire. You should wear your hair like that all the time. It looks simply wonderful. And that gown becomes you much better than it did me. Why, you look quite pretty this evening."

"Thank you, Priscilla."

"Come along, Sylvester. You promised me a crab patty."

"Yes, Mrs. Pringle."

"Priscilla," Claire heard her say coyly. "You know I keep telling you to call me Priscilla, Sylvester, darling."

When Mrs. Pringle whacked Sylvester's arm playfully with her fan, Claire was shocked. My goodness, could the flirty widow be setting her sights on Sylvester Addison-Addison? If she was, it might be just as well for the citizens of Pyrite Springs. If Sylvester married a rich woman, he wouldn't have to work anymore and Mr. Gilbert might hire a polite clerk to work in his mercantile establishment.

"Claire!"

She swirled around to encounter Dianthe, wafting toward her on Jedediah Silver's arm, her white-and-black-speckled dress fluttering around her like a butterfly's wings. Dianthe had her arms outstretched, and Claire clasped Dianthe's hands in hers, her earlier uncharitable thoughts engulfed by genuine affection for her friend.

"Your ode was wonderful, Dianthe, and your dance utterly charming."

"Wasn't she magnificent?"

Claire wasn't sure she approved of the look of devotion in Jedediah's eyes. Nevertheless, she said, "Indeed she was. Why, the poem was so—so—so appropriate."

Jedediah subsided into silent worship, and Dianthe blushed. Now Claire was sure she didn't approve. If Tom Partington was in love with Dianthe, it would never do for Dianthe to take a liking to Jedediah Silver. As envious as Claire was of Tom's possible regard for Dianthe, she would never wish him to suffer from unrequited love. As Claire herself did.

"Well, Claire, dear," Dianthe said, her face alight with gaiety, "I suppose we must be off. It is an artist's duty to mingle with her patrons, you know."

"Of course, Dianthe. Have a good time."

"Thank you. And thank you for planning this, Claire. I know it was your doing."

"It was nothing, really."

Dianthe gave her a sisterly kiss on the cheek, and Claire lifted her hand in farewell as Dianthe and Jedediah drifted away. She wondered if she should have tried to pry him away from Dianthe. With a sigh she decided Tom Partington, who was so very clever at everything, must be much more adept at love games than plain, dull Claire Montague. He'd just have to wrest Dianthe away from Jedediah himself this evening if he wanted her.

The party was quite jolly. Everybody seemed to be having a splendid time, laughing and chatting. Claire was both relieved and pleased. Even if Tom had held the Artistic Evening merely to humor Dianthe, it was a wonderful way to introduce himself to his new neighbors. She watched him smile and converse with Mrs. Humphry Albright and her husband, Humphry Albright, two of Pyrite Springs's wealthiest citizens, and knew a moment of complete satisfaction. He seemed to have a natural talent for friendly intercourse.

Well, of course. Why wouldn't he? He'd met and chatted with all classes of people in his career. Claire well remembered Gordon's reading her the newspaper article describing a Russian archduke's hunting trip, guided by Tom, into the vast American plains. He'd even been in the party that had gone along with the president on his first visit West. He'd certainly had a lot of practice hobnobbing with people of high social standing. Why, Tom was a blue-blooded southern aristocrat himself, by birth.

Even if he hadn't enjoyed the artistic renditions as much as he might have, the evening seemed a complete success. Deciding she really mustn't stare at Tom all night, Claire began to mingle, happy in the knowledge that Tom had established himself as the new master of Partington Place and therefore a force to be reckoned with in the community of Pyrite Springs.

Tom was about ready to cut and run by the time he finally managed to slip away. He'd been trying to catch Claire's eye for an hour or more because he was much more comfortable in her company than he was in babbling nonsense to a bunch of strangers, but she was being elusive as hell. When he couldn't stand it a moment longer, he maneuvered himself over to the bank of windows, scooted behind a heavy curtain and sneaked out the door without anybody catching him. He felt as though he'd managed an escape from behind enemy lines.

"My God," he muttered, peeking at the curtain to make sure he hadn't been spotted and chased down. Nobody emerged, and he sighed with relief. Freedom at last. Sinking wearily against the balcony railing, he pulled out one of his cheroots, snapped his thumbnail against a sulfur match, lit up, and inhaled blissfully.

"My God," he murmured again as he turned and rested his arms on the rail.

The balcony overlooked the grounds of Partington Place and revealed a view that was magnificent in the daylight. Even tonight, with the weather as cold as a witch's tail and the stars and the moon washing the world in pallid silver, Tom felt a sense of soul-deep satisfaction as he surveyed his kingdom.

He supposed he should at least try to get used to these artistic shindigs. Claire set a great deal of store by them, and he'd recently discovered that her happiness was very important to him. How odd! He'd never particularly cared about another person's happiness before; it gave him a funny feeling to know he cared about Claire's.

She'd had her hair done too. Tom knew it was probably arrogant of him, but he couldn't help believing she'd done it in part for him. The idea pleased him. He wouldn't have cared if she'd maintained her severe demeanor, but she really did look prettier, more feminine without those damned rattlesnakes coiled over her ears.

She was really something, Claire was. This whole setup was something.

His cigar smoke hung in the frosty air like a puffy cloud, and Tom grinned. He began making smoke rings for the hell of it. God, he loved being rich. He'd never even imagined he'd be rich one day. This legacy from his uncle was a miracle, a damned miracle.

Tom wondered if Uncle Gordon had known what he was doing when he left him Claire. Naw. He couldn't have.

Because he'd lived too hard for too long, Tom turned to face the direction of possible danger. He didn't want anybody silently slipping through those windows and sneaking up on him. Propping his elbows on the railing, he leaned back and crossed his legs at the ankle. His new evening shoes gleamed in the moonlight, and he sighed happily when he looked at them. Damn, he hadn't worn anything but ragged old boots for years.

He wondered where his uncle had gotten the idea that he'd been used to fancy social doings. Probably from his mother.

A niggle of irritation thrust itself into Tom's mind at

the thought of his mother, and he decided not to think about her or his idle, worthless father this evening. After he got used to his new life, had started his Appaloosa breeding program, and knew exactly how his finances stood, he could tackle the formidable problem of his indolent, indigent parents.

He'd bet Claire could help him think of a suitable way to deal with them. She could do anything. The thought of the able, clever Claire made him feel dreamy.

Suddenly a movement caught the edge of his attention, and he jerked his head to the left. There, two windows down, a figure emerged from the crowded, stuffy ballroom. It didn't take Tom any time at all to realize it was Claire. He smiled and decided the fates were playing right into his hands tonight.

She didn't know he was there but stood still, her gloved hands loosely gripping the railing, and peered up into the chilly December sky. He stuffed his half-smoked cigar into a sandbox, thoughtfully provided by the ever-helpful Claire, and walked toward her quietly. He didn't want to give himself away too soon.

She didn't notice him approach, and he paused to observe her for a moment. Washed by moonlight and star-shine, her face looked sweet and faintly mysterious. Tom took a deep breath.

"Aren't you chilly, Miss Montague?"

She jumped, startled, and pressed a hand to her breast. Tom wished he could do that.

"Mr. Partington! I didn't realize you'd come out here too."

She was utterly charming, looking up at him with those big eyes of hers. Even her spectacles were adorable—because they sat on her nose.

"I confess I had to escape for a moment, Miss Montague. Too much hobnobbing taxes my social skills. I had to recruit my strength."

She laughed softly. "I don't believe it for a minute, Mr. Partington. Why, you won the hearts of everyone here tonight, I'm sure."

He cocked his head. "Did I win your heart?"

Colors were lost in the moonlight, but Tom knew she blushed as she turned to look into the sky again. "Don't be silly, Mr. Partington," she said lightly.

"Seriously, Miss Montague, aren't you cold? Would you like me to fetch you a wrap?"

"No, thank you. It was becoming intolerably warm in the ballroom, and the cool air feels refreshing."

"It does, doesn't it?" Tom decided to look at the sky with her since she apparently didn't need him to hug her and make her warm. Maybe later.

Orion prowled the sky, too conspicuous a fellow, decked out in all his brightly twinkling stars, to sneak up on the bear or the dog sharing the heavens with him. Tom said softly, "At night on the prairie sometimes it almost felt like I could reach out and grab a handful of stars. They seemed even thicker and closer when we were hundreds of miles away from civilization than they do here, although they're still beautiful."

"It must have been magnificent out there in the wilds of the limitless American plains."

"It was."

"Do you miss all that freedom, Mr. Partington?"

"A little."

"So many of us have never had even a taste of freedom." She sounded very wistful.

"Well," said Tom, hoping to make her feel better, "it was a pretty hard life most of the time."

"I suppose it must have been. But you've had so many

thrilling experiences, Mr. Partington." Claire put a hand on his sleeve. "And before you protest, I know you don't consider your exploits to have been grand. But to those of us who have never seen the Great Plains or been farther away from civilization than a walk in the woods, your experiences seem quite exciting."

Tom considered the little hand on his arm for a moment before he covered it with his. That she didn't pull away he took as a good sign. "I suppose you're right. It seemed to me that I was only doing my job, but maybe there was something special about it. After all, now that the railroad has cut the country in half, nothing will ever be the way it used to be. There's no going back to reclaim the wilderness. There's very little left on this gigantic continent that's unknown to us. The Indians are on the run; the buffalo are dying or dead; settlers are moving west by the thousands. In some ways I reckon I'm partly responsible for taming all that vastness." Tom shut his eyes for a minute. "I'm not sure I'm proud of it."

When he opened his eyes again, he found Claire watching him, her expression solemn.

"I believe I understand what you're saying. But you know there's no way to stop the onward thrust of progress. If you hadn't helped them clear the land for the railroad, somebody else would have."

"You're right, of course."

Tom forgot about Orion and the plains and the railroad as he gazed into Claire Montague's sympathetic face. She seemed to understand his feelings better than anybody ever had. It was funny, he thought, that he'd never missed this aspect of civilization, a partner in life. Perhaps that's because he'd never been exposed to anyone like Claire before.

"I think you performed a great service to your country, Mr. Partington."

Sweet Claire. Always his champion. He wondered if anybody had ever bothered to champion Claire. She deserved a hero—a hell of a better man than he. He wondered how she'd come to be such a sensible, vital woman, what circumstances had molded her into the appealing person she was today.

It surprised him when he heard himself say, "I think I need to kiss you for that, Miss Montague."

Her eyes opened wide. "You do?"

Her tiny, shocked whisper fluttered in the air and caressed his ear.

"I do."

"Oh, my."

He settled one hand lightly on her shoulder and another on her soft cheek, guiding her head toward his. His lips barely skimmed hers. She didn't know a thing about kissing but kept her lips shut tight. She was scared, Tom could tell. He whispered gently, "Open your mouth a little, Claire."

She did. When his lips touched hers again, he found them soft and meltingly sweet under his. He kissed her very delicately, very tenderly, in a way he'd never kissed a woman before. He kissed her as though he cared because he did. After a moment he felt her begin to sway against him, almost as if she were dissolving in his arms. Tom groaned as his body tightened with desire.

He slid his hands over her almost bare shoulders, feeling her cool, silky skin. "Put your arms around me, Claire," he commanded softly. After a second's hesitation she complied.

Nothing could have prepared him for his reaction to having Claire Montague in his arms. Her tentative response ignited him, and he discovered himself wanting to teach her the art of love, to coax her secret passion into fire.

She would catch fire; he knew it. Underneath her modest exterior beat the heart of a hopeless romantic. She tried to hide her ardor, and Tom wanted to uncover it. He wanted to make her burn for him as he burned for her.

Groaning again, he pulled her more deeply into his embrace. His lips left hers to travel over her chin and onto her bare throat. He heard her gasp and covered her mouth again. Her hands were still on his shoulders, but he felt her fingers dig into his evening jacket as though she couldn't help herself. He wished she'd forget her reserve and relax for him.

"You taste like sweet wine, Claire. You intoxicate me," he murmured as he nipped at her ear.

"Oh!" she exclaimed breathlessly.

Tom had to kiss her again for that, and he did. This time he was more daring and allowed his tongue to outline her lips briefly. She gasped.

Then, just as Tom had hoped she would, she seemed to kindle into a small flame. She was still uncertain, but her fingers stopped digging into his shoulders, and her arms slipped around to squeeze him tightly. Her mouth opened to his gentle probing, and she allowed his tongue to play with hers. After a moment hers responded.

Tom couldn't recall ever having his arms around a total innocent before, nor could he recall ever being so near to losing control. But he knew he had to be careful. Not for the world and everything in it would he frighten Claire.

No. He wanted to tantalize her feminine hunger out

into the open, to show her unmistakably that he considered her a lovely, desirable woman. He knew she thought little of her charms, but he knew her to possess charm in abundance. He wanted her to know it, to take delight in herself and in him and in the magic they could create together.

If anybody had told him on his first night at Partington Place that he would soon be making mad love to his housekeeper, Tom would have scoffed. He wasn't scoffing now. He couldn't recall ever feeling so aroused.

His arousal was not entirely carnal, either, but owed a good deal to honest affection and tenderness, two emotions that had been foreign to him until he met Claire. They made this experience deeper, more meaningful than any sensual encounter he'd had before. Until this evening he'd never kissed a woman he cared for, would never have guessed how exciting an experience it could be.

"Claire, Claire," he murmured as his lips blazed a trail across her shoulder, kissing and nipping. He tongued the pulse at the base of her throat. Her head fell back, and Tom saw the twin small perfect swells of her bosom and dared to kiss lower, until his lips pressed one of those delightful swells. He heard her gasp again and hoped she wasn't shocked.

He realized he'd overstepped propriety when, with a mighty effort, Claire pushed herself out of his embrace.

Her hand flew to her swollen lips, and she cried, "Oh! Oh, no!"

She looked aghast, and Tom's conscience smote him mightily even as he held out his arms and ached to have her in them again. "Claire, come back. Please."

She cried, "Oh, no!" again. Then she cried, "Oh, my God!"

Tom saw tears pooling in her eyes and began to worry. Certainly she couldn't be afraid of him. Could she? "Claire, please listen to me. I'm sorry, Claire."

"How in the name of mercy could I have done such a thing?"

Tom took a step toward her, and she backed up. Then he realized what she'd said. How could *she* have done such a thing?

"Claire, you haven't done anything. It was my fault."

She began shaking her head, and she looked almost wild. Tom was afraid she was becoming hysterical and could hardly believe it of his staid, dignified Claire. He said, "Claire," again, only to have her back up another step.

"Good heavens, what have I done?" she whispered, as if mortified beyond endurance.

"Claire, please listen to me." She backed up yet again, and Tom was afraid she'd bolt. He'd seen frightened horses look like that. "Don't run away, Claire. Please. Listen to me!"

His words were for naught. With one more horrified "Oh, my land!" she spun around and dashed through the open window into the ballroom as though pursued by demons.

"Damn!"

Tom raced to the flapping curtain, hoping to grab her, to make her listen to reason. He stopped abruptly as the bright lights of the ballroom struck his eyes like a blow. Clinging to the curtain and squinting hard, he perceived a sea of milling people and looked quickly to his right and then to his left. With a sigh he saw a swatch of golden yellow fabric disappear as the hall door closed and knew he was too late to catch her. He tried anyway, sidling along the curtained wall, only to find himself hailed from the ballroom floor.

He muttered another bitter "damn" and turned to see who had called him. He wasn't sure what he'd have said or done even if he'd managed to catch up with Claire, but he knew he had to talk to her. It would have to be later, though, because he'd never escape now. Mr. and Mrs. Humphry Albright bore down upon him. Gritting his teeth, he resigned himself to another hour or two of social insipidity.

Even as he mouthed the vapid nothings required of a gentleman of wealth and stature, his brain seethed with worry over Claire. He escaped outside again as soon as he could and stared up at the bedroom windows on the third floor, wondering which one was Claire's.

❧ 11 ❧

Claire clattered up the stairs, flew down the hall, and rushed into her room, pushing her door so hard the knob slammed against the wall. She yanked it shut, locked it as if all the devils of hell were pursuing her, and only then realized that the doorknob had knocked a hole in the plaster.

Covering her mouth with her hands, she gaped at the plaster on the floor, and her mind registered the appropriateness of this latest dismal reflection of her nature. She stood there for a full minute or more, quivering like an aspen leaf and staring at the damage, before she flung herself onto her bed and burst into tears.

Everything she'd ever feared about herself was true: She did have a genetic weakness in her constitution. There was a flaw in her makeup, a crack in her character, a blight on the family tree. Dress her up in frills, fix her hair into anything but prudish braids, and her virtue flew right out the window. Blood will tell; it had told tonight in no uncertain terms.

And Mr. Partington had fallen right into her wicked

snare. The poor soul, primed by Dianthe's beauty, had found Claire flaunting herself on the balcony and succumbed, just as her father used to tell her a man would do.

"But I'm not pretty, Father," she used to wail, hoping he'd not force her to dress in the awful, indecorous costumes she used to wear.

"Don't matter," he'd answer with a wink. "Gents don't think with their heads, Claire. Their brains are in their breeches."

His disgusting assessment of males had been correct. Claire used to think her father was wrong, that "gents" must be different from the types of men her father lured into his medicine show, but she guessed they weren't.

Tom Partington was as much a gentleman as Claire had ever known, and he'd been willing to sacrifice his honor with her this evening; she knew it. Given the lure of a strumpet, even a gentleman could be tempted. She hated knowing it.

After her flood of tears had subsided, Claire rose from her bed and looked at herself in her mirror. She despised what she saw: a woman with no moral backbone. A plain woman who'd had her hair cut and frizzed and forced into fashion. A dull woman in a gay dress, trying to be something she was not, a person of merit.

She had no merit. She was a vile schemer. A hussy, a strumpet, a carnival attraction who would think nothing of throwing herself at an honorable man in a mad moment of frailty.

Well, she acknowledged with scathing contempt, perhaps that was not entirely true. She was thinking of it now; no mistake.

What had she done? How could she ever face Tom Partington in the morning? How could she have deserted her post this evening, leaving him to fend for himself among that throng of people downstairs? But she couldn't possibly return to the ballroom. She simply couldn't. What on earth would they think of her?

Bitterly she decided they undoubtedly wouldn't think of her at all. Unless she was throwing herself into some man's arms, nobody ever seemed to notice her.

Would Tom fire her? Had she sunk so far beneath his reproach that he would turn her out of his home? The thought didn't bear thinking about, yet she couldn't stop thinking about it. How could she stand to leave Partington Place and Pyrite Springs?

This was the first place in the world she'd ever felt at home or had friends. She'd never stayed in one place long enough to form friendships when she was a little girl. It hadn't taken her long to realize no decent parent would allow his or her child to befriend her anyway.

Who could blame the parents? Who would want to play with her? Her! Claire Montague, daughter of a devious, double-dealing medicine show quack! Claire Montague, whom her father had dressed in seductive costumes to tempt the customers!

Turning away from the mirror in despair, Claire went to her window and flung it open. Sadly she dug her handkerchief out of her pocket, wiped her eyes, blew her nose, and stared into the same sky she'd observed moments before with Tom Partington. Only now the heavens no longer looked beautiful. They looked merely beyond Claire's reach. As was Tom Partington. And happiness.

Tom knew a gentleman wouldn't stand in the middle of his lawn and stare up at Claire's window. Nor would he debate the propriety of rushing up there and falling on his knees at her feet. Or trying to shake some sense into her. But then, he'd never pretended to be a gentleman.

Watching her stand there clutching her handkerchief and occasionally blotting her eyes almost broke his heart. What had he done? How could he have been so infernally clumsy?

It had been easy, he thought glumly as he flung down his cheroot and ground it into the cold earth beneath his feet. Years earlier he'd lost the knack of performing according to society's dictates. His mother would have been appalled at him for this evening's work, and for once he wouldn't have blamed her.

He watched Claire until she slowly shut the window, her every movement an affirmation of her despondency. Then he knew he had to return to his stupid party and his stupid guests in his stupid ballroom, so he did.

Not too long later, giving every appearance of affability, he shook hands and bade his guests a friendly farewell, promising more than once to hold another party soon. He didn't voice the worry in his heart: that he had driven Claire to leave him, thereby not merely precluding another Artistic Evening but withering his happiness forever.

Dianthe St. Sauvre, carefully overseen by Jedediah Silver, Tom noted wryly, shook his hand and asked, "Wherever did Claire go, Mr. Partington? I wanted to thank her again for suggesting you continue with these delightful entertainments."

Tom thought that was an interesting way of putting it, considering she had been the main entertainment of the evening—if you could call an insipid poem and a ludicrous dance to some decidedly odd music entertaining. Before he could think up an answer that didn't reveal the truth, Sylvester Addison-Addison spoke.

"You know Claire, Dianthe. She probably thought she had to rush to the kitchen and see to the washing up or something."

Sylvester's tone was supercilious, but Tom decided not to punch him because he'd replied to a question Tom didn't know how to answer. He said, glaring at Sylvester, "Yes, Miss Montague is exceptionally efficient and competent. She is truly a treasure."

Dianthe smiled winningly and purred, "Oh, yes. She *is* a treasure, Mr. Partington."

Tom thought he detected sincere appreciation in Dianthe's voice and demeanor and guessed she wasn't entirely witless. Anybody who admired Claire must have some redeeming virtues.

He deliberately squeezed Addison-Addison's hand too hard because Sylvester was a weakling and had been rude to Claire twice tonight. Although he knew his display of strength to be childish, he was mildly gratified when Sylvester winced. He was flapping his hand in the air when he exited the house with Priscilla Pringle hanging on his arm. Tom watched with satisfaction and hoped the widow would smother him.

After the last of his guests had left, he walked slowly upstairs, trying to think of something appropriate to say to Claire. Stopping at her door, he paused and drew in a deep breath before he knocked, very softly.

Claire, huddled in her bed with her quilt pulled up to her chin, had heard his soft footsteps. She knew who it was in the hall; nobody but Tom and she slept upstairs. When she heard his knock, her heart almost stopped and she held her breath even though she knew he couldn't hear her breathing from behind the locked door.

Everything was silent for what seemed forever, and

Claire had just begun to relax when she heard his soft "Claire?"

She stiffened up again and sat as still as she could, considering her heart was thundering so hard she was afraid she'd swoon. She comforted herself with the knowledge that even if she fainted into a dead heap, her soft bedclothes would muffle the plop.

Surely he would wait until tomorrow to fire her, wouldn't he? She hadn't known him very long, but she knew him full well enough to be sure he possessed a kind heart.

Claire had thought her tears were all spent, but as she sat in her bed, frightened and miserable, they came again. They coursed down her cheeks when she heard another whispered "Claire?" She wanted to fling herself out of bed, race to the door, and throw herself into his arms. She wanted to beg him to kiss her again, to teach her the joys of his touch, to have his way with her.

Truly, Claire Montague was a fallen woman.

Tom knew what he had to do when he awoke the next morning. In the night inspiration had actually stricken him almost dumb. In fact, when the first fingers of daylight dared creep into his room and flicker across his eyelids, he sat up, stunned.

He, Tom Partington, heir to Partington Place, frontier scout, boy general of the Lost Cause, had fallen head over heels in lust with his housekeeper. Not only that, but he honestly liked her a whole lot too. Why, Claire Montague was the most splendid female he'd ever encountered.

He wanted to keep her around. For a long time. Maybe even—well—forever.

At the very least he was going to do his best to make her agree to be his mistress.

Good heavens. Tom had never had a real, honest-to-God mistress before. The thought frightened him.

Rubbing his eyes and leaning back against his headboard, he decided he was being absurd and determined to think about it before he did anything irrevocable. This apparent overnight insight was only the result of the erotic dream that he'd just had and that had been interrupted at an extremely inopportune moment. If he'd stayed asleep another minute or two longer, he might have been able to experience what he'd primed himself for last night in Claire's arms.

Tom gave himself a mental punch in the jaw and told himself to behave. He had some serious thinking to do.

After devoting a good forty-five minutes to the task, he sighed and mumbled, "I don't want her to leave me." The thought of her leaving Partington Place and him filled his very soul with dread.

The revelation was not particularly welcome. He'd never considered needing another human being the way he needed Claire. It seemed like such an unmanly thing to do.

On the other hand, he'd come to value Claire's practicality, companionship, and sweetness. The notion of wanting to keep her by his side wasn't entirely idiotic.

The thought of marriage paid his brain a brief visit but was so appalling to Tom, whose memories of his parents' marriage had left an indelible blot on his soul, that he buried it immediately. Hell, Claire already lived with him; he couldn't see any reason to commit so rash a folly as marriage.

No, there was no need for him to marry her. If he played his cards right, he was sure he could get her to fall in love with him. Then she'd want to stay, and he wouldn't have to do anything stupid.

Frowning, he swung his feet over the side of his bed and realized with annoyance that his nightshirt had gotten tangled up around his waist again. Damned irritating inconveniences, nightshirts. He wondered if Claire would mind if he slept naked after they became lovers.

Then he realized how silly he was being. He'd jumped from hoping she'd fall in love with him to worrying about sleepwear after they were lovers. First, of course, he'd have to convince her that it would be in her interest to have him, and Tom didn't have a clue as to how to go about that. Especially not after he'd lost his head last night and scared her to death.

"I guess I'd better apologize first."

He didn't know what he'd do if she felt she had to leave his service, but he knew for sure he wasn't about to let her get away.

Damn, but civilization was difficult to deal with. There were so many cursed rules. Out on the prairie if a man needed something, he just tracked it down and shot it. He didn't have the leisure or the need to bother with finesse. Here in the damned civilized world he had to woo it first, to tame it. Taming virgins was a new experience for Tom; he wasn't altogether sure he was up to it.

Nevertheless, he knew he'd bungled badly the night before. Poor Claire was a delicately nurtured female, and he'd all but mauled her, right on his own ballroom balcony.

As he buttoned his vest and straightened his tie, Tom muttered, "So be it." If he had to court Claire Montague, then by God, he'd do it.

All the way down to the breakfast room he cudgeled his brain, trying to remember the arts his mother had drilled into him when he was a boy. He wished he'd paid more attention.

He paused at the door, trying to think of a suitable apology to offer her this morning. Deciding his best course would be honesty, he pushed the door open, intending to beg Claire's forgiveness and try to persuade her to let him make it up to her properly.

His intention was thwarted immediately. She wasn't there.

"Where the hell's Claire—er, Miss Montague?" She couldn't have left him already, could she?

Jedediah looked up from the eggs he'd been shoving around on his plate. He was the only other person in the room.

"Oh, hello, Tom." Jedediah sighed dreamily. "Beautiful morning, isn't it?"

Frowning, Tom muttered, "I guess so. Where's Miss Montague?"

"Your first Artistic Evening went splendidly, Tom. Wasn't Miss St. Sauvre brilliant?"

"I guess so. Where's Miss Montague?"

"Her 'Ode to the Spotted Horse' was truly an homage to Appaloosas, wasn't it?"

"Is that what it was? Where's Miss Montague?"

"I don't think I've ever met a lovelier woman in my life. She's the epitome of everything I've ever even imagined in a female. Don't you think she's wonderful?"

Perceiving at last that his companion was paying him no mind, Tom peered at Jedediah closely. The man looked moonstruck. He'd been in the presence of lovesickness before and knew one had to proceed carefully around its victims. He sat down next to Jedediah and put a hand on his shoulder. You had to capture their attention first or they were of no use at all.

"Jed," he said, shaking his shoulder, "Jed, look at me for a minute."

When he was certain Jedediah was looking at him, he said, enunciating carefully, "Do you know where Miss Montague is?"

"Miss Montague? She was here a minute ago. Didn't eat a thing. Then she went away again."

"She didn't eat?"

"No. I don't think so."

Jedediah sighed soulfully, and Tom knew he would soon be lost to him again. He said quickly, "Did she go to her office?"

"Hmm? Who? Oh, Miss Montague? I don't know."

Good grief. Deciding he'd have to hunt Claire down on his own, which shouldn't be too difficult for a professional scout, Tom rose and prepared a plate of fluffy biscuits, bacon, butter, and jam. When he found her, he was going to be damned sure she ate something. He wasn't about to let her waste away on him.

Claire had tried her level best to braid her hair into her usual two braids. She wanted to get her old, prudish self back if at all possible so that the wanton creature who had invaded her body would go away and never rear its evil head again.

She'd had no luck. The curls Miss Thelma had ironed onto her bangs were, well, curly. And the back tresses had been cut and were now too short to braid properly. The only way she could possibly fix her wretched hair without help was to knot it in the back and leave the front curly. She'd never rued her hair's tendency to wave naturally as much as she did this morning. Even when she tried wetting those devilish curls, they persisted in bouncing back and taunting her with their verve. Their wretched gaiety.

Claire didn't feel gay. She felt awful. At least she could dress properly, so she did. Selecting the dullest, brownest, plainest frock from a closet full of dull, brown, plain frocks, she buttoned it up to her neck and tiptoed down to breakfast.

She must have stood at the breakfast room door for a good five minutes trying to bolster her courage before she dared enter the room. She almost fainted with gratitude when she encountered only Jedediah Silver. When she'd finally managed to get his attention, he'd told her Tom hadn't been down yet.

Thank heaven.

Now she sat at her desk, wringing her hands and wishing she hadn't been too craven to meet Tom in the breakfast room. He might go more gently on her with Jedediah in the room. But no. She'd run away like a coward, and now she was alone. When he came, there would be only the two of them. There would be no third party to mitigate what must surely be his total denunciation of her morals and manners.

So involved was she with self-censure that when his soft knock did come at her door, she jumped and uttered a soft cry. Then, too frightened to speak, she pressed her hand to her bosom and stared at the door as if it were about to devour her.

When it slowly opened, she began to tremble.

"Miss Montague?" came Tom's voice from behind the partially opened door. He sounded friendly, and Claire could scarcely believe her ears.

"Y-yes?" she managed to say weakly.

"May I come in for a minute?"

Might he come in? Why was he asking her that? This

was his home. She cleared her throat and said, "Of course, Mr. Partington."

The door opened, and Claire beheld Tom Partington, a penitent smile on his glorious face, a plate of biscuits and jam in his hand, his incredible eyes twinkling like sapphires. She nearly fainted.

"Will you ever forgive me, Miss Montague?"

"F-f-forgive you?"

"For frightening you so badly last night. My behavior was unforgivable."

His behavior was unforgivable? Claire opened her mouth, then shut it again when she realized she didn't know what to say.

"I know how I must have frightened you, Claire. Miss Montague. May I call you Claire?"

"I—you—well, of course."

"Will you call me Tom?"

Thunderstruck, she gawked at him for several seconds before she murmured, "Good heavens, no. I simply couldn't."

He looked disheartened and shook his head. "I'm sorry. I had hoped we could mend our fences this morning. May I at least join you for a little morning chat?"

Gaping at him like the fool she knew herself to be, Claire murmured, "Of course."

"Thank you." Tom looked down at his plate. "I brought you some breakfast. May I please ring for coffee? You should eat something."

Suddenly Claire knew what she must do. She stood in a flurry of brown calico and resolution, determined to get this over with.

"Mr. Partington, my behavior last night was insupportable. I behaved in a manner not merely unseemly but—but depraved. Why, you must conclude me to be beyond forgiveness. Indeed, I can scarcely believe it of myself. I'm sure you have no reason to believe this, but truly I'm not given to—to behavior of that sort."

To her absolute horror, tears began to sting her eyes. She swallowed the ache in her throat, determined not to cry and humiliate herself further.

"You what?"

Tom looked astounded, and Claire almost stamped her foot in frustration. Surely he wasn't going to pretend that nothing had happened between them, was he?

She sucked in a deep breath. "Do you want me to leave your service, Mr. Partington? I would not blame you if you desired me to do so, although I—I had hoped we could come to an understanding." She would not cry. She told herself so as she dug in her pocket for her handkerchief.

"Me? Want you to leave?" Tom stood as still as a plaster statue of a waiter, the plate held stiffly before him. "Do you want to leave?"

She couldn't hold his gaze a second longer. Hers dropped as she whispered, "No."

Expelling a gigantic breath, Tom said, "Well, then, let's not even talk about it. Of course you don't want to leave. Last night—well, it was a momentary breach of propriety, Claire, and it won't happen again."

She was afraid to look at him for fear she'd find he didn't mean it. "Thank you." She almost jumped a foot when he plunked the plate down on her desk.

"Thank *you*, Claire. I was afraid I had ruined myself in your eyes forever."

She did look at him then, a swift glance to ascertain if he was joking. It didn't seem like a joking matter to her, but she guessed an honorable gentleman like Tom might have a large tolerance for disgusting behavior. He looked only relieved, and Claire began to believe that he truly had forgiven her and that she really would be allowed to remain at Partington Place.

"Now," he said bracingly, "will you please ring for coffee so we can eat some of these good biscuits? I'm hungry, and Jed said you haven't eaten anything yet either."

Although her stomach rebelled at the very thought of food, Claire whispered, "Of course, Mr. Partington." She pulled the bell cord and sat down at her desk once more, feeling a little more secure with several feet of furniture between herself and Tom.

Tom popped a piece of bacon in his mouth and began to butter a biscuit. "Hope you don't mind, Claire. I'm used to getting up and eating a lot earlier than this. I'm not used to these city hours."

Surprised yet again by this declaration that he wasn't the sophisticate she'd always believed him to be, Claire blinked at him. "Of course. Please eat."

Scruggs knocked, opened the door, and walked slowly into the room. He looked as if his best friend had died overnight, but he always looked like that. Claire was used to it.

"May we please have some coffee in my office, Scruggs?" she asked politely.

With a look at the food on her desk and then a look at Tom, Scruggs said at last, "Very good, ma'am."

Right before the door shut behind him, she heard him mutter, "A perfectly good breakfast room, and where do they decide to spread the crumbs?"

She felt guilty. If she hadn't been such a coward, they would be eating in the room designed for such practices instead of in her office.

After swallowing his bite of biscuit, Tom said, "Uncomfortable sort of fellow to have around, old Scruggs, isn't he?"

Gripping a pen in her hands to keep them from shaking, Claire said, "He's simply accustomed to orderliness and routine, Mr. Partington. I'm sure he doesn't mean to be uncivil."

With a beautiful grin Tom said, "I don't mind, Claire. I think it's sort of fun to have a death's-head butler on my staff. Makes the place more interesting."

A smile trembled at the edges of Claire's mouth, and Tom said gently, "That's right, Claire. Please smile for me. I won't feel so much like a brute if you smile for me."

Of course his kind words made her want to cry again. Fortunately a knock came at the door, and she managed to salvage her composure by jumping up to answer it. She took the coffee tray from Scruggs's hands.

"Thank you, Scruggs."

"Think nothing of it, Miss Montague. I'm sure I'm used to having my morning chores interrupted by trivial requests."

Scruggs shuffled off, and Claire brought the coffee tray over and set it carefully on her desk.

"All right. Your turn, Claire. You must eat something. I won't let you not eat."

Looking at the biscuits this time with the knowledge that Tom didn't plan to dismiss her from his service, Claire actually began to feel a faint quiver of hunger. She sat down and took a biscuit.

"Mrs. Philpott's a very good cook, Claire. I'm glad she's over her fuss."

As she buttered a biscuit, Claire murmured, "Mrs. Philpott is an artist in her own way, I believe. I expect all artists are temperamental from time to time."

"A brilliant comparison. I do believe you're right." He kept smiling at her, and Claire felt nervous. "You don't seem to be temperamental, Claire. Your disposition seems to be remarkably even."

If you only knew! Claire cleared her throat. "I'm not an artist, Mr. Partington." She didn't suppose her *Tuscaloosa Tom* novels counted as an artistic endeavor.

"I don't know. It seems to me that there's an art to keeping an estate of this size running as smoothly as you do it. You make your job appear effortless, and I know it's not. You have to juggle a million different things, yet you do it so smoothly your management appears invisible."

"Thank you."

Claire tucked in her chin and took a bite of biscuit, aware of her cheeks turning hot. She'd never been complimented so prettily on her efforts at housekeeping before; indeed, she didn't think anybody even noticed how much effort went into making the running of the place appear effortless.

They ate in silence for a few minutes, Claire feeling nervous, Tom apparently relaxed.

"Tell me, Claire," he said after a while, "have you ever ridden?"

She looked at him in surprise. "You mean, horses?" she asked, then berated herself. Of course he meant horses!

"Yes. I wondered if you used to ride as a child or anything."

"No. No, I never had the opportunity to learn to ride, Mr. Partington."

The two or three times her father had managed by foul means to get his hands on a piece of horseflesh, he'd immediately sold or gambled it away. Claire felt her mouth tighten and made an effort to relax. She'd have loved to ride as a child; it had almost broken her heart when she'd seen those pretty horses go away again.

"Well, if you would allow it, I'd like to teach you."

"I beg your pardon?"

"Would you allow me to teach you to ride? I'd enjoy—I mean I'd appreciate it. I—I think you could help me a great deal in my horse ranching endeavors if you wouldn't mind. If you have time. That is—"

"Mr. Partington, nothing would give me greater pleasure than to be of service to you in any way possible."

"Yes. Your value as an employee is measureless." He smiled almost ruefully. "Are you sure you'll have time? I know you're busy. I'd be happy to hire another person to help you with your housekeeping chores if you need one."

"No, please. I'm sure that won't be necessary. Why, I've always wanted to ride. It will be a joy to assist you." It would too.

Claire knew that after Tom married Dianthe, the beautiful poetess would never enter into his interests as she herself did. If she could make herself even more useful to him, perhaps she'd never have to leave Partington Place. Granted, it would be difficult to see her best friend married to the man she loved, but Claire could do it. She'd spent her entire life watching others have the things she wanted; she was an expert by this time.

"Wonderful!"

Tom sounded happy with her acquiescence, and Claire was pleased.

"I shall visit Miss Thelma today and order a riding skirt, Mr. Partington. I don't believe any of my present clothing would be suitable for riding."

"Let me pay for it, please, Claire. After all, you'll be doing me a favor."

Shocked, Claire exclaimed, "Oh, no! I couldn't possibly allow you to buy clothes for me, sir. Why, it would be most improper!" She blushed, recalling the very improper kiss she'd participated in a mere few hours earlier.

"Well . . ." Tom didn't look particularly resigned, but he finally muttered, "All right. But you must promise that you'll allow me to buy your boots. After all, you can't ride without boots, and they're expensive items."

She smiled grimly, aware that she had already earned more money than she could spend in three lifetimes, thanks to her books. "Please, Mr. Partington. Indeed, I have a good deal saved up. I should not dream of allowing you to buy boots for me. You will be giving me one of my life's fondest dreams when you teach me to ride."

"Will I really?"

Tom looked genuinely pleased; it only confirmed Claire in her opinion that he was a truly wonderful man.

"Indeed you will, Mr. Partington. I used to long to ride when I was a girl."

She refrained from telling him about the brief period during which she and her father had tagged along with the circus. Ten-year-old Claire had haunted the ring where the bareback-riding lady used to practice. The lovely woman had never even bothered speaking to the carnival hack's scrawny daughter, but Claire had been in awe of her. With a sigh she told herself to stop remembering her dismal childhood and to concentrate instead on her much more agreeable present.

"Well, then, good. It's settled. I look forward to your first lesson, Claire."

"Thank you, Mr. Partington. As soon as I have the house organized, I'll set off for town."

Tom rubbed his hands in pleasure. "Jed and I will be seeing to the stables, Claire. The first horses will be delivered the week after Christmas. That's only four weeks away. By that time maybe you'll be able to help me break them."

She looked at him blankly, and he elaborated. "Tame them. Calm them down enough to take a saddle."

"Oh. Of course." She felt foolish.

"Don't worry, Claire," he said, putting a hand on her arm. "You'll soon learn the language of horses."

Her skin caught fire under his touch. Good grief, she simply must suppress this infatuation of hers.

❧ 12 ❧

Tom wanted to take Claire to town himself, to storm into Miss Thelma's and order all the prettiest gowns and bonnets in the place. He wanted to deck her out, to show Pyrite Springs exactly what he saw in Claire Montague: a lovely woman of rare merit in a world filled with fools. But the minute he'd set foot inside her office, he'd sensed he had better move very slowly, very carefully.

Poor Claire had been almost frozen with terror. Her red-rimmed eyes told him more clearly than words what she had suffered overnight. Not only that, but she'd obviously tried to subdue her new curls this morning. And she was back to wearing those ugly brown gowns too. It was as if she had struggled with all her might to suppress her natural feminine instincts.

He didn't understand her motive for hiding her true beauty any more than he understood her reaction to the wonderful kiss they'd shared. Any of the painfully proper females his mother used to fling at him would have already begun planning the wedding if he'd kissed one of them the way he'd kissed Claire. Claire obviously had been reared according to principles far different from those of his parents, yet another reason to value her.

When she'd apologized for the kiss as if it had been all her fault, his puzzlement grew. Something besides mere innocence was at work here. He didn't know what it was. When she asked if he wanted her to leave his service, he'd begun to perceive that the job of persuading her to become his lover would be formidable.

He'd certainly like to get to the bottom of her fear, whatever it was. Had she been the victim of an unlucky love affair? Had she been exposed to brutality in her early years? Had some scoundrel trifled with her or disparaged her sleek, trim elegance? The very thought made Tom's blood boil. Whatever it was that had frightened her so, Tom vowed he'd unearth it and lay it to rest, no matter how difficult the job proved to be.

Ah, well. Tom Partington had never shrunk from a challenge in his life, and he sure as the devil didn't plan to shrink from this one. In fact, as he stepped outside and drew in a bracing breath of crisp winter air, he smiled and knew he was looking forward to the wooing and winning of Claire Montague.

Jedediah Silver joined him a moment later. Clapping Jedediah on the back hard enough to jolt the spellbound look from the accountant's face, Tom said, "Come with me, Jed. We're going to the saddler's this morning to buy Miss Montague a sidesaddle."

Trying to catch his breath, Jed gasped, "We are?"

"Yep. She's going to be helping me with the horses."

"Didn't know she knew anything about horses."

"She doesn't. I'm going to teach her."

"Oh." The look in Jedediah's eyes was eloquent.

Tom ignored it. Pulling Jedediah along, he set off at a

spanking pace toward the stables. "Tell me, Jed, what do you know about Miss Montague's background? What did she do before she came here to work for my uncle?"

Still trying to regain his lost breath, Jedediah almost had to run to keep up with Tom. He panted, "Miss Montague? I don't know. She was working for your uncle when I became his man of business five years ago."

With a conspiratorial look at his companion, Tom said, "Well, Jed, I have a new job for you. After we discover where Uncle Gordon hid his *Tuscaloosa Tom* profits, I want you to tackle Miss Montague's background. Only you must be absolutely discreet."

Wheezing by this time, Jed managed to gasp, "Discretion is my middle name."

They had arrived at the stables by this time. While Tom laughed, Jedediah sank onto a hay bale and eyed him in some surprise.

The accountant's scrutiny didn't bother Tom. He was glad Claire had work to do in the house before she went to town because it would give him time to visit Miss Thelma's before she did. He planned to make good and sure Claire's riding habit, at least, was crafted in a color other than brown.

Claire stared in dismay at the forest green serge draped over Miss Thelma's arm.

"This is quite the latest thing, Miss Montague," Miss Thelma said with a twinkle, "and it will look ravishing with your hair and complexion."

Since the very last thing in the world Claire wanted was to look ravishing, Miss Thelma's words filled her with consternation. "I was hoping you'd have something suitable in brown or black, Miss Grimsby."

"Nonsense. Why, I have it from the highest fashion

authorities that serge is the ultimate fabric for riding, and it comes only in this beautiful green or in the cherry red over there. I think the green would suit you better."

"Oh, dear." Claire looked dismally from the beautiful green to the beautiful cherry red and felt trapped. "Can it be made in a demure fashion?"

"Well, I should like to know how a riding habit can be anything but demure, Miss Montague," Miss Thelma said somewhat tartly.

Brightening minimally, Claire murmured, "I suppose you're right."

"We also have some lovely new batiste and lawn for blouses, and I have a perfectly stunning scarlet sateen that would make a gorgeous gown for Christmas. In fact, I have one made up in blue if you'd like to try it on." Miss Thelma waved vaguely toward the back of her shop. "And we have some delightful plaid and striped calicoes for skirts. You *did* say you wanted to brighten your wardrobe, if I remember correctly."

Claire looked with real longing at the magnificent peacock blue sateen gown draped over a dress form. "I believe I did, yes, but I'm not certain brightening my wardrobe is a good idea any longer." Her voice sounded stifled. She felt stifled.

"Nonsense!" Miss Thelma declared roundly, surprising Claire, who had assumed the customer to be always right. "Why, I have it from an unimpeachable source that the young Mr. Partington desires his staff to look fashionable."

Narrowing her eyes suspiciously, Claire asked sharply, "Who told you that?"

Miss Thelma gave her a triumphant smile. "None other than Mr. Partington himself, Miss Montague." Seeing Claire's eyes widen in shock, she continued. "Yes indeed. He came in here himself and ordered new paisley shawls as Christmas presents for the female staff at Partington Place—except you, my dear, for whom he has something entirely different in mind. He said that he has an image to maintain and wanted his staff to look fashionable."

"He said that?" Claire was so startled that she didn't even pause to consider how different Miss Thelma's Tom Partington sounded from the one she'd come to know, the one who claimed not to know beans about fashion and to care even less.

Almost smugly Miss Thelma nodded and said, "He most certainly did, Miss Montague. And if I may be so bold as to give my opinion, I must say I agree with him. Why, Partington Place is the grandest estate in the county. It's only fitting that you, as its most visible representative, dress accordingly."

After a moment's thought Claire muttered, "I suppose so."

Botheration! A sense of ill usage bubbled up in her, and she resented Tom Partington's officiousness for a good solid minute or two. Still, if he wanted a fashionable staff, Claire guessed it was her duty at least to try to be fashionable. But how could she possibly repress her base urges if she dressed fashionably? Those awful urges seemed to take over her personality unless she was dressed in the severest of modes. This was all so very troubling!

Straightening, Claire told herself to stop being idiotic. Wearing a colored skirt could not possibly betoken a wanton nature. There was certainly no evil goblin lurking just out of sight waiting for her to don a hint of red so it could take over her soul and make her do lascivious things. Why, the very thought was laughable.

She knew herself to possess a strong inclination to do right even if she hadn't been bred for it. One tiny lapse did not a hussy make. After all, she *had* escaped from her past and for ten long years had done nothing even remotely indecorous. Certainly she could maintain her strength of character if she were to wear the occasional color.

That pretty plaid, for example, was quite nice. And the blue gown Miss Thelma had pointed out was exquisite. Scarlet of course was out of the question. But the blue . . .

"Perhaps you're right, Miss Grimsby." Claire hesitated another several seconds before she threw caution to the wind and asked, "May I try on the blue gown? Do you expect it might fit me?"

Miss Thelma, who knew quite well it would fit Claire since after her long conversation with Mr. Tom Partington this morning she'd had her assistant add a lengthening flounce to its hem and take in the waist, said, "I do believe it might, Miss Montague. Let's just see here."

Claire could hardly believe what she'd done an hour or so later when she left Miss Thelma Grimsby's Frocks and Bonnets. Not only had she purchased that gorgeous blue gown to wear at the open house on Christmas Eve, but she'd ordered a riding habit in forest green serge; three blouses, two of batiste and one of lawn; and three skirts, one in a dark green plaid with a dashing stripe of red, one in blue-and-white-striped calico, and one in a crisp, frivolous rust-colored sprigged muslin.

Claire pulled her plain, dull shawl more tightly against the December chill and walked blindly away from Miss Thelma's. She was in such a flutter of excitement and trepidation as she dashed across the street toward the Mercantile that when she heard a nearly forgotten voice call to her, she thought for certain it was her conscience taunting her. She was so shocked she tripped and had to grab on to the hitching rail to keep from falling down.

The voice called to her again, and Claire's heart executed a series of crazy stumbles and then crashed like a boulder caught in an avalanche. Turning, she whispered, "Oh, no!" and fought the urge to weep in despair.

"Claire!" came yet a third jovial cry, and Claire saw him: Claude Montague, master rogue, unscrupulous medicine show huckster, gambler, libertine, thief, cheat—in short, her father.

She whispered, "Oh, no!" again, and frantically looked around for somewhere to hide. In only a second she recognized the idea to be futile. She could never escape now that he'd found her. She could, however, prevent herself from being seen talking to him on the public main street of Pyrite Springs, where she was known as a good woman, a straitlaced woman, a woman of strong moral fiber and impeccable decorum.

She rushed over to him and grabbed him by the coat sleeve. "Come into the alley," she ordered, and almost upended him as she dragged him between the Pyrite Springs Mercantile and Furniture Emporium and LaVira Pitts's Ever-Fresh Bakery.

There, immersed in the delicious smell of freshly baked bread, Claire demanded, "How did you find me? What are you doing here? What do you want?"

Claude frowned. "Now, is that any way to greet your long-lost father, my child?"

Since she'd known him since her infancy, Claire snapped, "Yes. Is Clive with you?"

"Clive experienced a bit of a misfortune in Seattle, Claire. I'm afraid he couldn't make the journey."

"In jail, is he? Well, that's good," said Claire of her

only sibling. "At least I have to deal with only one of you. Now what do you want? I know you wouldn't have come here unless you wanted something."

Twirling his mustache, Claude peered at Claire critically. "You look a sight, child. Why on earth are you dressed like that? Why, you're a regular dull dog. You never had any looks to begin with, you know, my girl. It's a damned shame to accentuate all your negative qualities the way you're doing. You need some color, Claire. You need a little frill here and there."

Claire was fairly seething with rage and frustration by this time. She stamped her foot, a silly thing to do in the dirt-packed alley, as she realized almost at once when a dusty cloud rose at her feet.

"Yes, Father. I recall very well your assessment of my looks. And what you used to make me do so people wouldn't notice them. How I choose to dress is absolutely no business of yours. What do you want? Don't even begin to think I'll go back to your awful medicine show."

"Pshaw, child, the things you say." Claude looked around with distaste. "Why are we standing here in this alley, Claire? Come with me, and we can have a nice cozy chat at the Fool's Gold Saloon, where I'm staying."

"I'm not going anywhere with you and wouldn't enter that vile establishment if my life depended on it," Claire said through gritted teeth. "I refuse to be seen with you. Now stop stalling, and tell me what you want."

Her expression was every bit as ferocious as her father's was sly. As she glared at him, she experienced genuine loathing. A handsome man, Claude Montague had traded on his looks for years. Women used to feel sorry for the plausible, good-looking reprobate who paraded his poor orphaned children around, feigning a solicitude for them he did not feel. Claire remembered bitterly the way he'd used her to lure unsuspecting women into his snare.

He'd never cared a lick about her except insofar as she could be useful to him. He'd left her to her older brother's care, and Clive had resented the duty. She had come to hate them both years before, and the ten years she'd been away from them hadn't softened her attitude at all. If anything, those years had given her perspective, and she detested them now more than ever.

"So you think you're too good for your old father now, do you?"

"I most certainly do."

Claude apparently hadn't expected exactly this reaction from his only female offspring. His eyebrows dipped. "I always did the best I could for you, Claire."

"Don't make me laugh!" she cried, as far from laughter as she'd ever been.

Splaying a beefy hand over his breast, Claude muttered self-righteously, "How sharper than a serpent's tooth it is to have one's child turn on one."

"As usual, you've got the quote wrong. Now stop blathering this instant and tell me why you've come here to blight my life."

"Well, I like that!" Claude declared, offended. "She hasn't seen her dear old father for ten years, and just listen to her."

"You listen to me, Father. The only reason you even kept me was that you could use me in your show and lure poor softhearted women into your clutches. I know you, and I know you have about as much family feeling as a barracuda. If you don't tell me what you want right this minute, I'm going to tell the sheriff, Mr. Grant, that you're wanted for fraud in the Colorado Territory."

Giving up his pose as a loving parent, Claude glared at his daughter for several seconds before he muttered, "Oh, all right."

Then he adopted the expression of cunning Claire remembered so vividly from her childhood. Her fallen heart began to shrivel even before he spoke.

"I met a friend of yours, my dear, on the train outside Omaha. A Mr. Oliphant. Remember him?"

Claire's insides began to twist painfully. She gave him one brief nod.

"We got to chatting over a bottle of brandy one night. He told me a most amusing tale."

Dear heaven. If poor Mr. Oliphant had allowed himself to drink with her father, Claire already knew why Claude had come to Pyrite Springs. She breathed deeply several times. The two words, "tangled web," danced through her head again, mocking her.

In the space of seconds she weighed her options and came to the only possible conclusion. Because she had no gun handy, she would have to pay her father blackmail to keep him from telling Tom Partington she was the author of those wretched books.

"How much money do you want to keep quiet?"

The wily Claude smiled. "Well, now, my dear, I understand you've managed to create a virtually limitless supply of funds with those dime novels of yours. You always were a clever little minx. I knew you'd do me proud one day."

"Stop slinging rubbish, and get on with it!"

Claude wisely ignored his daughter's outburst. "Since it was I who saw to your upbringing and education for all those years, it seems only fair that you provide for your poor old father in his old age. Don't you think so?"

Furious, Claire exclaimed, "No, I certainly do not! Why, you unscrupulous old fraud, you never cared a thing about me! You never saw to anything but your own welfare. If it wasn't for those poor deluded women who used to think they were in love with you, I'd never even have learned to read and write!"

Disconcerted at having his past flung so candidly into his face, Claude muttered, "Now, Claire, that's not true."

"It is so. Oh, you make me sick!"

Claude frowned mightily. Since, however, he was a shrewd man and knew better than to argue with his clever, sharp-tongued daughter, he said, "Two thousand dollars, and I'll never darken your door again."

"Two thousand dollars? Why, you miserable old charlatan! I ought to go to Sheriff Grant right this minute!"

"Ah, but you won't—will you, Claire?—because your high-and-mighty Mr. Tom Partington wouldn't like it." Claude looked quite smug as he twirled his mustache and smirked. "Anyway, from what Oliphant said, two grand is peanuts to you. I should think you'd consider it a small price to pay to get rid of me."

Staring at the man who had fathered her, Claire couldn't help feeling sorry for her own mother. Undoubtedly she'd been one of Claude's long list of victims. She'd probably died just to get away from the awful man. Now Claire was to be added to the list.

Well, so be it. Claude was right. Two thousand dollars was a small price to pay to get rid of him.

Poking him hard with her forefinger, Claire said coldly, "Stay right here, and don't move. If you go out into the street, I'll pretend I don't know you."

Without waiting for him to reply, she stormed off, leaving him in the alley. She deliberately scuffed her shoes in the dirt so that dust would puff up into Claude's face. Even his sneeze did not mitigate her fury.

When she made her withdrawal at the Pyrite Springs Bank, her expression must have been black because Mr. Twitchell, the teller, didn't even try to make small talk. After stuffing the money into a large envelope, Claire stalked back to the alley where Claude was lounging, smoking a fat cigar. He greeted her with a bland smile as though they were mere acquaintances and not mortal adversaries.

Slapping him in his paunch with the envelope, Claire snarled, "There. Now get out of my life and stay out."

"Tut-tut, child. I really think you should treat your old father with more respect than this."

"Just be grateful I don't walk around town armed."

Claire had the satisfaction of seeing Claude's eyebrows arch in genuine surprise right before he snatched the envelope from her fingers and marched away, striving for a dignity she knew he didn't possess. She watched him until he turned down the street and out of her sight, a hand pressed to her forehead, her heart a raging cauldron of despair. The stagecoach rattled past, and Claire had a mad impulse to scramble onto it and go wherever it would take her.

If only she could be certain her father would keep his word and leave her alone.

Silly Claire. Of course he wouldn't keep his word. She knew that. Blackmailers were never satisfied; it was a well-known fact. She'd read terrible tales about blackmailers and the resultant despair they wreaked upon unlucky souls who harbored black secrets.

For heaven's sake, blackmail was one of the novelist's

best friends; she'd even used it herself once or twice in her books. Blackmailers always came back for more. Especially this blackmailer. Her father was the worst man she'd ever met in her life; she didn't trust him an inch.

"Dear heaven," she moaned softly. "Please, Lord . . ."

But she didn't know what to ask. Even if she'd thought of something, she didn't expect God would look with much favor upon a woman who was perpetrating a beastly deception on the man she loved. Claire sank back against the wall of the Pyrite Springs Mercantile and Furniture Emporium and fought the urge to shriek her frustration to the heavens.

Tom had sent Jedediah Silver back to Partington Place earlier in the day, since he had some inquiries to make of the farrier, Colin MacDougall. Now, his business successfully concluded, he rode the placid Ebony down Pyrite Springs's main street, feeling grand. He'd opened an account at the bank expressly for his horse enterprise, wired his breeder in Montana, made arrangements with a builder to assess his mansion for the laying of gas lines, and chatted with several people who just seemed to want to offer friendly greetings.

Since he'd become an adult, Tom hadn't lived in any one spot long enough to make friends. He did of course boast a flock of comrades who were fellow scouts, but they hardly qualified as the types of settled associations he seemed to be acquiring in Pyrite Springs. The idea of living here, of having an abundance of casual friends and acquaintances gave him a gooey, warm feeling in his chest.

His conversation with Miss Thelma this morning had gone even better than he'd expected too. She was on his side when it came to convincing Claire Montague that she was an attractive, desirable woman.

He pulled his horse up short when he saw a portly gentleman stride out of an alleyway, twirling his waxed mustache and grinning like a cat who'd just caught a big fat mouse.

Tom didn't care about the portly gent. What had caught Tom's eye was Claire Montague, staring after the retreating man and looking as miserable as he'd ever seen a human being look.

Her expression tore at his heartstrings, and he found himself wanting to kill the self-satisfied gentleman walking away from her. He leaped from his horse just as the stagecoach rumbled down the road in front of him. When it passed, Claire no longer stood in the alley, and he had no idea where she'd gone off to. Nor was the mustachioed fellow anywhere to be seen. Damn.

He was troubled as his horse carried him down the road toward Partington Place. Try as he might, he could think of no suitable way to approach Claire with his worries. Her private life was not his concern; she'd have every right to tell him to mind his own business if he asked, damn it.

Worry plagued him, though. He didn't like his Claire to be so upset about anything. Most particularly, oddly enough, he didn't want her upset about a man. Who could the fellow possibly have been? Resolving to consult with Jedediah Silver on the matter, Tom made his way back home.

Somehow Claire managed to walk calmly into the Pyrite Springs Mercantile and Furniture Emporium before she collapsed. Dianthe St. Sauvre, who had been critically studying some delicate eyelet lace, rushed over to where

Claire had sunk, trembling like a leaf, onto a cracker barrel.

"Claire! Whatever is the matter? Are you ill?"

Even Sylvester, who had been brooding over a particularly troublesome passage in his book and ignoring Dianthe, put down his pencil, flipped open the hinged countertop, and walked to her side. "What's the matter, Claire? You look like hell."

Dianthe scowled up at Sylvester, who shrugged.

"Oh, my God," Claire whispered, "I'm doomed."

Dianthe's eyes opened wide. "Whatever can the matter be? Please tell us, Claire! Perhaps we can help you."

Claire dug into her pocket for her handkerchief. "Nobody can help me," she declared dramatically. "It's too late."

"Good God, you're not consumptive, are you?" Sylvester began backing away from Claire, his expression one of terror. "Don't cough on me, Claire, please."

"For heaven's sake, Sylvester, don't be absurd."

Claire had never heard Dianthe sound so resolute and cranky. Her friend's attitude gave her courage, and she swallowed the tears she had begun to shed. By Jupiter, if the fluffy Dianthe could be firm in a catastrophe, so could Claire. Of course Dianthe had no idea what the catastrophe was, but that didn't matter. Her friends cared; their solicitude gave Claire strength.

Sitting up straight and gathering her shredded composure around her, Claire said, "It's my father."

"Your father has consumption?" Sylvester began to look less terrified and more puzzled.

"Did something happen to your father, Claire?" Dianthe asked sympathetically.

"Yes. He came to Pyrite Springs."

As her voice conveyed none of the joy generally associated with such a family reunion, Dianthe merely blinked at her. Sylvester looked more interested, and he walked back to her side.

"Um . . ." Dianthe began, obviously unsure of herself, "are you and your father at odds, Claire, dear?"

"At *odds*?" Claire uttered a brief, harsh laugh. "He's the most loathsome human being on the face of the earth, Dianthe! He's a fraud and a cheat and a vile, despicable villain! He's a blackguard, a scoundrel, a charlatan, and a vile pretender!"

"My goodness," Dianthe murmured, stunned.

"Really? Tell us more, Claire." Sylvester pulled up another barrel and, fascinated, plopped himself down on it.

"I couldn't believe it when I heard his voice. I know God is punishing me for deceiving Mr. Partington. I know it!"

"Nonsense!" Sylvester said roundly. "Tell us more about your father. Maybe I can use him in my book. Ow!" He glared at Dianthe, who had pinched his arm.

"Can't you see that Claire is terribly upset, Sylvester? Forget your stupid book for a minute, can't you?"

"Forget my book? My *stupid* book? Why, I like that!"

"Oh, I didn't mean anything, and you know it," Dianthe said crossly. "But let's see if we can't help Claire before you use anybody's father in your book."

"Yes, please help me," Claire begged. "I need your help. I don't know what to do. He's threatened to expose me!"

Tapping her delicate chin with an equally delicate finger, Dianthe murmured, "Well, now, before he can do that, perhaps it's time you told Mr. Partington yourself, dear. I get the impression he's quite taken with you, you know."

"Me?" Claire cried, shocked.

"Claire?" Sylvester cried, also shocked.

Dianthe looked peeved. "Yes. Claire. I don't know why you both seem so surprised. It was obvious to me, and I should know."

Claire and Sylvester shared a glance. Dianthe's idea was so absurd Claire almost forgot her miseries and laughed. Almost.

"You're very sweet, Dianthe, but I know Mr. Partington only cares about me as a housekeeper. Perhaps," she added, daring to dream, "he might even think of me as a friend." She couldn't make herself admit the truth aloud: that no man, least of all her hero, Tom Partington, could possibly look at Claire when Dianthe was in the room.

"Well, perhaps," Dianthe conceded—rather too quickly, in Claire's estimation. "But I still think you should tell him yourself now, Claire. It would spare you all this worry and anguish, and then your father would have no further hold over you."

"Is he really so bad, Claire?" Sylvester asked, all ears. "You must tell us more about him."

"I don't want to."

A glance at her friends, however, both offering her their services out of the goodness of their hearts—well, out of the goodness of Dianthe's heart, at any rate— made her decide it would be unfair of her to keep her past a secret any longer.

"But you have to promise me you'll *never, ever* tell another single soul in the world what I'm about to tell you."

"Can't I even use it in my book? If I promise to change the names?" Sylvester began to look sulky.

"Oh, all right, as long as you change the names. It's a sordid, awful story, though."

The Author's demeanor brightened at the word "sordid." He went over to lock the front door so they wouldn't be disturbed.

So Claire related an edited version of her childhood to Dianthe and Sylvester, ending with her father's sudden appearance and blackmail demand that very day. Dianthe looked suitably appalled. Sylvester smiled ecstatically and rubbed his hands.

"Besides the late Mr. Partington, you two are the only people in the world I've told about my novels, and you're the only people in the world I've ever entrusted with the story of my childhood. You must honor my secrets. I—I don't think I could ever live it down if anyone else were to discover my shameful past."

"Oh, Claire!" Dianthe hugged her tightly. "None of what you've told us is your fault. None of us is given the opportunity to choose our parents. You should never, ever feel ashamed of what you've come from. Why, just look at you today. You've made yourself into a wonderful, responsible woman, and you've done it all by yourself! You should feel proud, not ashamed."

Claire had never heard Dianthe speak so feelingly or with such incredible common sense. All at once, hearing herself being stoutly defended by her friend, she began to cry again. She forgave Dianthe every inch of her beauty and talent and hugged her back.

Sylvester looked as if he didn't quite approve of the two ladies' emotional display. He did say, however, "Dianthe's right, you know, Claire. It's amazing that you didn't end up soliciting on the streets of San Francisco, given your background and—ow!"

Glaring at Dianthe, Sylvester massaged his foot where she had stamped on it.

After blowing her nose and wiping her tears away, Claire asked shakily, "So, what should I do?"

Dianthe tapped her chin again. "Well, you know, Claire, I don't think you'll have to worry about your father for a while yet. You just gave him a substantial amount of money. Surely it will take him some time to run through it, and by then we'll undoubtedly have thought of a splendid plan. Or," she added with a sly, knowing look, "Mr. Partington will have declared his intentions, and you'll feel able to confess to him."

"Never!"

"We'll see." Dianthe gave her a catlike smile.

By the time Sylvester unlocked the front door again, loftily ignoring several upset citizens, Claire felt better. Nothing had been resolved, it was true, but she took Dianthe's kindly words to heart. By the time Claude came back to demand more money, she'd certainly have thought of a good way to get rid of him.

She knew she'd never be able to tell Tom Partington she was in reality Clarence McTeague.

❧ 13 ❧

*I*n a determined effort to put her corrupt father out of her mind, Claire hurried home and threw herself into decorating Partington Place for the Christmas holidays. That very afternoon she took Scruggs and Dolly, one of the housemaids, into the attic and began to haul boxes downstairs.

"Are you certain Mr. Partington will approve, Miss Montague?" asked a reluctant Scruggs, eyeing a large carton with disfavor.

"Mr. Partington will be thrilled," Claire replied. "I'm sure he'll enter into the spirit of Christmas just as the late Mr. Partington used to do."

Scruggs allowed himself a doubtful "humph." He did, however, pick up the carton and cart it off.

She had everything taken to her downstairs office, where she and Dolly set to work emptying the boxes. Since Claire had never really enjoyed Christmas as a child with her roving father, she almost forgot her worries in the excitement of the season.

"Look at this!" she cried at one point, hauling out a

spool of red velvet ribbon. "I'd forgotten all about this. We can make red bows and tie them to the banister posts on the staircase."

"They'd look lovely, ma'am," Dolly said deferentially. All the servants, with the possible exception of Scruggs, treated Claire with the utmost respect.

"And we can make paper garlands too, Dolly, to string between the bows, and maybe drape some pine boughs above the garlands."

"Oh, ma'am, it sounds very pretty."

"Good. Then I think I shall take a walk to the woods this afternoon and cut some boughs."

"Need any help?" came a deep voice from the door.

Claire almost jumped out of her skin. She and Dolly leaped to their feet. "Mr. Partington, I had no idea you were there!"

"I hated to interrupt. You looked like you were having such a good time."

Feeling her cheeks catch fire, Claire tried to smile. "We were having a good time. We're decorating the house for Christmas."

Tom's eyebrows arched over his beautiful blue eyes, and Claire couldn't maintain his gaze. "I hope you don't mind, Mr. Partington."

"Mind? I think it's a wonderful idea. I'd never even have thought to do such a thing."

"Really?"

"Really. We weren't much for decorating on the frontier. Not that we had anything to decorate."

"Oh. Of course not."

Dolly, obviously nervous in the presence of her grand employer, murmured, "Perhaps I should start on the parlor, Miss Montague."

"Fine, Dolly. Thank you. Put the glass angels out on

the mantelpiece and set to work making bows from the ribbon. I'll be outside cutting greens. There's another box we haven't even opened yet. I think the crèche is in there, along with the Father Christmas Mrs. Gaylord made last year."

"Mrs. Gaylord? Is it made of marigolds?"

Claire managed to smile at Tom's teasing tone. "No. For once she forsook marigolds and created a lovely Father Christmas, just for Partington Place. It's crafted using a process called papier-mâché and then painted, and I hope you'll like it."

"I'm sure I shall." Tom held the door for Dolly, who fled with a box full of glass angels, the spool of red velvet ribbon hooked over her arm. "Now, where exactly did you plan to cut these famous greens?"

Claire felt uncomfortable now that they were the only two people in the room. She tried to keep her hands busy by lifting things out of one of the cartons. "There are some pine trees along the path leading toward the meadow where you plan to build your new stables. And I have two pyracantha bushes in the garden. Their foliage is lovely at Christmas. It looks very like holly. I planted a holly bush last spring, but I wouldn't feel comfortable taking cuttings from it yet as it's still too young."

"I see."

Tom's tone was soft and sweet, and Claire realized she'd been rattling on in an embarrassing manner. Clearing her throat, she said, "Yes. So, shall we be off? If we leave the house through the kitchen, I can grab my gardening gloves and cutters."

"Of course."

Tom had never seen Claire so nervous, and her attitude worried him. Either she was upset about that man he'd seen today or she was still fretting about last night's kiss.

He wanted to kick himself for being so clumsy a prospective lover. But hell, he'd had no experience with proper females before he met Claire. He didn't know the first thing about wooing. The loose women who used to follow the railroad had no truck with coyness. They were happy to spread their legs for anybody, as long as they were paid.

Claire set a spanking pace after she'd gathered her shears and gloves. Tom made her relinquish the clippers to him, although she was reluctant to do so, and then he almost had to run to keep up with her.

Because he wanted to lull her into letting her guard down so he could question her, he said, "I can hardly remember the Christmases from my boyhood, but I do recall that they were fun. We used to go over to my cousins' house. They were twins, Freddy and Emma, and we'd sing songs and play games."

He looked at Claire, hoping she'd offer a Christmas memory of her own. She didn't, and Tom decided to try again.

"Yup. My other uncle and aunt, their kids, and both sets of grandparents would all gather at my aunt Ruby and uncle Paul's house. There'd be a real gang of us, all right. I remember Aunt Ruby used to crumple up white paper and make it look like snow, and I always wondered why, since Jesus was born in the desert. Nobody ever gave me a reasonable answer either."

He glanced at Claire once more. She looked worried. Again she offered not a word to support the conversation, and Tom felt like huffing in frustration.

Deciding a direct approach was his only recourse, he

asked, "What about you, Miss Montague? What did you do as a child at Christmas?"

Tom was appalled at the apprehensive look she shot him and wondered what he'd said to disturb her. Everybody had Christmas memories from childhood. Did that constitute an improperly personal question? Even though he didn't know much about polite society, he didn't think so.

After a moment or two Claire cleared her throat again. "Actually, Mr. Partington, my—my family did not celebrate Christmas. Much."

"Oh." Well, hell. "Er, did your parents have religious objections to the holiday?"

Was it his imagination, or did Claire's face register the briefest hint of irony? It was gone now. Tom couldn't be sure.

"No, Mr. Partington. I never knew my mother, you see. My father—well, my father didn't—he didn't have time for such things."

"He didn't have time? How could he not have time for Christmas?"

"I'm afraid you'd have to ask him that."

Claire spoke more sarcastically than she'd intended to, Tom judged, if her quick flush was any indication.

"Oh. Did, er, did you have friends to spend the holidays with?"

"Good heavens, no."

Tom was taken aback by Claire's tone, which was faintly horrified. He narrowed his eyes as he concentrated. Had that fellow this morning known her in her youth? Was he a friend of her father's? Somebody whom Claire held in aversion for some reason? Had he attempted something unsavory with a young Claire? Tom's hand tightened around the clippers.

"Was that an acquaintance from your childhood with you today, Miss Montague?" he blurted out. Then he cursed himself as an addlepated idiot when Claire stopped dead in her tracks and her cheeks drained of color. She looked as if she might faint, and he quickly took up one of her hands.

"I beg your pardon, Miss Montague. I didn't mean to pry. But I saw a portly fellow with a waxed mustache walking away from you this morning, and you looked quite distressed. I didn't like to think of you being troubled, you see."

"Oh."

"Was he someone out of your past?"

Claire seemed to recollect her wits after only an instant. Snatching her hand away from Tom, she attempted an airy laugh. "Good heavens, no, Mr. Partington. Why, I haven't seen anybody I knew in my childhood for years and years. And no, I had no conversation with a portly man in town today. If I looked troubled when you saw me, it was . . . because I'd just received some bad news. Yes indeed. It was just, er, some unfortunate news, was all it was."

She was lying. Tom knew she was lying about something, but he had no idea what or why. "I trust the news wasn't terribly bad."

"No. No, it had to do with an—an investment."

"I see." Tom examined Claire's face for another second before deciding he'd alienate her by pressing further. He did, however, decide he'd pay a visit to Pyrite Springs this evening after supper. There were a very few places in town where a stranger might stay overnight, and that man had missed the last stage out of town. Tom hadn't been a scout for nothing.

Determined to put Claire at her ease, he turned the

conversation back to greenery. With a good deal of effort on his part, eventually Claire seemed to relax. With a little more effort, she actually began to enjoy herself in his company. He hadn't completely lost his ability to charm, he guessed. Thank God. For perhaps the first time in his adult life, Tom mentally thanked his mother for her insistence that he learn the art of inconsequential small talk.

Soon Claire was actually laughing at his silly jokes. Her cheeks grew pink with exertion and the brisk winter air, and she looked extremely pretty. Tom was enchanted. This was what he wanted out of life: a home, his horses, traditions, and Claire.

They ambled back to Partington Place together, dragging several large pine boughs behind them. The urge to kiss Claire plagued Tom, and he tried to mitigate it with more conversation.

"Miss Montague, I want you to know how much I appreciate the way you take care of me and my home. Decorating for Christmas is a wonderful idea. You're a real treasure, you know."

"It's my pleasure to decorate the place, Mr. Partington. Partington Place has been my own home for a good many years now, after all."

She smiled at him, and Tom's urge blossomed like bluebells on a summer's day. He dug his fingers into his bough and prayed for strength. If there was one thing Claire didn't need, it was for him to perpetrate another clumsy attack on her person. He smiled, not daring to open his mouth for fear of what might emerge.

The scent of fresh-cut pine was strong in the clean air, and the silence about them was broken only by the crunch of their feet and the rustle of branches. Tom looked up into a cloudless slate blue sky beginning to

pinken in the west as the day crept toward evening. He
wished he could think of something to say that would
take his mind off his base desires. He was surprised when
it was Claire who broke the silence.

"I used to dream about Christmas, though," she said,
as though continuing a conversation they'd been having
for hours. "Even though we never celebrated it."

"You did?"

"Yes. I used to dream of going off into the woods and
cutting pine boughs and decorating a house prettily.
Not a grand house like yours. Just an ordinary house.
But I'd have decorated it with ribbons and angels and
boughs. It would have smelled of pine and cinnamon
and winter." Giving Tom a little sideways peek, she
added shyly, "It was just a silly childish dream, you
know."

"It doesn't sound silly to me."

Indeed it didn't. In fact, it sounded downright normal
to Tom, who'd never thought to dream about having
Christmas because he'd lived it. Glancing at Claire, he
saw her looking incredibly wistful and totally desirable.

His bough slipped out of his fingers and plunked to
the dirt with a rustle. Claire looked at him, surprised.

"Why, Mr. Partington, what's the matter?"

Tom clenched his fingers into tight fists and fought a
major battle with himself. The desire to sweep Claire
into his arms and tell her she'd never miss Christmas
again, that he'd make up for all the unhappy Christmases
of her youth, battled with common sense, which told
him she would be shocked by such a bold overture. If
she fell into a faint at his feet, he wasn't sure he'd be able
to control himself.

Stiffly he stooped to reclaim his fallen bough. "Nothing's the matter, Miss Montague. I only dropped my branch."

"Oh."

And after he'd visited Pyrite Springs and determined who or what the evil man was who had disturbed Claire's peace so greatly, Tom would slay him. He *knew* that man was responsible for Claire's unhappiness. Anybody who caused his Claire distress deserved only one fate. It would be Tom's great pleasure to mete it out.

He, Claire, and Jedediah dined in the breakfast room that evening. Tom wondered if Scruggs, foiled in his attempt to keep them in the dark, decided to serve in the breakfast room because he found no more joy in serving dinner in the dining room. He might have decided the supposition unworthy had not Scruggs's demeanor been even more dismal than usual.

"He looks like he just lost his dog," Tom muttered as he watched Scruggs's rear end disappear behind the door.

Claire smiled. "He doesn't like to have his little kingdom disrupted. The new lanterns in the dining room have knocked his senses all askew."

With a laugh of genuine amusement Tom said, "Do you think that's it? I've heard of regimented lives, but old Scruggs takes the cake."

"I suppose he does at that."

"You and Dolly certainly did a bang-up job of the Christmas decorating," Tom said, hoping to generate a lively dinner table chat. "The place looks wonderful. I really like the pine bough wreath with the candle in the middle. It's charming. Don't you think so, Jed?"

But Jedediah was staring off into space at the moment, a faraway expression on his face, his fork dangling limply from his fingers. He obviously hadn't heard a word that had been spoken thus far at the table.

Chuckling, Tom whispered to Claire, "Still under the intoxicating influence of Miss St. Sauvre, I presume."

He'd expected Claire to share in his amusement. She didn't. She jumped, in fact, and stared at Jedediah aghast. "Merciful heavens, I'm afraid you may be right, Mr. Partington," she whispered with what sounded like anguish. "But I feel certain she doesn't return his infatuation. I'm just sure of it."

"I don't know why not. They were with each other all last evening, after that silly—er, that ode of hers was finished. I wouldn't be at all surprised if it was love that's captivated our practical Jed."

"It can't be! But—but if it has, I'm sure Dianthe doesn't reciprocate."

Tom was a little worried about Claire's obvious chagrin but chalked it up to whatever had upset her this morning. With a little shrug, he said, "No? Well, that's too bad for Jed then. I must admit that while I don't have too much use for Miss St. Sauvre's alleged poetry, she does seem like a nice enough person. I'd never have pegged her for a flirt."

Claire's owlish expression charmed him. She blinked rapidly several times and seemed to be at a loss for what to say. At last she avowed seriously, "I'm certain Dianthe would never flirt with a gentleman, Mr. Partington."

"I'm sure you're right, Claire."

Apparently his smile was a little too warm for her because after blinking another couple of times, she turned red and dropped her gaze. A big sigh from Jedediah caught Tom's attention, and he smiled at his love-struck accountant.

"What do you plan to do with your evening, Claire? I have to go to town for a while, and it doesn't look as though Jed here's going to be much company for anybody."

"I'm not certain, Mr. Partington. Perhaps I shall read for a while."

"Sounds peaceful."

Claire thought about Tom's assessment of her planned evening's entertainment as she crept off to her office and sank into her chair. Peaceful! She would never know another moment's peace as long as she lived; she knew it. Her delight in Christmas had faded between the time she and Dolly had finished decorating and dinner, and Claire had had plenty of time to revive her worries. They plagued her now as she stared out her window and hoped for lightning to strike her.

So fervently was she praying for a bolt from heaven that when a knock came at the outside door, it jolted her out of her chair. Her father! It must be her father, back with more demands. Claire flung open the door to reveal Dianthe and Sylvester, and her sigh of relief was so hearty she was surprised it didn't blow them both over backward.

"Oh, I'm so glad it's you!" She felt not quite so desolate, knowing her friends were on her side.

"Evening, Claire." Sylvester sauntered past her, bearing a lily and several sheets of foolscap. He looked happier than Claire had seen him in months.

Dianthe drifted into the room as if borne on a fairy cloud.

"Claire, you must let me read you the first few pages of my latest book, *The Wily Turk, Adolphus*. I've modeled him entirely after your father, and I think it's the best work I've ever done. After you left this afternoon, all I did was write!"

"My goodness," Claire said weakly. She wondered how his customers had fared if he'd done nothing but write. It was a wonder Mr. Gilbert hadn't gone out of business before now, with Sylvester manning his Mercantile and Furniture Emporium.

"I still don't think Adolphus is a Turkish name, Sylvester," Dianthe murmured.

"Nonsense! Who cares anyway? It's my work, and if I say his name is Adolphus, who can say me nay?" He whirled around to confront Claire, who was closing the door. "What do you think, Claire? It's an author's privilege to name his characters, isn't it?"

"I suppose so." She'd named hers, and look at all the trouble it had caused.

"Well, I still don't think it sounds very Turkish." Dianthe looked a trifle miffed.

Sylvester waved his lily languidly as he took up his customary pose next to the fireplace. "It doesn't matter. It's a work of art."

Claire wished she could be so sanguine about her own work. She sat with a sigh, glad at least to have company to take her mind off her troubles.

As if reading her mind, Dianthe leaned forward and placed her hand over Claire's. "We decided to visit you this evening to give you courage, Claire, dear. You were so upset this morning."

"Yes. Although why that should be I have no idea. Just think of all the raw material you have to work with—from your own family! Why, I should think any novelist worth his salt could write stories forever on your father alone."

Sylvester's handsome features spoke of disdain. However, disdain was so common an expression on his face that Claire did not take exception. Not that it would have made any difference. She wished she possessed Sylvester's talent for ignoring anything but his art. Her own problems squatted in her heart like evil, sharp-clawed ghouls.

Yet she was awfully happy to have these kind friends visit her. "Thank you very much, both of you. I feel extremely fortunate to know I can rely on you for support."

Sylvester lifted a brow, but Dianthe smiled sweetly, and Claire felt better.

Before Sylvester could begin to read from his latest manuscript, Dianthe, looking faintly embarrassed, asked, "Is Mr. Silver still staying with Mr. Partington, Claire?"

Claire's brief bubble of security burst instantly. Did Dianthe return Mr. Silver's obvious affection? This could prove to be a catastrophe for poor Tom Partington. On the other hand, how could she stand in the way of true love if that was what this turned out to be? She decided to proceed very cautiously.

Ignoring Sylvester's pointed glare, she murmured, "I believe he plans to stay through Christmas, Dianthe."

Lowering her eyes, Dianthe murmured, "He's a most appealing gentleman, isn't he, Claire?"

"Mr. Silver?"

"Yes."

"Well, yes, I suppose he is. Of course he doesn't hold a candle to Mr. Partington in manners or address or countenance." As soon as she'd spoken, Claire frowned and wondered if she'd uttered the truth. Actually Mr. Silver was quite handsome, had perfect manners, and was polite to a fault.

With a breathy giggle Dianthe said, "But you have Mr. Partington all sewed up, Claire."

Claire felt her eyes open wide. This was the second time today Dianthe had said something of this nature. Claire couldn't imagine what maggot could have gotten into Dianthe's head. "That's absurd, Dianthe," she said tartly. Then she wished she hadn't spoken so harshly since Dianthe was trying to help her.

With a huge sigh Claire went to fetch her mending basket and settled into her chair. "Let's listen to Sylvester's new book, shall we, Dianthe?"

"All right, dear."

Before Sylvester could do more than draw in a deep, dramatic breath, a knock at Claire's hallway door was answered to reveal Jedediah Silver, who had come to keep Claire company for the evening. Claire welcomed him into her office with resignation. Well, why shouldn't her plan to attach Dianthe to Tom Partington fail too? After all, everything else in her life had already gone wrong.

When he visited Pyrite Springs after supper, Tom was dismayed when he unearthed neither hide nor hair of the portly, mustachioed gentleman he'd seen striding away from Claire earlier in the day. He asked at the Pyrite Springs Hotel and the Gold Nugget Inn, to no avail. It wasn't until after he'd tried the telegraph office, the stage depot, the post office, been frustrated at all three, and decided to stop in at the Fool's Gold Saloon for a beer that he found his quarry.

By that time the evening was well advanced and the man was embroiled in what seemed to be an endless poker game. Tom couldn't imagine Claire's becoming involved with a fellow who gambled. Observing from his

post at the bar, he grinned at the barkeep and said art-
lessly, "New face in town, I see."

Bruce Bing, the sociable barkeeper whose own mus-
taches were waxed almost as prettily as those on Tom's
prey, swiped at the counter with his damp rag. "Yup.
Come to town yesterday on the stage. Friendly feller."

"Looks like the game's been going on for a while."

"Yup. They been playin' durned near all afternoon.
That new feller keeps chinnin' and grinnin' and keepin'
'em all in stitches. Reg'lar comedian, he is."

"Know his name?"

"Well, now, I ain't so sure. He's stayin' upstairs."
Bing winked hugely. "A guest of Miss Mildred, you understand."

Tom gave a suitably sly grin. "Fast worker, is he?"

"I reckon. Never seen him till yestiddy, and he's already Miss Milly's guest." Another wink let Tom know
just how much Bing appreciated such a slick operator as
the poker-playing, lively old comedian.

"Maybe I'll mosey on over and see what's going on at
the table." Tom flipped a coin to the barkeep, who
smiled at his generosity.

The conversation around the poker table was animated. Tom sipped his beer and watched the man
closely. The fellow was as smooth as a polished marble.
His brown eyes twinkled, his teeth flashed, and he kept
up a steady stream of amusing anecdotes, making sure
his fellow poker players were constantly off guard but so
diverted that they didn't object. If Tom didn't suspect
the man of having hurt Claire, he might have been entertained. He wished he could talk to the damned fellow, but the game seemed destined to go on for hours.

Patience was a virtue he'd developed on the plains,
however, and he used it now. Pulling up a chair, he

straddled it, settled his arms over the back, and watched the game for what seemed forever.

It wasn't quite forever. In fact, Tom's patience was stretched only another hour and a half or so. At last the game broke up, and the man stood and stretched.

Grinning, Tom said, "You won quite a pot there, sir."

The fellow grinned back, and Tom could have sworn he was being assessed acutely. He felt like a side of beef for a minute. It was an uncomfortable feeling, and he counteracted it by standing and holding out a hand. "Tom Partington here. I enjoyed watching you play. You're a skillful hand at poker, sir." Tom was sure it wasn't his imagination that made him think the man brightened when he divulged his name.

"Indeed I am, Mr. Partington." He shook Tom's hand. "Claude Monta—Montenegro here."

Montenegro, huh? Strange name. "In town for long, Mr. Montenegro?"

"Alas, no. Just passing through."

"I thought I saw you earlier this morning outside the Mercantile, chatting with somebody. Now, let me see . . . Who was it? Ah, yes. Miss Claire Montague, it was. You a friend of hers, Mr. Montenegro?"

"Montague. Montague." Claude put on a show of thinking hard. "No, can't say the name's familiar."

"No? My mistake. But come to the bar, Mr. Montenegro. Let me buy a stranger a drink. I don't play much poker myself anymore, but I enjoy watching a skilled cardplayer, and you're one of the best I've seen in a long time."

Claude's grin was as toothy and benevolent as any Tom had ever seen. He didn't trust the man already. What on earth could this slick customer have to do with Claire? The awful thought struck him that he might be a former lover. Had he come back to plague her to return to him? Could it be this man whom Claire had been fleeing when she came to work for his uncle? Had she been fleeing anything? She was such a starchy, straitlaced woman it didn't seem possible somehow.

Yet such a scenario might explain some puzzling things about her. Tom settled against the bar, called for drinks, and prepared himself for a long, interesting evening.

Although he awoke the next morning with an aching head and a sick stomach, he had to admit the evening had been interesting. Entertaining even. He'd seldom met anybody as amusing and engaging as the man who called himself Claude Montenegro.

He'd learned absolutely nothing, however, about his relationship with Claire Montague.

❧ 14 ❧

*T*he slippery scoundrel twirled his waxed mustache and smiled at Miss Abigail Faithgood. His expression might have been taken as benevolent by anybody unfamiliar with his black heart. Miss Abigail, however, knew the dastardly man well. It was he who had hired the band of villains from whom she and Tuscaloosa Tom Pardee had just escaped. It was he who threatened to kill her sheep so that he could take over her ranch.

"Good afternoon, Miss Faithgood. What brings you to town today?"

Miss Abigail squared her shoulders. "I imagine you are surprised to see me, aren't you, Mr. Maguire? But your scheme bore no fruit, as you now know. I still live."

His greasy smile still in place, Oliver Maguire murmured, "Now whatever can you mean, my dear girl?"

"I mean you're a vile, despicable, evil human being who doesn't deserve to exist on the same earth as the rest of us," Claire muttered savagely.

Her pen dropped to her blotter, she put her elbows on

her desk and cradled her head in her hands. Beneath the manuscript page she was writing lay the telegram she'd received this morning from Mr. Oliphant, warning her about what had transpired on the train and apologizing abjectly. As if an apology would make a difference now.

"What am I going to do?"

She'd been doing her best to borrow a helpful tip from Sylvester and use her conniving father as a novelistic device. At least that way he'd be good for something. It hurt to write about him, though, even this little bit. What Claire wanted to do was forget he even existed.

But how could she do that if he kept turning up? Granted, he'd turned up only once so far, but Claire knew that now he'd found her, unless she was prepared to flee Pyrite Springs, change her name, and take up residence elsewhere—preferably a foreign country— she'd never be rid of him again.

At a tap on her door Claire snapped her head up, whisked her novel from the blotter, and crammed it into the drawer, wishing she'd never brought it downstairs in the first place. She glanced up in time to see Tom Partington, looking not quite in perfect health, watching her curiously as he closed the door.

His grin was as beautiful as ever. "Hiding evidence of your embezzlement activities, Claire?"

She looked down at the corner of a manuscript page sticking out of the closed drawer and wondered why the fates seemed to hate her so much these days. After quickly opening the drawer, stuffing the paper all the way in, and closing it again, she looked up and donned a bright smile. At least she hoped it was bright.

"You caught me," she said lightly. "And here I was hoping to keep my nefarious scheme a secret for a little while longer."

Tom chuckled and then winced. Claire's heart lurched. "Are you not feeling well this morning, Mr. Partington? You didn't join us at breakfast."

"No. No, I wasn't quite up to breakfast, I'm afraid. I went to town last night, and I fear I overindulged a trifle."

"Oh." Claire knew exactly what sort of overindulgence Tom referred to. Her father had euphemistically called his occasional bouts of drunkenness overindulgence. She'd never have suspected Tom of such regrettable habits. She felt her mouth tighten and made an effort to relax. It was not her place to judge her hero. That is to say, her employer.

"You look grieved, Claire. Please believe me when I say that such excesses are not at all commonplace, and I certainly don't want to disappoint you." He looked longingly at the chair across from her desk. "May I sit? Or have I sunk myself so far beneath reproach that you wish to be rid of me."

Good heavens, did she appear that disapproving? Striving for an easygoing smile, Claire said, "Of course you may sit, Mr. Partington. And I assuredly do not disapprove of you, nor would I ever wish to be rid of you. I was just going over the, er, household accounts."

Sinking into the chair with evident relief, Tom sighed and asked, "I don't suppose Uncle Gordon hid his book profits in the household accounts, did he?"

Not quite daring to meet his inquiring smile, Claire murmured, "No, he did not."

"Pity."

Tom rubbed his forehead with thumb and fingers, and Claire felt a moment of compassion. It was only a moment, though; she didn't approve of the type of indulgence that resulted in headaches and mean tempers.

She'd been victimized by gentlemen in such a condition too many times in her youth.

"Whew, I'm really not used to drinking, Claire. I like a glass of brandy or something every now and again, but I can't even remember the last time I had a head like this."

Claire deemed it prudent not to respond. She began to fiddle with her pen.

"But you see, I met this very intriguing fellow last evening when I stopped in at the Fool's Gold Saloon, the same one I thought I saw you with earlier in the day. Turns out he goes by the name Claude Montenegro."

Claire's pen fell to the desk, and she snatched it back up again. An odd numbness invaded her body, and she began to perceive Tom as if she were looking through the wrong end of a telescope. Suddenly he seemed very far away. She dropped her pen again and clutched the edge of her desk so as to remain seated and not faint and slide into a heap on the floor.

"M-m-montenegro?" she whispered, and frowned because that had sounded wrong—entirely too soft and shaky. She cleared her throat and tried again. "What an odd name!"

Tom winced once more, and Claire realized she'd spoken too loudly.

"I don't think it's his real one." He shaded his eyes and looked as if it hurt to speak.

He'd been consorting with her father! Claire wasn't sure she could stand hearing about it. On the other hand, she knew she couldn't stand *not* hearing about it.

"Er, why should he be using a false name, Mr. Partington?" She schooled her face to betray none of the panic rampaging in her heart.

"I think he's a confidence man, Claire, a bunco artist."

"You do?" She stared at him, awed. She'd never known anybody to come to such a quick, shrewd, and accurate assessment of her miserable father. Then again, she'd never spoken to anybody about him before either.

"Yes. I wonder why he's in town."

Was it Claire's imagination, or did Tom look at her with a too perceptive gleam in his eyes? She dropped her gaze. "I'm sure I wouldn't know, Mr. Partington."

"No? Are you absolutely sure you don't know him, Claire? Was he the one responsible for your unfortunate investment?"

Unfortunate investment? Ah, yes, she remembered that lie. Claire tried to laugh, a difficult thing to do with her mouth dry as cotton. "Good heavens, no, Mr. Partington. I have no idea who the gentleman is. Was. Is."

Tom shrugged, a gesture that seemed to hurt. "Are you sure? I was certain I saw you with him yesterday morning."

Claire tried to swallow the lump of cotton wadding in her throat. "Saw him with me? I mean, me with him? Goodness gracious, no, Mr. Partington. Whatever would I be doing with a confidence man?" She tried to appear innocent. She felt guilty as sin.

"Well, now, Claire, I don't know. That's what I was trying to find out because you sure didn't look happy when I saw you."

"I didn't?" Claire said in a very small voice.

"No. You didn't. And I was sure he was walking away from you at the time."

"Is—is that why you went to town? To meet the—the portly gentleman you thought had been with me?"

Was Tom Partington actually saying that he'd tried to

track her father down for her sake? Because he was worried about her? Searching his face for clues, Claire saw only the features she'd loved for so long; she couldn't read his mind, more's the pity.

"I don't like to see you unhappy, Claire," Tom said, his smile rueful.

"Thank you, Mr. Partington." Nobody had ever told Claire that he didn't like to see her unhappy. It was undoubtedly the kindest thing anyone had ever said to her. She deemed the truth too pathetic to admit aloud, so she said, rather unsteadily, "May I fix you a remedy I've heard is good for your particular ailment?"

The least she could do for this wonderful, wonderful man was mix him up a dose of her father's physic for when he'd overindulged. She hadn't thought she'd ever find anything she'd learned as a child useful, but perhaps she'd been wrong.

"You know a hangover tonic?" Tom sounded incredulous.

"A housekeeper's duties are many and varied, Mr. Partington," she said vaguely.

"It's hard for me to imagine my uncle Gordon getting himself into this predicament."

"He never did." Tom looked at her curiously, and Claire scrambled for purchase along the slippery path of her many deceptions. "I, er, I learned it during the course of another employment, you see." It was the truth, more or less, Claire told herself.

"You worked for somebody less sober than my uncle, I presume."

"Yes." That was definitely the truth.

"Thank you, Claire. I'd appreciate a dose of your cure."

"All right. Then it would be best if you were to lie down for an hour or so with your eyes closed."

He sounded almost meek when he said, "All right."

So Tom drank Claire's concoction. It tasted vile, and he didn't dare ask what was in it. Then he allowed himself to lie down on his bed with a cool, damp cloth over his eyes, even though he'd wanted to discuss horses and stables with Jedediah Silver.

When he arose an hour later, however, his headache gone and his stomach no longer rebellious, he mentally added one more feather to Claire's cap. The woman was incredible, and he wanted her more than he'd ever wanted anything—even his horses.

Somehow or other he was going to discover what was troubling her and eliminate it. Along the way he was going to win her love.

The two and a half weeks between the reemergence of Claude Montague into his daughter's life and Christmas passed quickly. Claire was terribly busy, and being busy allowed her to submerge her problems under activity. Besides, she loved the hustle and bustle attached to the season. As the days passed and her father stayed away, the threat of exposure seemed to fade. Claire supposed she was living in a fool's paradise, but she decided to enjoy the peace while she could and resume worrying about her problems later.

It didn't take her more than a couple of days to get used to her new hairstyle after her initial unsuccessful attempt to tame her curls. She even admitted, to herself, that the soft "do" flattered her more than those braided coils she'd had tacked to her head for ten years. One morning she actually found herself admiring the way the sun brought out the red highlights in her hair and made it glisten.

Of course, when she realized she was primping, she stopped at once and lectured herself for fifteen minutes about vanity, the wages of sin, and the need to be ever vigilant lest her bad blood show. Until Tom complimented her on her appearance. Then she forgot all about vilifying herself and wondered if Miss Thelma had her plaid skirt ready yet. She was ever so pleased to discover that not only was the plaid skirt ready, but the blue sateen evening gown and one of the blouses were also waiting for her when she paid the modiste a visit.

That evening, when Dianthe came to dine at Partington Place, she, Tom, and Jedediah were very kind in their praise of Claire's new style in dress. Claire felt pleased with herself and not at all as though she were a fallen woman parading her wares. After all, her new plaid skirt and blouse were extremely modest; in no way could even she, her severest critic, convict herself of putting herself forward unbecomingly.

She started to relax and enjoy feeling attractive for the first time in her life.

For years Gordon Partington had held an open house at Partington Place on Christmas Eve. The entire village of Pyrite Springs used to drop by for eggnog and fruitcake. When asked if he cared to continue the tradition, Tom agreed with a fair show of enthusiasm.

"Why not?" he'd asked after a moment's thought. "Why not act like the landed gentry? I reckon that's what I am after all."

Then he'd laughed, his blue eyes twinkling gaily, and Claire had caught her breath and wondered yet again how any one man could be so perfect.

So she set to work getting the front hall and the parlor

prepared, and she helped Mrs. Philpott bake ginger-snaps, tiny pecan-studded meringues, shortbread, and brandied cherry drops to augment the traditional holiday fruitcakes, which had been packed away in the basement months before and were now awaiting the day.

Scruggs directed the setting up of the Christmas tree and the stacking of firewood with his usual glum efficiency. He also saw to the resurrection of several bottles of Gordon Partington's best wine and cognac. It wouldn't do for the mayor and the other leading citizens of Pyrite Springs to be entertained with mere eggnog. Tom was glad he wouldn't have to drink the rest of Uncle Gordon's fancy stuff all by himself. He'd already ordered some liquor more to his taste from San Francisco.

The piano tuner was called in from Marysville to make sure the grand piano was in voice. Claire and Dianthe sang Christmas carols for one whole day as they made paper and popcorn ornaments for the tree. Tom and Jedediah found them in the parlor that afternoon, flushed and happy, with mounds of paper garlands coiled at their feet and a tubful of popcorn between them. They'd asked to join in the fun, and Claire didn't think she'd ever been happier in her life than she was then.

After supper they'd sung more carols, and Claire discovered another childhood trick was useful in her present life. She could play the piano. Claude Montague, of course, had never owned such an expensive instrument, but she'd been made to learn in a variety of unsavory establishments. Her father had found her musical ability useful in his various rackets.

That evening Claire was glad for her skill. She played from a Christmas songbook, and Tom turned the pages for her while Jedediah and Dianthe decorated the tree.

For once Claire didn't bother to worry that the accountant and the poetess seemed to be on remarkably friendly terms. She smiled at Tom, he smiled at her, and she felt herself as close to heaven as she would undoubtedly ever get.

Tom kissed her again on Christmas Eve. A light snow had fallen earlier in the day, but it didn't keep the citizens of Pyrite Springs from attending the annual open house at Partington Place.

"Wonderful party, Mr. Partington," Mr. Gilbert, the mayor, said, slapping Tom on the shoulder in a show of hearty brotherhood.

After he'd recovered from the staggering blow, Tom said, "Thank you, Mr. Gilbert. I find I'm enjoying these traditions my uncle established."

"Good thing, tradition." Mr. Gilbert puffed out his chest as though accepting credit for the tradition of traditions.

Tom didn't figure he'd argue. He only smiled.

It was just as well he'd armed himself with a smile because the next person to walk into the parlor was Sylvester Addison-Addison, complete with flowing red silk scarf draped around his literary neck, a bouquet of white lilies tied up with a red ribbon—for Claire, he said—and Mrs. Pringle firmly attached to his arm. If he hadn't already been smiling, Tom might well have gaped in astonishment. He was sure the Author would never have stood for that.

"Good evening, Mr. Partington," Mrs. Pringle cooed, never releasing Sylvester from her talons.

"Good evening." Tom nodded to them both. He received a frosty inclination of the head from Sylvester and a spirited flutter of lashes from Mrs. Pringle.

Mrs. Gaylord had forsaken orange this evening in deference to the season. She was swathed all in red when she waddled in with a brooding Sergei and a happy Freddy March a few moments later.

Tom sneaked a peek at Claire, who was pulling duty at the punch bowl and looking absolutely ravishing in her peacock blue evening gown. She gave him a glorious conspiratorial smile, and he winked back and decided his life was truly abundant and that Mrs. Gaylord's red looked superb.

Dianthe floated in on a cloud of white silk and lace. Almost immediately Jedediah snatched her away to the Christmas tree. Later in the evening Tom saw the two of them disappear out the side door and return a good twenty minutes later, Dianthe flushed and more ruffled than he'd ever seen her and Jedediah looking positively moony. He grinned and blew several smoke rings because he was happy.

The disappearance of his accountant and Claire's best friend gave him ideas too. He wondered if Claire would take more kindly to an overture from him this evening than she had the night of the Artistic Evening. He'd been showering her with respect and friendship these past few weeks and hadn't tried to sneak a single kiss or one improper embrace. He considered he'd been acting with incredible nobility since although he was a master at patience, sexual restraint wasn't one of his more solid virtues.

Looking back on their brief encounter on the balcony, he decided his kiss that night had been premature. Yes indeed. Entirely too impetuous. That was the reason she'd been scared; he'd jumped the gun and attacked her without notice. He should have buttered her up first. Fired a warning salvo over her head, as it were.

He was getting better at this society stuff. He now

realized a lady required time and preparation. He figured three or four weeks were probably long enough, considering they lived together and therefore undoubtedly knew each other better than most people did before they kissed. Or even got married, for that matter.

Not only that, but the very season required exuberance. A kiss was exuberant, wasn't it? It could be considered part of making Christmas truly merry. What was all that mistletoe for if not for kisses?

Tom had never hesitated to kiss a female before; his hesitancy in this present instance troubled him. He discovered himself staring at Claire from across the room while she played Christmas carols at the piano.

She had suspended her spectacles on a blue satin ribbon pinned to her bodice but had slipped them on now so she could read the music. She was surrounded by a choir of Pyrite Springians, and he shook his head and told himself not to be a fool. He'd never had trouble attracting women before. Granted, Claire was a bit more straitlaced than most of the women he'd dealt with in his life. She shouldn't require *this* much thought. Should she?

Perhaps it was true the other women he'd kissed had been ladies of the evening; still, women were basically all alike, weren't they? Besides, his mother had thrown him together with several belles the few times he'd dared visit her home in Alabama, and they'd seemed to like him. He frowned, recalling his mother's concerted attempts to get him to marry one of those feather-brained twits.

"Tom!"

Tom nearly dropped his cheroot in surprise when Jedediah slapped him on the back.

"Evening, Jed. Having a good time?"

"I'm having a wonderful time," Jedediah said, reverting to dreaminess for a second. He snapped right out of it. "But what's going on here? You looked unhappy."

"Did I? I'm not unhappy at all, Jed. As a matter of fact, I can't remember the last time I had such a good time."

Jedediah looked at him closely. "Are you sure? I distinctly saw you shudder."

"Oh, that." Tom chuckled. "I was thinking about the delicate females my mother used to throw in my face back home, that's all, and thanking my lucky stars I don't have to put up with that nonsense anymore."

Jedediah followed the path of Tom's gaze. "I notice you're looking at our Claire as you have these thoughts," he said, sacrificing slyness with a wink.

Tom sighed eloquently. "Do you think she cares for me at all, Jed?" He caught himself up short and stared at Jedediah in amazement. He'd never asked such a ridiculous question of another man in his life. What in God's name was the matter with him?

Jedediah evidently didn't mind. In fact, he laughed. "Tom Partington, I think Claire is madly in love with you."

"You what?"

"Well"—Jedediah now equivocated, embarrassed about having spoken so boldly—"I actually don't think that. Dianthe's the one who thinks that."

"Does she really?" Tom was vastly intrigued. "They're best friends, aren't they? If she thinks so, there must be a reason."

Jedediah went dreamy-eyed for a second, apparently having gone into a trance at the mention of his beloved. Tom grabbed his shoulder and shook him. "Don't you think so, Jed?"

"Hmm? Oh, Claire." The accountant frowned, as if

trying to recall the topic of their conversation. "Oh, yes. Claire! Well, I suppose so. I guess Dianthe should know if anybody does."

"Yes. Yes, I guess she should."

The notion pleased Tom inordinately. Could Claire really be in love with him? If so, that would solve all his problems since he was about to die from wanting her in his bed. If she loved him, then she must feel some carnal desire. He wasn't altogether sure how these things worked, but it seemed to him that if two people—one being female and the other male—desired each other, then there should be nothing to stand in the way of kisses. Lots of kisses. And more.

The thought of more almost made Tom salivate.

"You think a lot of Claire too, don't you, Tom?"

Tom had forgotten all about Jedediah. He jumped to hear the accountant's voice so close to his ear. "Of course.. Of course I do. I'm very—very fond of her. Yes indeed."

"Do you think you'll ask her to marry you?"

"Marry her?"

"Sure."

Good Lord, Tom had conveniently skipped over that step in his lurid fantasies about Claire.

He said, "Er, um, well . . ."

"I'm thinking about asking Dianthe to marry me," Jedediah confided softly.

"You are?"

With an enormous, happy sigh Jedediah said, "I certainly am. To have that treasure to myself for all eternity is just about the finest thing I can imagine. Permanence. A family. Until I met Dianthe, I never thought about marriage or a family. But if a fellow meets the woman of his dreams, I reckon he begins thinking about establishing something for himself. And his heirs. I've actually been thinking about heirs." He laughed as if he couldn't believe it of himself. "Yes indeed. Marriage is the answer in such a case, I reckon."

Tom nodded. Of course. He'd conveniently forgotten about marriage. Marriage had always looked like such a dreadful, deadly trap to him. He'd forgotten that any proper female would expect marriage before she'd even consider the part that came after kisses. What an appalling thought!

He reminded himself that Claire Montague and his mother were entirely different women. As he and his father were entirely different men. Why, the two sets of them—Claire and Tom and his mother and father— might as well belong to different species entirely.

"She'd be a wonderful wife for the master of Partington Place, you know," Jedediah continued. "She seems to belong here. Sometimes I used to think Gordon might marry her, but he either didn't want to or never got around to asking her." Jedediah didn't notice the look of shock on Tom's face. "I wonder if she'd have married him if he'd asked."

"Of course she wouldn't!"

Now it was Jedediah who looked shocked. Then he grinned. "Why, Tom, I do believe you're jealous."

"I am not!"

"Well, if it's any comfort, I'm sure Claire had no feelings of that nature for Gordon."

"Of course she didn't. She says he was like a father to her."

"So do you think you'll ask her to marry you?"

"No. I mean, I'm not sure." Tom swallowed and made himself say, "I—I don't know."

"You don't know?"

Jedediah roared with laughter. Tom was miffed. "Well, I'm not used to this living in civilization nonsense, you know, Jed. Marriage is a pretty stiff penalty to exact from a fellow."

"Ah, but it's worth it."

"How do you know?"

Jedediah frowned. "I just know. The thought of making Dianthe, the lady I love, my wife, why, it would be wonderful. To love and cherish and protect her. To have all the rights and privileges of a husband . . ." His voice trailed off, and he was apparently too moved to speak of those rights and privileges.

"Yeah, that's right." Tom looked at Claire again. Yes indeed. All the rights and privileges. Still, there were other ways of achieving those rights and privileges, ways not as irrevocable and frightening as marriage. Shoot, the very word sent shivers up his spine. Of course, if a body were married, he wouldn't have to worry about consequences. If little baby Partingtons were to result, for example.

God, what a thought! It made Tom cringe. As he pondered Jedediah's words, Tom tried to envision having children, but his imagination wasn't up to it.

What on earth was he doing, thinking about children, anyway? He'd never thought about children in his life.

Dianthe momentarily blocked his view of Claire, and he frowned. Then he looked at Jedediah and shook his head. For the life of him, he couldn't figure out how a smart cookie like Jed could prefer the silly, ode-writing Dianthe St. Sauvre to the stable, practical, delightfully useful Claire Montague. Then he grinned again. To each his own.

And Claire's practicality of nature might work to Tom's advantage too. Why, certainly she'd understand that a body didn't just rush into marriage. No. A sensible person would understand the merit of practicing first, to make sure the fit was right. Yeah, that's what she'd do.

Anyway, if Jedediah was right and Claire was already in love with him, half the battle was won. He'd take her outside, where he could ravish her sweetly with intoxicating words, kisses, and caresses. Maybe even ask her tonight to be his mistress. Why not? She already lived in his house; it would be a perfect arrangement. Perfect. By the time Jedediah meandered off, Tom was primed and ready to sweep Claire off her feet.

Unfortunately Claire was not on her feet. She was solidly planted on the piano bench with at least a dozen melodious guests warbling Christmas carols as she played. Tom sighed, resigned. Patience, he cautioned himself. Patience was an art he'd learned well and thoroughly.

He did, however, plan to put a stop to that lecherous Alphonse Gilbert leering at Claire's cleavage. He stalked to the piano and stepped in front of Gilbert.

Smiling sweetly, he said to the startled mayor, "Miss Montague and I have a pact, Mr. Gilbert. She plays, and I turn the pages."

The mayor was not the only one startled. Claire looked up in astonishment and could have sworn she detected a hint of jealousy in Tom's eyes.

Quickly returning her attention to "God Rest You Merry, Gentlemen," Claire told herself not to be stupid.

She felt a heady mixture of exhilaration and sorrow when she and Tom waved all but the last two guests away a couple of hours later. She'd had such a good time. For a while she'd even allowed herself to pretend that she was the mistress of Partington Place and Tom her husband. Silly Claire. Still, it was Christmas. If she were ever to allow herself to dream, she guessed Christmas was the best time to do it.

The only guests remaining were Jedediah and Dianthe, who were chatting cozily in front of the fire. Claire sighed as she gazed at them. She had removed her spectacles, deciding to let them dangle on their satin ribbon, and the two lovers looked like little fuzzy lumps. She wondered if their obvious affection for each other was breaking Tom's heart. She hoped not.

"Would you like to stroll in the garden for a moment, Claire?" Tom asked softly at her elbow. "It's cold, but the night's beautiful."

She turned to find him beside her, holding a beautifully fringed and flowered shawl. "How lovely!" she exclaimed, forgetting all about Tom's question.

"It's my Christmas present to you, Claire. I was going to have it wrapped up but decided to give it to you this evening so you'd feel obliged to humor me by wearing it as we stroll in the garden."

Claire could no more resist his beautiful, sparkling blue eyes than she could stop the world from turning. With a warm smile she said, "Thank you very much, Mr. Partington. You're absolutely right, of course. No woman could resist such a temptation."

"The shawl or me?"

Tom settled the shawl over her shoulders, and she breathed in his masculine scent, a potent combination of bay rum and something uniquely his own. Her knees trembled, and she wanted to tell the truth. Instead she laughed softly and didn't answer at all.

They strolled along the neatly raked paths through the bare garden for a few moments, Claire's hand resting comfortably on Tom's arm, her new silk shawl feeling like heaven on her bare flesh. She'd never owned anything so grand.

Tom drew them to a stop at a little stone bench. He covered her hand with his, and Claire felt a jitter of alarm. She quelled it, reminding herself that she had not misbehaved once tonight, that nothing in her present behavior or dress in any way reflected her past, and that Tom could not possibly misinterpret her actions. The night of the Artistic Evening she'd obviously been sending out lures. Since then she'd guarded her behavior meticulously. Nobody could possibly mistake her for a former medicine show shill.

"Claire," Tom said softly, looking down into her eyes in a way that made her spine turn to jelly, "that night when I kissed you, I realize I blundered badly."

She couldn't maintain his gaze. "Please, speak no more about it, Mr. Partington. We both blundered that evening. I assure you I've completely put it out of my mind." *Liar, liar,* her conscience said, taunting her.

"Well, that's more than I've been able to do."

Claire, surprised, looked up at him again.

"I haven't been able to think about much else."

Oh, dear. He hadn't come to the conclusion that she did that sort of thing all the time, had he? She'd been so circumspect recently, so extremely proper. She swallowed and didn't know what to say.

"In fact, I've been wanting to do it again ever since then but haven't wanted to scare you."

Thought fled. Claire, stunned, could only gape at him. He cupped her chin in his hand, and she gasped.

Then, in the absolute certainty that she couldn't escape her past if she lived to be a thousand, Claire burst into tears.

❧ 15 ❧

"**C**laire! Claire, for God's sake, what did I say?"
Tom felt helpless as he watched big, fat tears course down Claire's cheeks. Good God, he hadn't meant to upset her. She groped in her pocket, looking for a handkerchief, Tom supposed, so he snatched his out and shoved it at her.

"Here, use this. Claire, please speak to me. Tell me what's wrong? Are you upset because I want to kiss you?"

To his consternation she nodded.

"You are?" Oh, Lord. "But—but why, Claire? Didn't you enjoy our kiss?"

She nodded. Then she shook her head no. Then she wailed, "Oh, no!" and sobbed harder.

At last he gave up trying to talk to her and hugged her tightly, hoping at least to give her some measure of comfort until she calmed down enough to tell him what was wrong. She struggled against his hold for an instant, then collapsed in his arms and wept onto his coat. He angled his head to see where her tears were falling and sighed when he saw they were of course landing directly on the polished silk of his lapel. What the hell. He was rich; he guessed he could afford another evening jacket.

After a while he began to wonder if she'd ever stop crying. Gradually, however, he began to make out strangled words struggling for air amid the waterworks and listened carefully.

"I tried so hard," he thought she said. "I tried and tried and tried, but nothing I did could ever erase my miserable past. There's no denying it, and there's no running away from it. It's found me out at last."

Tom squinted, thinking furiously. Her miserable past? What the hell was she talking about? And what did it have to do with his wanting to kiss her?

"I knew I couldn't do it. You simply can't make a silk purse out of a sow's ear. I knew it! I knew it! Oh!"

A silk purse out of a sow's ear? Was she comparing herself with a sow's ear? Was she comparing *him* with a sow's ear? Cautiously Tom murmured, "Claire? Claire, what is it? Please tell me."

She shook her head violently, and he clutched her more tightly, fearing she might make a break for it. He wasn't about to let her go until she explained herself; he didn't care if it took from now until New Year's Day.

"It's all my fault," she moaned, "all my fault. If I hadn't flaunted myself, none of this would have happened."

Flaunted herself? Claire? Claire Montague? She of the prim brown gowns and rattlesnake tresses? Tom frowned. This was getting ridiculous. Ever so lightly he shook her.

"Claire. Claire, stop crying and listen to me. You must tell me what the matter is. Now." He used his brevet general voice, the one he'd used to keep fifteen- and sixteen-year-old recruits in line.

That voice had worked during the war, and it worked now. Claire's tears sniffled to a stop. She tried to step away from him, but he wouldn't let her, so she had to mop her eyes on his coat sleeve. Tom sighed, but he didn't mind.

"Now will you tell me why you're so upset, Claire, darling? I can't stand seeing you so upset."

She nodded, so he dared release her. While she blew her nose on his handkerchief, he guided her to the door that led to her office. He wanted to get out of the cold. Also, he didn't relish having an audience when he and Claire spoke, and he had a feeling Dianthe and Jedediah were probably still in the parlor, oblivious of their surroundings or the fact that all the other guests had departed.

Very tenderly he led her to an armchair and bade her sit. He pulled up the chair that usually resided in front of her desk. Sitting directly in front of her so she couldn't escape, he took up her hands.

Her nose was pink, and her eyes were swollen and red-rimmed. Her face looked pale except for a couple of hectic red splotches blooming on her cheeks. She was really a mess, and he had to squash the urge to hold her tightly and soothe her in his arms. Later, he told himself, after he'd discovered and dealt with the problem.

"Now, Claire," he said gently, "please tell me why you're so upset. Is it because I wanted to kiss you again?"

Apparently not trusting herself to speak yet, Claire nodded. Then she shook her head no. Then she moaned softly, and Tom stifled the urge to shake her until she came out with it. Why were females all so perverse?

When a fellow had a problem, he'd either tell you what it was or shut up about it. Why did females always have to dance around things so hard and so long?

Suppressing the unkind thought, he said, "Yes and no? You're going to have to make up your mind, Claire, because I can't read it for you, you know. I think I deserve to know why you're so upset. It hurts me to know that you don't want me to kiss you when I want to kiss you very badly."

Her head jerked up, and she looked at him in honest horror. "Oh, I'm so sorry!" Her voice sounded raw.

Tom cursed himself for being a blundering ass. "I didn't mean it that way, Claire. I'd never do anything to frighten you, at least not on purpose. I do want to kiss you, but not if it's going to hurt you like this."

Shaking her head miserably, Claire mumbled, "It's all my fault. All my fault."

His eyes narrowing in thought, Tom tried to make sense of the few clear snippets he'd heard Claire say in her distress. She'd said it was all her fault several times. She'd said something about silk purses and sow's ears. Had she said something about a bad background? He searched Claire's bowed head for clues.

"Look at me, Claire," he commanded very softly, nudging her under the chin with a bent finger.

After a moment she complied, and he studied her face hard, trying to read her emotions. He recognized distress; that was easy. He was sure he read fear in her eyes too. And was that shame? Was she ashamed of her behavior? But she hadn't done anything. Surely she couldn't blame herself for his kissing her. Could she? Leaning closer and examining her face very, very carefully, Tom guessed maybe she could.

"Claire, why do you think it's your fault that I kissed

you? For that matter, what's wrong with kissing? If a man and a woman care about each other, kissing seems a logical thing for them to do. At least it does to me."

"C-c-care about each other?" Her big brown eyes held a world of wonder.

He nodded. "I care about you anyway. I don't know what you think of me. Maybe you hate my guts. That's what it looks like from here."

"Oh, no, Mr. Partington, I could never hate you."

In spite of himself, Tom smiled. Claire's confession had sounded so pathetic. It thrilled him, though. *Yes!* he thought. He'd known she wasn't indifferent to him.

"I'm relieved to hear it. Now, will you please tell me what you think is your fault and why you consider my kisses so repulsive?" A dreadful thought struck him, and he felt his innards reel crazily. "Is there somebody else, Claire? Do you love another man?"

"Good grief, no!"

Tom's relief was so great he had to shut his eyes for a minute. "Good," he whispered. "Good."

"But—but I'm not that sort of female, Mr. Partington. Truly I'm not."

His eyes snapped open. "You're not what sort of female?"

She sucked in a big breath. "I'm not a hussy. Honestly I'm not. I know I must have given that impression, but I'm truly not. I've tried so terribly hard to be a lady. I— I've tried so hard."

Her last sentence wobbled badly at the end. Tom's mouth fell open in astonishment. "What?" he barked, too startled for finesse.

Claire's fingers tightened around his handkerchief, and she peered at them instead of at him. She had to blow her nose again. Tom continued to stare at her.

"Mr. Partington, I greatly fear my background is—is not very good. I'm afraid there are things in my past that are too painful for me to speak of, but please know that I've left all that behind me. For the past ten years I've striven to be a good person. I've tried so hard to become a woman of strong moral fiber and character, to be chaste and pure and good.

"And now I know I've failed! They say one can never overcome one's past, and I guess they were right because you obviously think of me as a—as a strumpet!"

Tom couldn't seem to shut his mouth. Nor could he speak.

Claire lifted her head and, big-eyed, watched him. She apparently drew the wrong conclusion from his thunderstruck expression. "But I'm not a strumpet! I'm not! At least I don't want to be! Oh, I'm so unhappy!"

Wrenching her hands from underneath his, Claire turned in the chair, folded herself into a knot around a cushion, and began crying again.

For several seconds Tom couldn't make himself do anything. He watched Claire weep as her amazing words spun through his brain. Claire? A strumpet? *Claire?* Good God. He shut his mouth with a snap and grabbed her by the shoulders. She tried to wrench away again, but he was too strong for her.

"Claire, look at me. Look at me, Claire."

She tugged. He pulled. She tugged again. He pulled again. Eventually she gave up and slumped in the chair, facing him, her head drooping as if it were too heavy for her to lift. He nudged her chin up once more.

"Claire, listen to me. I never, ever, ever thought of you as a strumpet, not by any stretch of the imagination."

She didn't believe him; he could tell.

"I have no idea why you think of yourself in such terms, but they're not true."

She still didn't believe him. Tom sighed and shook his head. Then he decided only the unvarnished truth would suffice, even though it seemed cruel to him. Eyeing Claire, he thought maybe she wouldn't think it cruel.

"When I first met you, I swear I thought you were a prim, stuffy old maid who'd never worn an improper gown or had an improper thought in her life. I took one look at you and thought you were boring, lifeless, and dull."

Her back straightened, and her chin went up all by itself.

"Whatever your background, you did such a good job of transforming yourself into a prudish housekeeper that it never even crossed my mind to think of you as anything else."

Her sweet lips parted slightly, and Tom eyed them with longing. He wouldn't kiss her yet, though. Not until they'd cleared this whole thing up.

"Do you believe me, Claire? I'm telling you the truth."

"I guess so."

"Good."

"But—but you kissed me."

"I sure did. And I want to do it again too."

Her brow wrinkled as she thought. "But—but why would you want to kiss me if I was dull? If you thought me plain and proper and practical."

"Because you see, Claire, you couldn't stop yourself from being you." He felt her stiffen in alarm and hurried on. "I don't mean that you, Claire Montague, are a trollop. I mean that you, Claire Montague, are a delightful, accomplished, amusing young woman with a charming personality and undeniable talents."

"I am?" She sounded utterly flabbergasted.

"You are."

After a pause long enough to make Tom wonder if he should try kissing her yet, Claire said, "You—you didn't think I was easy?"

"Easy?" With great effort Tom stopped himself from guffawing. He definitely did not want to hurt her feelings. "Claire, nobody in the entire world would ever believe you were easy."

She stared at him hard for almost a full minute before she shook her head and said, "But you kissed me."

"Well, of course I kissed you! I kissed you before, and I want to kiss you again!"

She looked at him reproachfully, as if he'd just confirmed everything she'd already told him and he'd just tried to deny. Tom scrambled to think of a way to explain what she obviously considered a paradox.

"Do you think every woman who is ever kissed by a man is loose? Do you think your friend Dianthe is loose?"

She shook her head. "Certainly not."

"Of course you don't, but Jed wants to kiss her. He may be doing it right now, in fact. Do you think Mrs. Humphry Albright is a strumpet?"

She shook her head again.

"Well, I distinctly saw Mr. Humphry Albright kiss his wife under the mistletoe this evening."

"Oh, well," Claire said with a gesture, "that's different. It's Christmas."

Tom snorted. "You can be blamed good and sure he doesn't wait a year between kisses, Claire. Don't you realize how foolish you're being? Men don't only kiss harlots or fallen women. They kiss women they care for. I care a lot about you, Claire Montague, and the desire to kiss a woman one cares about can be mighty blasted strong! Can't you understand that?"

Her mouth fell open, and her eyes went as round as billiard balls.

Tom jumped to his feet, so frustrated he wanted to punch something. He settled for running his hands through his hair and pacing. "Damn it, I'm not doing this right."

Claire stared at him. "You—you care for me? You? Care for *me*?"

He whirled around and glared at her. "Why do you find that so damned hard to understand, Claire?"

"But—but you're Tom Partington. You're a hero."

He snorted again and rolled his eyes. "Oh, for God's sake!"

"Why would you care for me?"

"Because you're everything I ever wanted in a woman and had begun to believe didn't exist. Because you're bright and talented and practical and can do things! Because you don't sit on your butt and expect the world to cater to you. Because you're lovely and sweet, and—and you grow flowers. Because you take care of this huge house and the garden and plan meals and entertainments and decorate for Christmas and don't simper and whine and expect the world to kowtow to you." He realized he'd begun to holler and took a deep breath. "Damn it all, Claire, I care about you because you're *you*!"

Claire blinked at him several times, and Tom held his breath. He hadn't meant to get mad.

She dropped her head again and seemed to stare at her fingers, once again tormenting his handkerchief. With a small frown she said, "I thought for sure you'd fall in love with Dianthe."

"Dianthe?" Tom cried incredulously.

"She's so lovely. She's beautiful and tiny, and she floats here and there, and she writes poetry and . . ." Her voice trailed off.

When she lifted her head, Tom realized she truly didn't understand his choice. He said, slowly and distinctly, because he didn't want her to misunderstand, "I think you are to be admired for your loyalty to your friend, Claire. And I know Jedediah Silver thinks the world of Miss St. Sauvre. Personally, however, I think she's got mice in her attic."

"Wh-what?"

"Her ace, king, and queen are missing. Her train got derailed. The squirrels ate her acorns."

"I beg your pardon?"

"Oh, God." Tom ran his fingers through his hair again and flung himself back down on the chair across from Claire. He swept her hands up in his. "Listen to me, Claire. I think it's wonderful that you set such a great store by your friends. Loyalty is another of the attributes I find extremely attractive in you. God knows, without the loyalty of my friends and mine for them, we'd none of us have survived when we scouted for the railroad. But Dianthe St. Sauvre is—is a pale imitation of the woman you are."

"She is?"

"She's nothing compared with you." He stood up again, his agitation propelling him. "What would a man want with a damned sonnet when he can have comfort, peace, and joy in his home? Why should a fellow want to watch some poet prancing around and chanting about spotted horses when he can have a woman who can offer sound suggestions to create a whole new business in breeding Appaloosas?"

Claire whispered, "Oh!" as if his words were a revelation to her.

He scowled at her. "Yes, 'oh!' What do you think a man like me would ever find enticing about a female who sits around all day and writes stupid poems?"

"You think her poems are stupid?"

"Well . . ." Tom waved a hand in the air. "Sort of. They're sort of—well—fluffy. If you know what I mean."

"You really think her poetry is fluffy?"

Her voice was very soft. Tom was afraid he'd gone too far. "I'm sorry, Claire. I know how much you value your friends. And it's not that I don't admire Miss St. Sauvre. I'm sure she's a good friend to you. And I have to admit she is pretty. I'm sorry I can't share your feelings about her poetry. I guess I haven't had much to do with poetry and stuff like that over the years."

"No, please don't apologize, Mr. Partington." She cleared her throat. "Do—do you really think her poetry lacks substance? Do you honestly think it's silly?"

"Well . . ." Tom tried to gauge Claire's emotional state but couldn't. He'd lived his life around rugged men. Female sensibilities—except those of ridiculous females like his mother—were as foreign to him as Gordon Partington's brandy had been his first night here. He decided to tell the truth. "Yes."

Time seemed to stand still for a moment as he looked at Claire and she looked at him. Then, in what seemed to Tom an explosion of blue sateen, Claire shot from her chair and into his arms like a bullet.

"Oh, Mr. Partington! Tom! How I do love you! How I've always loved you!"

Tom didn't have time to brace himself. When Claire plowed into him, his arms closed around her, and he staggered backward. He smiled when he fell onto the sofa, though. He smiled and laughed, and his heart was near to bursting with satisfaction. When he kissed her this time, he had her full cooperation.

Claire wasn't entirely sure she believed Tom's assertion that he cared for her. Nevertheless, he'd said such sweet things, had declared his fondness for her with such passion, and had said exactly what she had always wanted to hear about herself and never believed she would— particularly from Tom Partington—that she couldn't seem to help herself. He even considered Dianthe's poetry fluffy! She kissed him back with all the gusto she'd kept suppressed for the ten years since she'd left her father. She hadn't realized she was capable of such boldness.

When he let her go briefly, she experienced a momentary fear that he found her enthusiasm repugnant. She looked up and discovered, however, that he was merely removing his evening gloves. When he renewed his embrace, fire danced on her naked skin where his bare flesh touched hers.

"My God, Claire," he panted, and she feared yet again that she'd somehow done something wrong. Her worries faded when he continued. "You feel so damned good."

She whispered fiercely, "So do you, Tom. You feel good too." He growled like a wild beast, startling her. Then he seemed to lose control entirely and began to ravish her with his mouth and hands. Claire had never felt anything so exciting in her life.

He was like a man possessed. He nibbled her chin and her cheeks and her ears, nipping her earlobes and outlining her ears with his tongue. Claire, who'd never even dreamed kisses could be carried to such extremes of passion or be felt in such far-flung regions of the human anatomy, whimpered with delight.

His hands were those of a madman, stroking every inch of flesh they could find. When they ran out of bare skin, they started to uncover more, an activity that momentarily shocked the innocent Claire.

Tom said, "Please, Claire, please. I want you so much. I've never wanted a woman as much as I want you. I need to feel you." She relented.

A gentleman had never spoken to her thus. If anybody had asked her a mere hour earlier whether she believed she could inspire such ardor in a masculine breast, she'd have replied with an emphatic negative. She might even have laughed, albeit with regret. Yet here and now Tom Partington, the hero of her very life, was showing her in no uncertain terms how much he desired her. Claire was thrilled.

"I've dreamed of this, Claire," Tom said raggedly. "I've dreamed of holding you and feeling you and—and seeing you."

When he got to the "seeing you" part, the last button on Claire's bodice gave way, and it fell to her waist, her ribbon-tied spectacles hitting the floor with a clunk.

Claire gasped, "Oh!" when she found herself suddenly bared to Tom Partington's eager gaze. Well, perhaps she wasn't exactly bare—she still wore her chemise and corset—but she was barer than she'd ever been in front of a gentleman, ever. Tom was close enough for her to discern his avid expression. Suddenly her father's unkind remark about men's brains being in their breeches came to mind. She tried to cover herself with her arms, but Tom caught her wrists.

"Don't," he rasped. "You're beautiful, Claire. You're so damned beautiful."

She wished she could speak words as easily as she could write them. She was sure Miss Abigail Faithgood would have been able to say *something* in such a circumstance. On the other hand, Miss Abigail Faithgood might have screamed. Claire definitely did not feel like screaming.

She saw Tom swallow convulsively several times. Then he lifted his gaze from the swell of her nearly naked bosom and looked into her eyes.

"You're so damned beautiful, Claire. I want to make love to you, but I don't want to frighten you."

"Oh."

"I want to—to take you to my bed, Claire. I want you to say right here and now that you'll share my life and never leave me. If you ever left me, I don't know what I'd do or how I'd ever carry on. We belong together, Claire, you and I. Certainly you must be able to see that."

"W-we do?" she stuttered, but she didn't consider that much of an improvement over "oh."

He nodded fervently. "We do. I've never met a woman like you before. I didn't think you existed for me, Claire. I thought I'd live and die alone. Being with a woman on a long-term basis never entered my head until I met you."

"It didn't?" Claire frowned. Surely she could do better than this!

"No. Please say you'll let me make love to you, Claire."

"I—I—"

He didn't give her a chance to finish but wrapped her in his arms, squeezing her tightly against him. It was just as well. She had no idea what to say. His hands renewed their exploration, sending shock waves of feeling through her, as his words reverberated in her brain. He wanted to make love to her! Her!

His hands sought the twin swells above her corset, and Claire almost shrieked with the excitement of feeling his touch on her sensitive flesh. Her mind was of no use to her at all when he grabbed her corset hooks and began to unfasten them.

"Mercy," she whispered.

"Make love to me, Claire. Make love to me and make me the happiest man on earth. Please say you'll make love to me. If you do, I'll take care of you always, Claire. You said you love me. You meant it, didn't you?"

His head jerked up, and he stared at her for a second, his expression suddenly wary, as if he suspected her of having been merely humoring him. Claire thought it was about the sweetest expression she'd ever seen.

"Of course I love you," she whispered.

"Thank God! Then will you make love with me?"

He went back to nuzzling her flesh. When the last of her corset hooks came free, Claire breathed deeply. Then her breath left her in a whoosh when she felt Tom's hands cover her breasts.

She cried out softly at his touch, startled to her toes.

"Does that feel good, Claire? You feel good to me. You're perfect, Claire. Perfect. Oh, Lord, you're perfect."

Claire, who knew her breasts to be round and firm, although small, was shocked yet perversely proud to have her feminine attributes praised by the man she loved. Somehow she managed to say, "Y-yes. Yes, it feels good," and he growled again. She wondered if gentlemen growled frequently when in the throes of passion or if it was a characteristic borne of Tom Partington's life in the wilds of the American frontier. His growls gave her a goosefleshy, excited-all-over feeling.

There was something about what Tom was doing with her breasts, Claire realized, that was extremely thrilling. The sensation was not confined to her breasts either. She began to feel a tingling, physical anticipation in her body that made her want to squirm. She moaned softly, and her head fell back.

That seemed to excite Tom, who immediately accelerated his assault upon her bosom. When Claire felt his warm, moist tongue lave her rigid nipple through the fine lawn of her chemise, she was grateful she no longer wore her corset or she'd surely have fainted for want of air.

"Let me make love to you, Claire. Say you'll let me make love to you."

Claire wondered what he was doing if he wasn't making love to her. He seemed very insistent, and Claire, who had again lost track of the conversation, tried hard to pay attention to his words. To encourage him to explain himself, she whimpered, "Hmm?"

"I want to make love to you. Please let me, Claire."

"Oh, Tom," she murmured, delighted at having the matter cleared up.

"Is that a yes?"

"Hmm?" He cupped her breasts and buried his face against them. In a shockingly bold gesture she ran her fingers through his beautiful golden hair and pressed his head closer.

"Love me, Claire," came, muffled, from the region of her chest.

Love him. He wanted her to love him. He was asking her to fulfill her heart's most fervent desire and love him.

Claire didn't think she could be happier if she discovered she'd been kidnapped in her infancy and sold to the man who called himself her father.

Tom wanted her to love him. In spite of her background. In spite of her father. In spite of her having grown up in a medicine show. In spite of her being merely a housekeeper. Well, Claire acknowledged with a faint spurt of pride, not *merely* a housekeeper. She was a wildly successful novelist as well.

She sat up straight so abruptly that she sent Tom sliding from the sofa to land on the floor.

"Hey!" he cried.

Claire's hands, which so recently had caressed her lover's thick hair, flew to her cheeks and pressed hard. She cried, "Oh, no!" and stared at Tom in honest terror.

He looked up from his seat on the floor, his expression registering alarm. "Claire?"

"Tom!"

"Claire?"

"Oh, no!"

"Claire, what is it?"

"Good Lord!"

In a frenzy she gathered her sateen bodice together and jumped up from the sofa. She cried, "I'm so sorry!" Without even pausing to stick her hands through her little puffed sateen sleeves or draw her gown over her bosom, she snatched up her corset and ran from the room, her spectacles sailing out behind her on their blue satin ribbon like a banner. The ribbon got caught in the door when she slammed it, and she had to open it and yank her spectacles out. The door slammed again, and she was gone.

Tom stared after her. "Claire?"

But she had fled, and Tom found himself staring at the closed door, as uncommunicative an article of carpentry as he could imagine.

Then, with his heart breaking and his trousers about to burst, he dropped his head back onto a sofa seat and muttered, "Aw, hell."

❧ 16 ❧

He genuinely cared for her! Claire slammed the door to her room behind her, locked it, and threw her corset against the wall in a fit of pique. She collapsed onto her bed, her eyes open wide in wonder, and she realized he'd told her he really, honestly cared for her. Could it be true?

Her body still singing from his caresses, Claire allowed her head to fall back as she sighed. What she wouldn't give to be able to live the last several weeks of her life over again. She wasn't exactly sure what she would have done differently, but she most assuredly would not have entangled herself in a snare of lies and deceit.

How could she get out of it now? How could she confess to being Clarence McTeague, the writer whose *Tuscaloosa Tom Pardee* books Tom claimed had made his life miserable for years?

He hadn't seemed to think Claire was behaving like a strumpet, even though he'd still wanted to kiss her. That was some sort of—of progress, she guessed. He'd explained carefully that gentlemen often wanted to kiss ladies who were not loose, even though those women weren't beautiful.

Thinking about it, Claire decided his explanation made sense. How else could one explain the world's ever-increasing population? After all, very few women were truly beautiful yet men still seemed to want to kiss them. In Tom's case his evident desire for her also indicated that he was both large-minded and benevolent. Her lack of beauty, though, however much she might regret it, hadn't exposed Tom Partington to ridicule. Her books, according to him, had, and Claire didn't expect he was making that up.

"What have I done?" she muttered, staring at her ceiling and seeing Tom's beloved face looking back in disapproval.

Tom sat on the floor in a state of intense frustration and absolute befuddlement for several minutes. At last, deciding he couldn't remain there all night pondering the mysteries of women, he got to his feet.

"Hell," he muttered, his unhappy gaze still focused on the closed door.

He didn't understand Claire's latest flight at all. Not one little bit. What in the name of God could possibly have spooked her this time? Things had seemed to be going so well there for a while. He should have known it wouldn't last. It never lasted with Claire.

But why? He slammed his fist down hard on her desk.

"Ow!" He glared at the desk as if it had leaped up and attacked him rather than having been the recipient of his own assault. His eyes narrowed as he recalled an earlier meeting with Claire, one in which she'd also become rattled when he'd displayed his interest in her.

He walked slowly around her desk and sat in her chair.

It made him feel not quite so removed from her to be sitting where he'd so often seen her sit.

She always looked perfect here, performing her duties in the businesslike and professional way she had about her. He admired those qualities. He'd seldom found them in men, much less in women, who seemed to be trained from the cradle in the art of silliness. Not Claire, though. There wasn't a silly bone in her slim, luscious, elegant body. Tapping his chin thoughtfully, he cast his mind back to their first kiss.

She'd been upset then too. Tom believed now, however, that some problem in her youth, perhaps something about which she felt a secret shame, had been the culprit. Whatever it was, it must have happened a long time ago. Her reputation since her arrival at Partington Place was absolutely spotless, and she'd been here for ten years. He didn't think she was much older than twenty-six or twenty-seven.

So whatever it was must have happened when she was very young. His fists curled in frustration. Damn. Whatever it was that plagued her, he was sure that portly gentleman from three weeks ago had something to do with it. Tom hadn't been able to find him again even though he'd gone to town to look. But the fellow had left Pyrite Springs, according to Bruce Bing, the day after he and Tom had sat up so late chatting.

Damn, damn, damn. Somehow Tom knew that man was the key. He wished he were here now so Tom could beat the truth out of him. Whoever that man was, he'd done something to Claire to make her feel she wasn't good enough, that she had to work harder and behave even more properly than most women in order to be worth the space she took up. Good God, if most of the men Tom knew felt that way, the world would be another Eden.

But poor Claire. She'd thought she'd somehow enticed Tom into behaving in an ungentlemanly manner.

In spite of his present state of disappointment and confusion, Tom chuckled. As if Claire Montague's demeanor could in any way be considered seductive. He frowned, remembering her tearful disclosure this evening.

Poor Claire. In his wildest imagination he couldn't picture her setting out deliberately to seduce anybody. Her nature was too naturally refined, her character too perfectly pure.

A thought struck him, and he sat up. Maybe that portly gentleman had seduced Claire and then blamed her for it! He'd read stories about girls seduced and abandoned, of girls lured into intimacies and then denounced by their seducers. Why, just think about poor Hester and her scarlet *A*. Or Clarissa. She'd stood firm in the face of everything that damned rake Lovelace had done to her, and who had died in the end? It sure as hell wasn't Lovelace. In fact, Claire's story was as old as the Bible.

That mustachioed gent was certainly a smooth enough operator to be such a villain. Tom wished he could remember some of the fellow's stories. They might give him a clue. His memory of the evening was unfortunately a little fuzzy. He wondered if Claire would ever admit to having been seduced and abandoned.

Tom wished he'd suspected about Claire's unhappy love affair when he'd been drinking with that shifty old charlatan. He'd have given him an earful. Maybe a gutful and a jawful too. Tom kneaded his knuckles in anticipation.

After sitting at Claire's desk and wallowing in his black musings for a good half hour, Tom finally stopped trying to make sense of things. Until Claire came to trust him, he'd never know why she got so skittish every time he tried to demonstrate his affection. His heart heavy, he dragged himself from her office and trudged up the stairs. He paused in front of her bedroom door, contemplating knocking and asking admittance.

After only a very few seconds he realized he wouldn't be able to chat coherently tonight, even if she were to answer his knock, as was unlikely. Seeing her again would just sharpen appetites better left unwhetted until they solved their problems. Whatever they were. With a sigh Tom dragged himself to his room.

Right before he drifted off to sleep, he determined to prove to Claire that he was the only man in the world for her. By fair means or foul, he aimed to have her. If that meant lulling her into complacency, weakening her with charm, and softening her up for the strike—much in the way he used to stalk game on the prairie—so be it.

He realized that in a few short weeks his goals in life had undergone a subtle change. Before his arrival at Partington Place, all he'd wanted was his horse ranch and enough money for comfort. Now the notion of achieving those same aims without Claire at his side made his blood run cold and his heart pound with dread. He couldn't let her go. He wouldn't let her go.

It was a wonder to Claire that breakfast on Christmas morning was not more strained. After all, she'd made a fool of herself—again—last night, when she'd run away from Tom.

He was in a jovial mood, however, and kept the conversation light. Since Jedediah Silver seemed lost in a romantic fog, Claire could only bless Tom for his savoir-faire, his light touch on a day that might have been nerve-racking if dealt with less adroitly.

How she loved him! Overnight she'd toyed with the idea of confessing her dastardly deed. After all, he'd told her he cared for her. Surely he wouldn't hate her just because she'd made a mistake and written those wretched novels.

Yes. With an aching heart she acknowledged that Tuscaloosa Tom Pardee had been a mistake. Those books had been a labor of misguided love, nothing more, nothing less. If Claire had possessed the slightest inkling that Tom would be embarrassed by them, she would not have written them. She would have been awfully disappointed, of course, but she wouldn't have written them.

All that was beside the point, however. She had written them and in doing so had hurt him.

Seeing him here now, though, his blue eyes sparkling with friendship and Christmas cheer, she knew she couldn't do it. Not today. In her present state of anxiety, watching the affection in his eyes turn to contempt and distaste would kill her. Claire resolved to put her mind to the problem later when she would certainly have overcome the worst of her nervousness. She applied herself instead to being a satisfactory Christmas companion.

After breakfast Tom visited the staff of Partington Place, gave each a very nice present and a Christmas bonus, and allowed them the rest of the day off. Then he asked Claire if she'd like to go horseback riding with him.

"When I saw Miss Thelma in town, she said you'd picked up your new riding habit."

Claire felt her cheeks get hot with pleasure and trepidation. "Well . . . are you certain you want me to go with you? I'm sure you'd have a better ride if a more accomplished horseman accompanied you."

"Ah, but I wouldn't have the pleasure of your company, though, would I, Claire? It's your company I want."

Immeasurably reassured by his words, Claire flushed hotter. "In that case I'd be delighted to ride with you. Or, rather, to have a riding lesson. For you do understand that I've never ridden a horse before." She didn't suppose the one time Charley Prince, the animal trainer at the circus, led her around the ring counted.

"Good." Tom rubbed his hands together. "Hurry then. I want to teach you all about horses, Claire, my sweet.

Claire, my sweet. Tom's honeyed words curled through Claire like fragrant steam.

The winter day sparkled around them, the air crisp and clean, the glorious Sierra Nevada rising in the distance to frame the day with grandeur. Clouds that looked as though somebody had whipped them with a fork piled high in the deep blue sky like meringue on one of Mrs. Philpott's lemon pies.

The horses, Tom assured Claire, were sluggish shadows of his favored Appaloosas but would be adequate for Claire to begin with.

"If they're slow and sleepy, so much the better," Claire murmured uneasily, looking down from her perch on the animal's back. It seemed a very long way to the ground.

Tom chuckled but assured her, "You'll do fine, Claire. As long as you understand that as soon as I get my ranch started, I'm going to get you the prettiest, liveliest little mare you can imagine."

"Really?" she said with some concern, but he only laughed again.

He went on about Appaloosas for several minutes, and soon Claire forgot to be afraid and devoured his words like candy. She longed to help him make his business succeed. She knew she could be a help to him too. Why, Gordon Partington used to tell her all the time that her ability with record keeping and business accounts was what kept him afloat. Of course he'd been exaggerating, but Claire did know she had a good head for business.

As she listened to Tom talk, she realized he was a solid businessman too, and her heart was happy. He was everything she'd ever wanted in a gentleman, just as he'd said she was everything he'd ever wanted in a lady. It still didn't seem possible he could have meant those words.

The specter of Tuscaloosa Tom Pardee reared its handsome head and drove her happiness away for a moment, but happiness has a buoyant quality and soon bounced back. Somehow, some way, Claire would think of something. "Something," a vague word, didn't lie quietly in the grave to which she consigned it. Nevertheless, she covered it up and determined to think about her problems later.

"I'm sorry, Claire," Tom said after a few minutes. "I didn't mean to bore you to death with my dreams."

"Your dreams aren't boring at all, Tom. I think they're wonderful. All my life I have yearned to be part of something permanent, to have something of my own. I don't blame you for dreaming about creating your own business."

She felt uneasy when Tom's gaze searched her face as if he craved answers to questions she hoped he wouldn't ask. She should have known better.

"What is it, Claire? What is it about yourself you aren't

telling me? Are you afraid I'll disparage you if you tell me you've made mistakes in your life? I won't, you know. I've made plenty of my own."

Claire concentrated very hard on the knee she had hooked around her saddle's leaping tree. She had to tell him. She couldn't tell him. She had to. She couldn't.

All of a sudden her brain fastened on her childhood. Her childhood was sordid and ugly, but while her books were her fault, her childhood wasn't. She cleared her throat. "Actually it's my background," she whispered nervously. "I'm afraid my origins were—were not at all refined."

He chuckled, and she glanced at him quickly. "You can't mean to tell me you're worried about having less than perfect origins, can you? If you are, just take a long look at my background. The only thing refined about me is my name, and that's elegant only if you live in Tuscaloosa, and then only historically. I'm afraid my parents managed to fritter away everything we ever had."

"No!" She was shocked.

"Oh, but yes. My mother and father are about the most ridiculous, flighty human beings the world has ever known. I expect my uncle Gordon never told you that part about my family, did he?"

"Good heavens, no."

"There. See? We're even."

She tore her gaze away from his dear face. "No. I don't think we're even, Tom. My own background is—is even less refined than that, I'm afraid. We were—we were terribly poor and traveled from place to place because we had no home. Our life was—was very uncomfortable."

With a funny little lopsided smile Tom said, "Mine was uncomfortable too, Claire, trust me. Half the time my folks couldn't even afford firewood. Neither one of them would ever stoop to chopping it themselves, of course."

"My land, I had no idea."

"Of course not. Uncle Gordon knew my mother in her silly girlhood; I don't think he realized she grew up to be an equally silly adult. My father was even worse."

"Oh, dear."

"But our parents aren't our fault, Claire. And if you think our childhoods were uncomfortable, you should have been along during my years with the railroad. You haven't lived uncomfortably until you've camped by a frozen stream without even a tree or a rock to break the wind whipping down from the poles."

Claire's grim mood began to lighten. She loved to hear about Tom's breathtaking adventures, and she couldn't wait to shift the topic of conversation away from herself.

"Good heavens." She shivered in spite of her warm serge riding habit.

Neither of them spoke for a minute. Then Tom said with a chuckle, "That might be an interesting plot for one of those *Tuscaloosa Tom* novels. You know, the flat prairie, the frozen stream, and the wind and all."

Claire, who had not thought about the *Tuscaloosa Tom* books for three or four blissful minutes, frowned. Tom was right, though, and she found herself filing the knowledge away, even though she didn't plan to write another *Tuscaloosa Tom* novel after she'd fulfilled her contract. She said with a fair show of lightness, "Too bad Clarence McTeague isn't with us."

"Yes. I'd like to have a chat with him, believe me."

Tom's sour tone seemed to drive the sun from the sky in Claire's world for a moment or two.

Then he sighed and said, "I meant what I said last night, Claire. I care for you and would be the happiest man on earth if you'd agree to an alliance with me."

Claire jerked the reins, and her horse protested. Tom reached over to settle it down again. She appreciated his concern.

An "alliance"? That meant he wanted her to be his mistress, she supposed. Well, he'd said as much last night.

"I won't press you, Claire. I—well, I know something's troubling you, and I wish you'd confide in me. You must know I'd never, ever hold anything in your past against you. What happened before we met is all over with. You've overcome whatever it is and become the woman I care about very much."

"Thank you, Tom," Claire whispered shakily. A little sadly, she wondered if she were simply not the sort of woman men married. Probably.

He took a deep breath and then blurted out, as if he could read her mind, "I suppose I should offer you marriage, but I—I can't do it. The only marriages I've ever seen have been like prison sentences. I can't do it."

His honesty caught her completely off guard. Her heart flipped over, and she opened her mouth, but nothing came out.

"I know I've botched things up by being too hasty. I'm sorry, Claire. You have some idea that I'm a grand southern gentleman, but the truth is I've been living like a heathen for fifteen years. I hardly remember all the things my mother used to try to teach me about polite behavior."

Looking into his handsome face, Claire realized he meant what he was saying. His frankness had shaken her, though, and oddly cheered her. She shook her head.

"You're a wonderful gentleman, Tom. You have a natural talent for the social graces, I guess, because you're—you're perfect."

He looked astounded by her assessment. "Good God. Do you really think so? My mother would be thrilled to hear you say it."

He smiled one of his glorious smiles, and Claire's breath snagged in her chest. "Any mother would be thrilled to have you as a son."

Tom snorted. "I'll have to tell you more about my family one of these days, Claire. I know it's disloyal to say so, but it's true. I've never met two more useless human beings than my parents."

"I'm sorry, Tom."

Apparently deciding the topic of parents was too glum for Christmas morning, Tom continued. "And don't forget that you can always talk to me, Claire. You can tell me anything. There's nothing you ever need fear from me."

His expression was so sincere, his eyes so somber, and his affection so evident that Claire began to weaken. If he could overlook the wretchedness of her past, perhaps he could forgive her for making a mistake and writing those books. He seemed to understand human foibles better than most people. Perhaps she could confess. Perhaps he would understand that she'd written her books out of love and had no idea they would hurt him.

"Um, Tom, I think it's very kind that you're not holding my humble origins against me."

"Good grief, Claire, a person can't be held accountable for his or her origins. Life's hard enough already. If we were expected to be responsible for our parents' faults as well as our own, we'd all be in the soup."

It was an effort, but she maintained her smile. "So—

so do you think people should be forgiven for making mistakes?"

"Depends on the mistake, I reckon."

Pretending to concentrate on guiding her horse around a dip in the grassy field, Claire said, "Well, I mean, if somebody did something in the misguided belief that he was doing a good thing and it turned out that it actually hurt the person it was intended to help, so you think that person could be forgiven?"

"I'm not sure I understand."

"Well—well, I mean, take Clarence McTeague, for example."

"I'd rather not, thank you."

Somewhat daunted, Claire cleared her throat and fumbled on. "Well, I mean, I'm sure Mr. McTeague meant his books as a—as an homage to you, if you know what I mean. I'm sure he didn't mean to upset you. I'm sure he had no idea you'd be inconvenienced or embarrassed by them."

"You're sure of that, are you?"

"Well, yes, I believe so."

"You were really fond of my uncle, weren't you, Claire?" Tom said softly. "I guess I can understand that, given your wandering childhood and all."

She wished he didn't think his uncle had written those books. It complicated things so. "Why are you so certain the late Mr. Partington wrote the books?"

With a shrug Tom asked, "Who else could have done it, Claire? Those books included incidents nobody else except my parents could have known about, and I know they didn't write them because they'd never expend so much effort on anything. I can't imagine them tackling something as time-consuming and difficult as novel writing."

"I see." Oh, dear heaven. "Your uncle was a wonderful man, Tom. He'd never have done anything to hurt you. He looked upon you as a hero. We all did. The *Tuscaloosa Tom* novels—whoever wrote them—were written by somebody who meant to honor you, not cause you misery."

With a laugh Tom said, "Yes, I know how much you like those books, Claire. It's one of the few topics about which I disagree with you."

"But if I'm right, don't you think you're being a little hard on poor Mr. McTeague, whoever he is—was."

Tom snorted again. "From what I hear, he's not poor at all." A smile broke across his face like the sun breaking through clouds. "Oh, all right, Claire. I'm absolutely certain my uncle meant no harm when he wrote those damned books. There. Are you happy now?"

Claire digested his words for a few seconds. She wished she weren't so dreadfully anxious. If her heart wasn't thundering and her brain shrieking, she was sure she'd be able to use her normally sound judgment to construct an appropriate confession.

But she was anxious, and her brain was shrieking, and if her judgment proved faulty, her whole future was in jeopardy. Yet she couldn't go on deceiving Tom; she knew that too. Throwing caution to the wind, she took a deep breath and opened her mouth to speak.

"Claire! Mr. Partington! Merry Christmas!"

The happy greeting surprised Claire into clamping her mouth shut. Daring to turn slightly in her saddle, she beheld Priscilla Pringle galloping toward them on a striking bay gelding, Sylvester Addison-Addison hard at her heels.

"Looks like we have company," Tom murmured.

She turned to find him smiling happily, and Claire

thrust her own problems aside. This was Christmas morning. She was riding next to the man she loved and, what's more, a man who claimed to care for her. She should be happy.

Consigning Clarence McTeague, Tuscaloosa Tom Pardee, and the poor deceased Gordon Partington to a corner of her mind, Claire felt a swell of contentment. She grinned when she realized the clever widow Pringle had provided Sylvester with a horse as black as soot, and mentally applauded her. The horse flattered Sylvester's darkly tortured poetic looks admirably.

Apparently Tom recognized the widow's tactics too because he said softly, "Looks like Mrs. Pringle's determined to woo the Author in a way he'll understand."

Claire giggled. "Now, now, Tom."

Out of the corner of his mouth he added, "I just hope she'll be happy with the bargain when she's got him snared. How'd you like to have him brooding over his coffee across the table from you every morning of your life?"

"That won't happen. Sylvester never partakes of breakfast. He consorts with his muse until all hours and seldom rises before noon, you see."

"Oh, my God."

Tom's expression was comically pained, and suddenly Claire felt bright and gay. She giggled again and called out a cheery "Merry Christmas, Priscilla! Merry Christmas, Sylvester!"

Priscilla's trilling laugh ornamented the brisk morning air. Sylvester scowled, and Claire was certain she heard him snarl a "bah!"

Not even Sylvester Addison-Addison could dampen her mood now, though. She and Tom exchanged a speaking look. Tom gave her a wink, reached for her hand, and briefly squeezed it. Claire didn't think she could get much happier.

Sylvester and Priscilla reined in their horses, and the two couples exchanged greetings and continued their ride as a foursome. Priscilla chattered away like a magpie, Claire smiled and added a murmured comment here and there, and Tom smiled graciously. Sylvester glowered at the scenery as if trying to ignore company he considered beneath him.

"Such a delightful party last night, Claire. Mr. Partington, I do believe your Christmas Eve entertainment was the grandest we've ever seen at Partington Place. I'm thrilled that you decided to continue the tradition."

"It was all Claire's idea, Mrs. Pringle."

"Bah!" said Sylvester.

"But it could never have happened without you, Tom. You're the one who was the inspiration for the evening." Claire smiled at Tom, who smiled back.

"I'm sure you're right, Claire, dear. Why, I told my darling Sylvester just this morning that the late Mr. Partington would have been thrilled to see how lovely the Place is these days." Priscilla smiled radiantly at Sylvester.

"Bah!" said Sylvester.

Priscilla laughed again, a gay, unrestrained laugh that amazed Claire, who would have been intimidated by so many of Sylvester's bahs. Not the jolly widow, who seemed oblivious to her companion's surliness.

"And will you maintain the tradition of Partington Place's Spring Open House as well, Mr. Partington?" Priscilla asked. "Claire has created the loveliest gardens anywhere around."

"A Spring Open House sounds fine to me, Mrs. Pringle. Claire," Tom announced with a telling look for her, "can do anything. She's absolutely superb, you know."

Claire blushed hotly.

Mrs. Pringle laughed with enjoyment.

Tom invited Priscilla and Sylvester to join him, Claire, and Jedediah for supper that evening. Dianthe joined them too, effectively bringing Jedediah back into the realm of the living. Claire and Dianthe prepared the meal, using leftovers from their Christmas Eve repast, which had been stored in Partington Place's specially fitted icebox.

The happy party sang Christmas carols far into the night. A light snow began to fall soon after supper, but nobody inside Partington Place cared. A fire blazed merrily in the huge fireplace, and Claire noticed with pleasure the significant looks passing between Dianthe and Jedediah.

Now that she knew Tom did not fancy Dianthe, she allowed herself to be happy for the couple. She also noticed Mrs. Pringle and Sylvester holding hands, although the widow looked more cheerful about it than the Author did.

As for herself, she was certain the way Tom kept smiling at her could have kept her warm if the weather had been ten times as cold.

❧ 17 ❧

Tunes swirled in Claire's head, and she forgot her usual reserve so far as to dance around the tiled foyer of Partington Place after the last guest had left. Jedediah was seeing Dianthe home, and Claire decided that tonight had been as close to perfect as a night could get. She felt free and happy and knew she was in love with a man who cared for her. If life wasn't perfect, if Tom couldn't ever really love her, if there were unresolved issues lurking in dark corners that might resurface to ruin her happiness later, at least she would have tonight.

Laughing, Tom swept her into his arms and danced with her. "Are you happy, sweetheart?"

"I don't think I've ever had such a wonderful Christmas!"

"Me neither."

"Thank you so much."

"For what?"

"For what? Why, for everything!"

Tom stopped waltzing but didn't remove his arms. He

held Claire loosely around the waist and gazed down into her eyes. Looking back at him, Claire was glad she'd removed her spectacles. Without them to clarify her world, Tom's face was a delicious blur. If she'd been able to see him clearly, she was sure she'd have become nervous. As it was, her heart sped up inexplicably.

"You needn't thank me for anything, Claire. You're the one who does the work that makes these occasions special. You're the one who plans and prepares everything. All I add is money, and as glad as I am to have it, you've taught me in a very few weeks how little good money is without talent and goodwill behind it."

"What a sweet thing to say! Thank you, Tom."

"Thank you, Claire."

His face was becoming clearer. Claire blinked when she realized this phenomenon was caused by his leaning closer to her. Her speeding heart executed an alarming athletic maneuver, and a crazy hope stirred within her.

Mercy, was he going to kiss her again? If he was, she swore she wouldn't run away this time. No matter what came of it, she wouldn't run away. Tonight, as everyone said, would be the night. He knew the worst—well, almost the worst—of her already; she had nothing to fear. The thought of being loved by him, the way a man loved a woman, almost made her knees buckle with longing.

Tonight the embraces between a man and a woman did not seem lewd to Claire. Tom's embraces were nothing like those she'd witnessed in her childhood because they were motivated by affection. What transpired between a man and a woman was sordid only if it was undertaken in a spirit of animal passion. The snide, cynical, lustful passions of a man like her father bore no resemblance to the sweet desire Tom stirred in Claire.

So she watched his face come closer with great anticipation. When he murmured, "I want you so much, Claire. I want you so damned much," her heart soared. She met his lips with hers and sighed in rapture.

Tom vowed to himself he wouldn't let her get away tonight. Tonight he was going to claim this woman and make her his beyond the shadow of any doubt. She was his, and he planned to prove it to her in no uncertain terms. She met his embrace so eagerly that he wondered if she had the same idea. He sure as hell hoped so.

Very gently, taking infinite care, he softened his lips and kissed her sweetly, praying with every heartbeat that she wouldn't resist. She didn't seem to be resisting. In fact, his eyes popped open when, after her initial sigh of surrender, she flung her arms around him and pressed her body against his.

"Claire?"

"I do love you, Tom!"

Her words were music to his ears, and he renewed his kiss with more vigor. He planned to take all the time she needed, though. He told himself to go slowly so as not to spook her. He wasn't sure he could endure another disappointment.

He felt her fingers slide into his hair and her foot rub his calf and almost lost control of himself. She certainly didn't seem to be feeling shy any longer.

His hands began to roam her silky skin as far up her arms as he could reach. He wished civilized females didn't feel compelled to wear so many damned clothes. This evening Claire had dressed in a simple woolen frock. The dress material was soft and supple, but underneath it there were so many barriers, some of which relied on whalebone to keep their shape, that Tom couldn't feel the softness of her sleek, elegant body. Slowly, slowly he explored in spite of the barriers.

Until he felt her trembling fingers fumble with the buttons on his jacket. Then he tossed caution to the winds and let his hands travel to her delightfully round derriere.

"Tom!" she cried.

A little worried, Tom looked at her. She wasn't scared. She looked delighted. Encouraged, he shut his eyes again and pressed her bottom. She caught on immediately, and Tom growled when he felt her get up on her tiptoes so she could feel his hardness against the juncture of her thighs.

"Please love me tonight, Tom."

Tom was sure that in the heat of his own desire he had misunderstood her. He gasped, "What?"

Smiling up at him, Claire discovered happily that all her inhibitions had disappeared. All she cared about tonight was learning what Tom's hands felt like on her naked flesh. All she cared about was feeling him kiss her. She felt beautiful for the first time in her life; she felt alive and vibrant, and she didn't care that tomorrow she'd be plain Claire Montague again. This man wanted her; he cared for her; tonight she even believed it.

"Love me, darling. Take me to your bed, take me anywhere, and love me, Tom. Please love me."

She saw his beautiful eyes open wide. She saw them shut. He groaned. Then, in a move so swift it made Claire squeal, he swept her off her feet and walked her straight to the stairs. As she rested her head on his wonderfully broad shoulder, she allowed herself a moment of amazement that he should be so strong and good and noble. He was going to make her his, to teach her the art of love, to show her what all the fuss was about.

Her toes curled, and she fought a giggle of anticipation. She wished she could use this new experience in one of her novels. Immediately she realized she must cease thinking about her novels if she expected to enjoy herself. And she *would* enjoy herself. Defiantly Claire clung to Tom, knowing that her life would change forever tonight, and glad of it. She would become his mistress, a delightfully wicked prospect.

No more would she be prim Claire Montague, housekeeper, who hid a sordid past behind a prudish facade and yearned for love and excitement. Tonight she would be loved for a certainty—and by the very man for whose love she'd longed these many years.

If he found he didn't care for her after her secret was out, if this episode was as painful as she'd heard it could be the first time, if she never experienced Tom's love again, at least she would cherish the memory of tonight.

She felt a thrill when Tom swept her past her room and down the hall to his. He was taking her to his own bed! For some reason his decision made her heart glow; it seemed somehow a confirmation that in some way he truly did care for her and wanted her in his life forever.

Not, of course, that Tom Partington was capable of wheedling a female into his bed with false promises. No indeed. Such despicable tactics were the tools of men like her father. Tom Partington would never do such a base and deceitful thing.

The door to his room opened with a crash since Tom was too preoccupied for subtlety. He growled, "Are you sure, Claire? Are you absolutely sure? I've wanted you for so long I'll never be able to stop unless you tell me now."

"I'm sure, Tom," Claire whispered.

It occurred to her what a nice thing Tom had just said to her. She understood that gentlemen in the throes of passion often made extravagant declarations. Still, Claire had never dared even dream that a gentleman would say an extravagant thing to her.

She whispered, "I love you, Tom," because it was the truth and her heart was full.

"Oh, God, Claire." Tom's voice sounded ragged as he dropped her on the bed. She bounced on the soft mattress and stared up at him.

"May I see you, Claire?" he asked shakily. "May I see your beautiful body? I've dreamed of it, Claire. I know you probably think it shocking of me, but you're so beautiful, you're so elegant and regal and wonderful. I want to see you."

He wanted to see her. Her! Skinny Claire. He thought she was elegant and regal. Her heart so full she could barely speak, Claire whispered, "Oh, yes, Tom. I want to see you too."

He obliged with such alacrity Claire was left gasping in amazement. She hadn't known one could shed one's clothing so swiftly. In a second or two Tom stood beside the bed, naked. She blinked rapidly several times, stunned, staring at the spectacular maleness of him.

"Mercy," she murmured, glad yet again she was not wearing her spectacles. She wasn't sure she could survive this much magnificence clearly delineated.

"I didn't mean to shock you, Claire." Tom sounded contrite.

"No. I'm not shocked," she lied. "You're just so—so beautiful." That part wasn't a lie. She'd never seen anything as awe-inspiring as Tom Partington in the buff, even if he did look fuzzy. Her myopic gaze raked his body. His shoulders were broad and muscled. She'd never seen such muscles. His arms were hard and corded with sinew. His chest rippled under a feathering of light brown hair that glimmered like gold in the candlelight.

She skipped over the part between his lean belly and his thighs and began her survey again from his toes, which resided at the end of long, well-shaped feet. Until this minute Claire never would have guessed feet could be exciting. His calves bulged with muscle—Claire hadn't realized how phenomenally well developed Tom was under the elegant city clothes he always wore—and his thighs did too. She saw dreadful scars on his legs and didn't wonder that he sometimes limped.

At last she dared peek at his maleness. "Good heavens!"

"Are you frightened, Claire?"

She noticed he had his fists clenched tightly at his thighs, as if restraining himself with an effort.

"N-no," she said, "I'm not frightened. Exactly. It's just all so new to me."

She saw him swallow and decided she shouldn't prolong his agony any longer. As he watched, she unbuttoned her soft woolen gown. His eyes grew round, and she felt herself blush even as his passion emboldened her. She flung her bodice open, ripped the gown from her shoulders, and lifted her hips to wriggle it down her legs.

Tom groaned.

Getting into the spirit, Claire unfastened her corset hooks and flung the instrument of torture to the floor, staring at Tom all the while. When she lay before him clad only in her camisole and drawers, she smiled. Very slowly she began to untie her camisole.

The provocative gesture seemed to jolt Tom out of his stupor. With a growl of pure lust he flung himself onto the bed next to her and took over the chore Claire had begun. Claire's eyes drifted shut when she felt his hands on parts of her body she'd never even felt herself except in the bath.

Tom's hands lit a fire within her, and his lips fanned it into an inferno. By the time he took one small, rigidly peaked breast into his mouth and began stroking her inner thigh, Claire was certain she would explode.

"That's right, Claire, darling. That's right. I want it to be good for you." His exploring fingers found the damp, hot seat of Claire's passion, and she uttered a muffled shriek and arched her hips.

"Yes," Tom whispered. "Oh, yes, Claire. You're so beautiful. So beautiful."

His hoarse, sweet words coaxed Claire to abandon herself completely in her quest to sate the pressure building within her. When release came, it did so swiftly and powerfully. Claire gasped, "Tom!" and she was gone in a paroxysm of small convulsions.

Claire's reason remained suspended for a terribly long time. When she finally became aware of her surroundings again, she discovered herself being held and caressed by Tom with the utmost tenderness. Her eyes fluttered open to behold his dear face smiling at her.

Her mouth was dry, and her body felt limp. She managed to mouth, "Mercy sakes," but it was an effort.

"That was the most beautiful thing I've ever seen, Claire," Tom whispered. "I hope this won't hurt you too much."

Hurt? He hoped what wouldn't hurt? From what seemed a great distance Claire realized Tom was positioning himself over her. When she felt his maleness prod her intimately, she remembered. Ah, yes, this was the part that was supposed to hurt. She smiled. She was ready; she didn't care. After what Tom had just done for her, Claire figured she could stand anything.

With one powerful stroke, he entered her. And she

still figured she could stand anything as long as she kept her teeth clenched.

"I'm sorry, Claire," Tom ground out. "I'm sorry, darling. I'll never hurt you again."

Daring to open her eyes, Claire realized it was taking a great deal of restraint on Tom's part to keep from moving now that he'd broken through her barrier. She managed a smile and said, "Please, Tom. I love you. It doesn't hurt," and knew she'd said the right thing when his countenance lost some of its rigidity.

Oddly enough, after a moment or two the pain began to subside. As Tom started to move within her and she realized how much pleasure he was taking from the act, she got caught up in it again herself. By the time he surged into her, roared his release, and collapsed on top of her, she was really quite enthralled, so enthralled indeed that she was almost disappointed that it had ended so soon.

There would be other times, though, she thought rapturously. There would be many, many other times.

The day after Christmas dawned crisp and clean and with a sprinkle of snow covering the landscape. When Claire awakened, she discovered herself in an intimate embrace with the man she loved and staring at a beautiful view outside his window, the curtains to which were drawn back. The sun sparkled on snowy fields like diamonds, and the fields seemed to stretch into infinity. The sky was as blue as Tom Partington's eyes, and Claire was sure she'd never be this happy again. It was a dead sure certainty that she'd never been this happy before.

"Good morning," a gravelly voice whispered in her ear. She felt Tom's breath fan her cheek, and a thrill shot through her.

"Good morning."

"Are you feeling all right, Claire? Did I hurt you? I didn't mean to hurt you."

"I feel fine, Tom," she murmured truthfully. "I feel simply marvelous."

"Good."

Tom was surprised at how good he felt this morning. Generally when he slept with a female, it had been in celebration of the conclusion of an assignment. Except, of course, when he'd been visiting his parents and had called on the fetching widow Columbine, with whom he'd had an understanding since his adolescence. This morning, however, he felt not merely clearheaded but energized.

Why, he felt as though he could climb mountains or conquer worlds this morning. He didn't understand it, although he was pretty sure his monumental sense of well-being had more to do with Claire than with himself. It felt right to have her in his bed. She belonged here.

Peering into her face, striped by the morning sun streaking through the window, he murmured, "You're so beautiful, Claire."

She was embarrassed by his words and tried to hide her face in his shoulder. He put his arm around her and chuckled softly. "You are, you know."

"Am not," came, muffled, from the pillow.

But she was. Her features weren't spectacular like those of Dianthe or Tom's mother, but her facial structure was pure and classical. Claire's face was one that would last forever. He'd bet any amount of money that she would still be lovely when she was seventy-five. He hoped he'd be alive to see himself proved right.

He nuzzled her neck. "Thank you, Claire. You've made me the happiest of men."

She said something, but he couldn't make it out because she was still speaking into the pillow. Feeling the need to see her and to clarify his future, he very gently pressed her shoulder until she lay on her back. Her cheeks were faintly flushed, and her beautiful brown eyes looked soft as a faun's. He had to kiss her, but he didn't lose track of his purpose.

"You'll stay with me, won't you, Claire? We make a wonderful team in every way. Surely you can see that. Why, a man's mistress is more important to him than any wife could ever be. You can see that, can't you?"

Claire sighed deeply, rapturously, and kept her eyes closed. Tom almost forgot his objective, but not quite. It disturbed him that she didn't rush to answer him affirmatively.

He shook her shoulder lightly. "Well? You'll stay with me, won't you, Claire?"

At last she opened her eyes and looked at him. He frowned when he saw wariness in her expression. Well, hell, she wasn't going to equivocate at this point, was she?

She reached up to stroke his stubbly chin. Her fingers were long and slender, just like the rest of her, and Tom reveled in the feel of them against his flesh.

"I—I'm very fond of you, Tom," she said. "Indeed I—well, I love you. You already know that."

Tom's heart swelled even as Claire began to look embarrassed. She'd told him so before, but every time she said it, he felt more secure. He was in fact outrageously pleased with himself. He must have done all right last night, in spite of having completely lost control. Turning his head, he nuzzled her palm and watched her gasp with pleasure.

"You're the most wonderful woman I've ever known, Claire," he told her, both because it was the truth and because it was infinitely easier to say aloud than the *L* word.

"Thank you."

"So it's settled then." He began to nuzzle her neck again.

"Y-yes. I guess."

He stopped nuzzling and looked at her sharply. "What do you mean, you guess?"

"I—I mean— Oh, heavens!" Claire sidled out from underneath him, sat up straight against the headboard, and pulled the sheet up to her chin.

"What is it, Claire?" Damn it all to hell and back again! Why in God's name was the woman wavering now? He tried to tamp down his frustration.

She cleared her throat. "I—oh, dear."

He glowered. She bowed her head and looked miserable.

"I'm so sorry, Tom. Can you give me just a tiny bit more time? There—there are some things you don't know about me yet, I'm afraid."

"Well, for God's sake, tell me!" Tom sat up too and ran his fingers through his hair. He was no damned good at this. When Claire flinched from his anger, he only got angrier. Hoping to calm down, he took a deep, soothing breath.

Attempting sweetness of tone, he tried again. "Please, Claire. We've told each other so much already. Surely you can't believe you can't tell me something." Unless—good God! "You're not married or anything, are you?" As soon as the words left his lips, he knew them to be absurd; she'd been a virgin, for pity's sake.

Her head jerked up so fast that Tom felt guilty. He patted her shoulder. "No. No, of course you're not. Sorry, Claire. But can't you tell me what the problem is? Don't you trust me at all?"

Claire's expression was one of exquisite soulfulness when she said miserably, "Of course I trust you. It's I who can't be trusted."

Oh, good Lord. Not this again! Through gritted teeth Tom said, "I trust you, Claire."

"Thank you."

Her voice was so quavery that Tom decided he'd better not push the issue, no matter how irritated he felt.

A clattering sound came from the hallway outside Tom's bedroom, and he saw Claire stiffen and dart a glance at the door.

"Good Lord, that must be Sally opening the upstairs curtains. What time is it?" The quaver was gone. In its place was alarm.

"It's just a little past six, Claire. You're not late yet."

"But I can't be seen here!"

She scrambled out of bed, taking the sheet with her. Tom grinned. "Sally won't come in here, Claire, believe me."

Tucking the sheet around her, Claire sounded panicky when she said, "But she might look into my room, and whatever will she think?"

Tom shook his head and guessed they'd have to deal with Claire's latest problem at another time. Maybe he could soften her up with another night of lovemaking. The thought appealed greatly, particularly as he looked at her now, wrapped up in that sheet, her cheeks blooming pink, her bare toes peeking out.

Good grief, he was besotted with the woman. "Don't worry about being seen, sweetheart. I'm the boss, and I won't let anybody fire you."

"Maybe I can tell her I went for an early-morning walk," she muttered, sounding distracted.

She looked like a Greek goddess with that sheet draped around her. He wanted to grab her, take her back to bed, and ravish her for weeks, but he figured she'd object. A slave to duty, his Claire. That, he reminded himself, was one of the reasons he wanted to keep her around.

With a gesture at her sheet he said, "Maybe she'll believe you and your friend Dianthe have taken to worshiping the sun in togas."

In spite of Claire's obvious morning-after embarrassment, she giggled. "Well, make sure Sally's through in the hall before I make a dash to my room, if you please."

With another sigh, knowing he still hadn't gotten to the root of Claire's strange, lingering uneasiness, Tom did as she bade. He watched her scurry to her room, dragging the sheet, and couldn't help smiling. He stretched sinuously in the beams of winter sunlight, thinking of Claire's beautiful, slender body, and laughed at himself when he realized he was fully aroused again. Lord, what that woman did to him! And she had no idea of her charms either. Maybe that was her greatest charm of all.

Well, it would be Tom's delight to teach her how desirable she was. He looked forward to it.

Claire blessed her housekeeping skills as she washed up. If she hadn't made it a practice to think ahead, she might have had to go downstairs and fetch water from the kitchen pump on this, the most momentous morning of her life. This morning, as every morning, fresh water awaited her in the pretty rose-covered porcelain pitcher on her dresser.

With a sigh she rinsed off the evidence of her deflowering. It hadn't felt like a deflowering. It had felt like a blossoming, her introduction to womanhood, something she'd never expected to experience. Claire had become so used to thinking of herself as an undesirable old maid—indeed had gone to great pains to make herself into one—that she still had trouble believing Tom Partington had desired her enough to carry his kisses through to their splendid consummation.

She drew back the curtains and stared out at the pristine day. A carpet of snow covered the meadow and crowned the trees. What perfect winter weather; how magnanimous of nature to have blessed them with the purity of all that white.

The snow stretched for as far as Claire could see, unsullied by signs of life. Later in the day footprints of men and beasts would chronicle the effects of civilization on that blanket of white, but right now Claire could pretend she and Tom were alone here in their world. She threw the window open and breathed deeply, almost freezing her lungs in her exuberance. She didn't mind a whit.

She felt wonderful. It didn't seem right to feel so good when she'd just risen from the bed of a man who wasn't her husband. The suspicion that her feeling of happiness was the product of her depraved upbringing nagged at her, only to be thrust aside.

"Nonsense," she said roundly to the sparkling day. "My father was beastly. Neither Tom nor I bear the remotest resemblance to my father. Why, Tom even wants me to stay at Partington Place forever."

She hugged herself and twirled around her bedroom before succumbing to gooseflesh and shutting her window. She had to don her woolen shawl before she could get her frozen fingers to curl around her hairbrush.

As she tweaked her new curls into a pretty cap above her brow, brushed her longer back hair until it gleamed and twisted it into a pretty Russian knot, her joy began to fade in spite of herself. Tom wanted her. She wanted him. One thing and one thing only stood in the way of her being the happiest woman on the face of the earth: *Tuscaloosa Tom Pardee.*

"I have to tell him," she whispered to her reflection, and cringed in reaction to the truth being spoken aloud.

Nevertheless, she knew the only honorable thing to do would be to confess. Immediately.

But when Claire descended the grand staircase at Partington Place to find Tom awaiting her at the foot of the stairs, the sweetest, most welcoming smile on his face, she hesitated. When he treated her with the most delightful deference at breakfast, selecting the prettiest hothouse pear for her, insisting she have the last remaining cinnamon roll, and begging her to eat some ham so she wouldn't waste away, her firm resolve began to waver.

Jedediah of course was too besotted to notice Tom's extraordinary behavior. Scruggs suffered from no such affliction. Claire saw him lift his brows in disapproval. When she visited the kitchen after breakfast to make sure Mrs. Philpott was apprised of the rest of the day's dining requirements, she discovered Scruggs had not dallied in spreading his suspicions, either.

"Is it true, Miss Montague?" Mrs. Philpott said, her eyes wide, her apple cheeks shining, her smile broad, and her hands clasped to her enormous bosom. "Oh, ma'am, is it true?"

Even though she knew the answer as she asked the question, Claire murmured, "Is what true, Mrs. Philpott?"

"Why, what Mr. Scruggs said, ma'am, about you and the master. I swear, I couldn't believe it when Sally came running down here while I was fixing breakfast and said how she'd heard your voice from the master's bedroom."

Claire stopped in the act of writing a note to herself, her pen suspended, her shopping list forgotten. "Good heavens."

"I boxed Sally's ears, I did, ma'am, but I reckon I'd better apologize now. After what Scruggs said about the master buttering your roll for you and peeling your pear and all, I guess we'll be hearing wedding bells at the Place yet."

"I don't believe the Place has a bell to ring, Mrs. Philpott," Claire said dryly. "I think you shouldn't pay attention to idle gossip."

The chubby cook winked at Claire and turned back to kneading her bread dough. "You can tease me all you like, Miss Montague, but I have eyes in my head too, and I've seen the two of you together." Her sigh was as huge as the rest of her. "It's love all right."

Claire escaped the kitchen soon afterward, shooting Scruggs a terrible scowl when she passed him in the hallway. As usual, he ignored her.

Later on that afternoon, however, her duties done and her beloved Tom gone to town to see if a wire had arrived from his horse breeder, Claire chewed the end of her pen and wondered if she'd lose her audience if Tuscaloosa Tom Pardee were to marry Miss Abigail Faithgood.

She slept in Tom's bed again that night. As he worked his magic on her body, she forgot all about her audience. She forgot about Tuscaloosa Tom Pardee and Abigail Faithgood. She forgot about everything but how Tom's skillful hands and lips made her body sing as he stirred her to ecstasy.

When Tom whispered that she was sleek and exquisite and lovely, that her skin was like satin and her lips like wine, all else was easy to forget. If such a thing was possible, she loved Tom even more for making her feel beautiful. In her twenty-seven years of life, Claire had felt insignificant, immoral, unpleasantly seductive, frightened, homely, and dull. Until Tom Partington entered her life, she had never once felt beautiful.

⁓ 18 ⁓

The first of Tom's Appaloosas, three mares and a
stallion, arrived shortly after the beginning of
the new year. Claire had never seen a man so
excited about anything, and she thought his reaction was
sweet. He didn't pretend sophistication or indifference;
he was ecstatic.

They were beautiful animals. Even Dianthe, invited to
view them by Jedediah Silver, who had elected to remain
at Partington Place for another several weeks, admitted
they were excellent horses. Claire was so pleased she
nearly burst her bodice buttons when she and Tom
stood on the balcony that evening and watched the sun
set over four of the loveliest horses either of them had
ever seen.

Tom squeezed her tightly. She could feel his heart
beating a rapid tattoo in his chest, and she knew he was
as happy as he could be. She was embarrassed when her
tears overflowed to trickle down her cheeks, but she was
so happy for Tom she couldn't help it.

By this time of course he'd told her all about his childhood, and Claire understood why he valued her practical nature. His parents had kept up the illusion of old southern wealth long after they'd lost everything—even before the war. Tom had learned to despise prevarications and pretense almost as much as he despised fecklessness. He told her over and over again that her honesty and her pragmatic character were what he admired most about her.

And that, she kept telling herself, was the reason she hadn't yet found the courage to tell him she was Clarence McTeague. She knew she'd have to tell him. Sooner or later he was going to find out anyway. Once again he'd mentioned writing her publisher to discover where his uncle had directed his proceeds from the novels.

Claire had even spent an entire evening mulling over various ways in which to persuade her publisher to lie to Tom. Mr. Oliphant admired her; perhaps he could be made to set up a false account or something.

She was ashamed of herself the following morning and visited Dianthe to confess and to beg advice. Her agitation was so great she didn't pay attention when she rounded the hedge leading into the Pyrite Arms's yard, and she nearly collided with Sergei.

"Arrrrgh!" Sergei followed up his bellow with a leap backward, ending in a crouch, his paintbrush lifted, brush end pointed like a knife at Claire's chest.

"Good heavens!" Claire leaped backward herself and pressed a hand to her thundering heart. "Oh, Sergei, I'm so sorry. I should have announced my presence."

The Russian was so relieved his legs gave out, and he collapsed onto the snow. His head dropped to his chest, and his brush fell to the ground.

"What are you doing outside painting in this

weather?" Claire glanced at the canvas set up on an easel. Long ago she'd learned to sneak up on Sergei's work and squint at it carefully. His paintings could be startling when approached directly. She saw at once that this painting wasn't too ghastly. Yet. "Whose soul are you painting today, Sergei?"

Heaving himself up and brushing snow off his rear end, Sergei said, "Mr. Partington."

Pleased, Claire exclaimed, "Sergei, how wonderful! I see you've discovered his soul to be, ah, not as tainted as those of most of the other people in town."

His brow furrowing, Sergei muttered, "It is a blue soul, the first blue soul in my experience. I know not if it bodes good or ill."

Claire patted his arm. "I'm sure it bodes good, Sergei. Mr. Partington is a fine man. A fine man."

She heard Sergei mutter darkly in Russian as she walked away but didn't bother to try to convince him. Not only was the weather too chilly for outdoor chats, but Claire had never yet known Sergei to be influenced by anything anybody told him. He was convinced that he alone could see into the souls of his subjects. Claire could only be grateful he hadn't yet perceived anything demonic about Tom's soul.

"How could he?" she asked herself with joy in her heart.

Her joy faltered when she took her problems to Dianthe.

"You mean to tell me you haven't told him *yet*?"

There was something about the way Dianthe asked her question that made Claire feel especially evil. Dianthe's was not a voice appropriate for censure, yet censure vibrated from every syllable. If Dianthe believed her to be at fault, Claire knew she was at fault.

"Oh, Dianthe," she whispered unhappily, "I just haven't found an appropriate moment."

"An appropriate moment?" Dianthe's eyebrows rose. "You've made love, Claire! In spite of what he says, he's trembling on the brink of a marriage proposal!"

"No, no. Certainly—"

"Certainly he is!"

Dianthe's vehemence made Claire blink.

"You must tell him, Claire. To do otherwise is wrong. Not to mention excessively foolish. It will certainly be worse if you wait."

"I know," Claire muttered, wringing her hands.

"You should have told him at the very beginning," Dianthe declared, making Claire stare. Dianthe was not given to bold declarations.

"I know. I know."

"The longer you put it off, the worse you're making it. You know he'll be upset that you didn't trust him enough to tell him sooner."

"But I do trust him!"

Dianthe looked skeptical, quite a feat for her. "Do you?"

"Of course I do!"

"If you trust him, then there's no reason not to tell him. Are you afraid of his reaction?"

Claire stared at Dianthe for several seconds as she tested her feelings. At last she whispered, "Yes."

"Well, then, it doesn't sound to me as though you trust him very much."

Claire felt defeated as she trudged down the lane leading from the Pyrite Arms to town. Dianthe was right about one thing: The longer Claire kept her dirty little secret to herself, the harder it would be to tell Tom the truth.

She was right about another thing too: Claire was afraid of Tom's reaction to the news she'd kept from him for so long. He was sure to be angry, and she wouldn't blame him. Right now he trusted and admired her. She wasn't sure she could bear to see his trust in her wither and die.

Halfway to town a dreadful plan began to form in her mind. It was so dreadful that Claire threw it out, only to have it bounce back again and take root.

But it would be evil, she told herself.

But it might work, she answered back perfidiously.

It was still evil.

It still might work.

Swallowing her scruples, knowing she was an arrant coward, vilifying herself as a wretched cheat, Claire hurried into the telegraph office. Powered by panic, she willed herself to think clearly and compose a message. Then, using all the artifice her father had taught her in her blighted youth, she smiled sweetly and bade Mr. Carter to send the message to Mr. Oliphant in New York.

Her heart beat so hard it hurt, and Claire knew she was a fool. No, she was worse than a fool. She was trying to keep the truth from the only man in the world she would ever love, a man who respected and valued her, who believed in her. She hated herself. Even as she hurried away from the telegraph office, she was phrasing her confession to Tom in her mind. She'd tell him as soon as she got back home, before she could lose her nerve again.

She was thwarted in her purpose that night because Tom and Jedediah had made a trip into Marysville and their return home had been delayed by the washing out of a bridge. A telegraph message arrived at Partington

Place advising Claire to expect Tom home as soon as the bridge had been repaired.

"The day after tomorrow," she murmured, staring at the wire. "Bother." She'd wanted to get the matter over with, to lay her sins bare before Tom and beg for his understanding. It was way past time she told him everything; he deserved to know.

With a deep sigh she folded up the wire and smiled at a dour Scruggs. "Why don't we take supper in the breakfast room, Scruggs?"

"Very good, ma'am." Scruggs stalked away from her as if Claire herself had been responsible for the collapsed bridge.

She had to content herself with continuing the very last novel in the *Tuscaloosa Tom Pardee* series that evening and the next. She missed Tom in her bed and slept poorly.

Tom was delighted to be back in his parlor at Partington Place and was only sorry Claire was out and couldn't rush into his arms and welcome him home. Truly, he couldn't recall another single time in his life when everything seemed to go his way as it was doing now. Life was grand. Life was good. He had his house; he had his horses; he had his Claire. Who could ask for more than this?

Claire was growing into a stylish horsewoman. Once she felt secure on the sluggish bay mare upon which he'd schooled her and he'd broken the prettiest Appaloosa mare to saddle, he'd presented it to her with a flourish. She'd been delighted. He'd even talked her into ordering another riding habit from Miss Thelma's.

Every now and then he wondered if Claire minded being his mistress. She was an extremely straitlaced sort of woman, and he sometimes got the feeling she didn't approve of herself for having succumbed to his seduction. Indeed he even got the feeling she still thought *she* had somehow seduced *him*. It might have been amusing if she didn't seem so troubled by the misconception.

He didn't like the idea of her feeling ashamed of herself. As if she had anything to be ashamed of!

That afternoon, as he waited for Claire to return from Pyrite Springs, Tom traipsed up to the ballroom balcony. Gazing out over his kingdom, he tested the name Claire Partington very carefully to see how it sat on his tongue. And if it affected his digestion.

"Claire Partington." He blew out a cloud of cigar smoke and donned one of his society smiles, the ones he'd been practicing on the mayor of Pyrite Springs, Mr. Humphry Albright, and his ilk. "Gentlemen, please allow me to introduce my wife, Claire Partington."

He swallowed some smoke and choked. Then he scowled. He was being ridiculous; he knew it. There was absolutely nothing intrinsically wrong with the institution of marriage. Just because his own parents were idiots, it didn't naturally follow that all married couples had to be idiots.

In his heart he knew that Claire felt she had somehow fulfilled her destiny by becoming his mistress. He was sure she thought being his mistress was all she deserved out of life. He knew her to be dead wrong on the issue too. Still, the very word "marriage" sent shivers up his spine.

He was being grossly unfair to Claire, and he knew it.

So he sucked in a breath of fresh air and tried again. "How do you do, General Lee. And may I introduce my wife, Claire Partington." Shaking hands with the invisible general, he continued. "Mrs. Partington is the one whom you have to thank for the evening's entertainment, General. My w-w-wife"—Tom had to pause and wipe his sweaty brow with his handkerchief—"is a lover of the arts."

She was his lover too, Tom acknowledged with a hardening in his nether regions. Without half trying, she could set his body aflame. He'd never had such a satisfying physical relationship. The straitlaced, prim-looking young woman who passed as the housekeeper Claire Montague during the day turned into a tigress at night in his arms. Her passion nearly consumed him.

As he gazed out over the frosty winter landscape, Tom did not feel cold. Just thinking about Claire in his bed was enough to heat him through and through. She was fire. She set him to burning with desire. She was every damned thing he'd ever wanted in his life.

But marriage? Tom shook his head and suddenly felt chilly.

"I know it's none of my business, Tom," Jedediah said later that afternoon, "but I think you should know there's a good deal of gossip about you and Claire in Pyrite Springs."

Jerking his head up from his newspaper and staring hard at his friend, Tom barked, "Gossip? What the hell are you talking about, Jed?"

Jedediah looked tense. "I guess the servants are spreading tales, Tom. They say she spends her nights in your room."

Tom's brows dipped, and he slitted his eyes in irritation. He'd always heard servants gossiped, but he'd never considered they might sling dirt about *him*. And Claire. For God's sake, they'd known Claire for years.

He said, "Well, hell," a response that he recognized as inadequate.

Pulling his collar away from his neck, which had turned red, Jedediah said, "Er, um, you know, Claire is well liked in town, Tom. Dianthe—er, Miss St. Sauvre, that is—said that she hates to hear her spoken of as though she were a—a fallen woman." He looked at Tom nervously. "Er, do you know what I mean?"

Scowling, Tom grumped, "Yes, I know what you mean."

Damn. They were gossiping about Claire! His Claire! Good God. Everything she'd ever feared about having a relationship with a man seemed to be coming true. It was all his fault. All his damnable fault because he was afraid of marriage. Him! The hero Tom Partington was afraid of a few lines on a legal document and the words "I do." Not very noble of him. Clarence McTeague would be dismayed. Except that his uncle was dead.

"Uncle Gordo'd be dismayed too," he mumbled sourly, eliciting an "I beg your pardon?" from Jedediah.

"Oh," said Tom, "nothing."

After clearing his throat once more, Jedediah ventured, "I've asked Dianthe to marry me, Tom, and she's agreed."

"Congratulations," Tom said absently.

Jedediah hesitated, as if waiting for Tom to say something more. When he didn't, he said, "Yes, well, Dianthe suggested that, well, if you wanted to, we might have a double ceremony."

"A what?"

"A double ceremony. You know, when two couples get married at the same time."

"Oh. I didn't know you could do that."

"You didn't?"

Tom took note of his friend's look of surprise and grinned in spite of his annoyance. "I've never been to a wedding, Jed. Folks didn't get married much out on the frontier. At least not the folks I knew."

"Oh, I guess maybe they didn't."

Both men contemplated marriage for several silent moments. At last Tom said, "When are you planning on this wedding of yours?"

"Dianthe wants to wait until April and ask you and Claire if we can use the garden at Partington Place. It's really pretty when everything's blooming."

"That's what Claire says too."

Jedediah licked his lips. He looked worried, as though he weren't sure he should be speaking so plainly. He forged ahead. "So, will you think about it, Tom? I—I hate to think of Claire's being ostracized in the town of Pyrite Springs."

"Ostracized!"

"Dianthe said that Mrs. Humphry Albright has been sniffing haughtily. I guess that means trouble."

"Damn."

Tom slapped his newspaper down on the table next to him and sprang to his feet. "This is abominable!"

Jedediah cleared his throat and seemed to brace himself. "Neither Dianthe nor I believe the fault lies at Claire's feet, Tom."

Tom went completely rigid for a second, infuriated by the accountant's blatant disapproval. Then he slumped when the truth smacked him upside the head. "No. Of course it isn't her fault. You're right. I'm the one who's to blame in this situation."

He didn't like knowing it either. He'd hurt Claire, and for no better reason than his own selfishness, his own bullheaded belief that because his parents were fools, the institution of marriage was wrong. What a damned coward he was!

Jedediah stammered an excuse and left Tom to stew in his bitterness. Stuffing his hands into his pockets, Tom scuffed his toe on the parlor carpet and brooded.

He felt bad; his heart hurt. Knowing Claire was suffering the humiliation of censure by her friends, the people she'd lived among for years, because of him sent waves of guilt knifing through him. Head bowed, he wandered out of the parlor and down the hall. It wasn't until he stopped in front of a closed door that he realized he'd headed directly to Claire's office. It was as if some instinct had led him there, to her. Everything he'd ever done in his life seemed to have directed him straight to Claire.

Pushing the door open, Tom peeked inside, hoping that she'd have come back from town and he'd find her bent over her desk, diligently working on accounts or menus or something. Everything she did in this room ultimately benefited him; she was his angel. And he'd hurt her. In his selfishness, foolishness, cowardice, and, yes, blind lust, he had led her into a role beneath her dignity and alien to her nature.

He was ashamed of himself. He ran a finger over the polished surface of her desk and looked at the result. Not a speck of dust sullied his fingertip; Claire would never allow dust to accumulate in his house. He sat in her chair and remembered the very first time he'd entered this room, bearing a bottle of port and a big empty place in his life. She'd filled up that empty place almost from the start with her sweetness and goodness and practicality. Damn, he appreciated practicality.

He'd been so blind. He should have known they couldn't keep their liaison a secret. No wonder Claire always seemed to be harboring some secret guilt, some deep sadness she tried to keep from him. She loved him; she even admitted it. Yet he'd never so much as hinted at how deep his affection for her ran. The very thought of life without Claire made his insides knot up and throb.

He shook his head, knowing he still hadn't hit upon Claire's secret. It was almost as if she were trying to hide something from him, something she thought made her less than a good person. That was ridiculous, of course. Tom had never met a better person than Claire Montague.

Leaning on the desktop, Tom picked up Claire's pen and idly flipped it between his fingers. A memory struck him, of this pen clattering to her blotter as they'd chatted one day, the same day she'd shoved those papers in her drawer and he'd teased her about being an embezzler.

The pen clattered to the blotter again, and Tom sat up straight. Good God! She couldn't truly be an embezzler, could she? Was that the reason she seemed to be so sad and guilty all the time?

"No, damn it," popped out of his mouth of its own accord. He glanced at the door to make sure it was closed. He didn't relish being discovered talking to himself.

Finding the door firmly shut against the rest of his household, Tom resumed brooding. The idea of Claire's being an embezzler was absurd. She could never engage in criminal activities; he knew she couldn't. Her principles would not allow her to do anything shady or devious.

But what was it she was trying to hide from him? What was making her nervous and sad? Was it just that she felt guilty about their relationship? Or was there something else? Something deeper? Something that had nothing to do with him?

Love notes? Had that idiotic puppy Addison been writing her love notes? Anger erupted in him suddenly, and he had to shake his head to clear it.

No. Addison was being firmly lured into the man-fishing creel of the pretty widow Priscilla Pringle. Besides, Addison was such a self-serving nitwit; he wouldn't write love notes to anybody unless it was to himself.

Still, and although it seemed illogical, Tom suddenly had a very strong hunch that those papers, whatever they were, had some bearing on Claire's discontent. Anything that kept Claire from pure happiness was a blot on his life too, and he resented it.

Shooting another glance at the closed door, Tom compressed his lips and then did something he'd never done before in his entire life: He snooped.

The drawer opened smoothly and without any betraying squeaks or scrapes. Of course he'd expect nothing less of a drawer entrusted to Claire Montague's care. Although he felt sort of sheepish about it, not at all the hero Claire had called him so often, after another glance at the door, Tom settled in to pry.

Everything was very tidy. He'd anticipated that it would be. After all, the drawer belonged to Claire. A pair of scissors rested neatly next to two pencils and a pen in a wooden tray. A bottle of ink, a piece of blotting paper, a rubber eraser, and a list of household items Tom suspected was a shopping list were laid precisely out next to the miscellany tray.

How like his Claire to keep such close tabs on things, Tom thought with a smile. God, he valued her; he'd never been in an establishment that ran more smoothly than did his estate. A sponge sat in a little dish ready to be filled with water to moisten postage stamps. A small envelope revealed the stamps as well. At the very bottom of the shallow drawer lay a brown folder tied with string. Carefully Tom removed the folder and untied the bow.

When he pulled out a sheaf of papers from the folder and glanced over them, their import escaped him at first. Claire's fine hand covered the sheets in tidy rows. He noted with interest that her handwriting sloped neither up nor down but trotted across the pages in firm, straight lines. He smiled. She was absolutely amazing. He didn't know another single soul in the universe, besides himself, whose regularity of mind allowed for such perfectly even rows.

But what was this? There were pages and pages here, all covered with Claire's beautiful cursive, unembellished with curlicues or fancy scrollwork. Her efficiency reflected itself in her handwriting, as it did in everything she did. Peering more closely, Tom began to read.

After a minute or two his eyebrows lowered. His smile faded. His forehead wrinkled. His eyes narrowed. A pounding started in his head. His heart began to thud heavily. He finished the first page, set it carefully down on the blotter, and began reading the second.

Suddenly he dropped the entire folder onto the desk and sat up straight. "Good God!"

This was one of those damned *Tuscaloosa Tom Pardee* novels! Right here. In Claire's desk. In her very hand.

What did this mean?

His frown left him, and his brow wrinkled harder as he concentrated. After a few moments of ponderous thought his worry eased.

"Of course," he said, and nodded.

His uncle Gordon used to dictate his books to her. That was what this was. This was the book his uncle had been writing when he died. Of course. Tom actually laughed, but the noise sounded too loud in the silence of the room, and he stopped immediately and swallowed.

He bent to the pages again. Why was the unfinished manuscript still in Claire's desk? Surely she wasn't planning on having it published, was she? Wouldn't she have told him? She and he had a perfectly open relationship, didn't they? She wouldn't have kept it from him, would she?

A dreadful thought began to creep around the edges of Tom's mind. It was so ghastly a notion that he didn't want to allow it in, so he only glanced at it sideways for a while as he concentrated on the story unfolding on the sheets of foolscap in front of him. The idea kept wanting to sidle past his guard and attack him, but he wouldn't let it.

"Jedediah couldn't find any trace of Uncle Gordo's records of his book sale profits."

Tom jerked up and looked around, wondering who had spoken. He realized with a start that it had been he who'd mouthed the significant words and frowned again. Once more he bent to read the pages.

"No wonder she was so scared."

Again his own voice startled him into looking around the room. This time, however, he knew who had spoken. He also had a fairly shrewd idea about what these papers suggested.

Allowing the manuscript to drift from his fingers, Tom stared straight ahead and thought hard.

He said, "Claire?" experimentally, hoping his reaction to her precious name would make him realize the total absurdity of what he'd just realized. He wanted inspiration to blind him with a truth completely contradicting the evidence. This afternoon inspiration was not Tom's friend.

"Hellfire," he muttered unhappily.

Claire Montague. Clarence McTeague. Good God, why hadn't he made the connection before? She'd even defended the idiotic novels on several occasions when he'd disparaged them.

Damn. No wonder she'd looked so disconcerted when he explained his lack of heroism. He must have burst her bubble with a vengeance.

"Poor Claire."

Wait a minute. Why was he thinking "poor Claire"? *He* was the one who had suffered from these blasted books! It was *he*, Tom Partington, who'd been made the object of Claire's girlish romantic fantasies! It had been *he* whose entire life had been made a living hell by her misplaced hero worship! *He* was the one who'd been teased beyond endurance by his fellow scouts.

She'd made him a damned laughingstock.

Tom sat back and stewed in righteous indignation for several minutes, his anger getting hotter the longer he thought about Tuscaloosa Tom Pardee.

Actually it wasn't the books themselves that angered him. It was the fact that Claire hadn't trusted him enough to confess her authorship. Her keeping mum about the books seemed somehow vile to him, a treacherous sin of omission. She'd hoodwinked him! She'd out and out deceived him. She'd kept a big, fat secret from him.

It wasn't just any secret either. It was a secret that had haunted him, waking and sleeping, for the last five years of his life.

She'd actually allowed him to believe that his uncle

Gordon had written those wretched books. She, who claimed to have loved Gordon like a father, had allowed Tom to believe something ill of him.

"Damn!" Tom felt more betrayed than he'd ever felt in his life.

Claire was the author of those damnable books! It had been *she* who had ruined his life! *She* was the one to whom he owed all that misery.

Resting his elbows on the desk, Tom sank his head in his hands and ran his fingers through his hair. Claire! The woman he cared for. The woman who claimed to love him. Good God!

Agitation bubbled in his breast like boiling water until it propelled him out of Claire's chair and sent him storming around the room. He kicked the magazine stand viciously, splintering its frail legs and sending a year's worth of *McCall's* slithering across the floor.

She'd tricked him. Little Miss Holier-Than-Thou Claire Montague had tricked him as if he were a green boy and she a practiced fraud! She'd written those trashy books and undoubtedly made a damned fortune. Trading on his name! Trading on his reputation and career! She'd used him as shamelessly as if she were a randy cowboy and he a two-dollar whore.

"Damn, damn, damn, damn, damn!"

It was unfortunate, Tom thought later, that Claire should have entered her office at precisely that moment. A smile lit her face, and she opened her arms to embrace him but stopped in her tracks when Tom whirled around and skewered her with the blackest scowl he'd ever hurled at anybody. Her hand flew to her breast, and she gaped, her eyes huge under her spectacles. Tom could plainly see fright war with bewilderment in those expressive eyes. Then her glance flickered to her desk, and she paled.

Lost to his wrath and in a voice dripping acid, Tom ground out, "Good afternoon, Miss McTeague."

❦ 19 ❦

*I*f she'd yelled at him or been defiant, she might have pricked Tom's defenses and he might have given her a chance. If she'd told him roundly that yes, she was the author of those books and she was damned proud of them, he'd probably have raged, but he'd have given it up in a moment or two. If she'd told him to go to hell or even demanded to know what he'd been doing pawing through her things, she might have thrown water on his anger.

When she just stood there looking like a frightened rabbit, her expression of patent contrition made him feel guilty. Him! Resentment flared in his breast, and his guilt only fed his ire.

"Yes, my dear. I found you out, didn't I? When did you plan to tell me, Claire? Or did you? Maybe you thought you could keep your little secret to yourself. Did you expect to feed off my name forever?"

"It—it's not like that, Tom," she stammered. "Truly it's not."

"No?" He sneered. Tom couldn't recall ever sneering

before, but he created a sneer on the spot and threw it at Claire. "What is it like, Claire? Please tell me."

"I—I meant to tell you. I wanted to tell you. But you hated the books so much." Claire hung her head. "I was afraid."

Tom's heart lurched. Claire's words hurt him more than he'd thought possible. She was afraid of *him*? "Because I've been so cruel to you, I suppose. Naturally you'd be afraid to tell me something like this." He swept his hand over the scatter of papers on her desk and said with biting sarcasm, "I'm such a cruel monster."

"You're not a monster," she murmured unhappily. "You've never been cruel to me."

"No? For a second there I wondered if I'd been beating you in my sleep or something."

She shook her head, and Tom saw tears gathering in her eyes. He wanted to run to her and throw his arms around her; he wanted to comfort her and tell her that it was all right and that he forgave her.

But her lack of candor had wounded him deeply, bitterly. He hated himself for what he perceived as his weakness. He held himself back from her, rigid, his sneer in place, wanting to injure her the way she'd injured him. He felt stiff, unbending, like ice.

"I'm sorry," she said. "I'm so sorry."

Even in his fury Tom hated to see Claire wringing her hands and looking so conscience-stricken. But damn it, she *should* be conscience-stricken. He'd taken her into his life and cared for her and told her all the secrets of his heart, and she'd betrayed him. He felt like an utter fool. She'd lacerated his pride as surely as if she'd taken a machete to it.

"How did you expect to keep the truth from me, Claire? What did you plan to tell me when another one of these abominations came out in print? Did you think your nasty secret would stay hidden forever?"

"No, I—I don't know. I don't know."

"You just figured that after we became lovers, it would be easier to gull me, is that it? You figured if you used your body to entice me, I wouldn't get mad at you for making an ass of me all those years?"

"No!"

She looked appalled, and he roared, "No? Well, then, damn it, why didn't you tell me?"

It seemed to Tom that his roar did her in. Her face crumpled, and she cried, "Oh, I'm so sorry!" She picked up her skirts and hared it out the door and up the stairs before he could draw breath to yell again.

For a second Tom was stunned by Claire's retreat. After he had gathered his wits together, he chased out of the office after her, but he was in time only to see her plaid skirt swirl around the upstairs banister. He knew she'd be in her room before he could catch her.

Seething with indignation, he stood at the foot of the stairs and glared at nothing in particular, his hands clenched at his sides, his chest heaving in outrage. The wicked, lying cheat. Damn her!

"A wire just arrived, sir."

Tom's heart almost stopped when Scruggs's lugubrious voice broke into his churning fury. He turned so fast the old butler staggered backward. Snatching the telegram out of Scruggs's hand, Tom said, "Thank you." His jaw was set so tightly it hurt to speak.

"It's for Miss Montague, sir," Scruggs said, as if Tom might not be able to read the envelope. "I was going to take it up to her."

"I'll take care of it."

Scruggs didn't speak for a minute. His eyes squinted

up, and he looked at Tom as if he didn't trust him to carry out the assignment. At last he said, "Very good, sir," turned, and dragged himself off.

Tom glared after Scruggs until he was out of sight. Then he glared up the staircase again and contemplated carrying this wire up to Claire. He didn't trust himself. He was afraid he'd shout at her again or, worse, grab her and beg her to forgive him.

Believing both those alternatives to be less than ideal, he stuffed the wire into his pocket and stalked off to his library.

"What have I done? Oh, what have I done?"

Claire allowed herself only a very brief while to lie disconsolately on her bed and weep. She knew tears didn't solve anything. Tears hadn't fixed anything when she was a child, and they wouldn't fix anything now. The only thing in her life that had ever been of benefit to Claire Montague was action.

She laughed bitterly and wished she'd taken action weeks ago and told Tom about those books. She hadn't, however, and now she was reaping the fruits of her deception. There was no going back; she had to live with what her lies had wrought.

Therefore, after she had willed her tears to stop, she stood up and contemplated her future. It did not lie here, at Partington Place, she realized with a stab of pain.

At least she had money. The last time she'd faced a new future alone, all she'd had was an advertisement ripped from the *Sacramento Bee* and boundless determination.

Her throat ached, and her heart felt as if somebody had scraped it with a rake. But she knew it wasn't broken. Hearts didn't break; her own heart had ached for years and years, yet Claire still lived. It surely would have broken by this time if such a thing were possible.

Dully she dug her old suitcase out from under her bed. Although she didn't have many possessions, she had much more than she'd arrived at Partington Place with ten years ago. Resolutely she decided to pack what she could carry in the suitcase and stow the rest in a carpetbag. She would send for the bag. She was sure Tom would not begrudge her the few treasures she'd collected during her ten years here. He was a kind, good, noble man. It wasn't his fault she was a cheat and a vile deceiver.

Another tear slid down her cheek, and she snatched it away angrily. It didn't take long for Claire to pack enough clothes and toiletries to last her a few days. Then she waited until she was sure Tom and Jedediah were at supper and slipped downstairs and into her office. There she almost broke down once more as she stuffed her latest work into its tidy folder and tucked it under her arm.

She'd write to Dianthe and Sylvester. She'd probably write to Tom too, once she was over the worst of her agony, and give him her new address. Not that he'd ever have use for it. She'd pen an apology now, though. She hadn't been able to voice it this afternoon. She'd have to word her letter so that it didn't sound as though she were making excuses for herself. There was no good excuse for not having trusted him enough to confess it was she who had written those books. Yet she wanted him to know that she had meant well when she wrote them. She didn't want him to think she'd consciously mocked him. How could she mock the man she loved?

As silently as a wraith she slipped out of her office and

into the crisp evening. Because she had come to love them so much, Claire paid a last visit to Tom's horses. She almost cried again when she stroked Firefly's silky nose. She adored the pretty mare Tom had given her.

"Good-bye," she whispered. The horse whickered in response. "Good-bye, Firefly. I love you. I'll miss you. And oh, how I'll miss Partington Place."

Then, before she could break down entirely, she hurried down the lane to Pyrite Springs, carrying her suitcase, her folder snugged under her arm.

"She wasn't feeling well," Tom said harshly in response to Jedediah's question. "I don't think she'll be joining us for supper."

"Too bad. I was hoping I could persuade her to visit the Pyrite Arms with me after supper."

Tom strove for a smile. "Going to visit your lady love, Jed?"

"Yes," Jedediah said with a sigh. "I'll go anyway, of course, but I know Dianthe and Claire are the best of friends. I thought she might like to go too."

"Yes. She might."

He hadn't given her a chance. He'd lit into her like a trout on a fly and hadn't let her say a word. He felt guilty as hell. Oh, he knew she was at fault. She'd lied to him. She'd deceived him. She'd kept a terrible secret from him.

Unfortunately for Tom, his innate honesty had been knocking for admission ever since he'd allowed his anger to run riot over Claire. It finally kicked him in the shins and made him pay attention.

Was her secret really so terrible? He knew she'd kept the truth from him only because she knew he hated those damned books and feared his anger. For good reason, as it turned out.

If she'd told him in the first place, he might have been annoyed, but he wouldn't have felt betrayed.

But he wouldn't have allowed Claire to get close to him either. He'd have missed out on the last several glorious weeks with her.

But those books! Those books were trash.

Trash, were they?

Yes. They'd made his life miserable.

Miserable?

Yes, miserable.

Really.

Humph. Tom scowled into his soup bowl. Well . . . all right. Maybe not miserable. If he were to be absolutely honest, perhaps he'd sort of enjoyed the notoriety.

A little bit.

And perhaps he *had* pretended a somewhat exaggerated umbrage when newspaper reporters had sought him out. He might possibly have been said to profit—indirectly, of course—from Claire's hero worship when he'd been given plum assignments.

The president of the United States had asked for him by name when he'd come West on a hunting trip. Said he'd read all about Tom in Claire's dime novels.

Maybe it had been kind of gratifying when that Russian archduke had insisted that nobody but Tom Partington could lead his expedition. Dime novels again.

If he were to be absolutely, unconditionally honest with himself, he might even have to admit that the silly books had boosted his confidence and turned him into a better scout. Not that he wasn't the best to begin with, of course. Still, when one had an image to uphold, one was apt to perform one's duties with more flair. People would be watching after all.

Humph. He shoved his soup bowl away, his appetite gone.

He guessed it might be true too that he hadn't bothered to wear those outlandish fringed buckskins until the first of the *Tuscaloosa Tom* books hit the stands. They were his trademark now, and he'd always feigned oblivion of his myriad imitators. In fact, he used to laugh inside when he saw people dressing like him. Well, actually, not like him. Like Tuscaloosa Tom Pardee. Claire's creation.

When Absolute Candor finally struck Tom, it hit during the roast beef course and with a humbling blow.

Great God in heaven, Claire Montague, his housekeeper, his mistress, his—his lover, had created a national icon. Not just any old icon either. She'd created an ideal of American manhood, a model of masculine virtues to which young boys aspired. What was it she'd said that long-ago day when they'd been discussing the books? That little boys in America who strove to emulate Tuscaloosa Tom Pardee were striving to achieve goodness and chivalry and—and—and—

Tom couldn't remember everything she'd said. He did remember, however, that at the time her words had struck him as ridiculous. Staring blindly at the long, polished table stretching out in front of him, Tom admitted to himself that her words no longer seemed foolish. He found himself strangely moved, in fact.

And she'd based her fictional character on what she perceived him to be.

"Good grief," he murmured, stunned, and swallowed an ache of maudlin emotion that had lumped up in his throat.

"I beg your pardon?"

Tom jerked and stopped staring into space. He'd forgotten for a minute that Jedediah was sharing the table with him.

"Oh, nothing. Sorry. Just thinking."

"Mmm." Jedediah returned to his own thoughts, obviously of Dianthe St. Sauvre.

Why, Claire must have loved him—or her image of him—before she'd even met him. According to her, she loved him still. Even after she'd come to know him. Did that mean he possessed enough of Tuscaloosa Tom's many fine qualities that she hadn't been totally disillusioned? It was difficult to imagine.

Taking great care, Tom ate what he could of the rest of his dinner. He skipped dessert. Since Jedediah was obliging enough to leave him after supper and go courting, he skipped port in the parlor. All Tom could think about was how hurt Claire had looked in the face of his rage.

He didn't know what to do. The memory of Claire's penitent expression as he'd yelled at her made his head ache. The thought that she might think he wanted her to go away was too awful to contemplate. He should apologize to her, but how? Should he wait until tomorrow, until she'd calmed down? If he waited, would she suffer all night? Would *he* suffer all night?

Yes, he decided, he would. The notion held no appeal.

As he slowly trudged up the stairs, his mind kept churning over the same problem and ending up in the same conclusionless muddle. Then he remembered the wire Scruggs had handed him before supper and pulled it out of his pocket. Turning it over in his hands, he stood in front of Claire's door, undecided.

Then, concluding he was being idiotic about this whole thing, he rapped sharply on her door.

"Claire? Claire, there's a telegram for you."

Silence greeted his announcement. He cleared his throat and tried again.

"Claire, please come to the door. There's a telegram for you from town, and we need to talk."

Nothing.

Tom stood at the door and frowned. Was she in there and avoiding him? Maybe she'd gone out for a walk. No; it was pitch-black outside and cold as a witch's—Well, anyway, he was pretty sure she hadn't gone out walking.

"Claire," he called more loudly.

Nothing.

This had been a hard day for Tom. His very satisfying new life had been kicked topsy-turvy by the woman who wasn't answering his knock, the same woman who had claimed to love him not three days earlier. Frustrated, he closed his fist and pounded on the door once, hard.

Not so much as a rustle of petticoats could he hear from the other side of that blasted closed door.

"Claire! Damn it! Here's a telegraph message for you. If you won't speak to me, at least look at your wire."

Furious when he got no response from this last caustic command, Tom declared, "Well, then, if you don't care what it says, I'll open it myself and tell you."

Knowing he was behaving like a thwarted schoolboy, Tom nevertheless yanked the wire out of his pocket and ripped it open. "Here. It says, 'Miss Montague, I regret that there is no legal way I can—' "

Tom stopped reading aloud and finished scanning the message silently. Then he looked at the door. "Claire?" He rapped several times, loudly. "Claire, whyever did you wire Oliphant to direct your royalties to my bank account?"

The unearthly silence finally made Tom's brittle patience snap. With one final thud on Claire's door with his fist, he barked, "Damn it, if you won't come out here and talk to me, I'll just come in there."

Although he expected he would have to break the door down since Claire was obviously planning to out-stubborn him, Tom rattled the knob only to have it unlatch silently. He pushed lightly, and the door swung open without a sound. Of course. There wasn't a door at Partington Place that squeaked, because Claire saw to them herself, every week, like clockwork.

He stood in the hallway for a moment or two, as still as a statue, dread gradually overcoming anger in his chest. Taking a deep breath, he stepped into the room. It was neat as a pin and empty of Claire. He sucked in a breath and, suddenly terrified, held it.

When he saw the carpetbag, packed and set neatly on Claire's bed, the last faint spark of hope in his heart sputtered and died. Aching, he walked to the bed, took up the note Claire had left on the bag, and read his name scripted in Claire's fine hand on the envelope.

His hands trembled when he opened it. He read it silently, unable to make a sound for the grief welling up inside him. The letter read:

Dear Tom,

Thank you for everything. You have been kinder to me than I deserve. Please believe me when I say I did not mean to hurt you with my books. They were written out of love, evidently misguided, and I regret any pain they may have caused. I realize I was wrong not to have consulted you before I used you as my model and not to have told you about my authorship after we'd met. I hope one day you will forgive me. I shall send for my bag when I am established elsewhere. May God bless you and keep you. You will always have my heart.

Claire.

Tom swallowed around a tremendous ache in the back of his throat. His eyes stung, and his head felt heavy. He lifted a hand and pressed his forehead as if that could keep the pain contained.

She'd left him. He'd driven her off. He'd hurt her, denounced the one thing she'd tried to give him, and she'd left him.

He whispered, "Oh, Claire," once, and then clamped his mouth shut for fear the next thing to emerge would be a sob.

Tom didn't know how long he stood there, dumbly staring at Claire's note. It seemed like hours. However long it was, he was eventually jolted out of his stupor by the clanging of the front doorbell.

Claire, he thought, his heart soaring for a minute before it crashed to earth again. It couldn't be Claire. She wouldn't ring the bell.

Unless she'd left her key behind. With that thought buoying him, Tom raced from her room, down the stairs, and sent Scruggs reeling against the wall when he dashed past him and wrenched the front door open.

"Claire!" he shouted into the face of the tall, portly, mustachioed gentleman who stood on the porch.

The gent smiled an oily, seductive smile that stabbed Tom in the heart as surely as if the fellow had used a knife. "We meet again, Mr. Partington."

Tom had seen his emotions in color before a couple of

times before. Once, in the heat of battle during the war, he'd viewed life through an orange haze. Once while being pursued by a band of Cheyenne warriors, he'd seen the world in shades of purple.

When he saw the mustachioed gentleman who had been walking away from a frightened Claire on the street of Pyrite Springs three months before, Tom's world suddenly turned red.

The man's greasy smile fled, his eyes bugged, and his mouth opened into a startled O when Tom grabbed him by the throat and began to throttle him.

"Where is she? Where is she, damn you to eternal hell? What the devil have you done with Claire?"

It took the combined efforts of Scruggs, Jedediah Silver, and a terrified Sylvester Addison-Addison to drag Tom away from Claude Montague before he could kill him on the front porch of Partington Place.

"I tell you, I'm Claire's father." Claude took another gulp of brandy and massaged his Adam's apple tenderly, as if he weren't sure Tom hadn't damaged it beyond redemption.

Tom ran his fingers through his hair. He had consigned Jedediah and Sylvester to the parlor and had taken Claude into his library. He didn't relish an audience while he questioned this slippery specimen, who he feared had more to do with Claire's odd behavior than he'd ever guessed. Her father! He'd believed they were lovers—that would have been bad enough—but her father! Good heavens.

"Why didn't she tell me?" His voice sounded pathetic. For good reason. He felt pathetic.

Rattled out of his usual aplomb, Claude swallowed

another mouthful of brandy and muttered, "Undoubtedly because she hates me."

"What?" Tom stopped pacing and stared at Claude. He couldn't imagine his Claire hating anybody, much less her father. Not even if he was this pernicious fellow.

Realizing how baldly he had declared his daughter's dislike, the wily Claude eyed Tom and seemed to draw himself together. "That is to say, our family life was disrupted when Claire was quite young, you see. We, er, fell upon hard times, and I greatly fear Claire blamed me." He splayed a plump hand over his chest and managed to look put upon.

Tom thinned his gaze and allowed himself to stop pacing and take in the full glory of Claude Montague. He remembered the sly fellow from the night they'd drunk together in the saloon. The man was a bottomless well of amusing anecdotes, but Tom hadn't trusted him then, and he didn't trust him now.

He shook his head. "No. You said she hated you. Why does she hate you? It can't be just because you had a hard time making a living. Claire wouldn't hate anybody without a good reason."

Rubbing his throat again, Claude adopted a melancholy expression. "I regret to say that Claire believed herself to be above her surroundings. I fear it has always been a grave fault in her, Mr. Partington. We, er, experienced a few hard times during and after the war, you see. Claire's dear mother passed on, and I was obliged to take up employment beneath my capabilities."

Eyeing him slantwise, Tom asked, "And what employment was that, pray tell, Mr. Montague?"

Claude lifted his chin, opening and closing his mouth several times as if testing to make sure his jaw still worked. Tom held on to his patience only by force of will.

At last Claude said, "For several years, my son and daughter and I traveled the roads, Mr. Partington. It was a perilous life, but I provided for my children the only way I could."

On the verge of throttling him again, Tom said very tightly, "What exactly do you mean, you traveled the roads?"

"I'm afraid ours wasn't a settled life. We led a rather Gypsy-like existence."

"What the hell did you do, damn it?"

Claude, never much for bravery, squeaked and pushed himself back against the sofa cushions. His answer, propelled by fear, came fast. "We traveled in a medicine show wagon."

Tom felt his eyes bulge. "You're a medicine show quack?"

Striving for dignity, Claude said smoothly, "I prefer to think of myself as an entertainer."

"An entertainer? A snake oil salesman?" Recollecting the few times he'd encountered medicine show swindlers, members of a species he considered particularly loathsome, Tom said, "You dragged your daughter around with you in a wagon while you bilked people out of their hard-earned money by selling them worthless remedies? You call that entertainment?"

Miffed, Claude said, "I was very entertaining as a matter of fact."

Tom's hands clenched and unclenched. He was finding it difficult to keep them from Claude's throat. He'd witnessed the result of a few medicine men in his day. Claude Montague and those like him sold gullible, sometimes seriously ill settlers medicines made from alcohol and doctored with everything from peppermint oil to rattlesnake venom. He'd helped bury more than one victim of a plausible medicine man's "sure cure." He despised Claude Montague and fakers like him.

Things were beginning to make a terrible kind of sense to him. "I suppose you used your children in your act."

"It wasn't an act!"

"Of course not. Let me guess. You dressed them in rags and made them pretend to be strangers. Then when you dosed them with your so-called cure, they were supposed to pretend to get better. They'd throw their crutches away and miraculously walk without a limp or be cured of pneumonia. Is that the sort of life you gave your children, Mr. Montague?"

It didn't look as though Claude trusted Tom's tone of voice, which was thin and strained. He edged down the sofa, away from his host, as though he were aiming to get as close to the door as he could in case Tom sprang at him. "Claire was never any good at the act. When she was older, she proved to be a little more useful, although she wasn't a very obedient child, I'm afraid."

Ignoring the last of Claude's whine, Tom snapped, "What do you mean, she was more useful when she was older?"

"Well, even then she wasn't worth much." Claude frowned at his fingernails and didn't see Tom stiffen. "She was such a prissy little prude. And such a snob. She didn't approve of the costumes she had to wear."

"What kinds of costumes?"

Claude flung a hand in the air. "Well, you know, she was female and therefore could have been an asset to the show, even if she was a string bean. Those costumes cost a fortune too." He sounded very disgruntled. "If she'd had any family feeling at all, she would have realized that a little flirting would only have helped."

Tom tried to say "flirting," but his tongue wouldn't work. He stared at Claude Montague and endeavored to imagine his sweet Claire in this monster's clutches.

Things began to click into place in his brain. Claire's terror of being thought a loose woman, her rattlesnake hair, her dull brown dresses, her belief that she was somehow unworthy, her trying so hard to be prim and proper. Her finding a hero in the man his uncle had told her Tom Partington was, a man who was the exact opposite of her father. Her turning Tom into a dime novel idol.

God save him. He closed his eyes for a moment, hurting for Claire. The very idea of her being used by this contemptible charlatan in his medicine show was repugnant to him. How she must have hated it! How his upright, splendid, wonderful Claire must have felt, being used by this—this—Tom couldn't think of a word bad enough to describe Claude Montague.

And Tom had made the woman his mistress! And condemned her for writing those books. His wonderful Claire. The only woman on the face of the earth he could ever love. He admitted it to himself now without even a hitch in his heart. He loved her. Of course he did. She exemplified everything he'd ever valued in a human being.

Well, by God, he was going to get her back. He was going to go after her and find her and bring her home and marry her and never let her go again.

He would deal with her father later.

He strode to the door, yanked it open, and bellowed, "Jed! Addison! Get in here right now!" Then he turned and pinned Claude Montague with a look that made the old fraud shrink into the sofa cushions again.

"My friends are going to stay here with you, Mr. Montague. They're going to stay here until I find Claire and bring her back. Then we're going to get to the bottom of this. If you manage to escape before I come back, I'll track you down and kill you." He gave Claude a smile that had been known to wither braver men than Claire's father. "I'm an ace scout, you know."

He had expected Sylvester to fuss at him and was prepared to deal with the simpering poltroon in no uncertain terms. He was therefore surprised but gratified when Sylvester, upon being apprised of the situation, cried, "Splendid! What an opportunity! I've longed for this moment."

"You have?"

"God, yes. Ever since Claire told Dianthe and me about her father, I've been longing to interview him."

"You knew this man was her father?"

"Well, not exactly. But she'd told us that her father was a confidence trickster."

"I beg your pardon!" Claude drew himself up and glared at Sylvester.

Tom shook his head. "Damn. She told everybody in the world but me, I guess."

"She didn't tell me," said Jedediah helpfully.

Tom wrapped his woolen scarf around his neck and began to draw on his riding gloves. "I plan to get the whole story out of her, but I don't want this prime article to get away before I do. Depending on what Claire wants me to do with him, I may let him go later."

Claude looked mortally offended and not a little frightened, but he didn't offer up an objection until after the door slammed shut behind Tom. Then he eyed his captors carefully before deciding Sylvester looked as though he'd be more responsive to his tales of woe than the disapproving, stuffy Jedediah Silver.

❧ 20 ❧

I t had gone dark an hour earlier, although some light crept through the window from the lantern secured outside the Wells Fargo coach. Mostly, though, Claire saw nothing but her own black visions as she stared out into the night.

Thank God she'd been able to purchase passage on the last stage to Marysville. She had no idea what she'd do once she got there, but she expected she'd be able to find a hotel room. If not, she wouldn't be the first passenger in the world forced to sit overnight with her baggage in the Wells Fargo office.

San Francisco was her ultimate destination. Fortunately her banking account was in the Pyrite Springs Wells Fargo branch. There were Wells Fargo branches in San Francisco, so it shouldn't be difficult for her to draw enough money out to begin her life anew.

The thought made the lump in her throat ache, and she swallowed in an effort to control it. It was amazing how physically painful emotions could be. Right now, for example, her chest ached, her throat ached, her head ached, and her stomach ached. Her legs and bottom ached too, but that was because of the dreadful bouncing of the stagecoach. She hadn't thought to bring a cushion with her as the other passengers did.

How many years, Claire wondered, *before I don't hurt anymore?* It was hard to conceive of becoming accustomed to life without Partington Place and Tom. Partington Place had been the only real home she'd ever known, and she loved it. And Tom was the only man she could even imagine loving.

"It'll be all right, dearie."

With a start, Claire realized that she'd sighed aloud and that the kind-looking woman across from her was smiling sympathetically. The woman was a stranger, and her amiable good-heartedness was almost Claire's undoing. Quickly she snatched out a handkerchief to catch any tears that might fall before she could sniff them back.

"Thank you," she whispered.

"Life can be very unkind sometimes," the woman said with a little nod, "but we females have to carry on. We're the strong ones, you know, dearie." She spoke confidingly and with a sideways glance at the other passengers, all men and all snoring.

The woman's declaration surprised Claire. She'd always been led to believe that men were stronger than women, but this stranger's words resonated within her, sounding a bell of truth. She sat up straighter and gulped the last remnants of tears welling up in her throat.

"I—I believe you may be right, ma'am."

The woman nodded again. "I know I'm right, dearie. We're the ones always left behind whilst the men go off and fight their fights and play their silly games."

Their silly games. Yes. Claire thought she understood what the woman was trying to tell her. It was always the females who kept the home fires burning. They reared the children and prepared the food. They were the glue that held society together. Claire belonged to a sister-hood forging the grit, the glue, the very backbone of civilization.

"Yes," she said. And even though her heart still ached for Tom and her lost home, and even though the thought of creating a new life filled her with trepidation, Claire knew she would carry on and eventually thrive.

The lady across from her held out a gloved hand. "My name is Myrtle Finchley, dear. Mrs. Edwin Finchley, al-though my darling Eddie passed on eight years ago."

Claire shook the woman's hand gladly. "Claire Mon-tague, Mrs. Finchley. Thank you for your kind words."

Mrs. Finchley shifted in her seat to lean closer, and for the first time Claire noticed the novel resting on the woman's lap. She could scarcely believe her eyes when she read the title: *Tuscaloosa Tom and the Outlaws of Oak Ridge Wallow.*

Mrs. Finchley saw where Claire's gaze had landed and smiled. "Oh, my, yes, dear. Some people frown on novels, but I say, if a body can't escape the hurly-burly of everyday life from time to time, then what's living for? I do so enjoy a rousing dime novel. They're just my cup of tea."

Claire swallowed and licked her lips. "And—and do you find Mr. McTeague's novels to be representative of the genre?"

"Oh, my goodness, Mr. McTeague's books are the very best, my dear. If you haven't read them, I highly recommend them. If you like that sort of thing, of course."

Mrs. Finchley looked a little guilty, but Claire hardly noticed. She, who had never known a mother, was suddenly engulfed by a burning desire to talk to the motherly Mrs. Finchley, really *talk* to her, as a daughter might talk to a mother in times of trouble. Taking a deep breath, she blurted out, "I wrote them."

Mrs. Finchley peered at her blankly and said, "I beg your pardon."

"I am Clarence McTeague. I wrote those books."

"You?" The woman's eyes opened wide, and Claire could plainly read disbelief on her face.

Sweeping a look at their traveling companions and finding them still lost to consciousness, Claire sucked in another enormous breath. Then, in a tumble of words, her story fell from her lips and into Mrs. Finchley's astonished ears.

She couldn't recall ever talking to a complete stranger the way she was now. Or anybody else, for that matter.

Spurred on by the compassionate older woman's frequent "oh, my goodness" and sympathetic clucks, Claire discovered herself revealing things she'd never told a soul. She skipped the part about Tom and her becoming lovers, but she admitted her affection for him and how hurt she'd been by his anger when he discovered her to be the author of the *Tuscaloosa Tom* books.

"But I wrote them because I loved him so, you see. He's—he was the hero of every one of my dreams."

"Indeed, my dear, I do see."

Dabbing at her eyes and sniffling, Claire said, "I know it was wrong of me to keep my authorship a secret, but I feared losing my job and—and his esteem. For he did esteem me, Mrs. Finchley. I know he did."

Claire's companion nodded soulfully and patted Claire on the knee. "Of course he did."

"But he was so angry. He said such—such awful things to me."

"If that isn't just like a man! Men are such absurd creatures. As much as I adored my darling Eddie, he used to get such odd quirks. He made me very angry many, many times."

"Did he really?"

"Of course he did. They're all alike, men are. Why, I think it's criminal, the way that man treated you! Oh, I know, I know," she said when Claire began to protest. "I know you kept something from him. And I know you love the fellow, my dear. But that makes it all the worse, don't you see? If he'd had a shred of compassion in his heart, he'd have known you wrote these wonderful books only because you value him the way he's always wanted to be valued. Why, I'll warrant he was secretly pleased to have been made the hero of your novels. Men!" she repeated in conclusion.

After a moment's thought Claire decided she might just agree. It felt so good to unburden herself, and she was so grateful to the motherly Mrs. Finchley, that the two ladies spoke far into the night as the coach rolled and bounced them along the road to Marysville.

As they chatted, Claire began to contemplate the completion of her last *Tuscaloosa Tom* novel. She'd pondered the idea of writing Mr. Oliphant and begging out of the one remaining book in her contract, but now she believed she shouldn't do so.

"A contract is a contract after all."

Mrs. Finchley agreed wholeheartedly.

"So I will finish *Tuscaloosa Tom and the Wool War.* Then I shall begin a whole new series." She nodded firmly.

"Bravo, my dear!"

"Why, I've already created one national icon. What's to stop me from creating another? I'll marry Tuscaloosa Tom off to Miss Abigail Faithgood and go on to bigger and better things. It will serve the bounder right to be shackled to that idiotic, screaming female."

"Exactly, my girl! You show him what he's giving up!"

Claire had never had a cheering section before, and she discovered she liked it. "Imagine, Tom Partington yelling at me. Why, I made him into a famous hero, and he actually had the nerve to condemn me for it!"

"The monster!"

By the time Claire became aware of a disturbance in the road, she was no longer near tears. In fact, she was fighting mad.

Mrs. Finchley seemed to be in a similar condition when Claire suddenly exclaimed, "Oh, my! Do you hear that commotion outside?"

"Mercy! It's probably some awful man holding up the stage or something."

"I wish I had a gun!"

The two ladies were prepared for anything when the door was wrenched open. Claire was ready to impale any would-be criminal with her parasol, and Mrs. Finchley had *Tuscaloosa Tom and the Outlaws of Oak Ridge Wallow* poised and ready to strike.

When Tom Partington appeared in the faint yellow lamplight, Claire gasped and dropped her parasol. Mrs. Finchley looked at her in surprise.

"Claire!" Tom cried. "Oh, my God, Claire! I thought I'd lost you!"

In her shock at seeing Tom here, Claire found herself sucking in huge gasps of air. He stared at her wild-eyed, his gorgeous hair disarranged under his hat, his eyes sparkling. Then, in a rush, her boundless grievances against the men in her life and Tom in particular exploded over her. She jerked away from his extended hand as if it were a poisonous snake.

She shrieked, "Don't you dare touch me!"

"Is this the cad who swore at you, Claire, dear?" Mrs. Finchley cried, appalled.

Unable to speak again, Claire nodded, and Mrs. Finchley brought *Tuscaloosa Tom and the Outlaws of Oak Ridge Wallow* crashing down, hard, on Tom's head. Fortunately for him it was covered by his hat.

In a flash Claire picked up her parasol and began stabbing at him. He staggered back, shocked to his core.

The other passengers in the coach had to varying degrees awakened during this ruckus. One of them muttered, "Here, here! What's going on?"

A bearded gentleman said, "Don't hurt that fellow, madam," and tried to grab Claire's parasol. Quarters inside the coach were tight, but Claire managed to elbow him in his stomach before she jumped down from the coach to confront Tom Partington. Mrs. Finchley finished the bearded gent off with her book and clambered down to support Claire.

Her parasol at the alert, Claire frowned at Tom, who was bent over almost double and staring at her as if she'd lost her mind. She realized she'd gotten him pretty solidly in the stomach with her weapon and felt a surge of primitive, and wholly improper, glee.

"What do you want with me, Mr. Partington?" Her voice was as frosty as the weather and hung in the air in a foggy clump between them.

"Mr. Partington?" Tom looked at her, disbelief sharing space with pain and helplessness on his countenance. If she hadn't been so irate by that time, Claire might have felt guilty about Tom's present breathless state. As it was, she didn't care. Chest heaving, she only scowled at him, parasol poised for another attack should he try to touch her again.

He straightened with difficulty. "Claire? Please, Claire, don't be mad at me."

"Why not, pray?"

"Because I'm sorry."

"You're *sorry?* You disdain my heart, my mind, my essence, the work of my soul, my very *meaning* in life, and all you can say is you're *sorry?*" She realized her voice had gone shrill, and she made an effort to control it. "And am I expected to fall down in a swoon because you're sorry, Mr. Thomas, the Boy General, Partington? Am I supposed to beg you to take me back and serve as your mi—mmi"—Claire took a deep breath—"house-keeper at Partington Place because you realize you were hasty and overbearing and—and horrid to me?"

"Please, Claire." Tom ran a hand through his hair and reached out to her.

Mrs. Finchley, bosom heaving in agitation, swung her pocketbook at his arm. "Don't you dare touch that dear child, you despicable fiend!"

Tom snatched his hand back and looked at Claire's champion in astonishment. Claire lifted her chin and announced defiantly, "You see, Mr. Partington? *You* might have forsaken me, but I still have friends!"

"But, Claire," Tom pleaded, being careful to keep his hands to himself, "I haven't forsaken you. I've come to beg you to come back and marry me. I can't live without you. I'm sorry I hurt your feelings, Claire. I—I— Damn it, I love you."

Claire's mouth dropped open, but nothing emerged. She wanted to stick a finger in her ear and clean it out.

Of course she did no such thing. Nevertheless she stood as if struck from stone. She couldn't believe what she thought she'd just heard, but she was afraid to ask him to repeat it for fear he'd tell her she was mistaken.

"Please, Claire? I love you so much. If you leave me, I don't know how I'll survive."

He sounded absolutely pathetic. Claire finally managed to shut her mouth, but she still couldn't think of anything to say. Frantically she looked at Mrs. Finchley, hoping to find inspiration in her staunch, albeit new, ally, only to discover Mrs. Finchley gaping at Tom too.

When nobody spoke, Tom looked nervous. He cleared his throat and tried again. "Claire, please come back to me. My conduct was unforgivable. If you can't find it in your heart to forgive me yet, at least give me another chance." He paused for a second and went on recklessly. "Your father came to the house tonight, Claire."

Mrs. Finchley, whom Claire had regaled with the full ignominy of her vagrant childhood, gasped, "Saints preserve us!"

Claire finally found her tongue, but she used it only to cry, horrified, "My father! Oh, no!"

"Yes. You see, I understand everything now, Claire. Truly I do. I don't blame you for making a hero out of Tuscaloosa Tom or for keeping the truth from me. You must have had a terrible childhood. You must have hated and mistrusted men until you met Uncle Gordon. I don't blame you for trying to forget your past and for wanting to make your present better. Or for writing those books. I understand why you needed a hero, Claire. I was wrong to take you to task. Please, please, Claire, come back to me."

Still wavering, Claire glanced once more at Mrs.

Finchley and found her peering thoughtfully at Tom. The older woman no longer looked as if she'd try to slay him if he made a move to touch Claire. Then Claire glanced at the stagecoach and discovered every passenger leaning out the windows and watching eagerly. One of them winked at her. She took umbrage and sniffed haughtily.

Still, Tom's words meant a lot to her. "Well . . ."

"Please, Claire?"

She'd never heard Tom sound this humble. She hadn't believed he had it in him to abase himself so thoroughly.

"Come on, young lady, tell the poor feller you'll marry him. It ain't right to leave them horses all standin' out here in the cold. Nor us neither."

She glared at the gentleman who had made the suggestion, but he only winked again.

"Perhaps," offered Mrs. Finchley cautiously, "you and your young man should continue on to Marysville and discuss the matter over a cup of tea, Claire, dear."

"Good idea," another fellow inside the stagecoach grumbled. He said a few more things about waking a body up in the middle of the night for no better reason than to carry on a lovers' quarrel in the middle of the road in the dead of winter, but Claire's ferocious glare quelled his mutters.

"Children," a roundish, cherub-faced man said, "as a minister of the Lord, may I offer my seat to the gentleman so that he and the young lady might speak to each other in the coach on the way to Marysville?"

He smiled sweetly at Claire, who had to swallow a sudden swell of sentiment. She shook her head, though, unwilling to share so intimate and confined a space with Tom Partington at the moment. She wasn't sure she should forgive him yet. After all, she didn't wish to appear easy.

Striving for poise, she said, "No, thank you, sir. Perhaps if he follows the coach to Marysville, I shall speak to him if he so wishes. You, sir, have no reason to relinquish your seat inside the coach. After all, you paid full fare for a coach seat to Marysville."

"I'll pay his fare, Claire!" Tom said, obviously nettled.

"It's a chilly night, Mr. Partington," Claire shot back. "You may find it advisable to ride your poor horse to death in the freezing cold, but that gentleman"—forgetting the manners she'd taught herself over the past ten years, Claire pointed at the cherry-cheeked fellow—"is not as young as you, nor is he as used to rough accommodations as you are. I feel sure of it."

"All right." Unhappy, Tom acquiesced. "But you must speak to me when we arrive in Marysville."

"Must I?" she asked, bridling.

"Please, Claire?"

He sounded desperate, and Claire relented. "All right. I shall speak to you in Marysville." She didn't like making the concession and stalked back to the coach and climbed aboard without so much as a backward glance.

Mrs. Finchley sniffed meaningfully at Tom before following in Claire's huffy wake.

The two ladies conferred the rest of the way to Marysville. One of their fellow passengers tried to offer a suggestion once but was glowered at so savagely by Claire that he subsided. The minister smiled sweetly at them and wisely held his counsel. The rest of the men went back to sleep as soon as they could.

Tom was almost frozen solid by the time the Wells Fargo coach finally rattled to a stop in front of the staging office in Marysville. He'd never been so happy to see civilization in his life. If he'd known he'd have to chase Claire all the way to Marysville, he'd have worn his buffalo robe, knitted head scarf, fur-lined gloves, and a second pair of woolen stockings before he set out. He hadn't felt this cold since he'd spent the winter of '73 in the Montana Territory chasing Indians away from the railroad tracks.

It would all be worth it, though, if Claire agreed to marry him. He opened the door and helped her and Mrs. Finchley to alight. Neither lady seemed especially pleased to accept his hand. He sighed and wondered how long it would take him to thaw Claire out.

"Do you need my support during your ordeal, dear?" Mrs. Finchley asked Claire, thereby winning herself a frown from Tom. She ignored it and him with exquisite disdain.

"I believe I can handle it. Thank you, Mrs. Finchley."

"I'll be taking tea in the coffee room if you need me."

"Thank you."

Crushed to his soul, Tom waited until Mrs. Finchley bustled into the coffee room before he burst out, "Why the devil do you think you'll need protection from me, Claire? Don't you know me better than that by now?"

Claire looked at him as if he were a particularly disgusting road deposit she'd just found smeared on her boot. "Mrs. Finchley," she said coldly, "is my friend."

Tom wanted to holler at her and ask her what she thought he was, but he held himself back. Refinement was what he needed here. Sadly, refinement was something he hadn't practiced much in his life.

Since it was past midnight and the stagecoach office was thin of company, he led her to a corner where a hard bench had been built against the wall. It wasn't an ideal trysting place, but Tom didn't guess he'd better risk asking her to share a hotel room with him yet. The other stagecoach passengers who had witnessed their performance on the road to Marysville peered at them curiously. Tom turned his back on them.

When Claire settled herself on the bench, her back as straight as a poker, her skirt folded precisely around her, and her lips pinched into two straight white lines, he sighed unhappily. He guessed he deserved her displeasure; he hadn't handled her well at all.

Meekly he said, "Claire, I know I hurt your feelings. All I can do now is to beg you to forgive me. I had no business shouting at you and no business being mad at you for writing those books."

Claire inclined her head imperiously, as if she were a royal duchess granting absolution to an errant knave. He knew he was taking a big chance, but he dared reach for her hand and was pleased when she didn't snatch it back again immediately.

"I love you, Claire. I know I've never told you so before, but that was because I've always been afraid to admit to having such emotions. I didn't trust love. The only people I'd ever loved before treated me like dirt and tried to suck me dry. I—I was afraid of being hurt, you see."

The truth, when it hit the air, scared the living tar out of him. Entrusting the secrets of his heart to another human being was a frightening proposition. His parents, the first people to whom he'd extended his heart, had not treated it gently. And here he'd just handed Claire his entire being.

Breathless, he waited to see what she'd do with his humble offering. As he waited, he experienced torment because he realized she'd already offered him her own heart, and he'd failed her, had thrown it back into her face as a matter of fact.

Claire, however, perhaps because she was female and therefore more accustomed to granting forgiveness than Tom, recognized the importance of his admission, which touched her. She had been inspired with the fire of self-worth by Mrs. Finchley, however, and didn't think it wise to let Tom off too lightly.

"I believe I understand," she said carefully. "As somebody whose heart and entire life's work were recently savaged unmercifully, I know how much it can hurt."

Tom winced as if she'd struck him. "I'm sorry, Claire. I'll never do such a thing again." He looked at her closely. "Claire, I didn't know your background. It never occurred to me that you might have been trying to overcome problems in your own past. If I'd known, I might have felt less betrayed."

She stiffened, and he hurried on. "I did feel betrayed, Claire. I had taken you into my life, and when you didn't trust me enough to tell me about those books and even let me continue believing my uncle had written them, it was like a slap in the face to learn the truth. I know it was wrong of me to jump to conclusions, but if I'd known Uncle Gordon hadn't written those books, I'd have felt more kindly toward him."

This time Claire winced.

"I didn't know then about your father."

Claire dropped her gaze. "No, of course you didn't because I didn't tell you. I understand. I—I'm sorry, Tom."

Thank God! She was back to calling him Tom. His heart soared, although he knew it was too soon to celebrate. "Can you tell me about it now, Claire?" he asked softly.

She hesitated for a moment, then sighed deeply. "I take it you know by now that I grew up in a medicine show. What you may not yet understand is that my father is a gambler and a confidence man and a terrible, cheating, awful, miserable, thieving scoundrel."

She paused, and Tom squeezed her hand for encouragement. "It was bad enough when I was little. In almost every town we passed through, the other children laughed at me and made fun of me. When I grew up, it was even worse because he made me dress up in lewd, hateful costumes and made me entice unsuspecting men into his trap."

Tom's heart gave a sudden twist.

Claire's composure began to crumble. "He never even let me wear my spectacles!"

Tom was stunned. He didn't know what to say. Memories of Claire pleading with him not to think of her as a strumpet washed over him, and he could only be ashamed of himself for not offering her marriage in the first place. Good God, his childhood problems were nothing compared with Claire's. And he'd undoubtedly done exactly the wrong thing in making her his mistress.

"The medicine show, cheating and conniving and running from the law—that was the only life I ever knew as a child, and I hated it. When I was seventeen, I ran away from my father and applied for a position at Partington Place. Mr. Partington took me in, even though I didn't know a thing about housekeeping. He was so good to me, and he taught me how to act like a lady and be proper and gracious—and to have friends. I made friends there for the first time in my life. I've tried so hard to live up to his expectations of me. I've tried so hard!"

His heart hurting for the girl Claire had been and the

woman she'd become, Tom said feelingly, "Believe me, Claire, in a million years, I wouldn't have guessed your background. Nobody would. I even asked Jedediah Silver, and he didn't know. He said you just showed up at Partington Place one day, and he never did know anything about you except that you were very genteel and took better care of the Place and my uncle Gordon than anybody else ever could have done."

"Truly? He really said that?"

Tom could plainly see how much Claire valued Jedediah's opinion. "Yes, Claire. He really said that. And he was right." Taking a deep breath and a daring chance, he said, "Will you marry me, Claire? Will you marry me and make me the happiest man in the world?"

Claire hesitated for so long Tom's heart began to shrivel in his chest. He was sure she was going to refuse him, even though he knew she loved him. Used to love him. Until he'd gotten mad at her.

He was on the verge of begging—and continuing to do so until he wore down her defenses—when her tiny yes kissed his ears.

"Yes?" He sucked in a ragged breath.

After a much shorter pause Claire said more firmly, "Yes."

Relief crashed through Tom with monumental force. She'd said yes!

"You mean it, Claire?" he whispered.

She peered at him so searchingly it was difficult for him to hold her gaze, but he did it and was proud.

"Yes."

Fearing to take anything for granted at this point, he asked carefully, "Then may I kiss you, Claire?"

She ducked her head shyly and whispered another tiny decorous yes.

When Tom swept her into his arms and crushed his lips to hers, both of them were startled by the tremendous cheer that sailed out from the door of the coffee room. Embarrassed, with Claire blushing furiously in his arms, Tom turned to discover everybody who had ridden in the Wells Fargo stagecoach, including Mrs. Finchley, applauding. Several beaver hats flew into the air, Mrs. Finchley waved her handkerchief, and the bearded gentleman stomped his feet in approval.

The cherub-faced minister was the first to approach them. He strode toward Tom and Claire with his hands outstretched.

"May I offer you my heartiest felicitations as well as my services, sir and madam? I am an ordained minister of the Southern Methodist-Episcopal persuasion, and I would be more than happy to perform the nuptial ceremony should you desire to take care of the matter immediately."

Tom and Claire exchanged a glance. Tom cocked his brow. Claire smiled. Then they both stood, hands entwined.

"We'd be happy if you were to perform the rites, Mr.—Mr.—" Tom felt foolish when he realized they didn't even know the man's name.

"Montenegro, sir. My name is Cyrus Montenegro."

The bride and groom laughed until tears ran down their cheeks.

By three o'clock that morning Claire had become Mrs. Thomas Gordon Partington. She had no bridal bouquet, no veil, no wedding gown, no bridesmaids, no three-tiered cake. What she had was a jovial minister, a supportive group of near strangers who stood witness, a man she loved almost beyond endurance, and a happi-

ness in her soul so great she was afraid she'd burst with
it.

Tom had behaved like a perfect dithering bridegroom
too. He'd spread money around like salt, fumbled his
lines, blushed scarlet, and even wept at one point. Claire
thought his conduct was so sweet she could hardly stand
it. Then he'd invited all their impromptu wedding guests
to a celebration of their nuptials at Partington Place and
took all their names and addresses so they could be sent
invitations when the event was organized.

After that he booked them a suite at the Marysville
Golden Fortune Hotel and sent two telegrams, one to
Partington Place. The other, he told Claire, was a secret.

She batted her eyelashes in mock dismay. "But, Tom,
how do I know you're not sending a wire to another
woman?"

"You'll just have to trust me, Claire," he told her with
a wink as he yanked off his vest and opened his arms
wide. "Come here."

With her cheeks warming and her heart full, Claire
went to him.

"I love you, Claire," Tom said when he'd wrapped her
in his arms. "I love you, and I won't let you leave me
again."

"I'll never leave you, Tom."

"I was so scared, Claire."

She knew he was telling her the truth because she
heard his voice catch and felt his heart thunder in his
chest. She thought about apologizing but decided an
apology would be poor strategy.

She, who had never thought about strategy in her entire life, had learned something very important today.
She didn't have to stand for being treated poorly by
anyone, not even the man she loved above all others. It

was a valuable lesson, one she planned to keep at the front of her mind at all times.

When Tom kissed her, however, she decided there were occasions when her newly perceived lesson could be relegated to the background. She kissed him back with all the enthusiasm in her heart.

There was something incredibly sweet about making love to her husband, Claire discovered that night. She felt a freedom to express herself in passion that she hadn't felt when she'd believed herself to be participating in something immoral. When Tom drove her to rapture, she surrendered to her climax with wild abandon, sending him over the edge in an instant.

For a long time they lay in each other's arms, neither speaking. After a while Tom admitted, "It's never been so good, Claire."

"Mmm."

Another several silent minutes ticked by before he said softly, "I'm sorry I didn't ask you to marry me weeks ago, Claire. It wasn't very noble of me to ask you to share my bed and not my name."

She snuggled up against him, glorying in the feel and scent of him and their recent lovemaking. "I understand how you felt about marriage, Tom. If I'd grown up as you did, with your mother and father, I'd probably have felt the same way."

He hugged her tightly. "That's kind of you, Claire, but I was selfish. It never even occurred to me that in making myself comfortable, I might have been wounding you."

Acknowledging the truth of Tom's confession silently, Claire smiled. Rather than rub his nose in his transgressions, she graciously—and honestly—murmured, "You had no way of knowing, Tom. I didn't tell you about my past because I was ashamed of it."

"You have nothing to be ashamed of, darling."

He squeezed her again, and Claire sighed in ecstasy.

With a chuckle Tom said, "And someday I'd be curious to hear some stories about your life in the medicine show too. After all, I've told you about life on the prairie."

"Never!" Claire shuddered. "I'd love to hear about how you first discovered Appaloosas, though."

So Tom talked about horses on his wedding night and gradually drifted into stories about his youth. Claire listened avidly. She didn't realize how clever he was at drawing her out of her shell until she discovered herself, safe in his embrace, actually telling him a tale from her own childhood.

In spite of her recent resolve never to speak of her early life, as she lay in the arms of her husband with the late-winter sunshine beginning to creep over the windowsill and splash onto the hotel carpet, episodes she hadn't spoken of for years began to spill from her lips. With Tom chuckling in real amusement beside her, the stories didn't sound merely sordid. Thanks to the softening effects of time and love, even Claire managed to find humor in some of them.

She was giggling so hard, in fact, when she recounted the tale of Claude Montague and the widow Casey's errant pillow slip that she nearly fell out of bed.

Catching her and pulling her back to his side, Tom said, "You mean to tell me she actually paid him to give her back her own pillowcase?" He had to wipe his eyes on the sheet because he was laughing so hard.

After she had caught her breath, Claire said, "Yes. And

I felt sorry for the poor woman because nobody in the world would ever believe that she and my father had done anything indiscreet. Why, she must have weighed more than two hundred pounds, Tom! In those days she would have outweighed him. And Father never favored plump women, you know.

"The poor thing was quivering with trepidation, though, worried that her neighbors might get the wrong idea. All because the wind had blown her laundry into our camp and my father was mad at her for having had us driven out of town. My father is—was—such a convincing old sinner he could have corrupted the pope."

"I believe it," murmured her husband.

"You know," she confided, "I used to hate it when he bribed people like that. But Mrs. Casey was so mean to us I didn't mind that time, even if I did feel a tiny bit sorry for her."

"She actually had you driven out of town?"

"Yes. And she wouldn't let her granddaughter play with me." Claire flinched when a spurt of pain clutched her heart even after all these years. To counteract it, she said lightly, "She was a nasty old biddy. She and my father deserved each other."

"Oh, Claire. I promise I'll make it all up to you." Tom hugged her hard, driving the pain right out of her and replacing it with love. "What a life you've lived! What a life we've both lived for that matter."

"Yes indeed, Tom. But yours has been elevating. Mine was only illegal half the time. Not to mention uncomfortable."

"Well, you'll never be uncomfortable again if I can help it, Claire," Tom vowed, punctuating his declaration with tiny kisses.

"I love you, Tom."

They proceeded to show each other how very much they meant their words until sated, they fell into slumber.

❦ 21 ❦

*T*hey slept until shortly after noon. After dragging themselves out of bed and consuming a hearty wedding breakfast, Tom rented a carriage to drive them back to Pyrite Springs. Claire bade Mrs. Finchley a tearful farewell and promised to send her a copy of *Tuscaloosa Tom and the River of Raging Death* as soon as she got home.

"I'll see you at your reception, dear," Mrs. Finchley sang out as the carriage pulled away. She waved her hankie furiously.

"Oh, yes! And I'll be sure you get a copy of the last book in the series too, when it's published," Claire called out the carriage window.

Patting her foolish tears away, she settled back into the carriage seat and found Tom gazing at her, an uncertain expression on his face. She knew why.

"There's only one more book left in my contract, Tom, and I plan to finish it. I won't break my contract."

"No. Of course not." He sighed, though.

"It's the last *Tuscaloosa Tom* book I'll ever write. I promise."

He grinned. "I know."

Claire wasn't sure what he meant by that, but she let it pass this time. If he tried to prevent her from writing books in the future, however, he'd get an earful. She might have agreed to marry him, but she'd be boiled in oil if she'd give up her writing career. She'd learned her worth and would never forget it again.

The rest of their trip back home was spent in deciding what to do about their respective parental problems. They batted ideas back and forth, ultimately settling upon a valid scheme for taking care of Tom's mother and father.

"I truly believe that you can't forsake them, Tom," Claire told him. "I know you're worried—for good reason—about their being unable to handle finances themselves, but if you were to hire a supervisor whom you trust, I'm sure that would mitigate the problem."

"I suppose so."

He didn't sound entirely satisfied. Claire understood. "You know, darling, you simply can't hold yourself responsible for their instability. All you can do is set up an income for them. If they can't manage, even with somebody overseeing their needs, there's not much you can do about it."

"I know. It just drives me crazy to watch them fritter their resources away."

Peering at her gloved hands, Claire said gently, "If you give somebody something, it belongs to that person. If he or she chooses to fritter it away, I suppose that choice is his or hers to make."

When she glanced up, it was to find her husband staring at her as if she'd just spouted an eleventh commandment. After a moment he said, "You're right. By God, you're right." Then he grinned. "You're right, Claire! They're not my fault!"

She shook her head and smiled. She loved him so much. And it was just like him to take on the cares of the world—or even those of his parents—and to consider himself at fault if the world—or his parents—decided to go to the devil in spite of him.

"As for my own dear father," Claire said, her smile fading, "I suggest you do absolutely nothing. He deserves nothing."

"I don't mind providing a small income for him, Claire. Truly I don't."

She scowled. "Well, if I knew he'd use it for something besides gambling and drinking, perhaps I wouldn't mind. I don't trust him, though."

"Remember what you just told me? About giving something away and its not being yours any longer?"

Vexed at having her philosophical words flung back at her, Claire muttered, "Touché."

"It would make me feel better to know we're at least giving both our parents a chance. If they waste it, that's their choice."

Claire actually glared at her beloved husband for a full minute until he chuckled. She realized she was being inconsistent and finally relented. "Oh, all right, Tom. But I think you're being much too kind."

"Well . . ." Tom hesitated, obviously unsure how his spirited spouse would take what he wanted to say. Then he seemed consciously to fling caution to the wind. "Actually I found him to be an amusing old scoundrel that night in the saloon. He's got a million stories, and he's quite a raconteur. I know he treated you badly, and I don't blame you for not forgiving him for it, but some people aren't cut out to be parents, I reckon. It's a shame your mother had to die so young."

A hot retort leaped to Claire's lips, but it cooled before she could scald Tom with it. He was right. Blast it, he was right.

Her father was about the most entertaining man she'd ever met in her life. In black moments given to deriding her talents as a dime novelist and wishing she were able to pen great, boring literature of the type Sylvester Addison-Addison wrote, she even owned—to herself—that she had inherited her storytelling skill from Claude Montague.

She didn't like knowing it. Her innate honesty made her admit, rather sourly, "Oh, all right." She sulked for another five minutes before she sat up and said, "But he'd better not settle in Pyrite Springs! I'll die if he does that."

Laughing, Tom reached for her hand. "My dear, if that's what will happen if he moves to town, I'll make sure he doesn't. I don't think he's very fond of Pyrite Springs, though. When we chatted that evening, what I remember of it, I got the distinct impression he considered our little town too small an arena for his large talents."

Claire said, "Humph."

When their rented carriage swept up the circular drive in front of Partington Place, Tom's favorite Appaloosa tied to the back, the entire household staff was lined up to greet them. Mrs. Philpott was crying. It looked to Claire as if she'd already gone through two handkerchiefs.

Dianthe St. Sauvre, Jedediah Silver, Sylvester Addison-Addison, Priscilla Pringle, and Claude Montague milled about in front of the tidy row of servants. They all were studiously ignoring Scruggs, who glowered even more blackly than usual at their overt levity.

Tom jumped from the carriage and raced around to open Claire's door. A cheer went up from the assembly when he lifted her down and swirled her around in his arms. Claire felt a thrill course through her when he carried her over the threshold of the house she'd lived in for ten years.

"Claire! Claire!" Sylvester dashed into the house hot on Tom's heels and snagged Claire's attention almost before Tom set her down in the tiled entryway.

Laughing, Claire said, "What is it, Sylvester?"

"Oh, Claire! Your father has given me enough meat for six novels featuring Adolphus, the wily Turk!"

Both Tom and Claire rolled their eyes. Claude Montague preened.

The marriage of Thomas Gordon Partington to Claire Elizabeth Montague was celebrated at a grand ball at Partington Place in April 1881. Claire selected April because her daphne hedges would be just beginning to flower, the wisteria would be glorious, the ranunculus and anemone would be in bloom, and everybody invited to the party would have had plenty of time in which to make arrangements to attend.

That was just fine with Tom, who had a particular reason for desiring postponement of the festivities. In fact, as the date approached, he began to worry that April might be too soon. Two weeks before the grand gala, however, he received a telegram from the New Mexico Territory and breathed an enormous sigh of relief. When the big day arrived, he was prepared.

Mrs. Philpott and two girls from the village prepared a delicious banquet, to which Tom and Claire invited their particular friends. Jedediah and a blushing Dianthe announced their engagement and impending nuptials during the main course. Priscilla Pringle waited until dessert before announcing that she and Sylvester, who scowled at the centerpiece during the entire meal, would also wed.

Tom and Claire exchanged a happy glance and squeezed each other's hands. Then, just after coffee had been served and the party was about to depart for the ballroom so that Tom and Claire could position themselves to greet guests, the dining room door burst open. Surprised, everybody turned toward the doorway to discern Scruggs, his eyes wild and a hand clamped to his heart. He was panting heavily and pressed his back against the door as if to keep it shut against an invasion of hostiles.

"Good heavens, Scruggs!" Claire had never seen the phlegmatic butler look so agitated. "Whatever is the matter?"

"Oh, ma'am," wheezed Scruggs. "Oh, my Gawd!"

Alarmed, Claire began to rise from her chair, only to have Tom place his hand over hers. When she looked at him, she was amazed to find him grinning from ear to ear.

"I'll take care of it, Claire. Don't worry. I think I know what the matter is."

"You do?"

Everybody jumped when they heard a tremendous crash issue from the other side of the door. Scruggs sidled away as if he feared for his very life.

When an enormous, uncouth voice shot through the heavy wooden paneling, demanding to know "whar that damned son of a buck Partington" was, Claire looked at Tom, her eyebrows raised in question.

"It's all right, everybody," Tom assured them, striding toward Scruggs.

Claire sat with a thunk when Tom flung open the dining room door to reveal a character the likes of whom she'd believed existed only in her brand of fiction. A huge man, clad in fringed buckskins, a wide-brimmed conch-bedecked hat, big boots, ammunition belts crossed over his chest, a holster filled with the biggest gun she'd ever seen, with side whiskers and a gigantic mustache, swaggered into the room and glared at the assembly.

Scruggs's knees gave way, and he slid down the wall to sit on the floor. Everyone else goggled at the invader.

Everyone, that is, except Tom, who embraced the unlikely fellow as though he were greeting a long-lost, and exceedingly dear, brother.

"Cable!" he cried.

"Tom!" the remarkable man cried back.

At least five minutes of backslaps, hugs, chortles, and masculine curses of an endearing variety ensued, during which Claire and her guests were left to exchange shrugs and puzzled glances. At last Claire decided she'd had quite enough, thank you, and rose from her place at the table.

At that very moment the two men broke their embrace, and Tom stood back, keeping a hand on the intruder's shoulder.

"Claire! Ladies and gentlemen!"

Claire was astonished to see tears in Tom's eyes.

"It's my very great pleasure to introduce you to my best friend in the entire world, Killer Cable Hawkins!"

An incredulous buzz rose from the table, but Claire did not heed it. Stricken dumb on the spot, she could only gape at the two men for a full minute until her rattled wits gathered themselves together again. Then, fairly quivering with excitement, she rushed to her husband's side. "Are you *really* Killer Cable Hawkins?" she asked in a voice rich with awe.

The giant ripped off his hat. "That's what they call me, ma'am." Claire was amazed to see his cheeks ripen with color.

"My wife is an aficionado of the frontier life, Cable," Tom said with a wink for Claire. "I invited you here especially to meet her."

Claire feared for the bones in her hand when Cable wrung it. She refrained from shrieking in pain only because she didn't want to hurt anybody's feelings.

"Ma'am, anybody what's got the good sense to marry up with this here varmint is somebody I'll meet come hell or howdy."

At his wife's blank expression Tom whispered, "He means he's glad to meet you, Claire."

"Oh! Oh, of course." She smiled at Cable again. "And I'm extremely happy to meet you too, Mr. Hawkins."

"My wife is a novelist, Cable, and she's been itching to start a new series of books about life on the frontier."

Tom met Claire's look of absolute incredulity with the most innocent face she'd ever seen. Then, her heart bursting with joy and her eyes filling with tears, she flung herself into his arms. "Oh, darling, *thank* you!"

"Think nothing of it, Mrs. Partington," he said. He winked at Cable and whispered in her ear, "Killer Cable boasts not merely a great name, Claire, but *he* has a limp in *both* legs."

Epilogue

The Legend of Killer Cable and its offspring proved to be bestsellers throughout the length and breadth of the United States. European rights garnered Clarence McTeague even more bounty. The public couldn't get enough of the invincible Killer Cable.

Even though Sylvester Addison-Addison's *Adolphus, the Wily Turk* and several subsequent novels did well, Sylvester's sales never matched those of Clarence McTeague, who had already proved his worth with a dozen or so *Tuscaloosa Tom* novels, published before he tackled *Killer Cable*.

Sylvester of course resented McTeague's success, although he didn't dare say so aloud to Claire Partington. Marriage to the wealthy Priscilla Pringle did nothing to improve Sylvester's disposition, but at least the customers at the Pyrite Springs Mercantile and Furniture Emporium no longer had to suffer his surliness, as Alphonse Gilbert was forced to hire a clerk with good manners.

Dianthe St. Sauvre and Jedediah Silver were married

shortly after Tom and Claire's April reception. Dianthe liked the "Silver" part of her new name but decided to keep the "St." part of her old one for poetic reasons.

Sergei Ivanov moved back to his native Russia in 1890. He claimed only another Russian could appreciate his works of the soul. Years later Claire was sure it was Sergei's face she saw in a photograph printed in the newspaper. He was one of a mob swarming the tsar's Winter Palace, and he had a paintbrush clutched in his upraised fist.

Freddy March finally learned to read music. Shortly thereafter he joined a band led by John Philip Sousa and took up the piccolo. The Sousa band played a concert on the grounds of Partington Place to celebrate Tom and Claire's fifteenth wedding anniversary. The entire town of Pyrite Springs was treated to the world premiere of "The Stars and Stripes Forever," which Sousa copyrighted in the following year, 1897. Claire wept with pride during Freddy's solo.

Tom's Appaloosa breeding ranch prospered, and the Partington horses soon became famous and much sought after in the equine world.

Claire was able to indulge her passion for gardening, eventually endowing the Partington Botanical Gardens with funding in perpetuity. Once Glorietta Garland progressed from marigolds to anemones and then on to roses, she became well known for her floral renderings of specimens in the gardens.

Mrs. Finchley became like a mother to Claire and acted as grandmother to the Partington children, Gordon and Lizzie. Royalties from Claire's books and profits from Tom's Appaloosa breeding operation provided both children with college educations.

Claude Montague moved to New York and then to

Los Angeles, California, where he became involved in the budding motion-picture industry. As Claire often told her husband, "Better on screen than in our home." Tom agreed with her and was grateful his own parents were content to squat in Tuscaloosa, overdrawing their bank account and dwelling on past glories.

Upon his release from prison in Seattle, Clive Montague joined in his father's celluloid venture and became wealthy until his career was cut short by Hollywoodland's very first "casting couch" scandal. Claire pretended they were not related.

"Thank God we don't share the same last name any longer," she muttered as she slapped the newspaper aside.

Tom grinned his wonderful grin at her. "I don't know, Claire. At least you don't have to go very far to find people to act as models for the villains in your novels."

She frowned at her husband over the top of her spectacles. "Tom Partington, my imagination is good enough to create villains. I don't need my brother."

His grin turned wicked. "I know all about your imagination, my love. It's been my inspiration and my delight these past twenty-five years."

Claire blushed. She did not demur, however, when Tom suggested they retire to their room for a little delight in the afternoon.

She felt much better afterward.

If you're looking for romance, adventure, excitement and suspense be sure to read these outstanding romances from Dell.

=========※=========

Antoinette Stockenberg
☐ **EMILY'S GHOST**   21002-X $5.50
☐ **BELOVED**   21330-4 $5.50
☐ **EMBERS**   21673-7 $4.99
Rebecca Paisley
☐ **HEARTSTRINGS**   21650-8 $4.99
Jill Gregory
☐ **CHERISHED**   20620-0 $5.99
☐ **DAISIES IN THE WIND**   21618-4 $5.99
☐ **FOREVER AFTER**   21512-9 $5.99
☐ **WHEN THE HEART BECKONS**   21857-8 $5.99
☐ **ALWAYS YOU**   22183-8 $5.99
Christina Skye
☐ **THE BLACK ROSE**   20929-3 $5.99
☐ **COME THE NIGHT**   21644-3 $4.99
☐ **COME THE DAWN**   21647-8 $5.50
☐ **DEFIANT CAPTIVE**   20626-X $5.50
☐ **EAST OF FOREVER**   20865-3 $4.99
☐ **THE RUBY**   20864-5 $5.99